Talbot Company

To my esteemed colleague N.J. Rockingham:

nihil superbus est te

"First came the Greycoats to eat all my swine,

Next came the Bluecoats to make my sons fight,

Next came the Greencoats to make my wife whore,

Next came the Browncoats to burn down my home.

I have naught but my life, now come the Blackcoats to rob me of that."

—Anonymous Poem from the Thirty Years War

Chapter 1

Livonia, Swedish Empire

"¿Como te llamas?"

"Good, now in French."

"Comment vous appelez-vous?"

"Good. German?"

"Wie heißen Sie?"

"And now English."

"Whut uus yaar nem?"

The tutor, her tired face wrinkled with age, sighed and placed her fingers on her temples. She knew that her student was trying her best, but what frustrated her even more was that she herself was no great speaker of the language of the Englishmen. Even so, she knew poor pronunciation when she heard it. Her student's words in that foreign tongue made her cringe.

"Crista," she said to her young student in their native Swedish, "we have discussed this time and time again. English is a language that requires you to enunciate and change the sounds of some letters. For example, the 's' in 'is' is pronounced

5

like a 'z'." she tried to sound like she knew what she was talking about, but she was unsure of even that.

Crista Stenbock sat in her bedroom chair, curling her long, flowing blonde hair with her finger as she lost her thoughts lost in the painted stars on her ceiling. Her eyes wandered about her room, with its silk curtains and wolf skin carpet. She glanced over to her large canopied bed; she would rather be napping under its covers than struggling over this language lesson.

Her father, Greve Olaf Stenbock, had hired a language tutor as part of her formal education. She would require many skills to be the intelligent and sophisticated future wife of a member of the Protestant nobility. She was expected to know how to speak the languages of the major foreign courts (especially French, as it was the lingua franca of Europe), be aware of her region's current political dynamic, and be skilled at the womanly arts such as painting, music, and crocheting.

"Sister Margret," she said, complaining to her tutor in English, "I practicing *engelska språket* for weeks, and it seem that I no be get any better unless I find good English teacher."

Sister Margret – the honorific made the old woman wince slightly. She had indeed, at one point in the past, been a nun, and preferred not to be called by that title anymore, but Crista insisted on using it as a form of respect.

Sister Margret had mastered many of the languages of continental Europe, translating Bibles for the French, Germans, English, and Spanish Catholics. She had left that life behind, however, leaving the convent after hearing about the 'evils of monastic life' from Lutheran preachers.

6

It also helped that the Church of Sweden decided to become Lutheran and sever ties with Rome. Her conversion and desertion of the monastic life had very good timing, too. That was thirty years ago, right before the wars of religion started. Now it was a dangerous time to be a Catholic, more so a nun in Sweden, just as it was dangerous to be a Protestant in Catholic Spain or Italy.

Ever since the Protestants and the Catholic league went to war over the ridiculous argument over who worshipped God correctly, a person's declaration of faith could be a death sentence.

Margret's primary concern now, though, was Crista and her English lesson.

"Child, English sounds much like Dutch, only less... erm..."

"Ergerlijk," annoying, Crista said, after which she switched back to Swedish. "I know you are trying your best, Sister, and I know you are trying to help me, but I think I might need some guidance from a real Englishwoman. I believe our lessons are over for the day. I bid you thanks, and I wish you well."

"I do not think your father would--"

Before Sister Margret could continue, Crista was out the door.

As she slowly descended the stone steps that led from her room in the solar to the great hall below, Crista's mind wandered as it often did, wondering what life must be like for the peasant girls that lived and worked in her father's county. Surely they did not have such a routine and boring existence as hers.

Every day it was the same thing – breakfast, usually some bread with lingonberry jam, seasonal fruit or some salmon,

7

followed by language lessons with Sister Margret, lectures on statecraft, dancing lessons, *fika* or coffee time with her father (which of course would be used to teach Crista about social graces), followed by crocheting, history lessons, and horseback riding, before a supper that usually consisted of warm salad, more fish, maybe some game birds or meatballs, and then bedtime, only to wake up and do the same thing again the next day.

It was enough to drive any seventeen-year-old girl insane. Certainly, living in a castle had the security and grandeur that a country home could not offer, but besides the horseback riding, it was terribly boring. Every window, every doorknob, every nail in the castle had been known to her since she was about nine.

Although she was free to come and go as she pleased, there was almost never any point to it. Her father was not the king, and his land holdings existed in name only, since by the new laws the land actually belonged to the king of Sweden alone, and he was merely its steward. The nearest large city was Riga, which was many miles away. Jarlsberg Castle was her home, in the easternmost corner of Sweden's new empire – but to her, the finely decorated walls and the same blue and ocher drapes and banners hung on the interior had lost their appeal years ago.

Jarlsberg was a castle by name, but in reality it was a Swedish *fästning* or fortress, constructed with lower walls and simpler defenses than a traditional castle. While the compound maintained a traditional keep that was surrounded by buildings like the smithy, stables, barracks, servants' quarters, store room, and chapel, its perimeter defenses were much simpler than older medieval fortifications.

Jarlsberg's walls were twice the height of a man and had earthen mounds built outside them to absorb the impact of cannon. The walls were constructed in a circle around the central structures, but the weakest parts of the wall were the gates that opened up to the western and eastern roads – their large wooden gates had enough room for three horses to walk through comfortably, but they had to be opened through a gatehouse that sat on top of them.

The most popular part of the castle was the courtyard, which was large enough to play badminton in, and indeed it had often been used for this purpose. It was also the garrison muster field. Crista had ordered that its edges be decorated with ornamental bushes and small trees to make it feel more "alive" as she put it.

Today, she thought, she would skip the lessons as she did every so often and head straight for the stables to tend to her horse, Sigfrid, whom she believed to be the second best listener in the castle, bested only by her friend Captain Sven Bjornsson, the garrison commander.

As she entered the great hall with its freshly mopped and scoured floor and richly decorated walls filled with paintings of the Swedish landscape in the summertime, she passed by Ratsherr Joachim Fegelein, a Baltic German councilman who acted as an adviser to her father and a teacher to her. In these times it was considered fashionable to invite foreign statesmen and dignitaries to "westernize" the "wild" lands of Eastern Europe, and Fegelein and people like him were doing a fine job in Sweden.

"Guten morgen, mein kleiner mausebär." Good morning my little mouse-bear, he said with a smile. He knew that she had no intention of attending his lecture on European politics, and he

was quite happy with that – it gave him more time to do more important matters, not that her education was not important, but running a county was no easy task. Taxes needed to be levied, labor needed to be allocated, and the grievances of peasants needed to be addressed. As soon as Crista went out the door to the great hall, he would proceed to his office to do some much-needed writing.

"Guten morgen, Herr Ratsherr." she replied with a curtsy in near-perfect German. She always felt that it was odd that the German people liked to use the word "mouse-bear" as a term of affection, but she never bothered to ask why. Brushing the thought aside, she proceeded out the door and into the castle courtyard, where she was greeted by the bright sunshine and the smell of daisies.

Dressed in her fitted pink and purple gown, she was more than a distraction for the soldiers that were assembling for their morning formation. Rows of helmeted heads turned her way as she sauntered towards the stables. She smiled back at the staring soldiers playfully, knowing full well that her presence was a pleasant surprise in the morning, and she was happy to know that she was boosting morale.

As she walked by the captain's quarters, she shouted a "good morning, captain!" through his window. Captain Bjornsson was a fine officer, although long in years, and acted like a second father to her, listening to her complaints and sharing her happiness while her own father was away on important affairs. It was unusual for him to be inside his quarters at this hour, but she thought nothing of it as she continued towards the stables.

Bjornsson awoke in a daze, thinking he had just heard the sound of a woman's voice; Crista's, possibly. Standing upright in his straw-filled mattress, he winced at the sunlight glaring down on him. As he ran his hands through his long blond hair and over his beard, he noticed that –

Sunlight? He was late for duty! Realizing what a fool he had been thinking that he could down eight tankards of mead like he was still a young man and make it to formation on time the next morning, he dashed out of bed and scrambled for his uniform and armor.

The laborious process of changing had begun: first came his blue trousers, tied off at the knees, followed by his silk stockings and boots; next, he hurriedly doffed his nightshirt and put on a cotton doublet, followed by a quilted blue woolen gambeson. He sighed heavily as he put on his blackened steel breastplate and combed helmet. In the time it took him to get dressed, a man could have eaten a good meal and closed his eyes for a nap.

Once he was satisfied, he grabbed his baldric, a belt worn over his shoulder that was used to carry his sword, and went out the door of his quarters, with the lingering feeling that he had forgotten something.

"Avdelning, giv AKT!" shouted the sergeant of the guard; a short, rotund man named Torsten. At this command, the mass formation of pikemen and musketeers slammed their left feet on the ground and stood at rigid attention, with their eyes facing forward, ready to be inspected by their commander.

Bjornsson walked in front of his formation and towards the sergeant, who was staring at his stomach.

"Sir," said Torsten, "your armor..."

Confused, the captain looked down himself and saw that he had failed to buckle his breastplate. He groaned in embarrassment. Sighing, he turned around and gestured for the sergeant to buckle him up.

"What are the reports from the watch, sergeant?"

"Nothing to report, sir."

"Very well. Have the men proceed with their usual morning drills and rotate through their designated guard positions." as Torsten finished buckling him up, he turned and faced him, tipping his helmet in a gesture of thanks. "Apologies for the tardiness – what I would not give to be a young man again. That much mead does not do my old head any good."

"Sir." Torsten said, not wishing to continue the conversation. He was about to turn to the men and give the first orders of the day when he heard a faint sound in the distance, like the fife and drums of a marching band.

Bjornsson turned to the watchman posted at the southwestern gate and shouted,

"What do you see?"

The watchman fumbled for his spyglass and rapidly scanned the horizon. Out of the corner of his eye, he could see a tiny red and white banner slowly approaching.

"Polish infantry company, sir!"

Chapter 2

Bjornsson swore under his breath. The Catholic Polish and their Lithuanian allies had been trying to push back Sweden's incursions into Eastern Europe for centuries, but they had only been at peace with Sweden until very recently. This was probably a desperate attempt to win back lost territory. Jarlsberg was a castle built on the borderlands between Livonia and Lithuania, but it had been guarded by several smaller outposts in the past. One of them had fallen, apparently, and now the enemy was at the gates and it was Bjornsson's duty to defend the castle.

"Musketeers to the southwest ramparts! Pikemen guard the gate! I want men on the cannons facing that general direction to begin shelling as soon as the enemy gets in range!" Bjornsson shouted as he dashed towards the ramparts to join the defenders. Jarlsberg had never been attacked before, but he was confident that he could defend it against a company-sized element of enemy troops with the artillery he had in place.

"Today, of all days, this had to happen as I suffer from a damn hangover." Bjornsson muttered to himself as he climbed up the steps of the ramparts. He took the spyglass from the watchman to look through it himself. The silhouettes of hundreds of foreign infantrymen crested the horizon beyond, with their pikes and muskets shouldered, standing still and awaiting orders.

Bjornsson recognized them by their uniforms to be Lithuanians – Catholic allies to the Poles and members of the Polish-Lithuanian Commonwealth. The Lithuanians were not particularly well known for the quality of their infantrymen. The discipline and tactics of Sweden's regular army would be more than a match for them, but Bjornsson had no wish to sally out of the safety of his own castle.

He ordered the guns, Swedish leather cannon, to adjust their elevations and concentrate fire on the Lithuanians. The smell of burning matches and gunpowder wafted up Bjornsson's long nose as he braced himself for the vibrations and noise of cannon fire.

With a series of loud thuds, the leather cannon propelled their fist-sized stone balls towards the mass of infantry. The rounds fell short several yards away from the big toe of the nearest enemy soldier.

"Sergeant Torsten!" Bjornsson cried out, "Adjust elevation to maximum!"

The sergeant repeated the order, and the gunners responded in the negative,

"That is all the range they have, sir!"

Bjornsson noticed movement on the horizon again. He looked through his spyglass and cursed at what he saw. The enemy was bringing in their own cannon: bronze six-pounder guns, with far greater range than his own. There were four of them, and all of them seemed to point towards the gate.

"Sergeant Torsten, prepare the men to sally forth."

As Bjornson finished this sentence, a synchronized volley of cannon fire sent rounds flying over the gatehouse with a loud whoosh, and four stone balls buried themselves in the wall of the castle keep. The enemy was most definitely within range.

Both Bjornsson and his subordinate stood petrified for a moment, staring at the keep's wall.

"I said move, damn you!" Bjornsson barked as he kicked Torsten to get him moving. The captain followed Torsten down the ramparts to the formation of pikemen guarding the gate.

Pikemen rushed to the gate and formed a square to prepare for the enemy's assault. A block of seventy-five bristling pike-wielding infantry stood at the gateway, muttering prayers and gritting their teeth in anticipation of mortal combat.

"Men!" yelled Bjornsson, "Embrace the fear in your bellies and the tears in your eyes! They are proof that you are alive! Turn that fear into hate, and rip..."

On the word rip, a cannonball tore through the wooden gate and flew straight into the mass of pikemen, turning a dozen soldiers into a mush of blood, flesh, splinters, and armor.

Bjornsson threw his hands in the air, "Lord God! At least give me a chance to finish my speech!" The captain turned to Torsten and growled, "March the men out into the field and deal with these Catholic bastards. Go!"

"Yes, sir! Gatekeeper, open the gate!"

As the gates rumbled open, the company drummer began playing his drum to the "preparatory" call – a long drum roll.

"Avdelning! Framåt... MARSCH!"

At this command, the drummer played a steady, rhythmic beat that bid the formation to march forward, even as the enemy's bronze cannons stared down at them in the distance. The enemy cannons chose to remain silent and the Lithuanians still refused to advance, knowing they would be in range of

15

Bjornsson's leather cannon. The captain rapped his fingers on his spyglass in restlessness and suspicion.

As his pikemen advanced on the enemy, Bjornsson heard the sound of rumbling thunder. Turning his spyglass to the direction of the sound, he scanned the horizon and saw what looked like a great dust cloud. Enemy cavalry – perhaps they were maneuvering to flank his pikemen.

The captain shouted for his pikemen to form a square to defend themselves against the approaching cavalry, but the formation was too far away for Torsten to hear him.

To Bjornsson's horror, the cavalrymen wheeled around the pikemen and charged straight for the castle's gate.

"In the name of God, close the gate!" Bjornsson yelled as he ran back up the ramparts to the gatehouse. The chains of the gate mechanism groaned as the men cranking it grunted and cursed that they could not make it move any faster. Bjornsson himself grabbed hold of one of the revolving spokes of the mechanism and exerted all the strength he could muster to make the rusted machine move. As the mechanism turned faster, the gate slowly closed. The massive wooden structure sealed shut as Bjornsson let out a satisfied sigh.

They were safe for the time being, the only damage to the gate being the massive hole that was left by the cannon round from earlier.

The foreign riders came closer. Lipka Tatars – distant cousins to the sons of Genghis Khan – Muslim steppe people famed for their excellent cavalry. These ones fought as mercenaries for the Polish.

16

As the Tatars came into musket range, the musketeers on the ramparts fired their weapons at them in a single volley and ducked behind the battlements to reload. Some of the enemy riders fell, while the rest responded with arrow fire with such volume that it effectively suppressed the Swedish musketeers, forcing them to remain behind their cover.

With the Swedish musketeers successfully pinned down, a few Tatars rode to within spitting distance of the fortification and grappling hooks through the hole in the gate. The riders, with the ropes of the grappling hooks attached to their horses, then rode at full gallop in the opposite direction, ripping off big chunks of the wooden gate.

The gate had been breached – a Tatar cavalryman sounded his horn.

Hearing their cue, the Lithuanian infantry formed a long, brought their spears to charge and slammed into the outnumbered Swedish pikemen, engulfing them on all sides. Torsten's company was effectively lost.

Crista was not trained in the arts of war. She knew nothing of shot or shell or concealment, but she knew that she had to return to the castle keep. Steeling herself, she bolted towards the keep's door, bumping shoulders with the flow of men that ran from the barracks towards the ramparts. It was made even more difficult by the fact that Crista had to run in a skirt. She muttered a curse to the fool who had invented it as she reached the castle gate and slammed her fist on it, ordering the doorman to let her in.

Crista put her ear to the door in impatience, wondering what could be taking so long. She heard the sound of heavy wood grinding on metal. The doorman was removing the large wooden bar that held the door together. After that, the doors immediately flung open and the doorman urged her inside, closing the door back up again as soon as she entered. Crista knew she would be safe for the time being. The stone walls and the soldiers defending the castle outside gave her a small measure of comfort, however now that she had gathered herself somewhat, she realized that someone was missing.

"Where is my father?" she asked the doorman.

"Mistress, your father went out on a hunting trip in the early hours of the morning." replied the doorman, his lips quivering. "I fear... I hope he does not return too soon, for his own safety."

Crista frowned. While it was a good thing that her father was safe, him being on a hunting trip also meant that he took a small number of soldiers with him from the garrison to act as bodyguards and dog handlers. Those same soldiers would have added strength to the garrison's meager force and would have possibly made a difference in the battle that was currently raging. But again, at least he was safe. All that Crista had to worry about now was herself. Where was the best place to hide?

The interior of the keep itself was large and offered many hiding places, but none appealed more to Crista than her own room in the solar. Not only was it comfortable and familiar, but there was also only one way in or out of it, through a narrow staircase that curled up and around a large stone column. She would hide there until the gunfire and screaming stopped outside.

The Tatars began pouring through the broken gate, trampling the musketeers that stood in their way to attempt a last-ditch defense. Bjornsson's tactical lapse in judgment had proven disastrous. He threw his arms up in the air in frustration

18

and watched as Tatars dismounted and came sword to sword with musketeers that were descending the ramparts.

He also heard a rumbling in the distance that was closing in at an alarming rate – definitely heavy cavalry. His pikemen, meant to protect against cavalry attack, were being hacked away by the Lithuanians several yards outside the walls. Every foe that was entering the walls was on horseback, and his men could not take much more of it.

A rider on a white horse charged through the open gate. The morning sunlight reflecting off of his plate armor, his face concealed by a closed faceplate, with his red lance couched beneath his arms. From out of his back, feathered wings bristled like those of an avenging angel. Dozens of similarly-attired cavalrymen followed behind him. Winged hussars – the pride of Poland's army and the greatest heavy cavalry in Europe.

Even as dust kicked up by the horses and smoke from the muskets obscured the battlefield, Bjornsson could tell that he was losing this battle. The next sensible course of action would be to organize a retreat. But to where? Riga? That was sixteen miles away, and there was no way that the garrison would be able to slip out of the fort safely without being slaughtered to a man, especially since the enemy was composed primarily of cavalry. As the musket balls whistled over his head, Bjornsson decided that it would be better off if he saved only the most important people at Jarlsberg, starting with the Greve's adviser, his daughter, and any officers that he could gather.

Scanning the chaotic scene at the courtyard, he could see that the hussars were making quick work of the musketeers he had placed there to stop them. Since they failed to put up a wall of pikes and were instead running around like rats on a sinking ship, the Polish hussars had their horses simply trotting around and were slashing at the retreating soldiers at their leisure.

The few swordsmen at the ramparts were faring no better. Tatars excelled at melee fighting, and many had brought shields with them, giving them a distinct advantage against the Europeans with their one-handed broadswords and tiny bucklers.

It was definitely time to go. Bjornsson sheathed his sword and hurriedly quit the courtyard, looking around him and making sure that none of his troops could tell that he was retreating back to the castle keep. He would never forget this defeat for as long as he lived, which would not be very long if he did not hurry.

As she huddled in the corner of her room, clutching a candlestick – more for comfort than as a weapon – Crista could hear the gunshots outside getting louder and more frequent. Her eyes darted around the room as if looking for a way out of this nightmare. Of course, she knew there was only one exit, but surely there was an alternative to descending the stairs into the hands of the enemy and certain death. The windows were reinforced with iron bars, so they were not an option; besides she could not fly. Hiding was not an option either – the enemy would search every room thoroughly for loot.

She looked back to the door. If she stayed here, she would be safe only if the battle below went favorably, and if the enemy was not allowed to enter the tower. What she could hear outside was not bringing her any sense of confidence in the ability of the garrison to defend either the castle or itself. If she left through that door, she had a small chance of making it outside and possibly escaping through one of the gates, if the soldiers were too distracted to try and catch her. She had to act soon though, while the fighting was heavy. If she waited too long, the enemy would overrun the garrison and she would definitely be captured. The door was the only sane choice.

Dropping the candlestick, Crista rose to her feet and bolted for the door. As she fumbled with the deadbolt, she realized that this could very well be her last day on earth. Seventeen years of nothing but boring parties, forced smiles, social tiptoeing and lessons... endless, frivolous lessons. Seventeen years wasted. She could not die like this.

The door opened, and in her haste, she almost slipped and fell down the stairwell. That would've been a slightly better, albeit more embarrassing death than bleeding out by shot or cold steel, but Crista had no intention of being bested by the work of a sloppy peasant blacksmith. She ripped her long skirt and removed her dainty shoes, running down the stairs barefoot. She was making good time. It would be insane to go through the front door into the courtyard, so she opted for the back door.

Just as she was about to sprint towards the small oaken double doors of the castle, a hand reached out from behind her and grabbed her by the arm, and another one reached for her mouth before she could scream. A man had pulled her behind the stairs. Panic gripped her. It was over – this is where she would die. She had many regrets, too many to think of, and tears started forming in her eyes.

"Bitte stehe schweigend auf mein mausebär." Please be quiet, whispered her captor, as he slowly removed his hand from her mouth. *Mausebär?*

"Herr Ratsherr? Ratsherr Fegelein? Thank God you are alive."
She whispered in German. Crista breathed a sigh of relief,
although her chest was pounding like a bird's.

"We cannot escape through either door." the councilman
said, his voice trembling with fear. "The Polish have attacked us
from both sides. Our only hope is to hide in the secret cellar
room and escape during the night after the Polish take the castle
and bed down."

Secret cellar room? Crista was sure she knew every inch of
the castle. She had never heard of a secret cellar room, but then
again she had never gone down into the cellar for too long. It
stank terribly, the air was musty, and there were always rats.
She hated rats, but she preferred to be surrounded by the vile
creatures rather than risk death.

"All right, I will follow you." she said after half a moment's
consideration.

Ratsherr Fegelein swallowed hard and wiped the sweat off
his brow with his silk handkerchief. "Good. Stay close by." he
said as he gradually stood up to leave their hiding place behind
the stairs.

No sooner had he gotten on his two feet than a loud bashing
sound emanated from the small backdoor while it started to
buckle. Loud shouts in Polish and Tatar came from the other
side. Ratsherr Fegelein froze, not knowing what to do. His
indecisiveness cost him.

The door burst open, letting in a flood of Tatar warriors and
a single winged hussar in shining golden armor. The Tatars ran
towards the petrified councilman, screaming their infidel battle
cries. Ratsherr Fegelein's pants suddenly felt a lot warmer.

The hussar in golden armor bellowed a command and the Tatars stopped short of skewering the councilman through his now empty bladder. The hussar dismounted from his horse and lifted the visor of his helmet to reveal the face of a man with piercing green eyes and a curled mustache.

"Czy to twój zamek?" said the hussar.

Ratsherr Fegelein's lips trembled. He opened his mouth to speak, to tell them he did not understand, but no words came out. He was going to die because of a lapse in translation.

"Nie. Ten zamek należy do mojego ojca." No, this castle belongs to my father, said Crista as she revealed herself from her hiding place. "He is my father's adviser, your grace." She continued in Polish. She stammered quite a bit. It was as if she was doing a recitation at gunpoint.

The hussar took a deep, respectful bow towards Crista and replied in Polish, "Where is your father, *kochanie?*"

"He is out hunting, your grace." she replied through chattering teeth.

"A pity. I would have liked to meet the man responsible for this valiant defense. I am Colonel Jan Casimir, of the Polish-Lithuanian Commonwealth, and I am here to respectfully request your surrender." as soon as he completed his sentence, he heard the sound of glass shattering.

Bjornsson could find no way to enter through the front door of the keep and had instead decided to leap through a ground floor window that had not been secured with iron bars. He had almost been shot twice and had been forced to dispatch a Tatar with his sword. He took in his surroundings, wild-eyed, in to find his lord's daughter and adviser surrounded by the enemy commander and his Tatar entourage.

He froze. Hopelessly outnumbered, there was no way he could rescue either Crista or Fegelein without getting killed himself. The Polish commander spotted him and raised his steel-gloved hand, signaling the Tatars to shoot him. He would have to move quickly – if he could either step back outside or jump behind one of the pillars...

Suddenly he heard the loud bang of a musket. A piece of marble from the floor must have nicked him in the leg before he realized that he was being shot at. His battlefield instincts kicked in, and he leaped behind a nearby column for cover. The next best course of action to take would be to run for the armory, maybe find a musket or a grenade to even the odds.

Bjornsson tried to make a dash towards the armory, but to his surprise, his right leg refused to respond. Looking down at it, he realized he had been shot. His blue pants were now turning dark purple. A sharp, burning pain pierced his thigh as the world slowly got darker around him. His last conscious thoughts before blackness overtook him were that he did not even have a chance to eat breakfast that morning.

Chapter 3

Four foxes, two boars, and an elk. Today had been a good day for Greve Olaf Stenbock, who had just finished his hunting trip and was returning to Jarlsberg castle with his catch and his small band of two dozen retainers. The greve was very pleased with himself. He had not only managed to utilize his hounds to the best of their abilities, hunting foxes, but had also managed to stalk and kill an elk on his own, for once choosing not to enlist the help of a retainer to make the kill easier.

But the sun was setting in the distance, and it was always a bad idea to hunt at night, considering the dangers of friendly fire and the wolves – armed as the group was, God had given the wolf the gift of night-eye, not man. Greve Stenbock did not like the idea of being hunted himself.

The group all rode on horseback at a slow trot, with the dogs, Smaland hounds, running happily alongside their masters, eagerly awaiting the fine meal they would have for doing such a good job.

Suddenly, the dogs stopped and smelled the air. Sensing something odd, the pack rushed ahead of the horses towards the direction of the castle as the dog handlers shouted at them to come back.

The greve had never seen them behave like this before. They were usually very well-disciplined and loyal animals, never deserting the hunting party and certainly never running so excitedly like this. He ordered his men to follow them, trusting their instincts, telling him that something was wrong.

As the hunting party followed the dogs to a small hill that overlooked Jarlsberg castle, the greve noticed large pillars of smoke billowing over the crest of the hill. His heart stopped.

The greve's retainers looked at one another and at him. They knew as much as he did that smoke could only mean destruction. Either a fire raged through the castle or they had been attacked. Everyone preferred to believe the former.

Greve Stenbock raced ahead of the hounds, his retainers trailing behind him, while the dogs barked incessantly, agitated at the sight and sound of the smoke. Thoughts raced through the greve's head like wildfire through a dry forest. What had happened? Who was responsible for this? Was everyone safe? How would he deal with the situation? And most importantly, what had happened to his daughter, Crista?

As he brought his horse to a fast gallop, his heart pounding in his chest, imagining the horrible things that could have happened to his estate while he was gone. He damned himself for prolonging his hunting trip as long as he did. If he could have come back sooner, he would have been there to stop whatever tragedy had befallen his home.

Drawing closer, he smelled an odor that was unfamiliar to him – it smelled very much like rotting meat, but it had a putrid sweetness to it. After riding a few dozen yards nearer towards the scent, he could tell that it was exactly what he had feared. Foreign soldiers were digging a mass grave and looting the bodies of fallen Swedish soldiers just outside the walls of the fort.

The greve brought his horse to a halt and sat in his saddle with his mouth agape. His retainers caught up to him and began whispering words of fear, repulsion, and anger.

The faint sound of boisterous laughter could be heard not too far away. The greve turned in the direction of the noise to see a group of Tatars with their padded clothing and funny fur hats, gathered in a circle around an injured Swedish soldier, limping about, armed with what appeared to be a candlestick.

Without another thought, the greve drew his sword and charged towards the Tatars and their prisoner. He might as well save one soul today if he was not able to save his castle.

The hunting party and its dogs descended from the hill. The Tatars were caught off guard and could not form a defense in time. They called out for help, but their screams were in vain. The only people outside were on the burial detail, and they were on the far side of the castle, where they could not see the slaughter. The greve's men made short work of the barbarians, slashing their backs with their sabers as they fled. The dogs bit into their necks and heels, while some of the men dismounted to finish what the dogs started. It was all over within the time it took to boil an egg.

The injured soldier wanted to show his appreciation but instead collapsed out of exhaustion.

With his hair matted in blood and his black armor stained with bile, blood, and urine, he was almost unrecognizable. As soon as his face was uncovered, he made a deep gasp for air. The greve recognized him as his garrison commander – Captain Sven Bjornsson. After he had been injured, the Tatars wanted to toy with him until they tortured and killed him. The greve had good timing indeed. If he had not been there to rescue Bjornsson, he would have surely died.

Two of the greve's retainers rushed to attend to him. His eyes were wide in fear and confusion, and he continued to gasp for air. Unable to stand on his own feet, the men had to hold him up as the greve approached him.

"Captain, what happened here?" said the greve, his brow furrowing with both disgust and worry.

The wild-eyed captain turned his head to his greve and managed to mutter, "Polacks... Casimir commanding... Crista captured..." before going limp in the arms of the greve's retainers.

Greve Olaf Stenbock would not stand for this blatant disrespect for both his home and the recently established peace between Sweden and the Polish-Lithuanian Commonwealth. These rogue Polish forces would be brought to justice, if not by their own king, then by the greve himself and an army of Western Europe's greatest mercenaries behind him.

Chapter 4

Bolingbroke Village, England

In other parts of the world, the sun would be shining and the birds would be singing their sweet melodies, filling the morning air. But when the Almighty created England, He decided, as a cruel joke, to make their summers miserable and wet. Instead of a bright and warm summer sun, rain clouds filled the gray and gloomy sky. Instead of birds singing, the loud pitter-patter of raindrops echoed off the wooden shingled roofs of English country houses.

The rain was not as hard today as it was on other days. The weather was being incredibly cooperative to woodsmen who were collecting firewood in the forest on the outskirts of the town, farmers who were tending their crops and did not mind a light shower, and hunters looking for rabbit and other small game to feed their families, all under the shadow of Bolingbroke Castle.

The hunters were using mostly English longbows since muskets were prone to getting their firing mechanisms wet in the rain, and a wet musket was a little better than an expensive club. Longbows had been put out of conventional military use a hundred years ago, but the peasants still used them to hunt, when their matchlocks could not be used. To prevent water from ruining their bowstrings, the English had them waxed.

It was quiet in the forest, save for the faint sound of water trickling off the leaves. A lone rabbit was grooming itself on top of a tree stump, its little paws rubbing against its puffy, gray-haired face. A few meters away, a little iron arrowhead protruded from a bush – except that it was not a bush, it was a man. Covered from head to toe in a smock covered with leaves and branches, the archer silently drew back the bowstring of his weapon and breathed out in a long, drawn-out breath in order to steady his aim. He did not want to miss this shot – it was probably the only chance he would get. If he missed, the rabbit would hop away into the woods and he would probably never see it again.

Confident in his aim, he released the arrow – it flew truly and swiftly... towards the tree stump. The rabbit, now alerted, bounded off into the ferns and shrubs to escape. The hunter, swearing, broke from cover and chased the rabbit, hoping against all odds that he would be granted a second opportunity to kill it.

His prey was fast; the hunter's clothes snagged on branches and thorns as he struggled to catch up with it. When he reached the first clearing, he thought, he would nock an arrow as fast as he could and pin this animal to the ground. Soon enough, the hunter and prey entered a clearing, and as soon as they did, the sound of a single musket shot rang loud and clear through the forest. The rabbit had been killed, but not by the man who had stalked it for half an hour and waited until it was still so he could put an arrow through its chest. No – it had been shot by a king's ranger.

The rangers watched over state property and made sure that no man would hunt on land that belonged to the king – which is exactly what the hunter was doing. Although the rangers themselves were supposed to protect the forest for the king's personal use, times were hard, and even the rangers needed to eat.

"You there – yeoman." the ranger called out, "What were you doing in the king's woods?"

The hunter did not respond.

Picking up the dead rabbit, the ranger then yelled, "Were you hunting in the king's woods? I shall have you know, sir, that what you are doing is a violation of the law."

Without another word, the hunter turned with a whirl of his smock and bolted off into the woods behind him. The ranger, shouting commands for the hunter to stop, clumsily reloaded his musket as he attempted to chase him. The two hurled themselves through branches, leaves, and bushes. The hunter was a quick fellow – he maintained a distance of ten paces from his adversary, even while moving. The ranger, still trying to reload his rifle, could not concentrate on the complicated procedure while running at the same time. A branch hit him in the face and he fell flat on his back. When he came to, the hunter he was chasing was nowhere to be seen.

Escaping his pursuer by the skin of his teeth, the cloaked man made his way to the edge of the forest and tried to catch his breath as he cursed himself for not being able to fetch dinner. He would probably have to go hungry again tonight unless he could convince some charitable soul in town to spare a loaf of bread – or he could try and go to the tavern and try to beg the tavern keeper for a meal. He decided that the latter option would hurt his pride less than the former – as he did not want to be seen as some common beggar – and made his way to the Black Horse Inn, the local tavern and public house.

The Black Horse was a simple looking establishment. The building was made of the cheap unpainted bricks and wood collected from the forest. The rusty sign that hung over the door depicted a rearing black stallion engraved with the words "Black Horse Inn" on its side.

The tavern was ancient, and some even speculated that its insignia was chosen because of its history of attracting recruits to the king's cavaliers. The bartender liked to claim that the pub was around when King Arthur himself wore the crown and that the horse was a symbol of the might of English cavalry that trampled the Saxon invaders.

Most of its patrons ended up serving in the army or in roving mercenary bands thanks to the recruiters that frequented the establishment. Many of the men that enlisted in the service returned to Bolingbroke in wooden boxes. Still, the money was good, and a life of soldiering was certainly better than a life of begging.

During the day, it was so quiet on the inside that one could hear the squeaking of the vermin that scurried about on the tavern floor. But at sundown, the place was so lively with the shouting of drunks and rogues that one could barely hear oneself think.

The hunter had arrived during the evening, keeping his hood up to protect his head from the rain outside. No one noticed him enter through the cacophony of song and drunken shouting. He approached the tavern keeper's counter, but before he could say anything, the tavern keeper sneered at him and said,

"James Fletcher. You dare to show your face here again?"

James did not respond but instead waited for the tavern keeper to finish. The large, bald man with a potbelly and a red nose produced a stick carved with notches from behind the counter. The notches almost covered the entire piece of wood.

"I am normally a very patient man, James – but you drive me too far. Do you see this tally stick? Each notch indicates a meal or a drink that you have promised you would pay for 'before the next harvest.' Well, we have passed harvesting season – twice." The tavern keeper paused for a moment, waiting for James to come up with some kind of excuse. He said nothing, so the tavern keeper continued, "I am sorry lad. I should have done this a long time ago, but I have to cut you off – I am trying to run a business here. And I cannot make any money for myself and my five sons – *five.*" He held up five fingers for emphasis, "unless you find some way to pay back what you owe me."

"How much do I owe you?" James said, finally. His voice was that of a youth – masculine, but gentle. Doffing his hood, the young hunter revealed a head of smooth black hair and piercing blue eyes, with good cheekbones, but a feminine jaw.

The tavern keeper ran his fingers through his own non-existent hair and grumbled. Every time he saw James's hair he was reminded of his own glorious locks – which he lost years ago.

"You owe me three pounds," said the tavern keeper, "Or a head of hair. The choice is yours. If you cannot pay me back, then I cannot serve you."

"Three pounds it is then." James said, without hesitating. He liked his hair very much. "If I cannot settle the debt before asking for my next meal, then you have my permission to shoot me."

33

The tavern keeper blinked in surprise and said, "If you are that eager to die, then I accept. You are hereby banned from the Black Horse Inn until you pay back your debt. Now get out."

James Fletcher dragged himself out of the Black Horse thinking that he had just consigned himself to death. Three pounds was the cost of a very nice warhorse. He had no idea where his next meal would come from – perhaps he was destined to live the rest of his life as a bandit – to hunt men instead of rabbits. Yes, that is exactly what he would do. Arrows were cheap and reusable. He would simply...

"Good morrow."

He was interrupted by a man wearing a cavalier uniform. A soldier! He was about to be arrested, then sent to jail – and hanged! He quickly turned and...

"You seem to be down on your luck, my fine fellow."

James stopped. He turned and faced the cavalier. The man's sword was not drawn, and he just stood there, with a smile on his face, as if he was talking to a friend. James was not sure whether to trust him or to proceed with his original plan and flee.

"May I inquire if you know about the dreadful war that rages on throughout Europe?"

James blinked at the mention of the seemingly irrelevant question and simply replied, "No, I have not."

"Then allow me to inform you, good sir," said the cavalier, "Seven years ago, his majesty King Charles decided to come to the aid of his beleaguered Protestant allies and declare war on the Catholics. Many men, myself included, jumped at the opportunity to enlist as soldiers in His Majesty's royal army – but five years later, disaster – for reasons unknown to us, the king withdrew from the war and now we are at peace! But an army without a war is seldom a good thing my dear lad, and thus we elected to continue fighting, and to continue earning our keep."

James did not understand. He was about to ask what the man's point was when the cavalier continued.

"You see, even though England is officially at peace by the declaration of the sovereign, we may still fight her enemies – as mercenaries in the service of her Protestant allies. Four florins a month – that is what we are getting these days. The continentals are rich, lad, and they pay quite well. The food is provided for, the beds as well. At nights, we sleep in warm cozy tents beside cozy fireplaces, and in the morning, the glory of battle awaits. You, lad, seem to need some money, quite badly I might add."

James's ears opened up at the sound of "four florins a month." He could pay off his entire debt in just six weeks of service! He did not want to hear anything more, not that he could understand the man anyway. He grabbed the cavalier's hand, shook it brusquely and said, "Whatever a mercenary is, four florins a month sounds fantastic. I accept your offer."

The cavalier smiled warmly and produced a document and a piece of charcoal from his coat pocket.

"Can you read, good sir?"

"No."

"Then make your mark on this document my good man."

James took the charcoal and made a big, black X mark on the sheet of paper. When he handed it back to the cavalier, he realized that he hadn't gotten the man's name, and asked him to introduce himself.

35

"Apologies – I am Thomas Warwick, formerly of the King's Life Guards, presently serving in the Talbot Company. Welcome aboard."

Chapter 5

Vienna, Holy Roman Empire

The clip-clopping of two horses echoed through the alleyways of Vienna's slums. It was around dusk, and the shadows of the horses and their riders hugged the cobblestone walls. The riders, one attired in a shining black suit of armor with a blackened, visored armet helmet, and the other clad in a puffed-and-slashed doublet with red and black stripes and a wide beret, conversed in a relaxed tone as a gaggle of beggars, thieves and homeless men trailed behind them.

"The Catholics are doomed to failure," said the armored rider on the left in German. "Who do they have supporting them? The Catholic League? Spain? These Holy Roman idiots?" His voice raised with the mention of each faction.

"Be careful, Otto, your accent is showing," said the comparatively plainly-dressed rider on the right, softly, "Do you want everyone to know that you are a damned Saxon? You may speak the same language as these Austrians, but remember that your states are at war." he continued as he glanced behind him to once again take account of the number of vagrants that they had brought with them. There were fifty-two.

Otto Koenigsherr and Gunther Jaeger were recruiters for Talbot Company, and they had been looking for fresh recruits within the Holy Roman Empire for two weeks. In the past, the two had worked as individuals, with Otto recruiting men from his homeland in Saxony while Gunther recruited from his place of birth in Bavaria, but now they had been ordered to work together and recruit men from Austria. So far, they had picked up a good number of men. The streets of the big cities were always littered with undesirables that reeked of the filth of the gutter who had death and disease hovering over their heads. These men were the opposite.

Otto was the son of a minor Protestant noble. Instead of investing his inheritance to grow his father's estate, the young Koenigsherr instead spent it on a fine suit of armor, a horse, and the best weapons he could arm himself with to participate in the wars of religion that raged throughout Europe. A cushy life on a country estate had no appeal to him. He preferred the excitement and romance of living a life out in the field with his brothers in arms and fighting for his coin instead of waiting for it to pour in thanks to the sweat and toil of other men.

Gunther Jaeger was a Catholic and a son of Bavaria. Originally the older of two children in a family of butchers, he, unlike Otto, did not choose to search of fame and fortune, but was instead impressed into the service of a mercenary group – the Talbot Company, just as he was doing to the men trailing behind him. Initially, however, due to his social status, Gunther was assigned as a lowly pikeman in the infantry.

In due time, though, he had proven time and again that he was not only one of the most difficult men to kill, but also one of the coldest and most calculating soldiers that his commanders had ever seen. He spoke little and preferred to lead by example, and this had earned him his place as a drillmaster in the company.

Fate had brought the two men into the service of the Talbot Company. Otto had deserted his unit after fighting alongside the Swedish at the Battle of Breitenfeld when the entire Saxon force was routed by a Catholic army flying the colors of the Holy Roman Empire. It was only later that Otto had found out that the Swedish had won the battle, and refused to rejoin his regiment in shame. He instead opted to join a company of free cavalrymen, who fought under no flag and for no cross. These men, he soon found out, were mercenaries for the Talbot Company.

It was here that he met Gunther – a low-born who had far more battlefield experience than he did, and whom he was instructed to treat as an equal. Although Otto's status permitted him to be the captain of a cavalry troop, he had no problem being put on equal footing as the man who trained *all* new recruits.

"Oh, it does not matter, Herr Jaeger," Otto said, dismissively. "I will end up killing a few of these Austrians eventually – or their sons, or their brothers, or their children. It would only hasten the process if they attacked me now."

"Oh yes, I relish the thought of being chased by every man in the city on top of the entire city watch, and possibly every dog from here to Liesenpfennig!" Gunther remarked with a snarl. "Your rashness will be your undoing. I suggest that you reign yourself in."

Otto dismissed his colleague with a wave of his gloved hand.

"Give me one good reason why the Catholics would be able to win. Just one," said Otto as they turned the corner into a wider main street.

"The Spanish can…"

"The Spanish still believe that we are in the previous century, my friend. Their army is composed primarily of men who fight in antique dress, and whose tactics could be thwarted by a general with half the brain of an ape."

"I was going to say that the Spanish can buy their way out of this war."

"How do you suppose they would do that? Oh, look." Otto said, cutting himself short as he saw a beggar curled up on the side of the street. "You there! Get up! Enlist in the honorable Talbot Company for four florins a month or die in the streets like a rat! The choice is yours sir!"

The disheveled beggar opened his weary eyes and looked up at the soldiers. He hadn't had anything to eat in days, and this was foremost on his mind.

"Good and kind sir, do you have anything to eat?" he said, his voice quivering.

Otto dismounted and strode over to the beggar, picking him up and standing him upright. "By God, you can stuff yourself with bread all you like when you join the company. Sometimes there will be sausage as well."

The mention of free bread and sausage was enough to make the beggar's heart skip a beat. It was either that or the muscle atrophy. He opened his mouth in a near-toothless grin and said, "Will I be clothed, fine sir?"

Otto struggled not to back away from the foul-smelling breath of the beggar and replied, "Oh, oh yes. Only the sturdiest raiment for company men. We will clean you up, put some armor on your chest, sir, and the ladies will flock to you." Otto rolled his eyes at his own comment. The man was in shambles. Even if they cleaned him up with all the soap in Europe, the stench of his breath would still be enough to put down an ox.

"What must I do for all this, sir?" said the beggar, almost pleadingly. He had lived almost his entire adult life out in the streets, and to him, this was the opportunity of a lifetime. No more stealing from honest, hardworking merchants, no more begging for coin, and no more rats for supper.

"Write down your name and make your mark on this roster." Otto said, handing the beggar a piece of charcoal and a book full of names.

The beggar stared at the book. His lips quivered – the one chance he had of getting out of this life and all he had to do was write his name – something he never learned how to do.

"Oh I see," said Otto, "Tell me your name, and I will write it down for you. All you will need to do is make your mark."

"Friedrich."

"Surname?"

"What is a surname, sir?"

"... I see." Otto muttered, simply scribbling 'Friedrich of Vienna no. III' in the roster, since there were two other men named Friedrich that they had recruited that week, neither of whom had family names.

Handing back the roster to Friedrich, Otto told him to make his mark, and he did so by holding the piece of charcoal like a knife and making a large X where Otto had indicated.

"Congratulations, my good man," said Otto with a smile, "Welcome to the company. Now fall behind with the others."

As the beggar ran behind them to join the other recruits, Gunther made a change to a roster of his own and added one more mark, making a total of fifty-three, one for every recruit.

"Do you know why your men were routed at Breitenfeld, Herr Koenigsherr?" said Gunther as he looked up from his roster.

"Yes," replied Otto, mounting his horse. "Because the officers put in charge over us were idiots and bed wetters, more suitable to an army of dolls and children's toys rather than regiments of horse and foot."

"Herr Koenigsherr," Gunther said, looking Otto straight in the eye, "the periodicals that mention the battle, written by the Swedes – whom may I remind you *won* that battle, mention that their flanks fell on account of 'Saxon troops of questionable quality'."

"I would watch my tongue if I were you, sir."

"Do not think that this is a personal attack on your own valor or strength of arms, Herr Koenigsherr. I wished to merely state the fact that the soldiers that your countrymen fielded at Breitenfeld were exactly like these men. You Saxons fed them, gave them armor and weapons, yes, but your officers severely neglected to instill in them the discipline that is essential for a regiment to function. This will not happen with these men."

Otto scoffed, "Oh? Why do you say that, Herr Jaeger? Even with you training them, I can plainly see that these men are more suitable to be cannon fodder rather than soldiers. None of them have any intelligence; I am absolutely sure none of them have held a weapon before, and I guarantee that they have no experience with even the most basic principles of drill."

"Perfect. *Tabula rasa.*"

"What was that, *Herr Jaeger?*"

"It is Latin for 'blank slate'. A man cannot make any bad habits if he has never acquired them."

The two riders and the men behind them approached a large building, built like a tavern, but with a stone wall surrounding it, built with embrasures – small windows that allowed weapons to be fired out from behind the wall. This was Talbot Company's Austrian guild house.

"Welcome to your new home, gentlemen," said Otto as he led the new recruits into the gates.

No sooner had the men entered the guild house's main hall than they were grabbed by other company men in uniforms, who stripped them of their rags and herded them into an open courtyard where they were doused with buckets of cold, soapy water to get rid of their stench.

The reception process had begun. The men would later be deloused, shaven, and equipped with fresh clothes and the white sash of the Talbot Company. Gunther would soon resume his duties as drillmaster and would beat the discipline into them until either exhaustion or death claimed them.

His men would not break like the Saxons at Breitenfeld. They would advance in their formations even as musket balls grazed their cheeks or as their friends died around them. They would come to fear the wrath of their commander more than the enemy, and the sound of his voice more than musket fire. This is what Gunther had been doing for years to all sorts of men – city dwellers and country folk alike. They would no longer be artisans, shoemakers, carpenters or farmers – they would be soldiers: disciplined, fearless, and violent. This is what the company expected of them, and this is how Gunther would mold them to be.

Chapter 6

La Scimmia Ubriaca Inn
Duchy of Milan, Northern Italy

Don Alfonso Villanueva y Santiago sipped his wine with a confident smile as he placed his feet up on his table. Life had been good to him so far. Fairly recently, the former Spanish soldier had been granted an *encomienda* or fief in the Viceroyalty of New Spain for his help in putting down a major insurrection in the Philippine Islands. For his service to the crown, he was put in charge of a vast tract of land on an island called Panay. Among his responsibilities as an *encomendero* for this land were the conversion of the natives to Catholicism, protection of the land from pirates and brigands, the propagation of Spanish culture and influence, and the exploitation of any natural resources. He devoted himself the most to this last duty.

Europe at this time was always hungry for new things from the new world that Spain had opened up for her – figuratively and literally. Spices, new fruits, animals, and vegetables flowed from the Americas and the East Indies into the markets of Europe and fetched hefty prices. Many enterprising Spaniards had been making substantial wealth from trading goods that were only produced in their new world possessions, like chili, potatoes, corn, and tomatoes – especially tomatoes. These would be planted and harvested by their native workers, given to their master as tribute, and loaded onto a Spanish galleon for transport to the markets of Europe.

For Don Alfonso, his *encomienda* produced sugarcane. Sugar was a luxury – sweetness was the one taste that the human tongue craved the most. The magical plant that was sugarcane, more grass than crop, grew like a weed in its native habitat.

The difference between a Spanish *encomienda* and a regular European fief was that the land actually belonged to the people living on it; however, the people owed service to their *encomendero*. Don Alfonso had put a humble and trustworthy native by the name of Gurung-Gurung in charge of the cultivation, harvest, and transport of the crop to Spain. If he did well, Don Alfonso promised him a substantial cut of the earnings – as soon as he returned from Europe.

Although he loved adventure, Don Alfonso despised the tropical heat of the East Indies. It frequently made him ill while he was there, and he was advised by his physician to return to Europe, where he would not have to endure the blistering tropical sun or the humid afternoons in the jungle.

Before leaving, the don instructed Gurung-Gurung to update him with quarterly progress reports, something the native had been doing with great efficiency and regularity. The native complied, sending letters to Europe without fail every four months – the time it took to get from the East Indies to Spain – for almost a year. The last progress report came about a month ago. It simply said *"Los barcos han salido del puerto."* the ships have left port.

Anticipating a gigantic windfall, the don left for Milan, one of Spain's possessions in northern Italy, not before notifying the House and Audience of the Indies, also known as the *Casa de Contratacion* of his change of address. This was where he would sell his goods. The Italians were the master merchants of

Europe. They would give him the best prices on the continent, and there would be no 20% tariff on precious metals that he would have to pay to the crown, unlike those other Spaniards who wished to flood the European market with gold from the New World.

Everything had fallen into place. God was good. In anticipation of his wealth, Don Alfonso had been issuing promissory notes to every shopkeeper, cobbler, tailor, and metalsmith he passed by, regaling them with tales of the massive income he would receive from his sugar shipment. The don had purchased a new suit of clothes, a dozen silk stockings, and a finely crafted spontoon and sword along with a full set of halberdier's armor, out of nostalgia for his old profession. He had even paid extra to have the armor delivered to the Scimmia Ubriaca Inn, where he was currently staying. The armor and weapons now rested up in his room – the finest room in the inn – in a rack he had custom-built for himself just the other day. It even had his name engraved on it on a large brass plate.

The Don looked up from his wine to notice a man had just entered the tavern. Much like the don, he looked out of place; another Spaniard in Italy, from his manner of dress. He seemed slightly lost, turning his head left and right, scanning every face in the tavern with a worried urgency.

"*Amigo.*" called out the don, "Come join me – perhaps I can help you?"

The man breathed a sigh of relief and weaved through the tables in the tavern to make it towards Don Alfonso.

"Are you Don Alfonso Villanueva y Santiago?" asked the man, seemingly out of breath.

"Yes." replied the don, his smile becoming wider. "Am I to assume that you are a courier from the *Casa de Contratacion?*"

"Yes, *señor.*" the courier said with a bow. "I am a messenger of the House and Audience of the Indies, and I have a message for you from the company."

Don Alfonso nearly snatched the letter out of the courier's hand in excitement. He peeled open the seal of the company to smell the letter. It was freshly written, and to him, it smelled like money. He opened the letter slowly, savoring his financial victory. His eyes widened as he read the letter:

Don Alfonso Villanueva y Santiago,

Esteemed señor, we at the House and Audience of the Indies seek to inform you that your ship designated as "La Bailarina del Mar", berthed at the port of Bobog, Island of Panay, chartered on a course from Bobog to Manila to Acapulco, with a final destination of the port of Cadiz, Spain, duly inspected and approved by the port authorities of the Audience in the Viceroyalty of New Spain, has delivered a cargo of **spoiled goods in the form of 500 tons of rotten sugar cane** *to the receiving shipping authorities at the port of Acapulco.*

There was more to the letter, detailing the weight of the cargo and the state of the ship and other damages, but don Alfonso's heart stopped at the word 'spoiled', and he could not read any longer. He had spent a substantial amount of money to grow the cane but had failed to realize that all of the other *encomenderos* who transported sugar refined their product in a sugar mill to prevent spoilage before sending it over to Europe. Knowing

48

nothing about sugar, and with Gurung-Gurung not knowing the distance between Bobog and Spain, he had skipped this crucial step and had paid for it dearly.

This was all the Indio's fault, he thought. If they had only calculated for how much time... no. It was his fault too. Plunging headfirst into a business he knew nothing about doomed him from the moment he stepped off the metaphorical plank. His accounts now suffered from a potentially life-ruining deficit thanks to all the frivolous spending he had done before his ship had come in, and for that, he could blame no one but himself.

If he had not been sitting down, the don's legs would've given way. Already he felt his palms moisten, and he started to tremble slightly. As the messenger walked away, he began to wonder what would happen to him. With a debt the size of the monthly income of a large village, authorities from the Audience would surely be after him. How would he settle his debts, where would his next meal come from... would he get in trouble with the law? Would he spend the rest of his life rotting in jail? What was he going to do? Where would he go?

Spain's possessions in both the old world and the new world were vast. There was nowhere he could go without running into a representative of the crown's law. Even here in northern Italy, he was unsafe. No Spanish citizen could step on a boat without the *Casa de Contratacion* knowing about it. He would be arrested the moment he stepped foot on any boat that flew the Spanish colors. The only options left were to leave Spanish-controlled lands. Travel to the wild lands of the east – Bohemia, perhaps even Poland or Russia. There he would live out his days as a fur trader...

Suddenly the sound of drums interrupted the don's spiraling thoughts. A gang of military recruiters had just walked into the tavern. Local Italians by the look of them. It seemed that God had placed a solution in his lap. Go to war or go to jail – the weighty decision rested on his shoulders.

"Friends and comrades, my name is Captain Emilio Toscana," said a recruiter, as he sat at a table while his companion played the drum beside him, "We of the honorable Talbot Company will pay a sum of four florins a month to any man who wishes to take up arms with us, in addition to any spoils you take for yourself! A life of adventure and excitement awaits you! You will never have to worry about your next meal or where you will rest your head at night when you enlist with the company."

People were beginning to mill around the recruiter's table at the sound of four florins a month. The pay sounded fair to Don Alfonso, and he had done soldier work before, so this was by no means an alien profession to him. He had decided. It was time to enlist with this 'Talbot Company' – since, realistically, the alternative was imprisonment and death. Better to die by the sword than by the slow, lonely and excruciating death of starvation.

Just as the don rose from his seat, the tavern doors swung open. A figure dressed in a very colorful blue, white, and red doublet entered the tavern, exhausted and panting. A rapier, leather kidney belt, and a steel breastplate made this person look like a mercenary, but something was amiss.

Chapter 7

The mercenary made a beeline for the recruiter's table, elbowing through the line, ignoring the complaints of the other hopeful recruits.

"My name is Lodovico Bianchi," said the mercenary in Italian, breathing heavily, "formerly of the company of Ernst von Mansfeld. I have served faithfully at the Battle of Dessau Bridge, and I am experienced in the use of smallswords, daggers, and rapiers. I have also served as a bravo-for-hire for various Italian nobles. You will hire me."

Captain Toscana looked at the colorfully dressed figure up and down and said, "What balls! Do you think I am an idiot, *signora?*"

She was desperately hoping for it, but this recruiter was no fool. He could tell that 'Lodovico Bianchi' was no man. Her long lashes, her small mouth, her delicately rounded and feminine jaw, her auburn shoulder-length hair, and a gentle pair of doe-like eyes that had clearly never seen battle before betrayed her for whom she really was – a teenage girl in a costume.

Don Alfonso looked on as 'Lodovico' desperately tried to plead her case with tales of bravado and her adventures with Ernst von Mansfeld, a German mercenary commander who was, a few years ago, considered the most dangerous enemy of the Catholic league. Von Mansfeld was known for his sharp wit and intelligence, as well as the uncanny ability to maintain unit cohesion even when the end seemed nigh. Such a man would never dare risk enlisting a girl into his ranks, let alone a girl like this... would he?

As her arguments caused Toscana to become more and more exasperated, to the point of the two beginning to shout at each other, the don decided that he had enough. Experienced mercenary or queen of shams, he would not allow this to continue. Seeing an opportunity to get into the good graces of the company, he resolved to challenge 'Lodovico' to a duel, demonstrating his weapons mastery and showing how clear of a fraud she was, if she was indeed a charlatan. This would, in turn, put Toscana at ease, and perhaps would earn him a position more suitable to his martial prowess among the ranks of this 'Talbot Company'. The don found it rather insulting to be enlisted as a mere pikeman. He had education, ambition, wealth... perhaps not wealth, but he was no one's cannon fodder. And if 'Lodovico' won the duel, then he would no longer have to worry about that massive debt he incurred, and she would be the one to worry about paying for his burial expenses.

Just as Don Alfonso rose from his seat, the tavern door swung open again. There was no fanfare this time. Three *convincing-looking* Italian bravos burst into the tavern, their eyes darting around the room. It took mere seconds for them to fix their eyes on their mark. 'Lodovico' stared back at them and immediately sprinted off, knocking down the recruiter's table as she went. The three bravos followed in hot pursuit.

The girl headed straight away for the stairs leading to the upper rooms and tried to run to the second floor, skipping three steps with her long legs every time she stepped up. However, she was soon stopped by a rather large man at the top of the stairs. It was the innkeeper.

Luigi Trotta, the owner of the Scimmia Ubriaca, had a keen eye for troublemakers, and that was what he saw in 'Lodovico'. If a trio of mercenaries had been hired to dispatch her, surely she had wronged someone, and Luigi was not about to let her escape from the arms of justice.

'Lodovico' turned and faced her assailants. The stairwell was narrow, forcing them to come up to her one at a time. The first bravo approached her slowly, his glowering eyes fixed on hers. Both drew their swords simultaneously and clashed against each other.

'Lodovico' had the high ground, being five steps above her opponent. His thrusts could not touch her, but her wild swings could nick him. As she swung her sword over her head in wild, reckless overhand chops, something her rapier was never intended for, her unprepared opponent winced as he tried to block her strikes with his limited reach.

The bravo could simply not find time to attack. His opponent's blows were quick, careless, but aggressive. If he came any closer, it would be like approaching a giant whirling needle, but he had to try it – he would not be paid otherwise. As the bravo stepped forward, there was a splatter of red. He clutched the side of his head where his left ear used to be and screamed in agony.

With her opponent disoriented, off-balance, and in extreme pain, 'Lodovico' thrust her sword into his neck – the smooth straight blade of her rapier piercing into his throat like a fork piercing a tender, juicy lemon.

'Lodovico' froze for a fraction of a second, realizing she had just killed a man for the first time in her life, but her survival instinct took over and she kicked the bravo's lifeless corpse down the stairwell, causing it to crash into his two companions below with a loud sound, like the cracking of bones.

If 'Lodovico' had been a better fighter, this fight could have been over much sooner. She had not even known that fighting from the high ground would extend her reach, make her strikes more powerful and give her a better angle of attack. Neither did she know that by fighting in a staircase, she eliminated the risk of having to face three opponents at the same time. However, all the veteran fighters in the room saw this as a clear indication of her 'experience.'

Before the other two bravos could recover to continue the assault, Captain Toscana stood up and yelled for a halt. 'Lodovico' peered at him from her place on the staircase, trembling, her eyes as wide as saucers, with her blade still held in a stance of attack.

Captain Toscana motioned for the girl to come to him. Even as she tiptoed down the stairs, not making the slightest noise, the eyes of the entire inn were on her, especially Luigi's. Who would pay for this mess?

'Lodovico' stepped over the bodies of her opponents as she approached Toscana, her sword still drawn.

"You can fight, *signora*." he said.

"I... I am Lodovico Bianchi. I am a man." she muttered, her senses slowly coming back to her, the realization dawning on her that she had taken a human life.

"And you have served under Ernst von Mansfeld?" he asked.

54

"Y...yes." 'Lodovico' said, frantically nodding her head.

"Did you have a commission?"

"Y...ah... yes." she said, not really understanding the question.

"Please understand that commissions granted in other armies do not carry over to the company. The price of a commission in the Talbot Company for a lieutenant of... swords, I believe your previous commission might have been in... is fifty florins."

"I have the money, of course." she said, quickly producing a bulging sack of coins from her belt. Again, 'Lodovico' did not fully understand what she was purchasing, she merely wished to keep up her quite transparent lie.

Captain Toscana grabbed the pouch and poured out about fifty gold coins. Frowning in suspicion, he bit one of them – the coin showed scarring from his teeth. It was real. With a shrug of apathetic resignation, he tossed a single coin to Luigi to pay for the damage to the inn, handed his roster over to 'Lodovico', had her sign it and said,

"Welcome to Talbot Company, lieutenant."

Toscana could see, clear as the light of day, that this was not a man. Fifty florins was actually the price of a captain's commission, but if she could afford it without even bothering to question it, then by all means, she could join the company and be ignored by the swordsmen she was appointed over. Coin was the only thing that mattered in the company, and as long as she had plenty of it, no one would ask any questions. The recruiter gave her a curt nod and motioned for her to take a seat as the line of recruits slowly started to form up behind her again.

The two surviving bravos that had been sent after her did not want to take the risk of being ganged up on by every Talbot Company man in the building by attacking her again, so instead picked up their fallen comrade and carried him out of the tavern, cursing her as they went.

The others around her stared at the fat sack of coins that 'Lodovico' had given to Toscana. Why was someone with that much wealth joining up with them? And more importantly, why were three armed men sent to attack her? Dozens of eyes stared at 'Lodovico', some curious, but mostly suspicious.

Don Alfonso sat at his table, pondering, with his eyes cast downward and his chin on his knuckle. He noticed something that the others had not. While everyone knew that 'Lodovico' was in fact, a woman, the brawl by the stairs made it seem apparent that she at least knew how to handle herself and could hold her own on a battlefield. Don Alfonso, however, saw the truth. 'Lodovico Bianchi' was one of the clumsiest swordsmen he had ever seen. While she was aggressive and apparently brave, she exhibited the grace and skill of an ape with a fire poker. However, since Don Alfonso knew this, he could use it to his advantage.

Naturally 'Lodovico' gravitated towards the only person in the inn that was not staring at her and sat at the don's table. She nervously clasped her small, soft hands together and decided to start a conversation... in Italian.

"So... I guess we are brothers in arms now, no?" she said with a fake chuckle. Luckily for her, Spanish and Italian shared so many words that they were mutually intelligible. Don Alfonso nodded and replied in his native Spanish,

"Yes, but you are no brother of mine, *señorita*. I have a few questions, if I may."

"Ah, you are a Spaniard. I do not know what it is like in your language, but in Italian, we use the word *signore* when we refer to men, and I clearly am a man. You may ask your questions, but the clarity of my answers depends on what those questions are."

"Why were those three men chasing you?"

"Well, this I can be honest about. Dead men cannot retort. I borrowed a very large sum of money from a bank here in Milan. I... may have gambled away three-quarters of it and spent much of the rest on these clothes and this weapon. By the time I realized what I had done I also realized that I needed to get out of this country. The money in my purse is all that remains."

Don Alfonso suddenly felt a strong connection with the girl. Both of them had the same financial problem since both had dug themselves deep into debt. He hoped that they would be able to find a way out of it together.

"A fine outfit you have purchased for yourself indeed, *señorita*." the don continued, insisting on using the feminine version of the word, "I would be terrified if the circus rose up in arms against us." he joked, without so much as a smile.

She sighed. "Is the disguise that bad?"

Don Alfonso nodded. "Not only is the disguise bad, but I can tell that you are lying about many things. For example..."

"*Signore*. I did not come here to be chided. In case you haven't heard, I am to be your lieutenant."

"And that is exactly what I am 'chiding' you for, *señorita.*" Don Alfonso said, taking another sip of the wine he had almost forgotten about. Its bitterness was magnified now that he knew he probably could not afford it. "*Señorita,* hypothetically, how would you feel if you were put under the leadership of a person who was completely without skill, know-how or experience?"

"I would be embarrassed, perhaps more than a little resentful. I might even resign from this imaginary position."

"And if this person was responsible for your well-being, your health, your very life, *señorita?* How would you feel?"

"I would feel terrified. I do not know what that question has to do with anything *signore,* because I know that I am a very capable leader and, as you have seen, quite a skilled fighter."

"Of course, of course, and you were put in charge of the swordsmen, correct?"

"Yes, that is correct."

"Then tell me, what is the purpose of a swordsman in modern warfare?"

"Why, they are there to fight of course."

"*Señorita,* everyone fights. Everyone from the dumbest pikeman to the haughtiest cavalier has a part to play in battle. My question is what role do your men, swordsmen specifically, play?"

"Well, I would say that the swordsman is responsible for fighting with the sword of course. Stop this nonsense; I know what I am talking about. I do not need to explain it to you!"

The don smiled, silently confident in himself and his judge of character. The girl did not understand the concept of a pike and shot formation – the most basic battlefield formation of any modern European army, and she was going to command one of its most critical elements.

"*Hija*," said the don, talking to her as if he were talking to a small child, "admit it. You know nothing about war or warfare. If you reveal this truth about yourself to your men, they will mutiny, and they will kill you. Soldiers do not like irresponsible, foolish leaders. Do you want to be killed by your own men?"

'Lodovico' quickly realized that the Spaniard was right, and she shook her head frantically, her eyes wide in fear from the realization of what she had gotten herself into.

"You are in luck, *hija*. I was once a commander of soldiers myself. I can teach you what to do, what to say, and how to act. I can turn you into a fearless leader of men and you can stand tall as a soldier instead of... whatever you are now."

"I suppose you are not doing this out of compassion for me, are you?" she said. The Italians were all naturally suspicious of the Spanish. The Spanish king was, after all, their distant, foreign master; and every proud son of Italy considered the Spanish as invaders.

"You read me well, *hija*. All I ask is one small favor. Give me enough coin to buy my own commission and my way out of this city, and I will take you under my wing and spare you from an embarrassing mutiny... and possibly death."

'Lodovico' looked around. Many were still staring at her, but the majority had gone back to whatever they were doing before she entered the inn. The air was still thick with suspicious murmuring, however.

"I accept, but if you are to train me, we must first trust each other," said 'Lodovico' as she narrowed her eyes. "You tell me who you are and I will tell you who I am."

"These life stories take many weeks to tell, *hija*. Let us save that for when we are on the road. Let us start with names. I am Don Alfonso Villanueva y Santiago. Who are you?"

"My name... my real name... is Sofia Fortezza di Milano."

The don smiled; content that he had finally been able to wrestle some truth out of this stranger. If he ever experienced a painful and horrible death because of her mistakes, he would know what name to curse in the afterlife.

"A pleasure to meet you, *Señorita Fortezza*." he said with a twirl of his hand and a slight bow of his head. "Now, as I said, you will never pass for a war veteran if you do not know the first thing about war. I ask you again – what is the purpose of a swordsman?"

"They are the first into the fray, the bravest and fiercest..."

Don Alfonso raised his hand, motioning for her to stop. "*Hija*, no. This is not how modern war on is waged on the continent. This is how you would fight if you were an infidel, a savage, or a Turk. When was the last time you heard of any of them winning a victory against a proper European army?"

"Well, the Turks have been winning major victories in Hungary..."

"My dear, the question was rhetorical." Don Alfonso interrupted. "Now, in modern warfare, the pikemen and musketeers, in the formation of a pike square, make up the most basic unit of a battle. It is strong from the front, but vulnerable to the sides. Your swordsmen are there to protect its flanks."

"I see, and how am I to do that exactly?"

"It would be best to demonstrate that in a marshaling field, *hija*. If you wish for the lesson to continue, I graciously ask for you to purchase my officer's commission for me so that I may have a company of men to demonstrate with."

Sofia made a slight bow with her head and took out her coin purse. It still bulged quite a bit, even after she gave Don Alfonso his fifty florins. The don smiled politely, barely containing his excitement, as he took the cash and presented it to Toscana.

"*Señor.*" he said to Toscana, "My name is Don Alfonso Villanueva y Santiago – I previously served under his majesty's..."

"Yes, yes, do you have the means to pay for your commission?"

The don dropped the pouch on the table, continuing.

"I previously served under his majesty's forces in the East Indies, as the commander of a halberdier company. I wish to offer my expertise to the company, as I believe that I would be wasted as a common foot soldier."

The recruiter looked at the don and could see that, unlike Sofia, he actually looked like he was telling the truth. Toscana saw the fine, well-kept clothing characteristic of the Spanish gentry, as well as the physical build that one might expect from a soldier. There was no need to bite the coin this time. He handed Don Alfonso the roster and instructed the don to write down his name and sign it. Don Alfonso was now a captain of the halberdiers.

Returning to Sofia, his smile as wide as ever, Don Alfonso sat beside her and gave her a brotherly pat on the back, saying, "We are either returning to the bank with chests full of coin or returning to our Heavenly Father. It is time for Sofia Fortezza the maiden to die and for Lodovico Bianchi the bravo to be born!"

Sofia had never really thought of death as a factor in the life of adventure she had made up in her head, but now there was no way to back out of her decision. So far though, she was falling in with the right crowd, and it looked like an auspicious start. She managed a fake, nervous smile and took a large gulp of Alfonso's wine, thinking, *What have I gotten myself into?*

Chapter 8

Rotterdam, Dutch Republic

The port city of Rotterdam was always a very busy place. The ubiquitous chattering of seagulls was drowned out by the noise of foreign ships being unloaded with fresh goods from all over the world and merchants eager to receive their new stock. The sounds of carts on cobblestone roads mingled with the cacophony of travelers and merchants shouting in different languages and livestock being sold at auction. The air smelled of cinnamon, tea, gunpowder and salt from both the sea and the stalls of the salt merchants.

The Dutch Republic was a trader's paradise. It boasted the lowest interest rates in the entire world and was home to the best business minds in Europe.

William MacRae was one of these minds. Though not a Dutchman himself, MacRae was a skilled businessman. While others worried about the rising or falling prices in the Dutch stock exchange, MacRae's fortunes were determined by the tides of war. As the leader and proprietor of the Talbot Company, MacRae bragged that he had the best and most diverse free company in all of Europe.

Within the ranks of the company were men from all over Europe – pikemen from Spain, Switzerland and the Holy Roman Empire, musketeers from France and Sweden, cavalry from Poland, Saxony and Russia, swordsmen from Italy, and various unspecialized troops from every corner of Europe, including Christian exiles from the Ottoman Empire and irregular troops from MacRae's native Scotland. These men were his product just as much as bales of cloth were the products of the textile merchant. And here he was, content to sit, like the other businessmen were, by the window of a dockside tavern, calmly smoking his pipe and nursing a glass of whiskey as he waited for his ship to come in.

The man himself looked nothing like a warrior at all, sporting a fashionable red leather jerkin over a doublet of the same color. On his head he wore a red cavalier hat with a single white ostrich feather in it, to show his wealth to the world. His features were angular and sharp, with deep, dark eye bags from long sleepless nights. What stood out about him though was the fact that he only had one true eye, having lost the other one in a duel with a rival clansman some five years ago. He had replaced it with a glass one, which did not move when his good one did.

His good eye now stared out into the harbor, as a ship flying English colors came into view, several miles out to sea. The aptly named "Fortune", when docked, promised to bring him a fresh batch of his countrymen from Britain, ready to put their swords and pikes to whomever their client willed. All of the recruiters he sent throughout Europe were ordered to muster today at the Rotterdam harbor with their fresh recruits behind them so that the company would be able to march to the main guild house as a group. Many men would be needed for MacRae's newest campaign, and many men had answered MacRae's call for adventure and money.

The stomping of boots in cadence interrupted the din of the portside markets. MacRae shifted his gaze to the source of the noise and found two of his officers, Gunther Jaeger and Otto

Koenigsherr, riding on horseback up the road towards the port, with fifty-three enlisted volunteers marching in tow behind them. The men who had once been beggars now wielded pikes that were ten feet long over their shoulders, purchased with company funds as an investment in an uncertain product. They marched with their feet in step and their heads held high. No one could have known that not even two weeks ago, many of the men were begging on the streets. It took twelve days of training on the march from Vienna to Rotterdam to mold them into the soldiers that MacRae saw before him. As soldiers, they were not fully capable of facing a determined enemy, but at the very least, they had been taught the basics of drill.

The two Germans rode in front of MacRae, dismounted their mounts, and saluted their master simultaneously. One could tell a lot about an officer's character by how he saluted. Gunther simply touched the brim of his hat with his fingertips and made a slight bow, while Otto removed his helmet completely and bowed as low as his armor would allow.

MacRae returned their salutes with a wave of his hand and said, "Are ye ready, me boys?" in a heavy Scottish accent.

"*Ja mein Herr.*" replied Otto, "We are prepared to march on your command."

Gunther remained silent, awaiting orders.

"Ye will have to excuse me. Ye are the foremost to turn up to me assembly. We will have to wait a wee bit more for the rest of the companies. Come, me lads, join yer colonel for a drink."

As the two Germans joined him, the stomping of boots came to an abrupt halt. Their men had come to a halt outside the tavern and stood at attention, dutifully waiting until they were ordered to move. The men were green as the grass though, and Gunther expected the formation to break ranks out of boredom within the next five minutes.

MacRae motioned to the bottle of whiskey that sat on his table, offering his officers a drink. Gunther respectfully declined, but Otto took a swig straight from the bottle without a moment's hesitation.

"What say ye of the quality of these men hither?" said MacRae, cocking his head in the direction of the men outside.

Gunther sat in stoic silence, letting his colleague speak for both of them.

"In all honesty, *mein Herr,*" said Otto, "the men themselves can be trained, however, I doubt they are of the sort of stock and attitude that we need for a sustained *kriegskampagne...* ah, campaign of war, sir."

"This is nary yer first time to recruit soldiers from among the scum of the earth, Master Koenigsherr. What makes these ones so different?"

"*Herr Oberst...* ah, colonel, if I may speak plainly, when I used to recruit soldiers in my home region of Saxony, I would always find men who had the hearts of warriors, who only needed the slightest reason to throw away his life for his cause – whether that be to defend his hearth and home, to avenge the death of a loved one or friend, or to simply stop the spread of foreign Catholicism. I see no such motivation in the men I bring here now. All I see is sickness, desperation, and poverty."

"But can they be trained?"

"It will be difficult but..."

"Good. As long as ye can prevent the men from turning tail halfway through the battles we will be encountering, the men should hold. Master Koenigsherr, these men are pikemen. They are nary meant to be skilled, smart, or washed. Up go the pikes, down go the enemy cavalry, while yer muskets and horse do all the other killing that needs to be done."

Otto nodded, deferring to the wisdom of his superior.

"It makes nary a lick of sense to subject the men to the elements while they could be quartered and rested for the long march ahead. We will have to wait a spell longer for the other companies to assemble. I suggest finding suitable lodging for them, Master Jaeger."

Gunther saluted and turned to address the men, many of whom were already slouching on their pikes. Two had actually broken formation and were sitting on the pavement.

Gunther groaned and yelled *"Gruppe! Stillgestanden!"*

The novice pikemen sloppily came to attention, while the two that were sitting on the ground scrambled to get back into formation, but not before being stopped by Gunther.

"Not you two. Stay here. The rest of you, follow me. We will rest in the tavern. The two that elected to sit down while in formation will stand at attention out here as our watchmen until they are relieved." he finished, glaring at the two.

Otto bowed to MacRae and joined Gunther in the formation.

"Some nice beer and a meat pie to regain our strength from a long ride sound nice right about now," said Otto.

"I will secure provisions and distribute them among the men," said Gunther, ignoring Otto's invitation. "Would you mind taking care of their lodging, *Herr Koenigsherr?*"

"Of course, *Herr Jaeger.*" muttered Otto, somewhat put off by his comrade's refusal to join him for a drink.

As the bottom tip of the sun's disc barely skimmed the edge of the water over the horizon, the ships in the harbor were secured and their cargo unloaded. The gangplank of the "Fortune" was lowered and men – soldiers, not sailors – marched off the vessel and into the port town. These were the Britons that MacRae had been waiting for so eagerly. There were men of all shapes and sizes, and speaking all manner of dialects. Irishmen, Welshmen, and Scots had formed bonds amongst their kinsmen during the journey, and came off of the ship in groups, laughing and cursing with each other. The English followed, descending the gangplank in noisy droves, urged on by their sergeants and recruiters.

James Fletcher clung tightly to his bow. He had been encouraged to bring it with him on the voyage. He had spoken to no one during the entire trip. The sewn cotton clothes and posh accents of his countrymen from the north were intimidating to a poor debt-ridden peasant like himself. He heard them speak of the fame, wealth and glory that they would have, and how they would return to England and buy new land for productive businesses. Fletcher simply wanted to escape his debts.

While others had their belongings stowed away in haversacks, rucksacks, and bindles, Fletcher had nothing but the clothes on his back and the bow slung over his shoulder. Fletcher had scarcely been out of Bolingbroke Village before, and he was amazed at what he saw here in Rotterdam. Leaning over the railing, he saw that the buildings were made of carefully chiseled and wonderfully painted stone and brick, the streets were crowded with people, and the unfamiliar but enticing smells of all sorts of wonderful spices mixed with the fishy odor of freshly caught seafood confused his nose. He did not have much time to take in all these new sights, sounds, and smells, though. The crowd of English mercenaries behind him carried him like a wave off the boat and into the port. Not wishing to get lost, he had no choice but to follow them to the tavern where his employer waited.

The mass of soldiers congregated around the tavern, with sergeants barking orders to keep the men in line. The more seasoned soldiers got into neat, orderly formations, while the novices like Fletcher milled about with mouths agape in confusion. Unlike the German-speaking companies, they had no opportunities to practice marching drills while out at sea.

Meanwhile, a different company was arriving by foot. The sound of their drums could be heard even over the frustrated shouting of the English sergeants. From a southbound road came the Mediterranean contingent of Talbot Company. Unlike the Germans or the English, these southern Europeans were almost all professional fighters, and it showed. These Italians and their Spanish comrades marched in step, shoulder to shoulder, with their eyes facing forward. The pikemen and halberdiers, with their armor glistening in the sun, shouldered their weapons, and the swordsmen marched with their weapons sheathed at their hips, or if they carried great swords, resting the backs of their blades on their shoulders.

The leader of the swordsmen looked out of place, however. Clad in a colorful blue, white and red doublet, this officer marched out of step and appeared to be following the lead of the men rather than the other way around. This odd officer also had very feminine features, especially for a warrior.

Sofia Fortezza was sweating from the long march. They had been on the march for twelve days now and she was amazed at how the men had managed to keep their spirits up this long. They had taken rest stops every ten miles or so, at the discretion of the commander of pikemen, the recruiter Captain Toscana, who led the formation. The last stop they had taken was at the village of Rijsoord, about six miles away. Now that they were finally at their destination, Sofia resisted the urge to simply faint. Her sword, as light as it was, felt like a heavy beam of wood as it rested on her shoulder. Don Alfonso had told her that this was the proper way to march with it. The Don himself was so much worse off, having to lug a spontoon while wearing a heavy suit of armor, but he seemed to enjoy the march, at what he called "a slow pace."

As the three hundred Italians and Spaniards assembled near the tavern, they blocked the streets around them with their formations, much to the chagrin of the Dutch locals. Their officers gave the command to rest, with Sofia repeating the command last, with more of a gasp than a bark.

Her men were not inspired in the least bit by her lack of military bearing and apparent weakness that she displayed during the march. Though she denied it at every turn, everyone knew that she was a woman, but none dared to speak against her because they knew that the company had a policy of executing mutineers. Many quietly talked amongst themselves that the company of swords was doomed to failure and death, but others hoped that there was still time for her to learn until the great campaign that they would inevitably undertake.

Sofia told her men to "stay put" as she broke ranks and walked slowly, gasping for air, to the front of the formation of halberdiers to meet with her mentor, Don Alfonso. The halberdiers gave her subtle condescending looks as she passed them. Some muttered in Spanish behind her back, and a few shook their heads in disgust.

These gestures of indignation only made her more determined to show them what she could do. She was not about to be replaced on her second week in command.

Upon reaching the front of the formation, she realized that Don Alfonso was gone. Panicking, she looked around rapidly for any sign of the Spaniard. Suddenly, she heard a whistle. Don Alfonso was calling for her from the tavern door.

"*Teniente Bianchi,*" *said* Don Alfonso, addressing Sofia by her masculine alias, "Come here and meet your colonel."

The Spaniard and Captain Toscana were already standing in front of MacRae, who was inspecting the troops from a distance.

"I see two officers when I should have three." the Scotsman said, "Where be the commander of swords?"

"*Signor!*" exclaimed Sofia as she ran up to meet them, heaving with her head hanging and resting her hands on her haunches. Her face remained obscured by her large hat. "*Mi scuso del ritardo, signor.*"

MacRae blinked once and turned to Captain Toscana. "Captain, did you no inform these folk that we speak English here?"

The Italian recruiter shrugged and said that he assumed that the other commanders already knew.

Talbot Company was an oddity within the mercenary companies of Europe. The universal military language was French, and almost every soldier drilled in that language and spoke it. MacRae, although he knew French himself, refused to speak it when he could, preferring the shorter, terser commands of the English language.

"Ye there," he continued, "what be yer name?" MacRae could not yet see her face, as her head still hung low.

"*Che cosa?*" replied Sofia.

"If you will pardon my interruption, *señor,*" said Don Alfonso, stepping forward, "may I be allowed to interpret?"

"Aye, ye may."

Turning to Sofia, the don said in Spanish, "He is asking for your name. Please tell me you know a tiny bit of English at least."

Sofia raised her head slightly and shook it. She knew nothing of the English language, but that was not going to stop her. She immediately stood upright and walked past the don to present herself before MacRae.

"Lodovico Bianchi, signor. Al tuo servicio." she said with a bow.

MacRae's one eye could not see very well, but he knew what he saw when he looked at Sofia.

"What by God's Blood is this? Who was the fuckin' eedjit that allowed a lass into the ranks and signed her up as a bloody fuckin' officer?"

Captain Toscana was sweating like a condemned man. The very thought that Sofia's poorly constructed ruse would trick MacRae made him curse his own stupidity. He shut his eyes tight and slowly raised his hand to admit his fault, fully expecting MacRae to stab him on the spot.

The Scotsman sneered at his officer. "Were there no other suitable candidates to lead the swordsmen? Is this bloody girl the best ye have?"

Captain Toscana nodded slowly, unsure of whether he would be called out for lying.

"Yes sir," he said. "She served under Ernst von Mansfeld during his Italian campaign. She has soldiered before."

MacRae glared at him with his one eye and said, "If it cannot be helped, captain. I hope she serves the company well. I will nary think ill of ye if she can prove to be a fiery amazon on the field of war, but if she falters but once, yer neck be upon me blade."

Toscana gulped and took a deep, grateful bow.

"And who might you be, Spaniard? Do not tell me that my fine Captain Toscana has set up a mere pauper with a stick to command my halberdiers."

"No *señor.*" replied Don Alfonso, "I am Don Alfonso Villanueva y Santiago, former servant of his Catholic Majesty, King Felipe IV, serving under his brave and true *regimiento de alabardas*, and now, by your benefaction, your loyal *capitan.*"

MacRae nodded with approval.

"It is good to know ye. I am Colonel William MacRae, the leader of this fine company, and I expect ye to serve faithfully under myself and the officers appointed over ye. I remind ye that this is not a regular army but a company of free folk. Ye may leave the company at any time after informing either myself or a fellow officer; however, while ye serve under me, I expect ye to obey me orders and to execute them to the best of yer ability."

There was at least one new officer with military bearing, MacRae thought. This other one, an Italian that spoke no English at all, would soon be a problem.

MacRae took small consolation in the fact that she was an Italian, like most of the other swordsmen, but was also apprehensive that the men might not want to follow a girl into battle, not that there was no precedence to this of course. An Italian noblewoman by the name of Caterina Sforza, merely a century ago resisted the mighty armies of the most powerful family in Italy, and before her, there was Joan of Arc, liberator of France, and Boudicca, whom Scots like MacRae considered a kinswoman. He wanted to be proved wrong because according to Toscana at least, he had no choice in the matter. This was his commander of swords, and she had to be at her best. The fate of her men depended on it.

"Master Spaniard," said MacRae, "Tell the lass that I bid her welcome to me company."

Don Alfonso opened his mouth to speak but was cut short before he could begin.

"Also, tell her that her ruse is as thin as the silk knickers she is wearing under her fuckin' armor."

74

Don Alfonso hesitatingly turned towards Sofia, whose eyes were wide open, eager to hear what the company's leader had to say to her.

"This is Colonel MacRae. He leads this company, and bids you welcome. Be careful with this opportunity, *hija.* You can be a good soldier, but only if you listen," said the don, making no mention of the fact that MacRae could see right through her disguise.

Sofia nodded and saluted MacRae with her sword.

The Scotsman nodded back to her and said to Don Alfonso,

"The lass must not rely on ye for very long. Teach her as much English as ye can. For now, the basic orders will suffice – attention, halt, charge, retreat, the facings and marching movements... I trust ye to fulfill this duty, Master Spaniard."

"As you will, *señor.*"

"We settle here for the night. This tavern has rooms and food for the officers, the rest can sleep outside under their cloaks. Tomorrow, we have a big day ahead of us – I have gotten a client from the north – willing to pay a vast sum for a grand campaign."

"Can you tell us any details, *señor?*"

"It would be best if I told the entire company all at once. Now rest yer men, Master Spaniard. I am leaving the good Captain Toscana here in Rotterdam to tend to Talbot Company's main office, but ah, for the rest of us, tomorrow will be a day of adventure and profit for all."

Chapter 9

The rays of the sun crept up the feet of the sleeping recruits as the men whom Gunther Jaeger put on night watch began to wake the other soldiers, who were sleeping everywhere from bales of hay inside barns to smelly alleyways and hard cobblestone streets. Pikes were picked up from the walls where they were left leaning on the night prior, and muskets were inspected and shouldered.

As the enlisted soldiers began their morning rituals, urinating in the streets and washing their faces in the horse troughs, the officers in the tavern began to stir as well.

Gunther briskly exited his room fully dressed and shaved. The gaunt German moved with haste towards Otto's quarters and knocked on the door.

"Enter," came the groggy response.

The wooden door to Otto's room creaked open to reveal the man out of his armor, urinating in a chamber pot, in full view of Gunther, who simply rolled his eyes and shook his head.

"Get dressed. As the two most experienced officers here, we will need to be at MacRae's side before anyone else. You know this."

Otto groaned while he shook off the last few drops of urine.

"Yes, yes, I will be there shortly. Was that all you wanted to say while you were in here? Did you want to play at being my mother? Well, good job. Now get out. I do not want you to see me changing."

Gunther shook his head at the man's twisted sense of modesty and shut the door.

During the night, a group of horsemen had arrived in Rotterdam from the far north. They traveled incognito, as to not reveal their wealth. Captain Sven Bjornsson had barely recovered from his injuries and could not run, but he could ride well enough, leading a group of survivors from Jarlsberg. While his captain rode off to hire mercenaries, Greve Stenbock had stayed in Sweden to ask for help from the king.

They had come riding several weeks behind a messenger that was sent to MacRae with a letter containing details of the campaign, and now they were in Rotterdam to assess the quality of men that Talbot Company was bringing to the fight. Bjornsson had barely gotten any sleep when he arrived in Rotterdam before he was awoken by terrible dreams about the attack on Jarlsberg.

Wasting little time, he bid MacRae assemble his officers in the lower hall of the tavern they were staying in. Time was short and valuable, and the sooner the men were briefed, the faster Jarlsberg would be back in Swedish hands.

"Good morning, Colonel MacRae." Bjornsson said as he limped into the tavern's hall, still half asleep. The fact that his leg had not healed was making this more difficult.

MacRae made a shallow bow and gestured that the Swede take his seat at a long table that they had conveniently set up at the end of the room, where the bards would usually play.

Bjornsson did not have to wait long. A mere minute after he entered, the early birds were eagerly filling seats in the tavern, anxious to hear about this new contract. They included Thomas Warwick, the recruiter and de facto leader of the Britannic irregular troops and the two recruiters from the Holy Roman Empire, Otto Koenigsherr, and Gunther Jaeger.

"Good morning, all. I hope we can end this meeting expeditiously, with the concerns of all men here present addressed."

"Bitte schweigen! Spricht jemand Deutsche, fremde Schweine!?"

"Beruhigen, Herr Koenigsherr."

"What the bloody hell is everyone saying?"

Bjornsson slammed his gloved hand on the table. The Babel-like cacophony fell silent.

"French." he said, in a low, growling, annoyed tone. "We will all speak French."

"*Très bien.*" MacRae muttered, drumming his fingers on the table. He hated this language but the client, who apparently spoke no English, gave him little choice. "Gentlemen," he continued in French, "this be the representative of our client, Captain Sven Bjornsson of the Kingdom of Sweden."

"The enemy descended on us in broad daylight at Jarlsberg Castle near the border of Livonia. They had a sizeable force with them, composed of Lithuanians and Lipka Tatars. I am here on behalf of my lord, Greve Olaf Stenbock to hire your company to avenge this insult to him and take back our castle. As we speak, my lord is appealing to the great King Gustavus Adolphus to send troops to aid us. In anticipation of his success, our two forces will meet at Jarlsberg Castle in twenty days. It will be a long journey by foot, passing through the Holy Roman Empire, then through Poland, where we are expected to meet heavy resistance before finally arriving at Jarlsberg at the border of the Swedish Empire. Does anyone have any questions?"

Thomas Warwick rose from his seat. "Yes – my lord, have you considered the possibility of a sea route? We could easily march through friendly territory, embark on ships at the Holy Roman port of Lübeck, and sail towards..."

"The point of a land route, Master Englishman," interrupted Bjornsson, "is to meet the enemy from the west while my lord meets them from the east, in a pincer movement. We are also going to make use of the opportunity to train on the march, something we cannot do while we are at sea. Furthermore, we will deny the enemy any opportunity of resupply from his own country by closing roads and restricting travel on them."

"We can also recruit more men as we travel through Deutschland." added Gunther, "Their men are good, professional fighters."

Bjornsson nodded his approval. Privately though, he was unsure if they had enough men and resources to attempt a siege. This momentary thought made him raise a question.

"What about cannon, siege works, carpentry equipment? Do we have those? The Tartars were able to take the walls with mere grappling hooks. It is doubtful that we will be as lucky."

As he spoke, the other officers entered the room. MacRae was visibly annoyed at their tardiness, but he said nothing in front of the client. This was the Swede's show now, since he carried the money.

Don Alfonso and a sleepy Sophia quietly entered and took their seats at the back of the room, followed by some lieutenants and their sergeants, who carried notebooks and pencils for taking down important details.

Warwick confidently assured his client that cannons could be purchased immediately in Rotterdam and hauled along with them. He also said that he had the best artillerymen in the company to man the said cannon, who were able to shoot a fly off of a mare's arse given good weather conditions. While the former statement was true – a Belgian gunsmith had set up shop near the company's headquarters last year – the latter was not. Warwick's men were irregular troops from the British Isles, who were perfect for skirmishing and harassing the enemy, but not so much for the precise work of a cannoneer.

Bjornsson gave a curt nod of approval and looked towards the newcomers. He then turned to MacRae and wordlessly asked for introductions.

"These are me officers for the field. Each commands a company of pikes, halberds, muskets or swords." MacRae said in Scots, "Do not trust the commander of swords though."

Bjornsson understood, although he did not have a perfect command of the language. He thought he was seeing things at first, but upon closer inspection, he could understand why MacRae did not have full faith in his commander of swords. That was no "sir." However, he did not wish to prolong the meeting with accusations and ridicule.

"Ordre de bataille." Bjornsson continued in French, "We will not fight in the standard formation. The Swedish battle formation provides superior and overwhelming firepower while enabling musketeers to defend our pikemen and vice versa. We

80

need about one thousand musketeers at the very minimum to make this work effectively and..."

"Sir," interrupted Warwick, "I believe the number of musketeers we may field is quite insufficient."

"You were in charge of the recruitment of these men, were you not, Master Englishman?" Bjornsson replied with a scowl.

"Yes, but..."

"You are relieved of command, sir."

As Warwick's jaw dropped, MacRae buried his face in his hands. There was nothing he could do. This man represented the client and the client was God. He could do whatever he wished. The loss of Warwick's command could prove to be a major weakness unless a more capable commander could be found.

"Command your artillerymen and irregulars if you wish," continued Bjornsson, "but I will take responsibility of the musketeers. We will need to buy muskets and shot in bulk before we leave Rotterdam."

MacRae winced. Never before had a client taken command of a section of his company, and he was hesitant about it. However, Bjornsson was a veteran soldier, and could very well be a capable commander. He chose to keep his mouth shut on the matter for the time being.

"Let us move on to the matter of payment then." Bjornsson said, pulling out a piece of parchment from his pocket and raising it up for all to see. "This is a letter of credit from Greve Olaf Stenbock, vassal of his majesty King Gustavus Adolphus of Sweden, authorizing Talbot Company to draw on his accounts one thousand florins payable immediately in gold for provisions, equipment and salaries, and a further four thousand florins

81

payable on the condition that Jarlsberg Castle is delivered back into his control."

He gently handed the letter of credit to MacRae, who received it with a smile and a low bow. The thousand florins would go a long way to ensuring that his men did not mutiny midway through the long march to Jarlsberg.

"Colonel MacRae, sir, I leave it up to you to determine the order of march, breaks for camp, purchase of provisions and so forth. If no one has any objections, we must spend the rest of today purchasing supplies and equipment for our long march. We leave at sunrise tomorrow morning."

MacRae was amused. Usually, a client would give what they considered a rousing speech to bolster the spirits of his men, and the men would humor them in turn by letting out a loud cheer. Not so this time. Here was a soldier who was all business and knew that, at the beginning of a long campaign at least, men were motivated by coin more than anything else. Hunger, weariness, and lust would be motivators further down the road. There was seldom any need at all for any grand speeches.

As the officers began to quietly leave the room, Sophia, who knew some French, began to realize what she had signed up for. She had traveled on long journeys like this before, although usually by carriage, not on foot. The journey there was at most a thousand miles. Would they be walking the entire way?

"*Signore Alfonso,*" she said, jabbing the Spaniard in his rib, "Will we be walking a thousand miles?"

Alfonso looked at her as if she were asking if water was wet. "Yes, *señorita,* we will be walking a thousand miles. Horses are only for the cavalry, artillery, and baggage trains. Are you a field gun, little girl?"

She did not appreciate the don's sarcasm. The prospect of a thousand mile journey without proper transportation bothered her. On a fast horse, the journey would take no less than five days, which meant that it would probably take them a little more than two weeks to do it by foot. She was going to have to get used to bandaging her feet.

Chapter 10

The Road to Gouda

Dutch Republic

The road from Rotterdam to Gouda was well made and comfortable to walk on, but extremely narrow, not allowing room for more than six men marching shoulder to shoulder. Six hundred and ninety-eight men marched shoulder to shoulder on that narrow road, with trees shading them on both flanks. MacRae and Bjornsson led the march from the front on horseback, followed by Bjornsson's musketeers, Gunther's pikemen, Don Alfonso's halberdiers, Sophia's swordsmen, and Warwick's irregulars and artillery, the former marching in loose formation. Otto and his cavalry brought up the rear and guarded the expensive six-pound cannons and the baggage train. The commanders of each company walked on the right side of their formation.

James Fletcher had no idea what was going on. He had been absent from the briefing since he was not an officer, and Warwick had simply been telling his men that they were going to march for a bit over two weeks, looting wherever they were allowed, before they were supposed to besiege some castle in some far away country.

As he stared down at his feet contributing to the chomp-chomp-chomp of the hundreds of marching troops, his mind wandered off to thoughts of the future. He owed three pounds to the innkeeper at the Black Horse Inn, but how many florins were in a pound? Or rather, pounds in a florin? He figured that he would simply show up with three gold coins since he doubted that the tavern keeper knew the difference anyway. But the whole point of this whole endeavor was to make sure he had food on his plate, and the last thing he ate was some salted eel and cheese on the...

"Vaffanculo! Guarda dove va, idiota!"

The ground was vertical, and his hands felt wet with mud. He had fallen, and...

"Alzati, contadino stupido!"

There was a girl screaming at him in a language he could not understand. He slowly got to his feet and tried to comprehend his surroundings. His head stung a bit.

He saw the screaming girl – her hair was drenched in mud, and she was holding what might once have been a colorful beret that was now stained brown. As she shrieked at him, she gestured towards her stained hat, somehow indicating that it was his fault.

Fletcher had gotten lost in thought, and while staring at his feet, he accidentally broke formation and had managed to march straight into the formation in front of him and knock over its commander – Sophia Fortezza.

Fletcher froze. He did not know whether he was going to be hanged or stabbed to death right there on the spot. He tried to stammer out an apology, but it was no use. The girl appeared content to continue yelling at him in her sing-songy language that seemed to be fond of the letter "z".

The chomp-chomp-chomping of men's boots gradually became a clop-clop-clopping of horses' hooves. Fletcher barely noticed Warwick passing him by, snickering as he passed by his fellow Englishman being chastised by a costumed teenage girl. The commander of the company of horse, however, would not take this so lightly. A black horse and similarly armored rider halted behind Fletcher's back. Sophia fell silent.

"You think this is a party where you can just mingle about, *herr Engländer?*" Otto said in English, his shadow cast over the two stragglers, "return to your company or I will have you whipped." he said to Fletcher.

"Lieutenant Bianchi," Otto said to Sophia in French, using her alias, "we will deal with this miscreant later, but I advise you to return to your men."

Just as Sophia wrung her hat and turned around to return to her men, a sound like thunder broke the stillness of the forest, followed by confused yelling and someone from far up in the front shouting,

"¡Emboscada! Ambush!"

20 Minutes Earlier

Graf Franz von Bulow was having a particularly slow day. The war had been hard on him and his band of cutthroats. They were once professional soldiers guarding his county but had since turned to banditry when the Holy Roman Empire was caught up in the flames of war, and pay and food became scarce.

The people he once warded over had now become his victims. Every day he neglected affairs of state to pillage the countryside or extort travelers on the road – anything to keep food in the bellies of his men. The last thing he needed was an armed mutiny.

He and his band of outlaws waited at their usual spot, hidden behind trees in a heavily forested area leading from his territory into the city of Gouda. Usually, they merely demanded a tax for travelers coming through this part of the woods. It was not good practice to kill one's peasants. Who would grow the wheat? However, something was different today.

Von Bulow heard them before he saw them – the clanking of metal armor and the thunder of a march. Soldiers were passing through his land – and they were probably here to do the same thing he was doing, except they would not hesitate to burn down entire villages to get what they wanted. He could not see clearly through the branches, but he reckoned that they were mostly pikemen. He could hear the shafts of their pikes rattling against each other in the distance. His men were mostly musketeers and swordsmen. He was outnumbered, but if he could confuse them enough, it would probably start a rout and disperse the entire force.

The two force commanders, riding on horseback, passed him by. Good – his force remained undetected. He noticed that they were followed by musketeers, and, as he expected, a massive formation of pikemen. He had to respond now – the pikes would get entangled in the trees and it would be easy work.

He whistled, mimicking the call of the koolmees bird, a signal to get ready for an ambush. His musketeers lit their wicks and aimed their weapons at the flanks of their unsuspecting victims.

The volley of musket fire tore through the left flanks of both Gunther's pike formation and Alfonso's halberdiers. The don raised the alarm and ordered his men to make a facing movement towards the enemy. At the very front of the formation, MacRae halted his horse and wheeled around, barking his commands,

"Company, halt! The company will advance, left turn!"

The company's professional musketeers halted and turned to their left in a synchronized, snappy movement. However, the novice pikemen who were taking fire began running into each other in a state of panic. Some broke formation, dropped their pikes and fled into the woods in the opposite direction, others took their pikes and charged into the woods only to be cut down by sporadic musket fire from an enemy that could not be seen. The majority, however, could not leave the formation since they were blocked in by the narrow road and their panicking comrades.

Pikemen were breaking into Don Alfonso's halberd formation, and men were being shoved around and pushed to the ground as cowardly novices struggled to escape the fight. The don would have none of it, however, and ordered his men to attack any soldier that strayed into his formation. These beggars with pikes would hold their ground or die.

Gunther tried to keep order by screaming at his men in their native German. He was desperately trying to get them to cover. When they would not listen, he presented his sword – a five-foot monster – and swung at them to make them back up into the woods behind them. This would make room for the muskets to get into position and return fire.

Bjornsson saw his cue and did not need to be prompted by MacRae as he bellowed,

"Mousquetaires! En rang de six! Tournez à gauche! En avant, marche!"

The sergeants repeated the same command in English and the musketeers formed a line of battle six men deep pointed towards the enemy, shoving Gunther's escaping pikemen out of the way to get into their formation.

There was a sudden lull in the enemy's fire. Bjornsson took this opportunity to order his men to load and fire into the tree line. Even though he saw nothing, he was sure that he would at least kill a few men.

"Présentez armes! Tirez!"

A single unified volley of musket fire tore through the trees. However, before a second volley could be let off, enemy swordsmen rushed out of the tree line, shouting and cursing in German at the unprepared musketeers.

Gunther was quick to react and ordered his pikemen to reform and charge, meeting their steel with his.

As all this excitement was happening, Sophia and Otto sat in the rear with their troops. Otto's cavalry were unable to move forward due to the narrowness of the road ahead. Sophia's swordsmen, however, had no such restrictions.

"Lieutenant Bianchi, order us into the damn woods!" a sergeant shouted at her, "We have a perfect flanking position!"

Sophia's head was throbbing. She had never been under so much stress before. She wrung her hat tightly in desperation and opened her mouth to speak, but no words came out, only wheezing.

"Luridi coniglio figlio di puttana!" Fucking cowardly son of a bitch, the sergeant cursed, "Men, I am taking command! Follow me!"

The sergeant drew his sword and led Sophia's men into the flanks of the enemy. Stuck between Gunther's pikes in front of them and the swordsmen engaging them on their right, the bandits were rapidly losing ground.

An arm wrapped around Sophia's waist and briskly pulled her into the bushes. She drew her sword in panic, but her arm got stuck on one of the branches.

"All is well!"

It was the peasant archer who had bumped into her earlier. His firm grip loosened and he held her by the shoulders. She did not understand what he was saying, but it sounded like he was trying to reassure her. She nodded out of instinct. He was telling her to hide and wait the battle out.

Warwick saw the swordsmen move in to flank the enemy, and bid his irregulars to finish the fight and draw the enemy musketeers out of the woods.

"Forward, lads! For loot and glory!"

A crowd of eighty Scotsmen, Irishmen, Welshmen and Englishmen shook the leaves with their guttural curses and jumped into the forest without any particular formation. Sword duels with the irregulars degenerated into ferocious murder as Highlanders bit off noses and Irishmen broke skulls with their

90

shillelaghs. The bandits' morale was broken, and they began fleeing back into the woods under a hail of musket fire. Talbot Company had tasted their first victory in this campaign.

Chapter 11

A wounded and dying bandit lay on the ground, his trousers soiled, with blood gushing from a stump that used to be his arm. He pleaded for his life as a Talbot Company irregular struggled to remove his armor. He had to hack through his limbs to make it easier. The wailing of men in similar predicaments filled the air.

"Twenty-three." counted Gunther Jaeger, as a Scottish irregular threw another bloody steel corselet onto a pile. He added another tick mark to his inventory list. "You, stop." he said, pointing to a soldier about to dump a heap of bloodstained clothing onto the pile. "Those go over there. This is for armor."

"I beg your pardon, sir?" the soldier raised his voice. It was hard to hear with the cacophony in the background. Dying bandits screamed while their corpses were hacked and looted as Talbot Company's men joked loudly or got sick and vomited on the bloody earth.

"I said those go over there! This is the wrong pile!" Gunther shouted over the chaos. He sighed in frustration. The noise of a battle's aftermath was something that he had gotten used to long ago, but the racket still made post-battle accountability annoying.

A rider approached. It was Otto, riding up to meet his comrade without the slightest dent in his armor from the battle.

"This is absolutely terrible," said Otto, raising the visor of his helmet.

"What do you mean?" replied Gunther, not looking up from his tally sheet.

"No jewelry, no gold teeth. Not a single one of these damn peasants has anything valuable. You would think they would at least have lockets or silver crosses or damn gimmel rings, but nothing!"

"Or it could be that these items were liberated from the bodies before you arrived on the scene, *Herr Koenigsherr.*"

"Perhaps. How goes accountability?"

"I believe we have sixty dead and counting. Thirty-eight deserted."

"What of the wounded?"

"I have not counted them yet. You remember how I deal with the wounded."

Gunther had a rather medieval way of dealing with the wounded. His sergeants scoured the field looking for those who cried out and offered them a choice – life or death. If they chose death they were stabbed on the spot; if they chose life, they would be hauled back to the baggage train and treated by the surgeon, who also happened to be one of the archers. They would most likely still die, but they would die as drunk as a lord since the surgeon liked to use schnapps to dull the pain.

A soldier walked up to the pair of officers, grinning widely.

"Sirs, I believe you will want to see this. I have found the enemy commander. We will get a handsome ransom from him, we will."

Gunther rolled up his tally sheet and tucked it into his belt.

"Show me."

After the three took a short walk through a field of the dead and dying, and into the forest beyond, they found the enemy commander, Graf Fritz von Bulow, standing there with his arms crossed, flanked by Talbot company swordsmen on either side.

"Good day," said Gunther.

"Good day," replied the graf in German.

"You did not run?"

Von Bulow said nothing but gestured towards his leg. He had indeed tried to run but had his leg caught in a badger hole, where he was now stuck.

Otto could not help but let out a good chuckle. Gunther, stern-faced, took the tally sheet from his belt and prepared to take notes.

"You are dressed in expensive armor. Am I correct to assume that you are a noble, sir?"

"You are."

Gunther jotted that down.

"If you are thinking of ransoming me, it will not do you any good, you know," Von Bulow said, with a tone of resignation.

"And why is that?"

"I am the lord of this county."

"And why should we believe you?"

"You passed by a boundary stone on the way here, did you not?"

"Yes, we did. It had the insignia of the local lord on it. There was a coat of arms with several yellow buttons in the shape of a triangle on a blue field."

"Behold," said von Bulow, and showed his ring, which bore the same mark.

"This proves nothing." Otto scoffed, "You could have stolen that from the real count."

"And what use would I have to keep it if I did? This would be very valuable to a politician, not some simple forest bandit."

"He is right." Gunther sighed, drawing his sword. "Since we cannot ransom you, would you like to die from decapitation or stabbing?"

"I would like to..."

Von Bulow's severed head hit the forest floor before he could finish his last words. Otto and Gunther headed back to the column while the soldiers surrounding von Bulow's body began stripping him of his belongings like vultures.

"You think we could have gotten something more out of him?" Otto asked.

"No, nothing." Gunther replied stoically, "Since we cannot ransom a robber baron to himself, the only other person we would be able to garner ransom from is the Prince of Orange himself."

"And why would the prince pay the ransom of a robber baron?"

"Exactly."

The two were quiet for a time. Crows watched them from the trees, drawn by the scent of death.

"Do you think MacRae will accept this high number of casualties?" Otto inquired as the two walked.

"No, of course not." replied Gunther.

"It is not as if we could have done anything about it."

"That is not what he will say. He will say that we should have drilled them more before we reached Rotterdam. The same can even be said of some of our officers." he added as he passed by the commander of swords, sitting motionless on a rock on the side of the road, being attended to by an archer.

Sophia stared at the corpses that lay sprawled on the road before her. The screaming was bothering her, but she could not seem to tear her eyes away or cover her ears. Perhaps she did not want to appear weak to her men.

"Her" men, she thought. They had just attacked without her when she froze in fear. This would not happen again. It was ironic since her last name meant "fortress" – something strong and unbreakable, something she was clearly not.

The corpses disturbed her in more than one way. It was not just that some of them were still 'breathing' with air escaping from their lungs, or that some of them had their dead, unblinking eyes fixed on her. It was that, in some strange sense of pareidolia, she was seeing familiar faces among the dead. The baker from the *panaderia* across the street from her old house in Milan had been stabbed through the neck; the boy she used to tease in the marketplace had an eye missing, and her uncle Giovanni had no arms left and was sitting naked against a tree.

96

But that was impossible. All those people were back home in Milan, and she was... where was she?

The sound of footsteps drew near. A young man approached. He spoke to her in a strange, funny-sounding language. She could not understand the words but she slowly turned her head towards the speaker.

It was that archer that pulled her into the bushes. He was looking at her worryingly, with his hands gently resting on her shoulders. He noticed tears starting to well up in her eyes, but she did not actually cry even as they rolled down her cheeks. His words and facial expression had a tone of genuine concern, but she continued to stare at him. She thought of nothing, but it was nice to feel that someone cared about her.

Still speaking, he gave her a kind smile and reached for something in his pouch. She recognized the word *"salame."* The archer produced a bit of sausage from his pouch and tenderly placed it in her hand. She thanked him in Italian and took a bite, then another larger one. She had not realized how hungry she had been. The archer smiled at her, satisfied and a little amused at the way she ate. A gloved hand suddenly grasped his shoulder.

"Lágarse, campesino." Beat it, peasant. Don Alfonso had arrived to check on his ward.

The archer was about to stand up and leave, but with a mouth full of salami, Sophia raised her hand to stop him. The don, confused, allowed the Englishman to stay but said nothing to him.

"Did your first battle go as you expected?" he said to her in Spanish.

97

"No," she said in Italian, wiping her mouth. "It was so quick. I did not know what to do."

"You did not know your father's things? What?" Don Alfonso said, confused.

Sophia laughed. Laughter was good, she thought. It was good to relieve some tension. She explained that the Italian words for "what to do", *cosa fare,* sounded like the Spanish *cosas padre*, or "father things", which made no sense. The don allowed himself a quick chuckle, but immediately changed his tone.

"*Hija,* you were clearly not ready yet. I am sorry that this had to happen to you before you could receive a proper discourse on drill. Also, who is this?" he said, gesturing to the archer.

"He is a peasant, one that hid me during the battle. A nice fellow, but he seems to be a bit of a buffoon. He does not speak like us."

"He is speaking English." the don replied, before turning to Fletcher. He looked the man up and down and told him sternly, in heavily accented English,

"Englishman, I would like to have a word."

"Certainly, milord." Fletcher humbly replied.

"I applaud you for your actions. It was brave of you to consider saving the life of your superior officer while putting yourself at risk. However, I am not entirely sure I can trust you. It is nothing personal. I trust no one. Can you see what is different about our commander of swords?"

"What about her?"

"Yes, exactly."

Puzzled, Fletcher tried to respond, but the don interrupted him.

"Do not do anything that would jeopardize your life or the sense of order that we have in the company. We have no women here, *señor,* only soldiers."

Fletcher was beginning to understand what he meant and responded with a meek bow.

A horn sounded in the distance. It was time for the company to regroup and continue the march. Fletcher bowed to both of them and scurried off to rejoin the irregulars as Don Alfonso wordlessly walked back to his men. Sophia finished the last bits of her salami and dusted herself off, once again thinking, what had she gotten herself into?

Chapter 12

Nordhorn Range

Holy Roman Empire

The march to Gouda was quick and unremarkable. So were the marches to Utrecht, Amersfoort, Voorthuizen and all the towns in Holland after that. The Dutch were a peaceful, generally quiet people. Or perhaps it only seemed that way since none of them wanted to stand up to an army of mercenary thugs that were marching through their lands, especially since Talbot Company was actually paying fairly for the goods that they were taking, instead of wantonly raiding like some of the other free companies did.

Now the company was eight miles east of the nearest settlement and had just crossed over into the territories of the Holy Roman Empire. Vast tracts of forest lay ahead of them, and Colonel MacRae had determined that an open field in the middle of a forest east of the town of Nordhorn would be a good place to set up camp.

The company was halted and the wagons from the baggage train were arranged in a circle around the camp to form a defensive position. MacRae would take his time here. There was no imminent threat of attack, and the men needed to cook, clean, and recuperate. Any fresh meat they had acquired in the towns had to be salted and preserved before it turned blue, and the surgeon had to be given time to check on his patients.

One by one, campfires flickered to life throughout the encampment as some men began setting their pots to boil their bacon while others went out into the woods to hunt for fresh meat.

Sophia Fortezza sat around a fire with Don Alfonso and Thomas Warwick. The Englishman set a pot of water to boil and produced a chunk of salt pork from his bag. Sophia looked at the pork with apprehension and said in Italian,

"By the devil, does he intend to kill us with all that salt?"

Warwick, who knew a smidge of Italian, commented,

"I am not certain about what you said but I would bet a pound Sterling that it was not anything good."

"What did he say?"

"Nothing important, *hija*." Don Alfonso said, reassuringly.

Warwick chucked the meat into the pot of boiling water and sighed.

"I was never any good at this, you know. It is a shame we are wasting these rations."

The don looked at him with uneasiness.

"Well, *señor,* man does not live on bread alone..."

"Yes, but, this is not bread is it... that would have been too easy. We will just have to see how it turns out."

"I am hoping for the best, *señor.*" Don Alfonso said as he stood up, "Excuse me, I think I will fetch some entertainment from the wagons. I will return shortly."

Salt pork was indeed an unpalatable substance unless it was soaked then boiled. Even then it was not the most pleasant meal

101

to have. By failing to soak it, Warwick ensured that the officers' meal would taste like the sea. Fresh meat would have been easier to prepare, which is why the irregulars like Fletcher were sent out to obtain fresh game from the denizens of the forest.

A hundred yards away from the wagon-enclosed encampment, James Fletcher had once again taken his bow and arrow to hunt for supper. He was part of a hunting party that consisted of himself and five other longbowmen, spread far apart from each other, but traveling in the same general direction to increase their chances of spotting prey. Several such hunting parties were scattered throughout the woods, looking for anything from deer and wild pigs to badgers and rabbits.

The five men walked slowly, with their heads down and eyes level with the shrubs that surrounded them. A slow tiptoe-like gait with carefully placed steps that avoided dead leaves and branches made them almost silent.

Suddenly, there was a rustle in the bushes directly ahead of Fletcher. Five arrows were nocked and aimed towards a large shaking bush. Whatever creature was hiding behind the bush made no sound of its own, but it was clearly rubbing itself against a tree that was directly behind the bush.

The arrows were loosed – and the creature let out a great roar of pain. A flurry of rippling reddish-brown fur shot out of the bushes. Four of the five members of the hunting party dashed up into the trees, screaming to God and the saints for protection. The great brown bear ran after Fletcher.

As fast as his legs could take him, Fletcher spun around and sprinted back to camp yelling,

"Bear! Bear! Bear!"

About thirty paces from Fletcher, two Spanish halberdiers stood watch. No one ever wanted watch duty. It was hard to stay awake and it always made the mind wander.

Isidro Gonzaga's mind wandered off to very strange places indeed, as he postulated to his watch-mate, Manuel Alarcon, that perhaps if one bathed in wine, there would be no need for soap.

However, before Alarcon could form a concrete counter-argument, he heard the faint sound of someone shouting in the distance. It was steadily getting louder and louder.

"Did you hear that?"

"Do not change the subject, Alarcon. You know that I have a good idea."

"No, listen... It sounds like someone saying, *ver...* but what is there to see?"

"*Ver? Nada que ver aqui.*" See? There is nothing to see, replied Gonzaga. "These foreigners trying to speak Spanish, *¡Dios mio, que horror!*"

A horrified looking Englishman broke through a thicket nearby, continuing to scream *"¡Ver! ¡Ver! ¡Ver!"*

"It is not ver! It is mira, idiota!"

The bear had no such grammatical restrictions as it thundered through the bushes behind the Englishman, closing in on him with alarming speed.

"Perhaps *ver* is the English word for *oso?*"

"He will die before he reaches the camp. I am in no mood to fight bears today."

"Eight florins says he can make it within view of the wagons before the bear kills him."

"It is a deal."

Fletcher continued to run even as branches smacked him in the face and thorns caught on his breeches. The bear was not slowing down at all. Fletcher could almost feel its breath on his neck, but he could see hope ahead. A wagon – he was approaching camp!

Don Alfonso was hunched over the side of a wagon, rummaging through common supplies that the company had procured on its trips through the villages. His hands found the neck of a guitar. Perfect. If his meal was to be bland, then at least he could play some good music to fill his soul.

Before he could even think of what song he was going to play, he heard the rapid pounding of footsteps, coming directly towards him. It was that peasant from earlier... and a bear?

Without thinking he dropped the guitar and quickly picked up his spontoon, bracing it as if preparing for a cavalry attack.

"Get behind me, *lunatico!*" he yelled out to Fletcher.

The Englishman readily obliged, putting Don Alfonso and his spontoon between himself and the bear.

The bear continued to charge, unwavering in its anger and blind pain. By the time it realized that it was about to impale itself on a long wooden stick with a pointy tip, the bear was not able to stop fast enough and was speared through the neck.

The great animal writhed in agony and started running around in panic as the don leaped away to avoid getting trampled under its powerful feet. As blood gushed from the wound in its neck, it turned and tried in vain to return home to the forest, but expired before it could take even five steps.

The don walked up to it and removed his spontoon from the beast. With great effort, he managed to tear it out of the neck, causing more blood to splatter on the ground and on his clothes. With a great sigh, he made the sign of the cross and began to pray,

"Saint Hubert, thank you for delivering me to victory; I dedicate this kill to you and our Heavenly Father, Amen."

When he finished praying, he turned to the Englishman hiding behind the wagon and urged him to come out.

"It is dead. You can come and see for yourself. Why is it that I keep seeing you around? What is your name, anyway?"

"It is Fletcher, sir. James Fletcher."

"*Leche?* Yames *Leche?* You are Milky Yames?" the don said, suppressing his laughter and letting his guard down.

Fletcher did not understand, instead choosing to politely smile and remain silent.

"Forgive me, *señor*," the don said, putting his hand on Fletcher's shoulder, "it is just that your name sounds... very awkward in my language. Permit me to say this but, I feel that we keep on meeting for a reason. I do not believe in coincidences, *señor*. Please, join me in camp. We will share a meal together." The don smiled, continuing, "Consider it my way of appeasing fate. You are welcome to join my companions and myself – we have salt pork. Ah, yes, I almost forgot," the don reached back into the wagon to retrieve his guitar, "there is nothing better to liven up the dullness of the forest than music."

105

Fletcher gave the don a wide grin and happily accepted. As the two walked back to camp, two disappointed halberdiers looked on from a distance.

Sophia slowly chewed the pork, wincing with disgust from its salty flavor, as Warwick eagerly awaited her assessment of his culinary skill.

"I pity the worms that have to eat my shit when I pass this through." Sophia said in Italian as she stared Warwick dead in the eye.

The Englishman, of course, did not understand, but could tell by Sophia's expression that he had once again failed at cooking. He gave a resigned shrug and dug around in the stew pot for a piece of pork for himself. As soon as he put it in his mouth he, too, looked like he was about to hurl.

"By Christ and all the saints, the best part of this pig's life was when it got slaughtered. Now it tastes like Lot's wife after Gomorrah!"

Sophia was determined to salvage the situation. She politely excused herself in Italian as she made her way towards the baggage train. She was going to get some ingredients she knew how to use and make something that at least she would enjoy. Maybe some cheese and diced tomatoes would go well with it too.

She suddenly lost her train of thought as she saw that English archer she met on the road and Don Alfonso heading back to camp together, with their clothes all dirty and bloody. She opened her mouth to ask what had happened but the don interrupted her, saying that they were both uninjured and that they would see her at camp. After seeing that neither of them was walking with a limp, she shrugged and continued on her way towards the wagons in the baggage train.

After digging around in the back of a wagon for some time, she was able to find and extract a sack of finely ground corn meal – the good stuff, bearing the seal of the *Casa de Contratacion* on the burlap sack. With some effort, she heaved the bag onto her shoulder and continued rummaging through the wagon in search of other ingredients. She was going to make polenta, a dish that Milan was famous for.

While Sophia prepared her ingredients, Fletcher sat by the fire with Warwick as Don Alfonso removed his bloody armor and clothing to wash.

"I remember you – one of the boys from Bolingbroke if I recall correctly." Warwick said as he absentmindedly poked his salt pork with a spoon. He resigned to fill himself up on coarse black bread for the evening.

"Yes, milord." replied Fletcher. He avoided saying anything further. It was improper for peasants to speak out of turn.

"Are you enjoying yourself on our little adventure? I am sure this is the furthest you have ever traveled."

"Yes, milord."

"You are quite the dullard, you know. No wonder peasants remain peasants. Master Spaniard, why did you bother bringing this man here?"

"I saved him from a bear," Don Alfonso said as he finished changing into a cotton shirt, "and this is the second time I met him. It could be fate."

"Well, fate has chosen a dumb mute." Warwick muttered, "Speak up, boy, say something clever."

"Do not pressure him, Warwick. He is probably just being polite." Don Alfonso said as he sat down with them.

"I... I am enjoying the journey, sirs." Fletcher managed to stutter.

"And God made man's mouth so that he may use it." Warwick said, smiling, "Bravo, Master Archer. Forgive me, but I forget your name."

"Fletcher, sir."

Don Alfonso snickered.

Warwick ignored him and said to Fletcher, "Yes, a pity there are not more of you longbowmen in the company. You can loose arrows much faster than the musketeer can fire his musket, and you have more ammunition than he does – twenty arrows in your quiver versus... how many boxes on a musketeer's collar, Master Spaniard?"

"Twelve, like the apostles."

"See. It is a wonder why we keep the musketeers around at all."

"Sir, if I may comment..." said Fletcher in a soft voice, "It took me six years of practice and hunting before I could truly master my bow, sir. I believe that the musketeers say that it took them less than a month?"

Warwick chuckled, "There is some truth to what you say, Master Fletcher, but if we in the company had musketeers that had only trained for a mere month, then half the front line of

Master Jaeger's pikes would have blown up during the battle on the road to Gouda."

Fletcher furrowed his eyebrows, not understanding what Warwick meant.

"Ah, you see, a musketeer has what is called a match – a cord of rope that burns at both ends that is needed to fire his weapon. During the heat of battle, this fiery candle wick is constantly burning while dangling near the cartridge boxes hanging from his belt. Far from being the only danger, but if a soldier applies too much black powder to his shot, then he will also blow himself up. I envy not the work of a musketeer."

Fletcher stared, still confused.

"*Señor Leche*," Don Alfonso said, smiling, "black powder explodes upon contact with fire. This is how muskets work."

Fletcher narrowed his eyes and slowly nodded, but before he could ask any questions, Sophia approached the camp, grunting, with a large sack slung over her back.

"*¡Señorita Fortezza! Este... ¡Señor Bianchi!*" said Don Alfonso, embarrassed that he almost gave away Sophia's real name. The English speakers were none the wiser.

Sophia dropped the heavy sack on the ground and, wheezing, said, "This man almost killed us with his pork that tasted of the sea. I will show you what real food tastes like!" She paused, regarding Fletcher for a brief moment, "The archer from the road? Why is he here?" she asked Don Alfonso.

"Fate." he shrugged.

Sophia smiled at him and offered her hand for him to kiss, but quickly remembering that she was supposed to be a man, flipped her palm to receive a handshake. "Lodovico Bianchi." she said, slowly and deliberately.

"James Fletcher. I remember you from the road, mi...lord." Fletcher replied, lightly shaking her hand, unsure of how to address a woman disguised as a man.

Sophia politely nodded, only understanding that his name was *freccia*, the Italian word for arrow. It seemed fitting, given that he was an archer. "Prepare to be amazed, my friends – I will not suffer the horrors of your English cooking that are best left for Satan and all his devils, but I will delight you with a simple Italian dish from home that will leave you craving for more!"

Don Alfonso chuckled and translated, "She says she is going to cook something."

"She?" muttered Warwick.

"Forgive me, *señor*. Slip of the tongue."

"Be at ease, Master Spaniard. The whole camp knows that she is a woman. It will be good fun to see how long before she notices that we know. It is too bad she does not speak our language, eh Master Fletcher?" he said, lightly jabbing Fletcher in the shoulder.

Fletcher laughed politely but secretly agreed with him. She was quite attractive even with that silly costume. She also had a lovely sounding voice and seemed to have a friendly, casual demeanor even after what had happened on the road to Gouda.

Sophia began by grabbing all salt pork out of the pot and throwing it out, to the objection of absolutely no one. With the water already boiling and salty, she started gradually mixing in the cornmeal. They would have a fine dinner that night.

Don Alfonso finally brought out the guitar and began to tune it. After a few awkward notes, he began strumming the strings – slowly at first, then at an increased pace. A beat began to form. The strumming was soon supplemented with the palm of the don's hand tapping against the guitar – percussion. The beat grew stronger and steadier. Shifting his hand on the fingerboard of the guitar, the instrument began to sing – its quick, happy tunes carrying the stresses of the day away like driftwood on rushing waves.

Warwick and Fletcher began to nod their heads to the beat. Sophia tapped her foot and began stirring her polenta to the beat of the music.

Don Alfonso, pleased with himself and his guitar, smiled a crooked grin and closed his eyes, saying, *"¡Canta para mi, mi angel!"*

The melody of the guitar grew even faster and more beautiful. If it was once a cleansing wave, it was now an irresistible howling wind that carried the sweet smell of Castilian roses.

Sophia slowly began to sway her hips. A smile formed on her lips. She could not resist the temptation any longer. She stopped stirring and dropped her spoon into the pot, practically leaping into the center of the group. Her feet moved like the ground was on fire, but the way she let the music carry her, it seemed like she danced around the metaphorical flames instead of stomping them out. She raised her hands, and her wrists and fingers moved like flower buds that bloomed and shut, following the sun. It was mesmerizing.

An audience began to form around her. Guards forgot about their watch, porters dropped their loads, and even Gunther

111

Jaeger, who was busy with his lists nearby, stopped brooding for about three seconds before gesturing for all the common soldiers to get back to work.

Sophia and Don Alfonso, oblivious to the world around them, continued their musical trance. Sophia grabbed Fletcher by the hand and pulled him up from his seat, drawing him close to her, their lips nearly touching. Fletcher grinned sheepishly as Sophia wrapped her arm around his waist and carried him into her world of swirling fire. Her eyes pierced into his, which were wide in fear and hesitation. She did not blink. In a whirl of frills and color, Sophia spun her partner, causing his free arm to flail, with a cheer from the audience around them. Sophia's body spoke to his, willing it where to go and how to act. As the howling wind reached its climax, Sophia locked Fletcher's leg with her own and let him slide gently into a dip, ending with her looming over him with a smile.

A roar of applause erupted from the crowd, followed immediately by the barking of sergeants and cries to return to work. Sophia's chest heaved with heavy breathing, and Fletcher's heartbeat raced as fast as a bird's. The two released each other awkwardly and shared a chuckle.

"My God," Warwick said slack-jawed, "that was the most powerful performance I have ever seen... by a woman."

Sophia, not understanding, took a bashful bow and returned to cooking dinner.

"Master Fletcher, I believe that the good lieutenant has just made you her dance-bitch." Warwick added. Everyone who understood the joke laughed.

Chapter 13

Jarlsberg Castle

Livonia, Swedish Empire

May it please Your Majesty,

It is my great honor and pleasure to inform you that, through our strength of arms, cunning, and the Grace of God, your loyal servants have managed to wrest power from the evil Swedes that occupied Jarlsberg Castle in Livonia.

The castle's armory and larder are fully stocked, and only the least bit of damage was sustained to the building during the assault.

I capture this castle in your name and for sacred Poland's lost honor. We shall take back the Swedish crown from that Satan-worshipping usurper Gustavus Adolphus and take back what is yours by divine right. Our defeat at Gorzno will be avenged.

If your majesty wills it, I humbly request that a grand army be assembled so we may take advantage of this surprise and drive the Swedes back to where they belong.

I remain your humble servant,

Colonel Jan Casimir

"What do you think, Radny Fegelein? Is it too short? Maybe it could use a little more embellishment?" said Colonel Jan Casimir as he poured more mead into his wine glass. The colonel was well-spoken, refined, and genteel, but the fact that he insisted on drinking mead out of a wine glass made Ratsherr Fegelein feel uneasy. He was also not used to being called *"radny"*, the Polish word for a man of his position.

Fegelein sat at his writing desk, taking dictation from Colonel Casimir as he slowly paced around Greve Olaf Stenbock's old council hall, which he had turned into his war room. The paintings of the greve and his family had been removed and neatly put away, replaced with maps and Polish banners. Muster rolls of Polish regular regiments, Lithuanian troops, and Tatar mercenaries sat in well-ordered stacks on the greve's old desk. The councilman and the colonel spoke to each other in German, which was Casimir's way of conceding to Fegelein's lack of knowledge in Polish.

"The letter is perfect, your lordship." Fegelein replied, not wishing to offend.

Colonel Casimir took a sip of mead and furrowed his brow, "This is excellent mead. Now then, sir, just because you are held captive here does not mean that you cannot criticize. You are a man of letters and I respect your opinion greatly. I am but a simple soldier. Are you absolutely certain that this letter is worthy of the king of Poland?"

"Well..." Fegelein said softly. He noticed the colonel raise his eyebrows, "Perhaps you can mention how you took the castle? It would paint you in a heroic light."

Casimir nodded his approval, "Excellent point. Write that down. Mention how I took the defenders by surprise, and how

114

the Tatars... no, that would make them look too important. Let us leave that out. Perhaps we can finish this later."

The sound of Fegelein's pen scribbling on parchment stopped.

"It does remind me, though, of something equally important. We need to write to that heathen so he can send us reinforcements."

"Heathen, your lordship?"

"Ah, yes, I never spoke about him at length. Imran Bey is his name. That is all you need to know. Could you prepare another blank sheet of parchment, please?"

As Fegelein carefully put away his letter to the Polish king, he wondered why a Christian such as Casimir would ever stoop to colluding with a heathen. He believed the letter he was about to write was going to reveal the answer to him. Taking a fresh sheet out of one of his desk drawers, Fegelein dipped his pen into his inkpot and began to write.

"Thank you," said Casimir, clearing his throat. "May the greetings of God the most gracious and merciful be upon you, oh noble Turk."

Fegelein's eyes widened at the mention of the Turks. They were the largest empire in the known world, and according to popular opinion, could crush Poland and Sweden both like insects. The only thing that stopped them from doing so was their war in Iraq, which they were winning decisively.

Casimir paused to think, twirling his mustache with his finger, then continued, "The Tatars that you hired out to us were brave and brutal fighters who were instrumental in the key victory we achieved at Jarlsberg. That being said, the treasure stores of the castle are now open, and the other half of your promised remuneration may now be collected. I look forward to dining with you again. Yours in Christ, Colonel Jan Casimir. Wait, no, I am sorry, do not write that last part down. Change it to yours in God instead. We cannot afford religious tension in such an uneasy alliance."

Fegelein frowned in confusion as he scribbled on the parchment. The letter still gave him no clue as to why a Muslim would ever agree to aid his bitter Christian enemy.

"As for the letter to the king regarding the battle of Jarlsberg, I trust you to write in all the details of the assault. After all, you were there. I remember you. You should have seen your face when I rode into the castle." Casimir said with a hearty chuckle.

Fegelein returned the laugh politely, although he recalled the event quite differently. The sight of a large armed man staring down upon him from the top of a war horse was not a memory he wished to treasure.

Escape had been the foremost thought on Fegelein's mind ever since the castle was taken, but the only escape plan he had was to hide in a secret cellar room and escape during the night – which was now impossible since Colonel Casimir had patrols all around the castle at all hours and there was always someone in the cellar drinking the castle's good wine.

It also did not help that he was too frightened to wash his soiled breeches, since Tatars had occupied the servants' quarters. The washerwomen could not do any laundry if they were being raped all the time.

"I am going to pay a visit to young Lady Crista," said the colonel as he threw on his leopard skin cloak, "Be very careful with that letter to the king, and remember we Poles say Zygmunt III Wasa, not Sigismund. Imagine the embarrassment of sending him a letter as if I were a Swede. Until we meet again, Radny Fegelein."

As soon as Casimir shut the door, Fegelein quickly pulled out another smaller piece of parchment and scribbled a message,

Jarlsberg Castle fallen. Polish, Lithuanian, Tatar troops occupying. Crista is alive. Polish commander has sent word to King Sigismund and is colluding with Turks. Send help immediately!

F.

Rolling it up, he made his way to a gilded cage sitting near a window in the corner of the room, where a small white dove lay cooing. Fegelein had managed to convince the colonel that this was his pet and not a carrier pigeon like all the others that had been killed and eaten. It helped that the bird was a white dove and not a gray homing pigeon like all the others. In reality, though, the dove was a special bird meant for communicating with Greve Stenbock's bank in Riga, where he was no doubt securing funds to hire troops to take back his home. Fegelein gingerly inserted the message into a capsule that he placed on the dove's feet and released it out the window.

"Crista is not in her room." Casimir said as he peeked his head through a half-opened door.

Fegelein shrieked at the sound of his voice.

"You scream like an old woman. I apologize for frightening you. Do you know where I could find her?"

"Check the library." Fegelein replied with a stutter.

"Ah, yes, how silly of me to forget, thank you. *Do widzenia.*" Casimir said as he silently closed the door. Fegelein's heart raced as he put a cloth over the birdcage.

Crista sat with Sister Margret in the castle library. She dreaded walking through the hallways, now constantly patrolled by Polish soldiers.

The courtyard was worse. The screaming of the washerwomen and her younger handmaidens as they were raped by the soldiers that occupied the castle was unbearable to her. She was lucky since Casimir ordered that no one should touch her under penalty of death. A small consolation this was, since her home was no longer her home, her handmaidens and the other female servants had been turned into sex slaves, there was a massive grave pit outside the walls that reeked of death, and her horse, Sigfrid, had been shot for kicking someone in the face when he tried to mount him. Several of the servants had already attempted taking their own lives to get away from what was rapidly becoming hell on earth.

Crista tried to forget about the reality of things by escaping into her books during her morning *fika*. Her hands quivered as she tried in vain to immerse herself in the book she held in her hands: a copy of Shakespeare's Macbeth in the original language. She had chosen poorly. The bitter taste of her coffee only seemed to emphasize the predicament she was in. She usually drank it with a lot of sugar, but the sugar was in the larder, and the Tatars were using heaps of it to blend with calamus roots to make a strange dessert from their land.

Margret, meanwhile, wondered if this were some sort of punishment from God for deserting Holy Mother Church. She was even considering returning to the fold since the Polish were Catholic and would not look too kindly on a disgraced nun, that is, if they ever found out.

The hard rapping of knuckles on the library's oak door disturbed their quiet contemplation.

"Come in." Crista said in Swedish, hoping that it was one of the remaining castle staff that still kept their sanity.

"I hope I am not disturbing you," said Colonel Casimir in Polish.

"Even if you were, your grace," Crista replied, switching to Polish, "I doubt anything I would say could prevent you from entering."

Casimir opened the door but did not enter, instead choosing to stand in the doorway, resting his shoulder against the frame.

"May I come in, your ladyship?" he said with a smirk.

Crista looked at him with an icy glare but gestured for him to enter nonetheless. Sister Margret simply sat where she was, scowling at the colonel, who ignored her.

"How may I be of service to your grace?" Crista said in an annoyed but nervous tone.

"I need nothing in particular. I just came to see how you were faring."

119

"I am well, and alive, unlike Anna."

"Who?" Casimir said, furrowing his brow.

"Anna was one of my handmaidens. You see, your grace, when you allowed your men to do as they wished with the castle staff, with all the looting..." Crista paused, taking a deep sip of her coffee, "and the rape, your grace, Anna's dreams were crushed. You ruined her wedding."

"What wedding?" Casimir scoffed, "I saw no tapestries or flowers or wedding vestments when we went through the castle stores."

"That is because, your grace, Anna is... what was the word for *bondeflicka* in your language... peasant? Ah, yes, *chłop.*"

"That is unfortunate, your ladyship, but I can assure you that I did not directly order her death. I specifically told my men that by killing the peasantry, they would be ruining this manor's economy. We want to present his majesty with a flourishing estate, not a desolate ruin."

"Oh, your men did not kill her, they..."

Sister Margret slammed her fist on the table, interrupting her lady, "They tore the flower of her womanhood from her before her husband had a chance to enjoy the bouquet!"

Casimir sneered at the old woman and drew his mace from the steel frog on his hip, placing it on the table with a loud thud. Pointing his finger at her as if he was accusing a small child, he said, "This is your only warning." and attempted to continue the conversation with Crista. "Before we were so rudely interrupted, you are accusing my men of raping and killing your peasant girl handmaiden, yes?"

Crista nodded silently and took another sip of her coffee.

"You should know, ladyship, that my men had been promised the opportunity to loot and raid, and I am simply fulfilling my promise to them. The alternative would be... ugly."

"Colonel, there are few things uglier than watching my friends fling themselves off of the castle balcony simply because they do not wish to bear the children of monsters."

"The alternative is mutiny and anarchy." Casimir replied, deepening his scowl, "An army that has been betrayed will rapidly turn into a storm of swords and violence. I am averting the wholesale slaughter and destruction of everything in this castle. Cannot you see I am trying to keep you safe?"

Crista furrowed her brow at him and asked, "Yes, why is that exactly? What use do I have to you, colonel, besides serving as your pretty little war trophy?" Crista was trying her very best not to scream at him.

Casimir's expression eased. He paused, curling his mustache thoughtfully. "I recall you saying that your father, the lord of the castle, was out hunting when I liberated this place? Well, it is logical to assume that he will gather allies and march on Jarlsberg to take it from me. You are my insurance."

"So you are expecting my father to refuse to lay siege to his home because his beloved little girl is trapped within?"

"Precisely. You should thank me for not letting you starve to death."

"And I suppose I should also be thankful for the screams and wailing I hear every night that come from the castle courtyard? What about the suicides, colonel? Did you know that

121

my people would rather kill themselves than be touched by your dogs?"

Casimir rubbed his temples in frustration. "I told you already. I must appease my men. I do not want them rampaging through the countryside like common brigands."

"And how long will you have to appease them for? Weeks? Months? An entire year?"

"I have asked for reinforcements from my king. Once they arrive, we will continue our noble campaign into the rest of your empire so we can put the Swedish crown back where it belongs, on the head of my king."

"This is your plan?" Crista said, confused, "Our kingdoms signed a peace treaty just last year and you already want to break it! King Sigismund will march on you and crush you as a rebel and a traitor!"

Casimir snarled raising his voice, "King Zygmunt would do no such thing! The Swedish crown is his by divine right, and I, his loyal servant, am helping him recover it, peace treaty be damned!"

Crista rose from her seat, "Help? You will be the death of your king! The wrath of every kingdom in the west will descend on the fool king that broke a peace treaty after just one year!"

Without warning, Casimir's open hand struck Crista on the cheek, causing her to collapse on the floor, bleeding from her mouth.

Sister Margret, enraged that this defiler of women would add further insult to her lady, flew to Casimir and struck him in the face with a slap of her own.

Casimir barely flinched and picked up his mace from the table. Despite her bravery, Sister Margret received a mace blow to her face, scattering her teeth all over the library floor and crushing her skull, killing her.

Crista, blood still dripping from her lips, picked herself up and ran over to her aged tutor.

"Margret? Can you hear me? Wake up!" she cried out to her old friend in Swedish as tears began to well up in her eyes.

Margret lay silent on the cold, hard floor as the blood from her head wound began to create a puddle around her.

Casimir dusted his hands off and murmured, "I am sorry it could not be helped. I will send someone to clean this up. In the future, it would be best for you to remember not to mock my king."

With this, he excused himself and left the room, leaving Crista sobbing over Sister Margret's body behind him.

Royal Castle
Warsaw, Poland

The weary King Sigismund III Vasa sat on his richly decorated throne as he and his Grand Crown Hetman, Stanislaw Koniecpolski, discussed the future of the kingdom over a game of chess.

"You were wise to sue the Swedes for peace, majesty," said Koniecpolski, gingerly moving his pawn.

"But at what cost? We have lost Riga and Livonia and our most important Baltic ports to the Protestants, and they force us to pay a tax on our trade in the Baltic? It is as if all our brave boys died for nothing." Sigismund wheezed. After his assassination attempt some years ago, he was no longer in the best of health. He thought for a moment and mirrored Koniecpolski's move.

"We must remember our role, majesty, as the guardians of Christianity in Europe. The Turkish wolf grows hungry as he sees the fire that rages in Europe. While the Holy Roman Emperor struggles to contain his squabbling heretic states..."

"We know," Sigismund interrupted, "The Turks will be waiting for the opportunity to strike and we Poles have the thankless task of being the wall which they break upon."

"Precisely, majesty. An end to the war will allow us to spend time recuperating and getting ready to defend ourselves against that devil Sultan Murad. Once he is done conquering Iraq, he will doubtless have nowhere else to go, and I believe that he shares the same mind as we do – the murder of the infidel leaves a slightly better taste in his mouth than the murder of his fellow Muslims."

A messenger entered the king's chambers and knelt before him, exclaiming, "A message from one Colonel Jan Casimir, your highness."

The king bid the messenger bring him the letter, and as he opened it and read it, his eyes grew narrow with confusion.

"This is odd. This man says he recaptured Jarlsberg Castle from the Swedes."

124

Koniecpolski furrowed his brow, "Does he not know the war is over?"

"And he has the audacity to ask us for an army to aid him."

"What are your orders, majesty?"

The Polish king sat in contemplative silence, resting his chin on his clasped hands. Four thousand souls had been lost to the Swedes in the last war. Vital seaports had been lost to them, and Poland had to pay a humiliating tax to trade in its own waters. This heralded the beginning of the end of Poland's golden age. Sigismund looked at the image of Christ hanging from a wall in his throne room. The king of Heaven gazed down upon His subject, His expression stern and fatherly.

"There is a way that appears to be right, but in the end, it leads to death." Sigismund muttered, quoting Proverbs.

"What was that, majesty?"

"Assemble the army. We shall take to the field one last time."

Chapter 14

Lingen, Holy Roman Empire

The city of Lingen was a short march away from Nordhorn Range, and the men of Talbot Company still had the energy to set up camp, which they were forced to do anyway since the walled city forbade large armies from entering the city. It was probably for the best as well, since the company was not sure which side of the war Lingen supported. This was not to say that they were forbidden from supplying here though, since eager merchants brought their wagons out to the men to sell various baked goods, sweetmeats, drinks, and trinkets. Unfortunately, Colonel MacRae was not keen on feeding his men pretzels and gingerbread for the duration of the campaign. While the men drank themselves into oblivion with the company's money, MacRae had sent Otto Koenigsherr and Gunther Jaeger into the city to secure supplies that they actually needed, like grain, water, dried meat, and salt, instead of wasting their time in some tavern on a street corner.

Otto Koenigsherr sat outside a tavern on a street corner, merrily nursing a tankard of ale, as Gunther sat across from him shaking his head in disappointment. This was his fourth tankard, and he was spending company money on the best ale in the house.

"You need to learn to live a little, *Herr Jaeger.*" Otto said, his speech slightly slurred.

"The only reason I am here with you is because I do not trust your sense of propriety. Do you expect me to believe that you will simply guzzle down all that ale, complete your task and haul a wagonload of supplies back to camp before sundown?"

"Yes!" Otto replied, raising his tankard.

"You have already had too much, we should go."

"No, stay awhile longer, have a pint yourself. It is good for your nerves."

"*Herr Koenigsherr,* my nerves are frayed because we were given a task and you are the obstacle that is preventing us from completing it."

"And you are... you are just a fun-killer."

Gunther sighed in exasperation and grabbed his colleague's arm, "Let us go."

"No!" Otto groaned like a stubborn child. His breath stank of alcohol.

"I have no intention of seeing you here tomorrow stinking drunk and robbed of your possessions. The sooner we complete this task, the sooner..."

"I challenge you to a duel!" Otto was clearly out of his mind, drunk. He regarded the way that Gunther looked at him, that disappointed scowl, that nagging tone. He probably thought he was better than him. This was no less than an insult, and Otto's honor had to be satisfied.

"What." Gunther said in confusion, his word more of a remark than a question.

Otto closed the visor of his helmet and repeated himself, "I challenge you to a duel!"

"I accept." Gunther said, rising from his seat to take his zweihander sword from the pillar from where it was resting.

"Excellent. This will be short and painless," Otto said as he staggered to his feet, drawing his broadsword, "for me."

"First blood, *Herr Koenigsherr*. If I win, sit down and shut up in the back of the wagon. If you win, I will drink with you until we are both arrested for disorderly conduct."

"Excellent terms, I agree." Otto said with a hiccup.

The two German swordsmen stepped into the empty street, away from the tavern. A small crowd began to gather around them. Duels were always fun to watch, especially when they were to the death.

Otto confidently assumed his combat stance, with his feet spread apart, one foot in front of the other. He gripped his broadsword in both hands and raised it high up like a priest offering the sacrifice at mass, ready to strike at Gunther's head.

Otto watched his opponent's movements carefully through the narrow eye slots of his helmet. Gunther frowned at him and changed his stance, holding his zweihander with its hilt below his waist, the tip aimed towards Gunther's helmeted face.

Now was Otto's chance. His opponent was defending from his waist while he was about to strike high. Otto leaped forward to move in for the kill, bringing his sword down onto his opponent's head – his blow was immediately blocked, and before he could react, Gunther had wrestled his sword away from him and he was on his back, looking at the sky.

The disappointed crowd dispersed and went back to drinking, while Gunther helped his companion to his feet.

"I think I am bleeding." Otto said as he opened his visor.

"Impossible. My blade did not touch you."

"No, I am very certain that I am bleeding. I think I bit my tongue."

As he got back on his feet, he felt a light tap on his shoulder. As Otto turned, he found a sword tip pointed straight at his face. As he looked down the length of the blade, he could see that it was being held by someone from horseback. It looked like Bjornsson, but he could not tell – the alcohol was impairing his vision.

"Förklara för mig," said Bjornsson in Swedish, "Var är mina leveranser?"

Gunther reminded the captain that they did not speak Swedish, and he sighed and switched to Low German, grabbing Otto by the visor of his helmet.

"My supplies, you idiot. Where are they? You have been gone for hours."

Otto giggled and responded in Saxon, "You sound funny. Do not worry, you old knacker, we will get your..." as Otto's speech trailed off, the sweet sensation of sleep overcame him.

Bjornsson was not amused. "Wake up!" he said, as he shook Otto by the pauldrons of his armor.

"It is no use," Gunther said as he put his zweihander away, "he will be like that for hours. However, sir, it does give us time to go to the market and take what we need."

"We might as well." Bjornsson agreed, "Come on, help me load this oaf into the wagon."

After the two men managed to heave the armored Otto into the back of the rickety wagon, the Swede hoisted himself up into the driver's seat as Gunther climbed up beside him. The stubborn Finnish horse made a reluctant snort as Bjornsson goaded it to walk to the marketplace.

"There is a matter that I wanted to discuss with you in confidence, *Herr Jaeger.*"

"Sir?"

"I was going over the muster roll of the company, and I noticed something about your recruits. The areas that they come from – Austria, Spain, Italy, Bavaria… do you realize what they have in common?"

"If this is a reference to the fact that the majority of our troops are Catholic, I do not see the problem. We will fight any enemy for you regardless of their religion."

"You may believe that, *Herr Jaeger,* but I trust no one. When I first met Colonel William MacRae I thought he was of the same faith as Colonel Alexander Leslie, a Scottish Protestant in the court of King Gustavus Adolphus. However a few days ago I heard him say, 'by our Blessed Mother' and I knew he was Catholic."

"What, precisely, is troubling you, sir?"

"If these men find out that they are slaughtering their fellow Catholics there may be a mutiny. We need to balance this out by hiring as many Protestant men as we can."

"Will the gold that we currently have be sufficient?"

"I have gone through the accounts. If we scrimp on supplies, we can afford to hire perhaps another one hundred and twenty trained men. The untrained will have to be paid in loot."

"I understand completely, sir. We will slash the rations appropriately."

"Yes, no more cakes, pretzels, wine or fresh beef either. All our meat will be dried or salted, and we will learn to subsist on the bare minimum."

Gunther nodded. Excessive leisure was bad for an army on the march anyway.

Bjornsson brought the wagon to a halt as they turned the corner into the market, and Otto was jolted awake, burping and mumbling.

"You are awake so soon?" said Bjornsson, "Good. There is a task I need you to help your companion with." Turning to Gunther, he continued, "I am going to do a bit of haggling here in the market. You two can go into that tavern over there and look for potential recruits. Tell them to meet us outside the walls to enlist. We shall have to do this in every town we encounter to balance out our forces."

Gunther dismounted the cart and grabbed Otto by the straps of his armor, throwing him off the cart.

"You sir," Otto hiccupped in protest, "greatly offend me. I challenge you..."

Before he could finish, Gunther slapped the side of his helmet, jarring his head. "Get up, we are going to the tavern."

"The tavern?" Otto said as he somehow regained his bearings and stood up on his own, shouting, "Joy and merriment! Ale, ale for every soul!" after which he immediately collapsed again.

Scowling, Gunther helped Otto up to his feet and stood him up straight. "Can you walk?" he said, more out of practicality than concern.

"Little children can walk!" Otto replied as he wobbled towards the tavern's front door.

Gunther rushed in straight after him and caught him just as he was about to slip and fall again. The patrons and the tavern owner gave them strange looks as they entered. It was not peculiar to see drunken soldiers gallivanting about the town, but Otto did not look like a common mercenary with his shining black armor and armet helmet.

The two found two empty spots on a tavern bench and sat down, receiving worried looks from the patrons around them, who whispered to each other in German.

"Do you remember what the Captain said, *Herr Koenigsherr?*" Gunther said, speaking slowly as if he were talking to a child.

"Recruit!"

"Good. But keep your voice down. Not everyone in the tavern has to know."

"Press gang the lot of them!"

Gunther sighed turning to the guests around him, "Excuse my friend here. He has had a bit too much to drink." Noticing that a few of the patrons had empty tankards, he smiled and called for another round of ale to be brought to their table. The men sitting with him still looked at him with a feeling of distrust.

Gunther opened his mouth to speak but was interrupted by a patron that sat across from him.

"You are recruiters, are you not?" he said in a deep baritone voice as he leaned in closer.

From the roughness of his hands and the size of his arms, Gunther thought he might be a field laborer or a blacksmith.

Gunther nodded, saying, "Yes. We work for the honorable Talbot Company. We pay four florins a month for a life of freedom and adventure."

"Which side do you fight for?" the large man said, scowling.

Gunther paused. He had to be careful. Even though this was Saxony, which was traditionally Protestant, there were still pockets of Catholicism scattered throughout the region. Declaring allegiance to the wrong faction could be fatal.

Otto slammed his fist on the table. "You are taking too long with this."

Before Gunther could stop him, Otto had climbed on top of the table with a tankard in his hand.

"Everyone!" he bellowed, "A toast to his holiness the pope!"

Dead silence. The tavern was so quiet that even the mice that scurried underneath the wooden floor stopped squeaking.

"Fuck the pope!" came a cry from the back of the room.

"Fuck off, you papist cunt!" screamed someone else.

"The devil take you! The devil take you and your armies to hell with him!" an old woman said, shaking her fist in the air.

Gunther grabbed Otto and sprinted for the door. Glassware, metal plates and someone's left boot hit the door just as they closed it behind them.

"You see?" said Otto laughing heartily, "My method was faster."

Gunther, panting, clapped Otto on his back. "Well done *Herr Koenigsherr*. Now we must tell them our true intentions before we start a riot."

Sophia lunged at Fletcher with her rapier, but the Englishman was able to see the blow with ease and stepped aside, letting her advance too far and trip herself on her own maneuver.

"Stop." Don Alfonso said in Spanish, pinching the bridge of his nose, "You were lifting your foot too high off the ground, *hija*. He was able to see you coming a mile away."

The three were practicing in an open field away from the main camp outside the wall, situated behind a grove of trees so that the common soldiers could not see them. Sophia was finally learning how to properly use her expensive Italian rapier, and Fletcher was getting practice with his old hunting sword while Don Alfonso dictated instructions.

"Right," said Sophia, panting, "Keep my feet close to the ground, but do not drag them, and, ah…"

"Quick, explosive movements," said the don, drawing his own blade to inspect.

134

"Yes, yes, quick and explosive." Sophia said as she practiced her movements at half speed.

"Did I do well, sir?" Fletcher asked in English.

"Oh, yes, superbly." Don Alfonso replied, switching to English for Fletcher, "Especially for someone who is untrained. Where did you learn how to fight like that?"

"Hunting boar in the greenwood, sir. Their movements are predictable, like hers, and she is just as ferocious and single-minded."

"You are lucky she did not understand that, *señor leche.*" Don Alfonso said with a chuckle.

"And where did you learn how to speak my language, if I may inquire?"

Don Alfonso smiled, "Once, when I was much younger, about your age perhaps, I worked as a ship's boy for the Spanish navy. One day my ship was intercepted by one of the vessels from your home country."

"Pirates, sir?"

"Well, yes, but they called themselves 'free sailors.' They were led by a very refined fellow, Michael Garlington was his name I recall. No frightening alias or gimmicks – he was as he was, a dandy highwayman on the high seas. Anyway, they press-ganged me into their pirate crew and I served them for several years, learning of your people's language and culture."

"And how did you ever manage to escape?"

"I did not escape, *señor.* I was eh... liberated. An entire Spanish fleet crossed paths with us once and forced us to capitulate. They repatriated us Spaniards back to the motherland and hanged the pirates."

"And you were not punished for piracy or brigandry?"

"The Spanish captain was very understanding, and frankly a bit of a racist." Don Alfonso chuckled, "He said that we were innocent by virtue of our Castilian blood. I am Asturian myself, but freedom is better than death."

Sophia walked up to them, frustrated with herself. "What are the two of you jabbering about in that ugly language? I want to go again. *Signor Freccia,* come, let us continue." she said, tugging on Fletcher's sleeve.

"Would you mind if I pry further, Master Alfonso?" Fletcher asked as he assumed his defensive stance.

Don Alfonso nodded his approval.

"Why are you training her? I thought she was already an experienced officer. I was clearly mistaken."

The don's smile faded. "No one must know that she is inexperienced. The lives of men depend on her. I am only helping her because she paid for my own commission and I intend to keep my word. Besides, she reminds me of my younger sister."

Sophia assumed her offensive stance and pointed her sword at Fletcher, waiting for instructions from Don Alfonso.

"*Señorita Fortezza,*" he said, switching to Spanish, "your opponent is reading your movement. Be unpredictable, use your feet. Do you remember how quickly you moved when you danced? Do that – but remember your fundamentals."

Sophia nodded and began to tap her feet on the dirt, giving herself a beat.

136

Curious, Fletcher looked down at her little feet making dust clouds in the dirt.

With no warning at all, Sophia glided towards her opponent, slapping the blade out of his hand with her sword like it was a lover that had scorned her, and brought the tip of her blade to Fletcher's throat.

Fletcher stood frozen in disbelief and fear until Sophia put her sword away with a smile cresting her lips

"Astounding," he said as he gave her a slow clap. "That was not an orthodox move, but it worked. It seemed almost... Fiorian."

"What?" she said, confused, "What does this mean, 'Fiorian'?"

"One of your countrymen, *señorita*. He was a very skilled master swordsman, known for his practicality, roguery, and deception. You should be fighting with a longsword."

"But I like this one – it is light and fast and it has my initials engraved on the side."

"As you say," Don Alfonso shrugged, "A warrior knows themselves better than anyone. Now, we shall refine this... dance technique of yours. And by the way, *señor leche*," he said, switching to English, "the sister that I am speaking about, my Catalina, was five years old when I last saw her. She shares her stubbornness and courage, but she was never very bright. Speaking of which..." the don paused and switched to Spanish again, "*Señorita,* what role do you believe your swordsmen play on the battlefield?"

"You have asked me this question before, *signore,*" she said with a confident smile, "and they are the first into the fray, the bravest and fiercest..."

"This is what you answered the last time, *hija,* and once more, you are wrong. I will explain again. The doctrine of modern war..." his speech trailed off as he drew his sword and began making a drawing in the dirt, "... is quite simple."

Fletcher and Sophia leaned in close to observe his diagram. It was a row of several large squares, with two smaller squares at the beginning and end of the row. The don also poked a series of holes in the dirt in an organized cluster behind the row of squares.

"For simplicity's sake," the don said with a sigh, "the large squares are the pikemen and musketeers. As I said before, they are responsible for taking the full onslaught of the enemy. Behind them, represented by the small dots, are the irregulars like *señor leche* here, the artillerymen and the cavalry. The irregulars have their uses – building bridges, pillaging, banditry, whatever they can do to make up their difference in salary from commissioned officers like ourselves. Now, the smaller squares are your swordsmen. They protect the flanks."

The don then drew squares overlapping the pike squares and continued, "If an enemy force draws near and entangles itself with our pikemen, what do you believe you should do?"

Sophia stuttered, but could not make an intelligent answer.

Fletcher put his hand to his chin in thought, "I assume these squares are armies, milord? Would it not be sound for the smaller squares here to turn and hit the enemy from the side?"

"I am thankful she did not understand that, but yes, that is exactly what the 'smaller squares' are for, *señor leche.*" he said with a smile, after which he switched back to Spanish. *"Señorita Fortezza,* you and your men will be responsible for attacking from the side to break pushes of pike."

"A push of what?" Sophia asked, dumbfounded.

"A push of pike is what happens when two companies of pike meet and realize that they hate each other very much – so much so that the field in front of them becomes a forest of pikes, with spear tips from friend and foe pointing at heaven, earth, and your nether bits. Your men are tasked with breaking this by charging at them from the side or 'flank' as we say."

"How would we go about doing that?"

Don Alfonso smiled and patted her on the shoulder, "Come, *hija.* I believe that tactics can wait until after you know how to fight. Let us continue the fencing practice."

Chapter 15

Talbot Company had been marching eastward for seven days, stopping at every village they encountered to resupply and recruit more men. The company's funds were by no means running low, but due to Bjornsson's austerity orders being enforced, the men were no longer getting the sweet treats and trinkets they were accustomed to in Lingen.

Sophia had been practicing sword and battle drills with Don Alfonso and James Fletcher, and had seen significant progress. She had also been rehearsing her marching drills with Fletcher, and she now knew the basic facing commands in Italian and, surprisingly, English, although she spoke with a heavy accent that Fletcher found adorable.

Gunther and Otto were becoming experts at ferreting out Protestants and persuading them to join the company for adventure and profit and had added a large number of trained and untrained recruits to the company's muster roll. Unfortunately, a few fights were breaking out amongst the more pious Protestants and the more zealous Catholics, and certain punishments had to be meted out to keep things in order. One such pair that found themselves at odds with each other was chained together at the ankles in order to force them to cooperate with one another. Measures like this proved effective at stopping fights but ultimately led to Catholic and Protestant groups congregating far away from each other in camp.

It had been a mere four-hour march from the last town they had stopped at to Schwedt, a town on the border between the German-speaking lands and Poland. The local militia had surrounded the battered walls of the town, under orders to not let anyone but traders and supply wagons inside. The town had been ransacked, besieged and plundered many times over the duration of the war, and the local burgomaster had had enough of it.

When Talbot Company arrived at the outskirts of Schwedt, they noticed that, strangely, other mercenary companies had congregated here as well. A veritable city of tents with different banners for each of the different free companies had been constructed outside Schwedt's city walls. Irishmen assembling under the French colors, bands of Portuguese adventurers, and the brightly dressed Swiss mercenaries among others gathered around their camps in a sea of tents that stretched for a mile around the city walls.

Colonel MacRae, being the businessman he was, did not like the fact that his competition was advertising louder than he was, and ordered Talbot Company to erect its tents in the center of the camp, taking some of the space away from a group of French mercenaries called the Blue Falcons.

"I want yon fuckin' dog's head to be seen from hither to Krakow!" barked MacRae as he gestured to the Talbot Company banner – a white dog's head on a red field – as a team of his men raised it high over the tops of the tent city.

Talbot Company's banner flew proudly over all the other insignias, especially because MacRae ordered that a spear be tied to the flagpole to make it even taller.

"Je vous demande pardon, Monsieur, si je vous interromps." came a voice from behind MacRae.

"*Va-t'en! Qu'est-ce que tu veux?*" What the hell do you want, said MacRae, turning around. He saw a man with wavy blonde hair dressed in an all-blue ensemble, wearing a shining steel breastplate decorated with gold-leaf. To accentuate his attire, he wore a white cape with fur trimmings. MacRae thought he looked like an absolute fop.

"My name is Colonel Dominique Sauvage, leader of *les faucons bleus*." the mercenary colonel said in French, "I would appreciate it very much if your men would kindly stay within the boundaries of your camp."

"And why the fuck is that?" MacRae said in a taunting tone, "Are your men afraid of being buggered in the arse like the wee jessies that they are?" he continued in Scots.

"I do not understand."

"Fuck off!" MacRae bellowed in French, "I am Colonel William fuckin' MacRae of Talbot Company, and me men go where they will! I am not about to fuckin' stop them from having their fun for some French woman!"

Colonel Sauvage gave MacRae a flamboyant bow and turned around with a whirl of his cape, walking away while cursing at the Scotsman in French. MacRae heard and understood every word, but only laughed and pointed at the Frenchman as he headed back to camp. Sauvage would not take this insult lightly.

Meanwhile, back at Talbot Company's camp, the atmosphere was one of merriment and anticipation. They were finally going to be able to enter enemy territory after this last stop for resupply. Soldiers boasted amongst themselves who could kill more enemies, and the rattling of armor was heard as Sophia's swordsmen practiced their strikes and footwork against Warwick's irregulars.

The tent city almost seemed like a town fair or a festival, with so much going on. Peddlers from Schwedt were hawking their goods to the mercenaries, and there was a lot of delicious-smelling fare that was tempting the noses of Talbot Company's more unrestrained men. However, Gunther and his sergeants were keeping an eye on everyone. Bjornsson's sumptuary laws still stood.

The matter of keeping the coin in the company's coffers was of so much importance that Gunther decided to place the company's gold under triple guard. What had normally been the duty of a single man now fell to two swordsmen and their commander, Sophia Fortezza, still known to them as Lieutenant Lodovico Bianchi, although everyone except her knew full well that she was a woman in disguise.

Sophia sat on a log next to a campfire they had built near the treasure wagon. The two soldiers with her, Vincenzo and Fabiano, were Italians like herself, both of whom hailed from Venice. Sophia felt somewhat at ease with them, finally having a chance to speak to people who shared her language, but on the other hand, she knew that they somehow did not respect her as a commander. She ran her fingers through the rings on her sword as she attempted small talk.

"So, gentlemen, what do you intend on doing with the gold we are getting from our little adventure?" she said with a faint smile.

"I do not know," Vincenzo said with a bored shrug, "Gambling, drinking, and whoring I guess. What about you Fabiano?"

"Definitely gambling, drinking and whoring. What else is there in life?" he chuckled.

"I..." Sophia hesitated, not knowing if they wanted to hear her opinion, "I have always wanted to have my own *sartoria*." she said sheepishly, referring to the luxurious Italian tailors found in Milan and Rome that created the waistcoats and dresses of the great and powerful men and women of the Italian courts.

The two Venetians said nothing but lay back against the wheels of the cart. One closed his eyes and the other one tipped his hat to cover his face.

"Hey, you cannot go to sleep on guard duty." Sophia said, trying and failing to sound authoritative.

"Fuck off," said one of the men as he drifted off to sleep.

Sophia sighed, frustrated. Even after all the sword and marching drills, she still could not be an effective leader of men because she had could not bring her men to respect her. She held her sword close to her and contemplated her journey so far. She had met a few new friends and gone through several hardships with them, but was this journey an adventure or just an affirmation that she was destined to fail in all her endeavors?

A gentle hand landed gingerly on her shoulder. Startled, she bolted up and drew her sword to strike. The figure took a step back and raised his arms in surrender. It was someone she had never seen before, dressed in a blue doublet with matching blue breeches, accented with a white cape and well-polished armor.

"Who are you?" she said, cautiously.

"Ah, an Italian," the man said in her language with a moderate French accent, "Good afternoon, miss. I am here to relieve you."

"Miss? How did you know?"

Sauvage stopped for a moment. It was painfully obvious to anyone with two eyes that this was a woman. But if she believed in the inconspicuousness of her own terrible disguise then he would humor her.

"I saw it in your eyes, miss. They are not soldier's eyes; they shine like sapphires – mesmerizing and beautiful."

Sophia, flattered, felt the rush of blood to her cheeks. It had been a long time since she had received a genuine compliment.

"You mustn't tell anyone, sir," she said, averting her eyes. "You must be the first person to notice my secret..." Sophia stopped short. Something was nagging at her about this man. "Pardon me for saying sir, but where is your sash?" she asked, referring to the white sash that all Talbot Company enlisted men wore to distinguish them from other mercenary bands.

The Frenchman furrowed his brow, confused, but quickly understood what she meant.

"My lady, I could say the same of you. Where is yours?"

It was true, Sophia wore no distinguishing sash because she was an officer, and MacRae knew all his commanders by their faces, thus he had decided to forego regimental sashes for them.

However, this was also strange since Talbot Company had such a small number of officers and Sophia thought she knew all of them.

"I am Dominique Sauvage, commander of the light infantry. I am not surprised you have never seen me before. I prefer to keep company with my men rather than with the dry and humorless officers."

His argument made sense to her, although she never heard anyone ever mention a "light infantry" contingent within Talbot Company. However no one really told her much of anything in the company – but they did tell her about her relief, and he was too early.

"I was told that my relief would arrive at dusk. The sun is still up, sir." Sophia said, putting up her guard.

Sauvage smiled and took a seat beside her.

"What is a few more hours? I arrived early, and there is nothing better to do in camp, I simply wish to fulfill my duty." as he spoke, he fingered a large medallion that he wore around his neck.

"What is that?" asked Sophia, eyeing the piece of jewelry. The medallion had a dazzling gold necklace with an impressive looking red stone set in its center. Sophia's eyes widened. It was the most beautiful piece of jewelry she had ever laid her eyes on.

"It is beautiful." she said, the glowing red stone reflecting in her eyes. She licked her lips and grinned at Sauvage, "I will play you for it." she said, producing a tin of dice from her belt.

Sauvage grinned back, "I accept."

146

Sophia had forgotten the predicament that got her landed in Talbot Company in the first place. She was unusually lucky at dice back in Milan, but her hubris had caught up with her, running her into debt. She was now in danger of making that same mistake all over again.

As the dice rolled in Sophia's little tin, she hardly noticed a pair of soldiers sneak into the cart behind her.

"Three ones, that is a thousand points." Sophia said, her smile wide with greed.

"I admit, that is pretty impressive," said Sauvage, looking at his two fives and a one, which gave him a mere hundred points. "Fair is fair. The necklace is yours. May I?" Sauvage asked as he offered to put the necklace around Sophia's neck.

Sophia grinned and nodded, closing her eyes as the Frenchman clasped the golden necklace around her neck. It looked beautiful on her.

"Now, if you will excuse me, miss, I must take my leave."

"So soon?" Sophia whined, "Stay awhile, let us talk."

"No," Sauvage chuckled, "I really must go. Look behind you."

Sophia whirled around and discovered two soldiers had mounted the treasure wagon. Before she could draw her sword, the wagon sped off, knocking the two Venetian guards over with the violence of its launch.

Sophia chased after the wagon, but could only helplessly watch as the soldier in the back of the wagon opened the treasure chest and began scattering coin at random. Money hungry mercenaries abandoned their posts and leaped at the ground, scooping up fistfuls of coin and brawling over the spilled cash like greedy vultures.

Sophia knew that she could do no more to salvage the situation. Her negligence had cost Talbot Company all its money.

Chapter 16

Sophia was terrified. Her actions had cost Talbot Company a devastating blow; one that most enemy armies could only dream of inflicting upon a host of mercenaries. She paced around in circles, pulling her beret down on her head as she did. Her companions, Vincenzo and Fabiano, had long since scattered and were now attempting to get as far away from Schwedt as possible.

Who would Sophia talk to without repercussions? If there were to be repercussions, how severe would they be? She had heard stories of armies punishing undisciplined or bad-mannered soldiers using whips and canes. The worst offenders were executed. She had so much to live for yet, and neither of these penalties were particularly appealing to her.

In her desperation, she decided to go and find Don Alfonso; he would know what to do. She had to find his company's command tent. The thumping of her heart reverberated through her head even though she was making the slowest, calmest steps towards the don's tent. She could feel her teeth chattering from the fear, and she had to grip the handle of her sword to keep her hands from shaking.

She did not realize it, but she was going around in circles again. All the tents looked the same to her in her state of panic. This only made her feel more helpless as she started breathing heavier. Her knuckles became white from gripping her sword, and she gritted her teeth as she walked faster and faster around the sea of tents, nearly forgetting what she had been searching for.

Suddenly, the thundering of hooves interrupted her thoughts. A horse stopped just short of trampling her. It gave a complaining neigh as its rider halted it. He was hauling along two prisoners behind him on foot, tied together with a long rope – two Venetians had been caught trying to desert the camp. Otto Koenigsherr dismounted and approached Sophia.

"Lieutenant Bianchi." He said in French, with a genuinely concerned tone, "Is everything all right?"

Sophia's lips began to quiver as she looked up at Otto. Before he could continue, she gave him a tight hug. Otto, taken aback, gently hugged her back, taking great care not to cut her with the couters of his armor.

"What is wrong?" he said, softly.

"I was distracted by a game of dice for this necklace," she said, holding up the dazzling red jewel on her neck, "and then some men came by and stole all our money." She pointed at the two prisoners Otto was dragging behind him, "Those two fell asleep and failed to stop the robbery."

Otto's face turned pale. A mercenary company with no funds was the beginning of a mutiny. He was thankful that many of these men were so far away from home that desertion would be hard for them, but the danger was still absolutely clear.

"We have to report this to Colonel MacRae." He said, "Also, this is faker than the kiss that Judas gave our Lord." Otto said as he examined Sophia's new necklace. "This is red glass, plain and simple. Also, this chain is copper. Lieutenant, you have just been arse-fucked." he said with a sympathetic grimace. Sophia looked up at him, her eyes red and swollen. She was terrified.

It was dusk. The blood-hued sun crested the rooftops of the City in the distance. While the other mercenary companies prepared their beddings and began to post night watches, the entirety of Talbot Company had gathered in a circle around a tall, thick wooden post, two nervous Venetians, and a scared teenage girl. Colonel MacRae convened with his officers and his client while Otto watched over the prisoners. The officers spoke in English, outside of everyone's earshot.

"Gentlemen," MacRae said solemnly, "This be an unprecedented act of treachery. Because of the negligence of three of our own men, we have lost our entire advance. The punishment meted should be fuckin' harsh and unforgettable."

"Hang them all." Gunther said, his expression stone-faced.

"We would be losing a valuable officer, sir," said Don Alfonso in Sophia's defense, "I suggest something more tempered. Perhaps we can simply deprive them of rations or throw them in a pit?"

"We have no time to build a pit, and everyone will be starving soon anyway." Warwick interjected, "We should just have at them with the cat o' nine tails."

"I propose that we hang the two common enlisted men and flog the officer," said Bjornsson as he scowled at Sophia, who was trembling nearby.

151

"All those in favor?" MacRae asked. His proposal was received by silent nods all around. Satisfied, the colonel clapped his hands with finality and had his circle of officers disperse to face the prisoners. Gunther marched over to Otto, whispered the sentence to him and walked back to MacRae. Otto shook his head in dismay.

"Vincenzo Rossi, Fabiano de Luca, Lodovico Bianchi." he said, without his usual air of sarcasm, "You have been found guilty of the crime of dereliction of duty. What do you have to say in your defense?"

Fabiano threw himself at Otto's feet, grasping at his boots with an expression on his face that could only be described as absolute fear.

"You would not execute a fellow Christian, would you signore?" Fabiano said in Italian, his grip tightening.

Otto looked down at him and replied, "That is not for me to decide. Now, do you want the whole company to think you are a sniveling cowardly runt or do you want to take your punishment like a man? Let go of my boot."

Fabiano relented and stood back up, while Vincenzo stood there angrily, gritting his teeth.

"All we did was fall asleep, God damn you!" he said.

"Yes," replied Otto matter-of-factly, "and this is one of the worst crimes a guard can commit."

"You will burn in hell for your injustice!" Vincenzo said, before he suddenly pulled a knife out of his boot and charged Otto.

152

The German mercenary deflected the blow of the blade with his armored gauntlet and delivered a swift punch to Vincenzo's gut with his free hand. The steel-clad fist delivered a blow like a mace and Vincenzo collapsed on the dirt, gasping for air.

Otto kicked the scoundrel as he was down for good measure and turned to Sophia.

"Lieutenant Bianchi. Do you have anything to say in your defense?"

Sophia's reply came in jumbled French. Her nerves had given up on her.

"I took good necklace from handsome man, and then he took box. I very sorry."

MacRae secretly breathed a sigh of relief. Sophia's confession was not made public, and before she explained herself in such an unintelligible manner, no one knew why she was even out there. Her French had become so bad that people thought she was being punished for taking a bribe, and the fact that the money was all gone was still a secret to everyone but the officers.

Otto, slightly confused, refused to respond to Sophia's questionable defense and proceeded to the sentencing.

"Vincenzo Rossi, Fabiano de Luca. For your negligence, you have been sentenced to hang by the neck until dead."

The two men began shouting all manner of curses as they were restrained and led to a nearby tree.

"Lodovico Bianchi."

Sophia stared at Otto, her eyes pleading with him. He did not acknowledge her.

"Given your status as an officer in the honorable Talbot Company, you are to be given thirty lashes with the cat o' nine tails, after which you are to be relieved of command. The company of swords is henceforth to be commanded by Captain Thomas Warwick."

Suddenly, a voice rose from the otherwise silent crowd.

"I have something to say!"

The officers turned their attention to the source of the noise in the crowd. They were surprised to see James Fletcher elbowing his way through the larger soldiers to make it into the center of the circle.

MacRae looked like he was ready to shoot this peasant for his insolence. Gunther waited patiently and listened to what the boy had to say. Otto stared at him with anticipation, while Don Alfonso and Warwick both wanted him to get out of there. He did not know what he was getting himself into.

"If I understood her correctly, my lords," he said in English, "she mentioned something about a necklace, did she not?"

Don Alfonso was visibly surprised. Perhaps all this time around the men had given the Englishman some knowledge of French. But why was he standing here at a court-martial mentioning the necklace?

"I was the one that gave her that necklace! Punish me instead!" he lied.

Don Alfonso slapped himself in the forehead. Warwick buried his face in his hands. They had both gotten to know MacRae by know and knew his sense of justice. This was just going to end badly.

Otto silently mouthed, *"Was zum Teufel"*, what the hell, before switching to English for Fletcher.

"Boy, do you have any idea what you are asking for?"

"Yes, sir. I take full responsibility for the consequences of my actions." Fletcher said, swallowing.

Sophia looked around, confused as to why everyone was suddenly staring at Fletcher.

"Gott verdammt. What are your orders, sir?" Otto said, turning to MacRae.

"If this boy was partly responsible for this heinous act, it be best to mete him equal punishment. Divide Bianchi's punishment in two – fifteen lashes for the lieutenant, and fifteen for the boy."

"What?" Fletcher shouted, "My lord, I must protest! This is unfair and cruel!"

MacRae crossed his arms and replied, "You asked to be fucked, boy. We now oblige you."

Don Alfonso, puzzled, wondered why he would want to do something as rash as this. The only logical explanation he could find was that perhaps he had feelings for Sophia, which was hard to believe since they could not understand each other.

"Pero es posible." he muttered.

The pair was led up to the pillar in the center of the circle as the roped were tied around the necks of the two Venetians by the tree nearby.

Sophia's eyes were fixed on Fletcher as they walked, her brow furrowed and her mouth agape.

"Che cosa fai, idiota?" What are you doing idiot, she said.

He merely smiled as they met in the center of the circle. His eyes spoke to hers, reassuring her that he would be with her. Her eyes only showed fear and confusion.

Gunther moved to join them, undoing the straps of his red and black gambeson as he walked. He removed the thick cotton jacket and the shirt underneath, tossing them on the ground to reveal a back covered with dozens of welts from punishments such as these. In his hand, he held the cat o' nine tails.

"Is this your first whipping?" he said to the pair in French.

Sophia nodded slowly. Fletcher struggled to understand. Gunther continued in French, seeing as the girl needed reassuring more than the Englishman did.

"Do you see these scars, Bianchi?" he said, turning around to show her the numerous welts on his back. "Six I received for dropping a bucket of water, twelve for calling my commanding officer a 'lout', and fifteen for drinking while I was on watch."

"The fool will never drink again." Otto chuckled as he looked on.

Gunther hushed him and placed his heavy hand gently on Sophia's shoulder.

"This is going to hurt, very badly. Cry, scream, curse, do whatever you want. No one is going to think any less of you."

Sophia nodded.

"Now, remove your breastplate and shirt."

Sophia lowered her head in shame. They were finally going to know the truth. The whole company was going to know that one of their members was a skinny teenage girl in men's clothing.

Gunther leaned closer to her and whispered, "We know. We have always known."

Sophia's eyes shot open. How had she not been chased away or executed?

"MacRae believes in giving chances. He did not care that you were a woman when he first saw you. Now, I am sorry to say this but you have failed him."

Sophia bit her lip. The shame came in tears that rolled down her cheek.

"Now, please, take off your clothes so that we can get this over with." Gunther said being as tender as possible. He said the same to Fletcher in English.

Sophia's heavy leather kidney belt and steel breastplate fell on the ground. With tears rolling down her face she took off her colorful cotton doublet and put her hands over her breasts to hide them in shame. A single lecherous howl erupted from the crowd.

Don Alfonso pointed towards the howling soldier and barked, "Who did that? Who did that!? Bring that man here!"

Two pikemen grabbed a teenage mercenary by the arms and dragged him forward in front of Don Alfonso. His eyes were wide in fear as he just realized the gravity of his actions. He was no older than fourteen.

Don Alfonso drew his sword and looked to MacRae for approval. With a nod of the colonel's head, Don Alfonso's sword

157

pierced through the boy's gut, causing blood to splatter on himself and the ground before him. The boy screamed and cursed in pain as the pikemen dropped him and returned to their places in the circle.

"We have no women here, gentlemen!" Don Alfonso yelled to the crowd as a pool of blood formed around the lifeless corpse of the slain teenager, "Only soldiers! Just because this particular soldier has different body parts does not mean she should be treated any differently!"

MacRae, patting Don Alfonso on the back, stepped forward himself to speak.

"Men, this be what happens when we fail in our duties."

Gunther tied both Sophia's and Fletcher's wrists to the pole with their backs facing him. Fletcher reached out and interlocked his fingers with Sophia's. He gave her a weak smile, which she returned.

"Let it not be said that I be an unjust man." MacRae continued, "Let it not be said that I be cruel or unkind. I make no favorites and treat all of ye based on merit. The just will be rewarded, and the lazy, the cowardly, and the treacherous will receive justice."

Gunther cracked the cat and stretched his arms.

"Executioners, perform yer offices."

As the two men hanged in the distance, their bodies writhing in suffocation, Gunther let loose his whip, striking Sophia first. She let out a piercing scream of anguish as her eyes, already wet with tears, gave way to more from the pain. Birds flew out of nearby trees in panic.

Fletcher was struck next. He too let out a great yell. His feet almost gave way to the shock, but he fought to keep balanced. Gritting his teeth, he braced for the next blow.

The whip alternated back and forth between the two of them. With each strike, they held each other's hands tighter until their knuckles were white. Their screams filled the air and woke some of the sleeping mercenaries from other camps.

As MacRae looked on, he said to himself, "I will fuckin' kill Toscana; sending me a sheep to do a wolf's job."

"I admire the way you run your company, MacRae," said Bjornsson in French as he looked on, "But we must endeavor to keep this lack of funding a secret from the men for a while longer. My liege will pay you gladly once we retake what is rightfully his. From here on, austerity and temperance must be our watchwords."

After thirty cracks of the cat, the whipping stopped, but the wailing and crying would not cease for another hour when the two were finally released from their bonds.

Chapter 17

As dawn broke the next day, Thomas Warwick climbed out of his cot, eager to taste something delectable from "Lodovico's Kitchen", but quickly became disheartened when he remembered that she had been whipped like a dog the day before. He had never even gotten to know her real name. Warwick sighed. Although the punishment she received was just, he could not imagine the pain she was going through – both physically and emotionally.

The English cavalier put on his uniform and went outside to stretch. He was now the commander of three companies. He would have some serious work to do. He could perhaps merge 'Lodovico's' old company of swords with his Britannic irregulars and form one massive shock infantry company. They would be less maneuverable, but far easier to command. He would worry about that later though. His primary concern now was food.

He approached the communal stew pot, surprised to find it already simmering with a fine-smelling soup. Someone had apparently been industrious enough to cook during the night while everyone was sleeping.

Taking a bowl, he scooped a good sized portion of the soup into it and took a taste – it tasted awkward, with a wave of bitterness, almost as if the cook dumped a bucket of spinach and a drum of pepper into the pot in anger. However, it was nearly balanced by the other ingredients: aromatic vegetables, lots of cheese and bits of bacon. Although it was cooked in anger, he easily recognized that cooking style – 'Lodovico.'

Finishing his meal quickly, Warwick ran over to the company drill area – a large flat piece of turf that MacRae had designated for drill practice, right next to the ground where Fletcher and Sophia were whipped.

Sure enough, there she was, dressed in her blue, white, and red clothes with her kidney belt and breastplate, standing in front of her swordsmen, prepared to hand them over to Warwick. But her expression had changed. Far from the usual cheery and energetic Italian, this girl stared at the distance with a scowl.

Warwick approached and gave her a flourishing bow. 'Lodovico' made a half-hearted dip in return and stepped forward, saying,

"Ils sont à vous." they are yours, she said in French with her usual Italian accent. She spoke softer now and did not look Warwick in the eye.

Bothered by her sudden change of demeanor, Warwick thanked her for her service and sent her to join her men in the back of their formation. He did not want to be looking into those empty eyes every time he faced the formation. The Englishman shook his head at this sad loss of such a happy soul, but quickly cleared the thought from his mind as he marched the company of swords over to join his irregulars.

Fletcher could hear Warwick's new men marching towards the irregular camp, but could not see them as he was lying face down on a wooden table, hissing with pain as the surgeon, an archer named Calvert, used a new experimental method to treat his wounds.

"Now hold still, I am trying to apply this ointment evenly." Calvert said as he brushed a mixture of egg yolk, rose oil and turpentine onto Fletcher's fresh wounds. "It is a miracle cure, I tell you. I have seen the results before; so much better than pouring boiling oil onto the flesh... Releases too much pus, you see."

"Stop. Talking." Fletcher said between gritted his teeth, "Finish. Treatment."

"Oh, yes, yes of course. All that is left is the bandaging. You whine too much. Your lady friend handled it so much better when I treated her last night. Not a sound out of her."

Fletcher suddenly raised his head at the mention of Sophia, but that caused him to bend his back, shooting pain back into his system. He cursed at the piercing sensation.

"Damn your ears. Now look what you have done." Calvert said, shaking his head, "I will have to apply the ointment all over again. I was just about ready to bandage you up too. Hold still this time."

"Calvert," Fletcher said, trying his best to speak in complete sentences, "how is she? Did she suffer much?"

"I will tell you what, boy. I have treated many torture victims in my time. Usually, after an episode like this, the victim becomes more docile, more... emotionally flat. Look at Gunther, for example." he chuckled.

"What about the girl?" Fletcher persisted.

"Ah, yes, the girl, of course. She ended up... different. I believe the experience hardened her. She seems angry at everything now; most likely her way of coping with the stress."

Fletcher let out a great sigh as the surgeon continued his treatment. He worried that whatever chance he had to know more about that sweet, innocent girl that grabbed his hand to dance during an impromptu guitar session was now gone. Whatever the torture had left behind was vicious and unfeeling. Fletcher closed his eyes as he heard the sound of marching feet getting closer.

Sophia's scowl hid the pain she was hiding as she marched. Not only the physical burning sensation from the whipping but the pain of her failures so far. As an officer she failed to lead her men in the bandit attack on the road to Gouda; as a soldier she had abandoned her duties in Schwedt; and as a friend she had failed to make any efforts to comfort *Freccia* or whatever the boy's name was, especially after he was tortured with her, for whatever infraction he had committed. She still was not sure why he was tied to that pole. He had always been the model follower – modest, unassuming, and servile.

But no more. A new person was forged from the blood of the cat o' nine tails the other day. With those fifteen lashes Lodovico Bianchi had died, and now Sophia Fortezza had to make a name for herself – one that she could be proud of. The new her had to be strong, competent, brave, and focused. Every waking moment had to be dedicated to proving to herself that she was more than just some rat on a sinking ship, scurrying away from her problems as the tide rose around her. This new life with Talbot Company was the storm that brought the tide, and she had to fight to stay above its waters. She kept the fake necklace around her neck as a reminder – never again would she fail as she did when she was guarding that wagon. She would not end up like Vincenzo and Fabiano who hung from a tree. She would embrace this new life and ride this storm to completion.

Don Alfonso knelt by his cot inside his tent. His helmet lay on his side while he clutched a wooden carving of Our Lady of Sorrows, made by the loving hands of native Christian craftsmen from his *encomienda* in the Philippine Islands. His eyes were closed in prayer as his thumb rolled over the cheeks of Mary, who had tears permanently chiseled into her wooden face.

"Oh sorrowful Mother," he prayed, "Let your servant Sophia be as your divine Son was when Pilate had Him scourged at the pillar. May the whipping not defeat her spirit, but may her pain awaken what is within her. I offer up her suffering and my own to you, gracious Lady, for we will need your protection during the days to come.

Also, bless that English heretic boy. He may not believe in your saving grace, O Glorious Lady, but allow what love he has in his heart to be nourished through your Son, Jesus. Amen."

As he finished, he crossed himself and opened his eyes. The Virgin had brought him comfort many times before, and she would not fail now. He kissed the image on its forehead and tucked it away in his pouch before putting on his helmet.

As he opened the flaps to his tent, he found that the other tents around him were being disassembled. The company was ready to begin marching again. He yelled for a sergeant to begin disassembling his own tent and went to find MacRae.

William MacRae stood on a small hilltop surveying the horizon with a spyglass. Otto and Gunther stood with him. Many of the other mercenary companies had left to march during the early hours of the morning, leaving Talbot Company behind with an Irish free company, the "Hearts of Eire", who were incapable of marching due to being too drunk from a night of debauchery.

"I cannot see bugger all," said MacRae as he looked through the spyglass. The colonel was trying to get a view of a bridge that straddled the Oder River, the calm body of water that divided Poland and the Holy Roman Empire. The terrain was relatively flat, and the city of Schwedt itself blocked the view of the terrain beyond.

"Are you looking for the other companies, sir?" Gunther asked as he looked through a spyglass of his own.

"No, just the one. Them French fucks that stole our money. We should have killed them in their sleep."

"How did you figure it was them, sir?"

"I pissed on precisely one person when we arrived here. It had to be him."

"Do you regret it, sir? Because of what happened with..."

"No. Nary a bit; just gives us an excuse to plunder the poor fucks." Collapsing his spyglass, he turned to Otto. "Mount up and tell the men to form a column in the prescribed order of march. I doubt we will face opposition whilst we cross the river."

Otto gave a nod and ran down the small hill to mount his horse. With a loud neighing and a whirl, the beast was off. Gunther descended the hill as well, leaving MacRae alone at the top, his brow furrowed in uncertainty of the sufferings yet to come.

Talbot Company's campsite was alive with activity. Men tore down tents as others rushed to join their formations. Warwick barked orders at his men while Otto rode around announcing that it was time to march. Gunther and Don Alfonso inspected their men as their sergeants slapped around soldiers who were still groggy from the night before.

Fletcher rose from his cot in the surgeon's tent, which was being dismantled. The pain shot up his back as he sat up, making him wince and hiss. Calvert, smiling, retrieved his own bow and quiver before handing Fletcher his.

"My lad, it is time to go." Calvert said as he put on his quiver, "I am quite sure that you can walk, even run given your localized injuries. As long as you keep yourself out of the melee of battle where the swordsmen and pikes are, you should be fine."

Fletcher thanked the surgeon and stepped outside to hear the clamor of orders and the shouts of men that were still dismantling and packing away the tents. He slowly made his way to the rest of the irregulars.

To his surprise though, the irregulars now stood in a formation. Normally, Warwick was content to have them march as a disorganized gaggle which befit their fighting style. Now that they had been merged with the company of swords, they had to match them in marching speed and tactics, which made them slower and less maneuverable.

The irregulars also looked very out of place. The first few rows of the new formation were composed of regular swordsmen, all of whom were outfitted with helmets, breastplates, shields, and swords; at the middle and rear of the formation, however, the irregulars began to mix in with them. Their wide variety of clothing and weaponry made them look like a heavily armed mob that was following the knight-like swordsmen. Scotsmen with

166

their great kilts mixed together with Irishmen and their conspicuous green garments with chainmail.

None of them seemed to know how a formation worked, though, and Warwick was having some difficulty keeping them in order as his sergeants had resorted to physically grabbing men by the shoulder to keep them in line. Fletcher was one of those men. He entered the formation from the side and elbowed his way into the center, whereupon a sergeant grabbed him, screamed at him for being wrong, and pulled him into a new position. Fletcher chuckled despite the pain he still felt in his back.

"I do not know what we should be doing," he said jovially to the soldier next to him, "what do you suppose we..." he stopped short, recognizing the blue, white, and red of the soldier from the whipping. "You!" he exclaimed.

The girl said nothing, but looked at him and acknowledged his presence. She did not even crack a smile. Now Fletcher truly understood what Calvert had meant by "hardened". As Warwick shouted the command to march, Fletcher wondered if he would ever get to see the sweet girl from that dance ever again.

Chapter 18

Bridge on the Oder River

Schwedt, Holy Roman Empire

MacRae had elected to march Talbot Company around
Schwedt to gain access to the great bridge that straddled the
Oder River. He did not wish to incur the wrath of the city militia
and have a thousand guns aimed at his men. The march was
not particularly hard, although Warwick was having some
trouble micromanaging his irregulars, some of whom had begun
shoving other soldiers out of formation so that they could walk
faster.

After a six-mile march, Talbot Company beheld the site of
the Schwedt bridgehead. Marching along the water's edge, the
men could smell the wet earth from the banks of the mighty
Oder. To their left was the city of Schwedt and the last neutral
town they were to encounter; to their right was the Oder River,
and beyond that Poland. In front of them lay the wide bridge
which they would use to cross into enemy territory.

It was curiously crowded with soldiers who were not
crossing the bridge. None of the men on the bridgehead were in
formation, and all of them seemed to be waiting around in
gaggles.

MacRae, who was riding at the head of the formation on
horseback with Gunther and Bjornsson, signaled a halt to his
men and rode to the rear to find Otto.

As he passed the throngs of soldiers, MacRae yelled for the musketeers to prepare their matches, the swordsmen to draw their blades, and the artillerymen to unlimber their guns.

Otto, surprised to see his commander galloping to the rear of the formation, rode up to meet him.

"Is there a problem *mein Herr?*" he said.

"Find out who these fucks are and why they be blocking our fuckin' bridge. I want no messing about, Master Koenigsherr."

"*Jawohl mein Herr.*" Otto replied as he galloped past his superior.

The German cavalrymen rode alone towards the bridgehead and slowed to a trot when he approached the disorderly mob of soldiers congregating there. From what Otto could tell, there were Irishmen, Scots, Belgians, and Germans among them but the majority of the group seemed to be French. A banner with a blue bird on a black field flew from a banner held by a bored looking standard bearer.

"Where is your commander?" Otto asked the standard bearer in French. The soldier pointed towards the bridge, where the baggage train of the company sat, held up by a broken wagon.

Otto carefully walked his horse through the crowd of soldiers, each of whom stared at him as he waded through the massive crowd of armor and pikes. When he approached the wagon, he found the group's commander kneeling down on the dirt, helping his men hammer a nail into the loose spoke of a wagon wheel. When he noticed a shadow of a rider looming over him, the company commander turned around and faced Otto.

"Oh, *bonjour monsieur.*" he said with a smile, "I did not see you there."

169

"Pardon me, my good sir, but am I to assume this is the reason why your men are blocking this bridge?" said Otto, returning the man's smile.

"Your assumption is correct. Do not worry, we will be done soon."

"Is there anything my men or I can do to assist you?"

"Well, we do happen to be short of a few nails. I hope you can spare some of your own. I would be in your debt."

"Of course – I will relay this to my quartermaster. Where is it you were going with this large army, at any rate?"

"Ah, as you know, beyond this border lies the wild country of Poland. It is no secret that the king of Poland is hiring real Europeans to augment his forces."

"I see. Well, I wish you the best of luck with the wagon. I shall return with those nails. To whom do I have the pleasure of speaking with?"

"Colonel Dominique Sauvage." the Frenchman said with a flamboyant bow.

"Captain Otto Koenigsherr. It has been a pleasure to make your acquaintance."

With this information in hand, Otto trotted out of Sauvage's way and rode back to Talbot Company's formation at a hard gallop. His horse skidded as it stopped by MacRae.

"Catholic mercenaries, sir." Otto reported, "A mix of nationalities but the majority are French. They're repairing their broken wagon."

"Did ye find their commander?"

"*Ja, mein Herr*, a Colonel Dominique Sauvage. He..."

"Form up in lines of attack."

"Mein Herr?"

"This was the fuckin' wankstain that deprived us of our treasure."

Otto's eyes narrowed.

"We'll grab them by the balls with our pikes and musketeers, then ye and yer cavalry boys can fall on them from the left flank. The river is to our right flank, they will have nary a place to run to. Keep the swords and irregulars in reserve until the pikes get tangled up in the push."

"Jawohl mein Herr."

Bjornsson drew his own sword and rode up next to MacRae.

"I want no conflicts in command. These are your men and you know how they fight. Direct my musketeers and myself as you please, colonel." the captain said in French.

MacRae smiled and made a slight bow of gratitude.

"I appreciate the amicability, Bjornsson." MacRae replied. His smile then collapsed into a stern scowl, "Move your fuckin' men to within pissing distance of the enemy and make nary a move till everyone else is in formation."

Bjornsson gave a swift nod and began to yell out his orders,

"Mousquetaires, en avant... marche!"

The sergeants repeated the command in English, and the drummer struck up the quick time march beat that told the musketeers to advance. Confused as to why they were marching towards a group of men repairing a cart, the musketeers did as

171

they were told. Gunther and his pikemen followed suit, leaving Don Alfonso's halberdier company little choice but to follow them.

Meanwhile, Otto raced back to Warwick to tell him the plan. The English captain nodded his acknowledgement, but as Otto rode back to rejoin his cavalry troop, Warwick privately sulked. If his men were not at the forefront of the fight there would be no glory for him.

Bjornsson kept his musketeers marching at a slow steady pace towards the French, who were now beginning to suspect something, with some of their commanders forming up their companies in lines of battle while the others simply stared in confusion and anticipation. As soon as Bjornsson judged them to be within "pissing distance", he ordered the company to come to a halt. The formations behind him stopped as well.

It was so quiet that the only sounds anyone could hear were the cawing of the crows hovering overhead and the grunting of an oblivious Frenchman who was taking a shit by the river.

Bjornsson's men were so close that they could whisper and the men on the other side could hear them. They could count the number of laces in their boots and see the decorations on their baldrics, but most importantly, they could see the terror and surprise in the eyes of their enemy.

A low thundering noise was heard on the left side of Bjornson's formation. Otto's cavalry was coming up on the side in preparation to flank, and only a fool would miss this.

"Compagnie!" was the last word a French sergeant said before Bjornsson gave the order to fire. Dozens of Blue Falcons were torn apart in a hail of musket balls, even as others who

were still standing rushed to light their matches and get into their formations. Lone brave souls charged Talbot Company's musketeers only to be stopped by the spearheads of Gunther's pikemen, who slowly advanced to protect the reloading musketeers.

Colonel Sauvage, upon seeing the chaos that was ensuing at the bridgehead, hastily summoned his bodyguards, numbering about twenty men, and bid them all jump into the river with him.

Any fool observing from the sidelines could see that Talbot Company was winning this battle. It was taking a lot of effort for Warwick to restrain himself from ordering his irregulars into a charge to take part in the slaughter. His men, however, had no such apprehensions.

"Ye see those bastards over there killing without us?" shouted a Scottish sergeant, "I say we show those wee cunts how real men fight! Up, you bastards, and split their heads open! *Buaidh no Bàs!* Victory or death!"

With this, the irregulars gave way to their impetuousness and charged into the fray, pushing the Spanish and Italian swordsmen out of their way. The swordsmen sergeants, along with Sophia, tried in vain to push them back but they spilled out of the formation in a tide of screaming, drunken chaos.

One of the Italians, not wanting to be outdone, burst into a spontaneous battle cry, "Let us show them how Italians die!" and ran into battle, goading his companions to follow him.

As the dust settled, the only soldiers that remained with Warwick were a dozen archers including Fletcher, the cannoneers and their guns, a few swordsmen sergeants, and Sophia. Warwick tugged at his hair in frustration.

173

"Bloody Scots and their damn brass balls," he said as he watched his men dive into the battle. Throwing up his hands, he commanded his archers to rain down arrows on the enemy to support his infantry while he directed the artillery.

Suddenly, a figure emerged from the riverbank to their right; several others followed. Frenchmen came out of the river, water trickling from their shirts and hair, with some holding daggers in their teeth. Colonel Sauvage had his bodyguards walk downstream under the water in a desperate attempt to flank Talbot Company. It had worked. Warwick was now trapped with twenty-two lightly armed fighters against Sauvage's twenty-one.

Sauvage himself then emerged from the water. Warwick could tell that he was a very strong man, being able to walk four hundred feet with only his head above the water, especially while in a breastplate. Hopefully, he and his men were weary from the long swim.

"Men, draw swords!" Warwick shouted, as his cannoneers ran into the woods behind them. Fifteen loyal men and one woman remained at his side. The Blue Falcons rushed forward, giving no chance for Warwick to draw his pistol. Sauvage himself fell on Warwick with his saber, swinging it at the Englishman's head. Warwick drew his own smallsword and parried just in time.

Elsewhere, the men were faring slightly better. Warwick's archers were having trouble keeping the Blue Falcons at bay with their longbows at short range, but the swordsmen were doing what they could as they bashed in faces with their shields and skewered men with their rapiers.

Sophia, far from the timid girl she was before, was now fighting for her life, aggressively slashing at the French soldiers whose movements sprinkled water at her face every time they struck at her. Sophia's strikes were uncalculated, but quick and strong; powered by her blinding rage. Blood decorated her armor as she swung madly at the exhausted French soldiers.

Fletcher, too, was fighting well. He had stabbed a man in the face with an arrow and was using his hunting sword to cleave through several opponents. His rabbit-like footwork helped him dance through the attacks of many of his enemies, who were slowed down by their waterlogged clothing.

The competence of his soldiers spurred confidence in Warwick as he thrust and parried with Sauvage, matching the Frenchman's technical swordplay with his aggressive English fencing style.

Sensing an opening through Sauvage's defense, Warwick thrust for the colonel's neck. He had him – this fight was over, or so he thought. In a quick, well-practiced movement, Sauvage covered the thrust with his own blade, the sparks of his saber and Warwick's smallsword flashing in both of their eyes. Before Warwick could counter-attack, Sauvage had stepped around him. Sensing that he was about to snatch victory from the jaws of defeat, Sauvage brought his opponent down on the ground with a pommel strike to the back of his head, reveling in the satisfying thud sound that the spherical pommel made when it hit the back of Warwick's head.

Warwick fell upon the wet grass, mud staining his face and uniform. His heart started racing. Defeat was almost certain. When he tried to bring himself to his feet, Sauvage slashed at his leg, making him scream in pain and staining his white breeches with his dark red blood. Warwick fell back down on the earth as Sauvage planted his boot on his back, pinning him there.

Exhausted, the panting Frenchman raised his saber for a coup de grace, just before a sharp pointed blade pierced through his throat, making him gurgle blood.

Sophia stood behind Sauvage with a maniacal grin as her trembling sword hand slowly pushed the blade of her rapier deeper into the back of his neck. The cathartic pleasure of killing the man that was the cause of her suffering felt almost orgasmic. A wave of emotion passed through her, part of it the glee of revenge along with the joy of victory and the thrill of battle.

As Sophia withdrew her blade in one quick motion, Sauvage's corpse fell on top of Warwick. Sophia could not hold back a maniacal cackle as she whaled on the back of Sauvage's armored carcass with the pommel of her expensive rapier.

No one but Talbot Company stood alive now. At the bridgehead, victorious, cheering men from Gunther's company of pikes were dragging crippled Blue Falcons to the water's edge and holding their heads below the water to drown them. Their satisfying gurgles as they breathed their last under the waters of the Oder River made many men laugh with gruesome delight.

Fletcher, his chest heaving with exhaustion, cautiously approached Sophia, who continued to pound at the lifeless Sauvage with her sword. Warwick lay groaning under him, unnoticed.

"He is dead. You can stop now."

She understood nothing.

"We need to tend to Captain Warwick."

She continued to pound away, giggling ever so softly.

Frustrated, Fletcher grabbed her shoulder, and in her surprise, she leaped up and pointed her blade at him. Her eyes were filled with tears, and her chest was heaving from all the physical and mental exertion. This was far from the same girl that Fletcher had saved on the road to Gouda.

Fletcher opened his mouth to say something, but he could not. He knew it would do no good, at any rate, she still did not understand his language. He raised his free hand up to her, as a man does when he is cautious with a wild animal. She refused to lower her blade.

Very gently, he put his hand on her wrist and wordlessly bid her to lower her weapon. The sword fell to the ground, making a soft thud on the muddy grass. Sophia looked into Fletcher's eyes. The girl that she once was wanted to return to being, but this wall of war and sadness were the bars to her cell that she could never escape.

Sophia's tears fell in torrents as she lunged to embrace Fletcher, the blood and sweat from her armor staining his shirt. He hugged her back, whispering that he missed her, but he knew that it would take time before she would ever be the same.

Two of Warwick's archers rushed over to him and threw Sauvage's body off of their commander. He struggled to rise, but he was alive. The pain in his leg was sharp, and every step forward was a punishment. He thanked his men and instructed them to carry him to a nearby log, where he sat to rest.

MacRae, meanwhile, rode up to the front lines to the cheers of his victorious soldiers. A Scottish bagpiper struck up a cheerful tune in celebration. It did not drown out the screams of the dying, but that too was music to MacRae's ears.

177

He galloped through the crowds of exhausted but cheerful soldiers to find Otto, who was helping one of his sergeants wrest a richly ornamented breastplate off of the carcass of a fallen enemy.

"I hope you do not mind a little blood on your trophy, my good man," said Otto, drawing his sword to cut the dead man's arms and head off.

"No sir, that simply gives it more character." the sergeant replied with a grin.

As Otto proceeded with the grisly task, MacRae called out to him,

"Master Koenigsherr, may I have a word?"

"Certainly, sir." Otto said as he stepped away, leaving the sergeant to finish off the body. MacRae dismounted so that he could speak to Otto in private.

"Find that fuckin' chest and get it back into our baggage train."

"I already looked, *mein Herr*. Not a trace."

"By Lucifer's hairy scrotum, that's fuckin' impossible. Bianchi herself told ye that these cunts absconded with the gold, did she not?"

"*Ja*, but it's possible, *mein Herr*, that they could have spent every single piece in one go. Look at the dead men around you."

MacRae surveyed his surroundings. Otto seemed to be right – every man in the Blue Falcons had uncharacteristically well-made armor and ornamented weapons fit for officers and nobility. The food that Talbot Company was finding consisted of fresh meat, game birds, and fish. The men were even finding real gold jewelry among the dead.

"Tongue up my fuckin' arse, we're buggered." MacRae mumbled, "Ye hold yer fuckin' wheest about this mess, Master Koenigsherr. No one must know."

Otto nodded as MacRae mounted his horse to ride away, shaking his head. Hopefully, they would be able to reach Jarlsberg before this new supply of wealth ran out.

Riding down to the rear of the line, MacRae could see from a distance that there were bodies near the artillery pieces and baggage train, where no one should have been. He was thankful that they did not belong to Talbot Company men. As he approached the wounded Warwick, he dismounted.

"What happened here, man? Our flanks were more secure than a chastity belt on an ugly virgin."

"They walked under the river, sir, and turned up on this side. But that is hardly our concern now. We have beaten the bastards."

"Can ye walk, Master Warwick?"

"I am not sure, sir, but I fear that I may not stir. The cut feels deep. However, I must add, sir, that if it was not for Bianchi, I would have been singing alleluias with the angels."

MacRae turned to find Sophia and Fletcher still locked in an embrace. Her wailing was loud and sorrowful. He was about to go and congratulate her but immediately noticed the body lying next to them. MacRae's face lit up with delight.

"Sauvage ye ball-munching, arse-licking, banger-gobbling toorie! It's good to see ye, mate!" he said as he dropped his

179

breeches in front of the corpse, leaving his manhood exposed. "This be for what ye've done to my money, ye French shitewraith."

A long and steady stream of warm Scottish urine poured over Sauvage's face and eyes as MacRae sighed in relief. Sophia stopped crying and Fletcher looked on in disgust.

"Ah, Lodovico Bianchi," MacRae said as he pulled up his breeches, "In light of yer recent actions, and as gratitude for pulling Warwick's English arse out of the fire, I hereby restore upon ye the rank of lieutenant."

"Sir," interrupted Fletcher, "your language."

"Nonsense boy, I uttered nary an oath... oh. I see." MacRae corrected himself quickly and restored Sophia's rank in French. The Italian girl managed a weak smile and wiped away her tears.

A vast and dangerous country awaited the men of Talbot Company across the Oder, and only a few of them knew that they were vastly undersupplied for the march ahead. If MacRae wanted to keep his band together, he would need a miracle akin to Christ's feeding of the multitude.

Chapter 19

Riga, Swedish Empire

Captain Henri Andersson sat on his cot in his dark room, lit only by the flickering light of a single dying candle. His green eyes watched the flame gently sway back and forth as his mind lay deep in thought.

The captain had originally enlisted as a volunteer in Sweden's Hakkapeliitta, and was well respected and treated fairly, even though he was a Finn. Normally the Swedish, who ruled his land, would talk of his people as if they were barbarians and savages who lived in the forest and did nothing but cut firewood and go ice fishing all day. This being said, his countrymen were also celebrated throughout the Swedish Empire as the best light cavalry in the world, but what lay heavily on his mind was the blatant cowardice of the Swedish aristocracy. The empire had twenty-three thousand fighting men under its command and eight out of ten of them were Finnish.

How he loathed those foppish dandies in their silk coats and ridiculous white collars who sent good, honest Finnish men to their doom. Peasants were taken from their homes in his native Åbo and thrust into wars they had no understanding of and no compulsion to fight in. In his mind, Sweden was ruining his country's economy by sending off Finnish sons to fight a Swedish war for no visible or immediate benefit to his people. The fields lay overgrown with weeds, the blacksmiths grew old and senile without anyone to pass their skills onto, and whole villages were depopulated just because Sweden did not want to spill Swedish blood.

A gust of wind from outside blew out Henri's candle as the door opened. A Swedish messenger entered his room clutching a piece of parchment in his hand. As soon as he stepped foot through the doorway, he began reading his message in a hurried and urgent manner,

"Sir, you have orders from Greve Olaf Stenbock of Jarlsberg. You are to assemble at once and..."

The messenger was stopped by a knife to his throat. It was a strange looking blade, very straight and angular, designed for chopping like a tiny axe.

"I can read, boy." growled Henri, "Now give me the paper and leave before my *hukari* decorates the floor with your blood."

The messenger dropped the rolled up piece of parchment and sprinted away. Captain Andersson never liked speaking Swedish, especially to people of lower status than himself, but the sight of the boy almost pissing himself made him feel all warm inside. He smiled at himself as he opened the letter and read it aloud, mocking the Swedish accent as he spoke,

Kapten Henri Andersson

Åbo och Björneborgs läns kavalleriregemente

Jag hoppas att du mår bra. Jag skriver för att berätta att... blah blah blah, surströmming köttbullar skit skit skit... **Jarlsberg Fästning, lettland.**

An assault on Jarlsberg Castle. Henri closed the door to his room and sat alone in the darkness. The Swedish elk bid the Finnish bear to fight his battles yet again. Cowards. The captain crumpled the letter in his hand and set his mind on the local inn, where he was to meet this Greve Olaf Stenbock, who instructed him to meet him there the next morning. Stenbock was no doubt some fat landed aristocrat who stank of herring.

He would make the greve wait and would travel the following afternoon by foot to make it even slower. For now, he would drink himself to sleep to make sure that he stank of alcohol, just for this meeting.

After a night of swilling cheap vodka and yelling incomprehensible Finnish words out of his window to passing locals, Captain Andersson was now hung over and on his way to meet his lord, moving without any sense of urgency towards the local inn, with his sword dragging on the ground behind him as he tossed his unsheathed *hukari* from one hand to the other. It was five hours past noon.

Kicking open the door to the inn, Henri was met by the greve and his entourage staring at him from a table facing the doorway. They all looked ready for battle; each wore their harnesses, jerkins, baldrics, and accouterments of battle. Henri only wore his tattered black doublet and riding breeches. He knew it was all for show – they were all either too old or too fat to fight in a war.

"You're late." Greve Stenbock muttered, gesturing for Henri to sit down.

Now began one of Henri's favorite games: playing the fool. A long time ago he learned that the aristocracy would never listen to anything he had to say, no matter how vital or how insightful his suggestions could be, so instead, he would merely sit there and speak as if he understood the bare minimum of the Swedish language.

"... and we will wait for reinforcements if we have to. Are you listening, Captain Andersson?"

"Yes, sir." Henri mumbled, his head still in pain from the hangover. Greve Stenbock glared at him but proceeded with his meeting.

"My lords, yesterday I received a message delivered to me via carrier pigeon. It released details previously unknown to me regarding the capture of my home. Thank the Lord that my daughter is alive."

The lords around Stenbock applauded, while Henri tapped his fingertips together, mocking their happiness. The greve gestured for them to stop and continued reading,

"However it also states, quite alarmingly, that the bastard that took my home has sent for reinforcements from the king of Poland, and that he is somehow, curiously, colluding with the Muslim infidels."

This news was met with gasps and murmuring amongst the lords, but a stifled yawn by Henri.

"I will need all of your men and our brave Finnish cavalrymen by my side if we wish to take the castle."

Henri could not help but roll his eyes. The vast majority of Sweden's infantry forces were composed of Finns who had absolutely no desire to be there.

"Captain Andersson."

"Yes, sir." Henri said dryly.

"How many of your cavalrymen can you field?"

"Hundreds, sir." That was a lie. He could probably muster sixty at best.

184

"Can we rely on you to support our flanks during the battle for Jarlsberg Castle?"

"Yes, sir." Henri actually wanted to tell the greve to 'fuck off back to Stockholm.'

"Thank you, captain."

"Yes, sir." A *hukari* would slide right through the old man's linen collar if he angled it just right.

"I should also state that I have hired the honorable Talbot Company to bear the full brunt of the enemy."

Henri sighed. At least some other poor bastards were dying besides his own countrymen – they were probably foreigners as well. The Swedes were trying their damnedest to avoid spilling the blood of their children. His blood boiled thinking he would have to sacrifice his life and the life of his men for a war that he had no business fighting. Captain Henri Andersson would not fight the way they wanted, but the way they deserved.

Chapter 20

Zalesie, Poland

Talbot Company had been marching for a little over three days, avoiding every village they could on MacRae's orders. The colonel reasoned that if they stopped to resupply at every village they went to, someone somewhere would rush to the nearest garrison and inform them of the company's movements. Although there was some truth in this, the real reason why MacRae was ordering his men to stay away from the locals was because he had no money to pay for provisions.

Bjornsson's sumptuary laws were now back in effect. The company was stretching the supplies they plundered from the Blue Falcons to the limit. Whatever fresh meat they once had was now gone, the little bread they had left was now rapidly turning hard and crusty, and the men were getting anxious. MacRae knew that food shortages would cause a blow to morale, and a decrease in morale usually planted the seeds of a mutiny.

MacRae would've continued to avoid villages if it was not for the village of Zalesie, which was unmarked on the map that he had purchased. The steeple of the village church was visible for miles, and there was no denying that it was there. Talbot Company had now been brought to halt a mile away from the village boundaries as MacRae gathered his captains around him and tried to think up a plan.

"Boys, I bring ye here to tell ye something in confidence. We be fucked. From what I can tell, we be low on food, low on mead,

186

and low on morale. One or two of the lesser men have already resolved to fuck us and desert in the middle of the night. We need supplies and we need them right fuckin' now."

"What are your orders, *mein Herr?*" Gunther whispered.

"The way I see it, we have two choices. Either we take supplies from the peasants by force and risk a Polish army riding up our arse, or we burn the whole fuckin' village to the ground, no survivors."

"And live with the guilt for the rest of our lives." Don Alfonso interjected.

"Master Spaniard, ye of all people should know that this is a necessity. Did ye not use force of arms to quell a rebellion in, what was the name of that wretched place? The Fellipaghns?"

"Las Islas Filipinas, señor. That was mandated by the viceroy, their blood is on his hands; and I did not enjoy taking the lives of defenseless women, children, and elders, regardless of the fact that they were heathens."

"What solution would you propose then, hm? Would you simply stroll up to them with your hand on your fuckin' Spanish balls and politely ask them to cough up food, water, and medicine?

"Sir, perhaps there is another way," said Warwick, who was now hobbling about on crutches, "We can make camp here and wait until nightfall, and steal some supplies from the village as thieves in the night. It shall be quick and painless if executed with good form."

"Master Warwick, ye cannot have a hundred people moving stealthily through a village."

"Not a hundred sir, but perhaps a dozen. My archers are capable of treading on leaves without making a sound."

"And if they fail?"

"They will not fail, sir."

"And if they fail." MacRae repeated, sternly.

"If they fail then we are justified in burning down the entire village."

MacRae found these terms agreeable, and the next few hours were spent in the woods outside the village, where the men quietly made camp, but were given strict orders to remain silent and hidden as to avoid suspicion.

It was no small feat to hide over a thousand men, in fact, several of them were spotted by the villagers, who ignored them, thinking that they were just another roving band of mercenaries passing through like so many others before them. There were even some children who waved at the soldiers as they played in the fields.

The lack of alarms and cries for help made some feel that MacRae's orders were unnecessary, even stupid. The men grew more restless with each passing hour until nightfall, when sleep was foremost on everyone's minds.

Everyone, that is, except for the few archers – Fletcher included – that Warwick had hand-picked for his daring nighttime raid. The twelve, like the disciples, gathered around Warwick's campfire as they listened to his instructions.

"You dozen are the fox-walkers." he whispered as the fire crackled, "You lot have lived in the greenwood all your lives and now is the time for you to make use of your God-given skills of finesse and stealth. The company needs food, blankets, tools, anything you can take. The plan is simple – sneak into the peasants' storerooms undetected and abscond with as many provisions as you can."

"But milord," asked Fletcher, "how would we haul off enough food to feed a thousand mouths?"

"An astute question, Master Fletcher. This matter will be left to Master Calvert."

"Bollocks." muttered the surgeon.

"His task will be to walk one of our horses into the town and harness it to a wagon."

"Is that all?" Calvert sighed with relief, "I shall be glad to do it, sir."

"I am quite sure you are. Now – as for the rest of you, what should concern you the most is the matter of loading as many goods into that wagon as you are able to. I want every carrot, every apple, every goddamn grain of rye that you find loaded onto that cart. If you run into trouble and wish to signal the others to retreat, mimic the sound of the owl. Master Koenigsherr has promised to rush in and help you."

The fox-walkers nodded and proceeded and began to ready themselves. These men were gamekeepers, yeomen, and hunters. Some put fresh bowstrings on their longbows while others removed their shoes for even quieter walking. Fletcher put on the old forest cloak that he brought from England but put it away once he realized that it would take too much time to put new foliage into the webbing of the cloak, and the leaves he had put in from the forests near Bolingbroke had browned with age long ago. He would not quite look like a walking bush in his green hunter's tunic, but it was better than what some of the other men were wearing with their red doublets and yellow waistcoats.

As last minute preparations were completed by the light of dimly burning lanterns, Calvert mounted his horse and quietly walked it into the town. It was time. The fox-walkers split up and slowly crept their way into the village from several directions, blending with the shadows, keeping their heads low and their steps silent. The rats that scurried through the villagers' houses made more noise.

Calvert had just finished attaching the yoke of a cart to his horse and stood by it, waiting for the others to return. Some men had found sacks of grain in the village mill, and others were finding butter in outdoor churns and salted meat in barrels that lay about people's houses.

Fletcher had found the main village storeroom. He walked towards it, his footsteps making absolutely no noise. As soon as he put his hands on the wooden door handle, he heard something from within – the creaking of wood, but not like the sound of a door handle. It was rapid and consistent, almost mechanical. Fletcher frowned. There was definitely something in there. He cupped his hands to his mouth to make the owl call, but decided against it. He could not be sure, and he did not want to enter the building alone.

Fletcher gave a hand signal to another nearby fox-walker, signaling him to come over. The fox-walker, a former thief named Nathan, silently came up by Fletcher's side.

Fletcher drew his knife and gestured for Nathan to do the same. Armed and ready for combat, Fletcher gingerly opened the door to the storeroom. It responded with a loud creak, but that was not all he heard.

"Oh, Jakub! Pieprz mnie! Aah! Aah!"

The two archers had chanced upon the village strumpet and a randy farm boy in the middle of their discreet midnight rendezvous.

As the couple continued to go at it, Fletcher's hand signals erupted into a flurry of fingers, insisting that the two should leave before they got discovered. Nathan, his eyes focused elsewhere, blatantly ignored his companion. Discounting Sophia, he hadn't seen a beautiful woman in weeks and he was determined to get his eyes full. Moving closer to the action with all the finesse of a hunter, he carefully placed his foot in a pile of hay, but did not see the cat that had chosen to nestle there for the night.

The cat's screech of surprise was immediately drowned out by the shrill piercing scream of the naked young lady, who still sat straddling her lover. Nathan froze in fear while Fletcher sheathed his blade and grabbed him by the collar, hauling him out the door.

Several yards away, Otto Koenigsherr sat on his horse, armored and battle-ready. He was so anxious that he even considered rushing his men into the village when he heard a real owl hoot. A scream suddenly broke the midnight calm, and a wide grin lit up Otto's face. It was time to pillage.

"*Truppen!* Move out!" He said with glee as he closed his visor and spurred his horse to full gallop, charging the village as the rest of his cavalrymen followed him, the thundering of their hooves waking every man and beast within earshot.

Lamps and torches flared in every window as the sound of Otto and his sixty cavalrymen drew closer. A few brave men

191

grabbed weapons and torches to defend themselves while the women and children fled to the safety of the church.

Nathan fled into the woods beyond the village while Fletcher made a run for the supply wagon, but Calvert had no intention of rescuing anyone. With a loud and panicked "hyeah!" the wagon sped out of town, throwing off one of the fox-walkers who had just placed a large bag of rye onto it.

"At least the supplies are safe." Fletcher said as he watched the rickety wagon speed off into the night. Suddenly, he heard someone shout something in Polish behind him. He wheeled around to find an angry Polish peasant running towards him raising a scythe, ready to slice him in two. Fletcher reached for his sword, but before he could do anything, a horse and rider came in between the two men. The dust that the animal kicked up from its gallop went into Fletcher's eyes.

After shaking his head and brushing the dirt away, Fletcher opened his eyes to see the villager with a sword slash wound across his back lying lifeless beneath the horse's hooves as Otto looked down at him from his mount.

"Well, Warwick had his little play at roguery, but now we do this like soldiers. *Oberst MacRae* has ordered us to raze the village and kill everyone."

Fletcher thought he had just misheard Otto terribly. At times, his German accent was hard to understand.

"I am sorry, milord, but I believe that I heard you say that you wanted to raze the village and kill everyone?"

"I see my English is improving. Yes, that is exactly what I said!" Otto replied with a nod as he galloped away, brandishing his sword, leaving Fletcher behind him coughing up a cloud of his dust.

Janusz woke up to the sounds of screaming women and laughing men. He could also hear the sounds of horses and fighting outside his simple wooden cottage. His heart beat faster at the implications.

As the village blacksmith, he was not trained in the ways of war, but there were two things he could bring to a fight – he made knives, farm implements and hunting weapons for the whole village, and he knew how to swing a hammer.

The blacksmith leaped out of bed and reached for his hammer – his Mjolnir that he would use to strike down these foreign attackers. As he headed towards the door, he remembered that he left some kvass to ferment in a large wooden barrel in the corner. One last drink before he died. Taking a swig from the barrel, he reasoned that he could use the barrel lid as a makeshift shield. Now he was armed like a warrior.

With his heart beating with all the fear and righteous anger in the world, Janusz kicked open the door of his hut and rushed out into the night, shouting the name of Jesus for protection and strength.

As the door burst open, Janusz was overwhelmed with the smell of smoke, the sight of fire, and the sound of his screaming friends and loved ones. His heart burned with hatred for the invaders – they would rue the day they set foot in his village to burn down his home and slaughter his people.

He turned to the first enemy he saw – a timid looking young archer who wore an expression of fear and bewilderment. Gritting his teeth, he clutched his hammer like a mace and swung at his opponent, who blocked it with his cheap sword. Janusz countered by striking him in the gut with the edge of his shield, causing him to fall over. He shouted in triumph as he raised his hammer to deliver the final blow.

Before the hammer could land home, it was met with the flat of a sword, wielded by a foreigner in black armor, like the paintings of the devil from the village church. He was probably their leader. If Janusz could kill him, the entire enemy force would rout. The fate of the village was in his hands.

As he recovered from the block, he assumed his fighting stance, with thoughts of the people he loved racing through his head, and whether this fight was worth his life. His breath came in great gasps as his heart raced harder. His opponent stood across from him, cold and silent.

Finding the strength within him, he spurred his feet to action and charged at the black knight, his hammer flailing in the air with all the fury and hate he could muster. He did not make five steps before he was skewered by the cold, sharp blade of a German broadsword.

"*Herr Engländer,* are you all right?" Otto said as he helped Fletcher to his feet. The madman that he had just run through with his sword lay writhing on the ground in his final death throes.

"I'm fine, milord." Fletcher said as he got up, grasping his aching stomach. "You... you're burning down this village?"

"*Ja*, and I took time to turn around and make sure that you were not hurt. I am glad I did."

"He was merely defending his home! Our men are setting fire to it!"

"Well, you are certainly ungrateful."

"Milord, I just..."

"You are to deliver the following message to the camp like a good little boy," Otto said, changing the topic, "We need reinforcements. We are outnumbered by the peasants, and they are slowly organizing. Defending is not feasible. Now – repeat what I just said."

"I... we need reinforcements and we are outnumbered by the peasants."

"That is close enough. Now, go – do not die."

Fletcher nodded obediently as he slipped away into the darkness while a mob of angry peasants with pitchforks and scythes descended upon Otto. The Bavarian grimaced and began hacking away at their unarmored bodies.

Meanwhile, back at camp, Don Alfonso had been awake all evening, listening to the sounds of the villagers screaming and watching the orange glow of the burning thatched roofs grow steadily brighter in the night. His men were awake as well. Some one hundred halberdiers stood by him, awaiting orders and the chance for plunder. Don Alfonso fought back old memories as he watched the smoke rise into the night air.

A figure came running up the road towards them – Fletcher. He was not bloodied but he was still holding his stomach and was clearly in pain. Don Alfonso ran to meet him halfway.

"Señor leche – what has happened to you?"

"I was attacked, milord. But never you mind that, Captain Koenigsherr is requesting reinforcements. The peasants..." he gasped for air, "...they are organizing, sir. They have us outnumbered."

Don Alfonso scowled. He knew that sixty horsemen against an entire village was a gamble, but he had no idea how resilient the Poles were, or just how fed up they were with the constant war.

"Go back to camp, find Lieutenant Bianchi – *este...* Fortezza. You know the one, the girl."

Fletcher furrowed his brow, unsure, but nodded slowly.

"It is very important that she not be here while we work, do you understand? This is a horrible but necessary thing we are doing, but seeing it in action, or worse, taking part in it, will scar her worse than she already has been. Do you understand?"

Fletcher opened his mouth to stutter out an objection, but Don Alfonso grabbed him by his collar.

"I feel like I need to explain this to you as I would to a small boy – I do not want to see a broken commander of swords on the battlefield. Find her and make sure she stays far, far away from the village."

With that, he released Fletcher and pointed towards the camp, wordlessly urging him to go as a father would urge his child. Fletcher, fearing the don's wrath, agreed. As the

Englishman fled back into the camp, the don made the sign of the cross and asked forgiveness from the Lord for what he was about to do.

Fletcher had little trouble finding the large blue command tent, even in the middle of the night. The moon and, eerily, the orange glow of Zalesie burning in the distance gave him ample lighting.

He opened the flaps to find Sophia lying on her cot, sound asleep. He approached her quietly, using the same walking technique he would use when hunting game in the forest as to not make the slightest bit of noise.

As he sat down on a wooden chest next to her, he thought to himself that he could sit here all night just listening to her breathe. It was soothing and deep, and he would've fallen asleep himself if not for the adrenaline still pumping through his veins. He was told to keep her away from the village, but he did not need to do that if she were here fast asleep.

Fletcher realized this was the first time he had seen her out of costume, and without that large beret she always wore. Her auburn hair covered her face, and strands of it moved as she gently exhaled. Without her puffy sleeves and armor, Fletcher could see that she was very thin, but not scrawny. Her arms did not have the muscles of a soldier, and her hands looked smooth, although she had a lot of dirt under her nails from the campaign. Her chest, covered by her bandages, rose and fell ever so slightly as she breathed. She mumbled something in Italian and turned over, showing her back to Fletcher.

Fletcher squinted and looked closer at the bandages – they were brown with age. He was certain that Calvert had ordered all of his patients to change their bandages daily. Sophia was probably instructed, but either forgot or never understood in the first place. Fletcher's were fresh from this morning, but hers needed to be changed soon. Perhaps if he were very gentle, then he could take them off without waking her.

With the slightest, slowest movements he could make, Fletcher stood up and opened the chest he was sitting on, silently moving objects around until he could find bandages or field dressing. His hand wrapped around something soft – linen wraps – perfect for bandaging wounds.

He turned to face the sleeping Sophia and stopped. How was he going to remove her bandages without waking her? He winced in apprehension as he eased forward to touch her shoulder.

As soon as his finger stroked her skin, she bolted awake and pulled her blanket up to her chest, her eyes wide open in surprise. She was ready to scream, but the pale moonlight was enough to help her recognize Fletcher's face.

"Cosa fai, Freccia?"

Fletcher swallowed. He had to use his rudimentary French versus her Italian to explain something that was complicated even in English.

"Eh... Je need to uh... changer de bandage on your derrière, mademoiselle."

Sophia raised an eyebrow, puzzled, and looked under her sheets. Her buttocks did not need bandaging, but then seemed to understand what he was saying. The bandages she wore were old, indeed, but to get out of them required her to expose herself to him, something that she was a little more than anxious to do, but for the sake of her health, it had to be done.

198

"*D'accord, vas-y.*" she said, switching to French for him, hoping he understood as she turned her back.

Fletcher understood nothing and assumed she wanted him to leave. Sighing, he placed his hand on her shoulder and said, struggling with his French,

"Mademoiselle, je... bugger... je ne pas abandon vous."

Sophia thought it was sweet that he said that he would never abandon her, but completely irrelevant given the context of what was happening. She wondered when he was going to start working. His hand just sat there on her shoulder. Giving him a confused smile, she put her hand on his.

"Vous pouvez commencer, monsieur freccia."

Fletcher was certain that he understood the word "commence", but started to tremble when Sophia's soft fingers ran through his. His teeth were chattering too, and he tried his best to hide it. Steeling himself, he patted her hand gently and proceeded to gently peel off the old bandages.

Sophia winced as the itchy bandages were peeled off her skin, exposing the red scabs on her back. The wounds were beginning to heal, but the dirty bandages were not helping. Fletcher was thankful they weren't infected. Reaching back into the trunk, he looked for something that he could use as a salve for her wounds. A jar of rose oil lay wrapped in a silk stocking for padding. This was perfect – this was the same substance Calvert had used on him.

As best as he could without resorting to speech, Fletcher urged Sophia to lie on the cot flat on her belly. He gently took her shoulders and pressed down on them. She willingly obliged, closing her eyes and positioning herself face down, while Fletcher opened the jar of ointment.

The sweet smell of roses filled the air as he poured the rose oil over her wounds. She hissed with pain but then gave out the slightest moan at the coldness of the oil.

Fletcher swallowed as he frantically searched for a towel to dab the oil with. Once he found it, he gently massaged the oil into her wounds, making her grunt with pain. Fletcher stopped for a while, thinking that he was doing her harm.

"Je vais bien, continue s'il te plait."

Fletcher understood "continue" and he pressed further, listening to her groan and watching her back twitch every time he applied the towel. He wanted to tell her that it was all right, that it was necessary, but he did not know the words for that. Instead, putting the towel away, he gently rubbed the uninjured part of her shoulders with his firm, calloused peasant hands.

Sophia cooed with pleasure. This was the first time anyone had touched her like this and she liked it. Her breathing became slow and relaxed as her muscles relaxed.

Fletcher bit his lip. He had little to no idea what he was doing but Sophia seemed to like it. He pressed harder, finding a rhythm, slowly gliding his oiled hands down the sides of her body, caressing her shoulders, ribs, and waist up and down. She let out a little giggle.

Fletcher felt the blood rise to his cheeks and to other parts of his body. He decided to straddle over her on the cot and continued to apply pressure over her sides and lower back, being careful to avoid her wounds. With a brave slip of his hand, he placed his hands on her buttocks.

200

She squeaked in surprise and flipped over, exposing her naked breasts to him. His heart beat like a bird's as he simply sat frozen and staring wide-eyed at her beautiful body.

She grabbed his hands and whispered, shockingly, in English,

"Us maybe die tomorrow."

Sophia placed his hands on her breasts as Fletcher started breathing heavily, leaning in to kiss her. The tent suddenly became much warmer.

Chapter 21

Don Alfonso was feeling a different kind of heat. The screaming had long since stopped, and the company of halberdiers had pushed the villagers back into the church, the only stone structure in the entire village; the rest of the buildings were consumed in an orange inferno around him as his halberdiers ran about, putting straw roofs to the fire, while the remaining cavalrymen formed a perimeter around the village, making sure that no one could escape.

He stared at the door of the church, where just moments ago, the parish priest had herded in the entirety of his surviving flock. They were probably going to wait out the raid in there. The don heard the clanking of armor behind him, signaling Otto's approach. His black armor had streaks of blood all over it.

"These Polacks are outrageous! They attack me with stones and… eh… *hirtengauner,* you know, the sticks they use for the sheep."

"Do you mean shepherd's crooks?"

"*Ja,* that's right. An outrageous thing, is it not?"

"When you are desperate to defend your home you will do anything. Back in the Indies, a native even tried to bite me once."

"What happened?"

"He broke his teeth on my armor then I disemboweled him."

"Good work, *mein Herr.* Ah, yes, I should tell you that *Oberst MacRae* has arrived to assess the situation. He is on the outskirts of the village, away from the smoke – bad for the horses you see."

"Of course, the horses." Don Alfonso said as he turned to leave.

Otto patted him on the back as he left and planted his bloody broadsword in the dirt to lean on it. His long day of killing was finally over.

MacRae and Gunther waited on horseback just outside the village, just like Otto said, watching the smoke billowing from the rooftops with stern expressions on both their faces. As Don Alfonso approached, they turned their steely gazes towards him.

"Master Spaniard, report."

"Sir, the villagers have been routed and have congregated inside the church. They should weather there until we complete our plunder and leave."

MacRae's brow furrowed, "How many villagers were left alive?"

"There were several dozens, perhaps. No more than thirty, sir."

Gunther shook his head, "That is still too many. A single soul reaching a nearby fortress would be a disaster for the company."

"Master Jaeger has a point. We shall weigh our options, but I want the opinion of all my senior captains. Master Jaeger, fetch Warwick out of bed."

Gunther silently nodded as he turned his horse around and galloped back to camp. MacRae looked upon the destruction he had ordered.

"This is never easy, Master Spaniard."

"I know it too well, sir." Don Alfonso replied as he set his eyes on a flaming chicken coop that was slowly collapsing.

MacRae dismounted and tied his horse to the village signpost.

"Come, we have much to discuss with Master Koenigsherr."

The two strolled through the dirt roads in silence as charred, blackened structures collapsed around them. A pile of unspoiled goods lay in the center of the village. Bales of cloth, cooking utensils, barrels of mead, and all sorts of useful things that had been appropriated from the villagers could now be used to aid Talbot Company on its campaign.

MacRae and Don Alfonso came upon Otto at the church, who was now busy trying to clean his sword with a raggedy shirt he had pilfered off a dead man.

"Guten Tag, meine herren." Otto said as he wiped off the last bits of blood, "As you can see we have truly done well for ourselves. This should last the company for a good while. Shall we assemble the men to march?"

"Not yet, Master Koenigsherr; there still be the matter of that to decide." MacRae said as he pointed towards the church.

"What of it, *mein Herr?* The villagers will surely move on from this place once we've left."

"Move on to where, Master Koenigsherr? Their wretched hides will flee back to their master, the local lord, who will no doubt wreak vengeance upon us with his militia."

"Are you suggesting that we slaughter them here and now?"

"Yes."

"Inside that church, *mein Herr?*"

"Yes!"

"But... this is a church."

"And you are a fuckin' Protestant! Do ye really care about the lives of the people that ye were so callously slaying nary half an hour ago? Do ye really care about the fuckers that were trying to kill ye?"

"Mein Herr..."

"Ye were up to yer fuckin' bridles in Catholic blood at Breitenfeld, Master Koenigsherr. Yer moral ground be about as high as the bottom of Loch Ness!"

Otto, firmly silenced, lowered his head and sheathed his sword. Gunther had just arrived from camp but had been standing around long enough to hear the entire exchange, especially since MacRae had the tendency to shout at the top of his lungs all the time. As he saw Otto being berated, he resolved not to let his friend be cowed,

"*Oberst MacRae,*" he said, breaking his long silence, "I fear that the burning of this building would have a significant impact on the morale of our Catholic troops, myself included."

MacRae threw his hands up in the air, "This is war, man! Are ye daft or are ye a fuckin' hypocrite? How many men begged Mary Our Blessed Mother to spare them before you cut them down? You, a fellow Catholic?"

Gunther said nothing.

"But suddenly we be here at this little church in a Polish village in the middle of fuckin' nowhere and ye decide to grow a conscience? Well, fuck me! But, let it be said that I be not a tyrant – if the consensus of you men is that the church shall not be put to the flame, and we should let a Polish army ride up our arse ten miles down the road and fuck us till we all be dead in the cold ground, then let it be so."

Just as the group turned to leave, Warwick came into view, hobbling along on his crutches. Otto muttered *"Scheiße"* under his breath as the group walked up to meet him.

"What did I miss?" said the Englishman.

"Master Warwick. Good, a fourth voice to the madness."

"I am not sure I follow, sir."

"The German boys and I had achieved consensus on whether or not to burn down this here church, but that was when there were only three of us to vote. I will not tell ye what consensus we came to, so that yer opinion will be fair and unbiased..."

"Sir, this building is a house of idolaters and heretics." he said, almost confused as to why anyone would *not* want to destroy it. "Burn it, or we will regret it immensely when the villagers leave this place and call for reinforcements."

MacRae's one eye shifted towards his German captains, "What in the name of Satan's burning cock are we to do now? Our vote is two to two."

"Herr oberst," said Otto, "Did you not ride in with *Kapitän Villanueva?"*

"The Spaniard? Aye, that I did." MacRae realized as he looked around, "But I discounted him since he not yet be a senior officer. It seems we shall have nary a choice but to garner his opinion on the matter. There he be."

Don Alfonso stood yet again in front of the church doors. He could hear the murmuring of the scared villagers inside, and could faintly make out the sobbing of their children. The Polish priest was saying blessings in Latin, and he admired the way that these people clung to their faith in such a trying time.

A gloved hand rested on his shoulder.

"Master Spaniard." MacRae said solemnly, "We require yer vote on a matter of grave importance."

Don Alfonso turned to see four officers staring at him, as if they were waiting for something. The expressions of anxiety, impatience, and sorrow on their faces were easy to read.

There was a long pause, as if no one wanted to tell him what they were going to vote on. He could hear nothing but the crackling of the fire burning away at weakening timber and dry grass. Someone cleared his throat.

"Do ye see this church?" MacRae said, finally breaking the silence, "The men are not decided on whether or not we should spare it or raze it like everything else in the village."

"Consider the fact, sir," said Warwick, "That if these people were to be released, they would have nothing to eat, nowhere to sleep, and nothing to sustain them without the mercy of their lord. If that lord is far away, then they would have to undertake an arduous journey towards his manor, and upon arrival, they would be treated as refugees. I dare say, some of the more desperate ones would turn to banditry. All this is disregarding the fact that if a single villager informs merely a passing Polish patrol, our jolly group is in danger of being attacked from the rear, or on the way back."

"If I may, *Herr Villanueva,*" interjected Otto, "These people are no longer a threat to us. It is true that they may wander but it is far more likely that they will stay here and rebuild. Who knows how long they have lived here, centuries perhaps. They would be loath to leave the homes where their fathers and grandfathers broke ground. Besides, consider that this is a house of God. Does not our Lord preach peace and goodwill, even amongst our enemies? And take heed, sir, these words come from a person whom your people consider a heretic."

Don Alfonso weighed his options carefully: on the one hand, Warwick was right that they would be suffering more if they were allowed to live. It was especially true that a displaced peasant population could very easily turn into an angry mob to demand action from their local lord, something that no lord would ignore, especially in a time of war.

On the other hand, Otto had an equally valid point. They would still suffer, but in time they could make the land ripe again. And Otto was right; this was indeed the Lord's house. It was obvious that a lot of love and care went into the construction of this building. It was easily the largest building in the entire village, and the best maintained. The Lord would surely strike down the man that dared to lay a hand on His sacred place.

The don stared at his boots in silent contemplation. Both his choices factored in the lives of a great many souls. If he spared the villagers, he potentially doomed Talbot Company, himself included, to an ambush. If he destroyed God's house, he would be killing innocent people that by and large did nothing to deserve it.

"Your vote, sir." Warwick said, impatiently.

"Señores…"

The officers leaned in closer.

"It is my personal belief that we are justified in burning down this village."

Warwick and MacRae breathed sighs of resignation, while Gunther and Otto glared at him coldly.

"The lives of our men are far more useful to God's cause than the lives of these peasants, and by sending them to Him, we will spare them the suffering of having to live their lives as squatters, refugees, and beggars in the streets." The don almost choked on his own words.

"Jesus Christ be praised." MacRae said with the slightest hint of sarcasm as he walked away, eager to have this day done and over with, "See that yer men attend to it, Master Spaniard."

"Si, señor."

Don Alfonso would not jeopardize the souls of his men in this heinous, blasphemous act. He had to be willing to do anything that he would order them to do, for such was the value of a true leader.

He turned towards the church and looked up at the simple belfry. The cross Christ had died on to save all the world stood above the flames in defiance of the destruction that raged around it. Soon it, too, would be nothing but black, smoldering ashes.

The Spaniard exhaled in great breaths, releasing his sorrow, as he went around the church to search for a piece of wood that he could use to start the fire. A large torch had fallen from an outdoor sconce and was still very usable. He did not deign to pick it up yet.

Removing one of his gloves, he traced his fingers along the wall of the sacred building. It was simple cobblestone, painted white, even between the cracks of the stone. The villagers had been meticulous.

He had once constructed a similar structure back in the East Indies, at the request of the local natives who had then recently fully accepted Christ as their savior. His church was made of limestone and mud brick, and it was not as large as this one, but it served its purpose. Every afternoon the faithful would stop all activity during the Angelus, proclaimed by the church bell. On Sundays, families would gather for the mass, and at times the congregation became so large that it flooded to the outside of the church, where fathers had to carry their little children on their shoulders. When the mass had ended, there would always be a large communal feast, where he was always invited to share in the natives' bountiful harvest; such things must have happened here once, but they would never happen again.

Picking up the torch, he lit it on the embers of a nearby building, rolling it around gently, making sure that the flammable cloth came to a good roaring flame so that he would not have to do this again. The roof of the church was made of straw hatching and was perfect for burning.

As Don Alfonso raised the torch to let the flames eat away at the edges of the roof, he thought he could hear something inside the church. It was faint, but it was definitely there. It sounded like a little girl – she was not crying or speaking, but singing. It did not take long for others to join her, and soon the whole

210

congregation raised their voices to the heavens in melodious song, even as the fire spread rapidly throughout the roof.

It was the Ave Maria.

Don Alfonso could not keep his eyes dry as he hurled the torch onto the rooftop of the building, causing the fire to spread faster. Soon, the singing turned to coughing, then choking, and finally when beams began to collapse, screaming.

The don turned away, as Peter did when he betrayed Christ, but chose to remain there while the church burned away so that he might burn the terrible deed into his memory as a reminder of his sin.

When night had turned to morning, and the flames had stopped, Don Alfonso still had not moved from his spot, even as the church behind him had turned to a burned down ruin, with the charred human remains of the villagers buried under the massive wooden beams that had crushed them, pinning them down as they burned alive.

The rest of Talbot Company had packed up during the night and was on the move. MacRae had ordered a few of Don Alfonso's men to stay behind and watch him after they had left for the night, and now the colonel himself had come riding along with a fresh horse in tow for him.

"We be leaving this place, Master Spaniard." MacRae said softly.

Don Alfonso nodded and mounted the horse that MacRae had brought him. He joined the caravan at a slow walk, staring at the burned-out rubble of the church he had put to the fire.

"Espere..."

Don Alfonso saw something sticking out of the rubble – a hand? Was it moving? The don leaped off of the horse and sprinted towards the ruin, hoping that there was probably someone he could save, someone he could apologize to, someone that could redeem him for his grave sin.

He grabbed the hand and pulled. The ash fell in a torrent from the figure – a stone statue of Our Lady of Sorrows had survived the fire, perpetually weeping for the sins of mankind, and his sins as well. The Virgin's gaze seemed to implore him for mercy.

Why would you do this to your Mother?

Don Alfonso released the statue's hand as tears streamed down his cheeks. He backed away, defeated, and started back towards his horse. Otto had held the reins for him while he went off. The rest of the caravan was a far ahead of them.

"I am sorry, *mein Herr,* but it had to be done."

Chapter 22

Slave Market

Caffa, Crimean Khanate

Atahan flung open his bedroom windows and breathed in the sweet mountain air. Today was going to be a good day; product flooded in like never before. The pointless wars that the Christians were fighting brought him many captives, and captives were always good for business.

After his morning prayers, and a quick breakfast of wheat pancakes and soup, he left his two-story house to venture into the bustling slave market. As a *yerliyya*, or local janissary, Atahan had enjoyed both the benefits of education and military training, something few people at that time could afford. The local vizier assigned him many years ago to assist with the business affairs of the notorious slaver Imran Bey, whose business was vital to the Ottoman economy in the area. His job as the bey's adjutant was something he took quite seriously.

The early risers were already out in full force, oiling the naked bodies of their products and making sure that there was not a louse to be found on a single scalp. Everything had to be perfect for the morning's sale.

"*As-salaam alaikum* esteemed Atahan," a merchant said as he came up to greet him. "How fares your lord Imran Bey?"

"*Wa-alaikum salaam,* Muzeffer Effendi. He fares well. Recent sales have been astounding, may Allah be content."

"Yes, but your lord does not have products as fair as mine." he said as he gestured towards a gaggle of naked slave women, huddled up for warmth. While their skin was indeed pristine and white, and their hair curled and perfumed, the women themselves shivered, due to the cold and fear.

"Damned Circassians." Muzeffer muttered, "Beautiful creatures, but weak constitution. They will live, though. I am not too worried."

Atahan chuckled, "Muzeffer Effendi, my lord does not deal in concubines, and you know this. It is as if we compare a tea house to a blacksmith."

"And I am the tea house?" Muzeffer asked with a sly grin.

"As you wish, effendi." Atahan said with a slight bow of his head as he continued along his way.

"Atahan Effendi, wait a moment." Muzeffer said, gently tapping him on the shoulder.

"One of your master's Tatars recently came bearing a message."

He produced a rolled piece of parchment from the folds of his cloak and handed it to Atahan. The seal, bearing the eagle of the Polish-Lithuanian Commonwealth, was still unbroken.

"Your master will remember my trustworthiness I hope?"

"I will be sure to mention your name."

Muzeffer smiled and made a low, grateful bow, stepping away to leave Atahan to his business.

As he continued through the slave market, Atahan continued to take in the sights and smells of the market. He now entered the finely decorated outer courtyard of the market where some of the slave traders resided. The neatly trimmed garden trees reached for the heavens like fingers, and the birds sang their sweet songs as they alighted on the cages of sobbing slaves.

Small children, secured in burlap sacks with only their heads sticking out of the bags, were being offloaded off of a wagon that had arrived just in time for market day. As he walked under a stone awning with intricately decorated arabesques, Atahan paused for a while and leaned on a pillar to observe the bickering between the Tatar slave raider and the Turkish merchant.

"What have you done?! I cannot accept these now – how am I supposed to prepare them in time for display?" said the slave trader.

The Tatar slave raider merely shrugged and said, "But they are fresh. Look at this one – I caught it just yesterday." pointing to a little Russian boy that was crying for his mama.

"Yes, well freshness like this is a bad thing in this business. You should know that by now. I will pay you but at half price."

"That is hardly fair."

"You were late and your product is riddled with filth. You are lucky I am not paying you at quarter rate."

As the bag of coins fell into the disappointed slave raider's hands, Atahan shook his head and smiled. These sorts of misunderstandings happened often; the rough Crimean Tatars had no mind for finesse, unlike Ottomans like himself and his lord. The opulent and magnificently decorated wooden doors that he now walked through could never be found in a Tatar home. Indeed, this was the house of Imran Bey, his master.

The bey had a passion for the color green. Silk curtains dyed with a vibrant shade of emerald decorated the walls, while geometric patterns painted in gold leaf seemed to swim across the roof and floor.

The bey stood in his reception room, richly attired in a green and yellow robe with a white turban wrapped around his head, inspecting a product recently brought in by one of his slave raiders, who was beaming with pride. The slave, bound in chains and wearing nothing but a loincloth, gazed with hatred at the bey who stood before him.

"What have you brought me, Dastan?" the bey said, as he circled the product, thoughtfully stroking his short beard.

"A most exotic specimen, effendi. The papers say it came all the way from Gao," the slave raider paused for dramatic effect, "in Africa!"

The slave's angry, cursing eyes followed Imran Bey as he walked around him. He had very dark complexion and curly hair. His wide nose and large lips did not make him particularly attractive in the eyes of the bey, but he had a well-muscled body, something that could be particularly useful for manual labor. However...

"Dastan, you have brought me a siyahî."

"You will pardon my ignorance, effendi, but this word you say... siyahî? I do not understand."

"A siyahî, an African slave, Dastan. I forget you Kazakhs do not have a word for them. There are few places for siyahî in the empire and you have brought it to the wrong market. It is not built for the cold climate of this place, and it is only suitable for

216

bodyguard work, which is readily provided for by the Russian and Moldovan slaves, which can be bought at a cheaper price."

The bey held the slave by the mouth to observe his teeth, but the African violently lunged at him, prompting Dastan to pull him back by his slave collar.

"Too aggressive." the bey said as he stepped back, "The only place fit for a siyahî like this one in the entire empire is in a harem to serve as a guard, but this one has not even been neutered yet."

Dastan sighed in disappointment.

"Do not worry, my friend. I will help you with the cutting presently. The sooner this is done, the sooner the wound will be able to heal. You will be able to sell this to some rich pasha looking for a dependable guard."

"I appreciate the sentiment, effendi, but I feel that a trained physician should handle this matter."

"Are you afraid that I might damage your product? Nonsense – I have done this many times before." Imran Bey turned and noticed that Atahan had entered the building.

"Ah, Atahan, my good and faithful adjutant." Imran Bey said, smiling, "Welcome. You are just in time to assist with the neutering."

"*As-salaam alaikum,* effendi. Muzeffer at the marketplace says that one of your men had come bearing a message."

"I am sure that whatever it is can wait." Imran Bey said as he produced a knife from a nearby drawer. "Do you know where we put the bandages, Atahan?"

"They are in the upstairs storeroom, effendi."

217

"I am loath to make that arduous trek for the sake of a slave. It will have to do without."

"But what if it bleeds out?" Dastan protested.

The bey gave an apathetic shrug and proceeded towards the African, who stared at the knife wide-eyed in fear.

"Dastan, Atahan, hold it down."

As the bey commanded, the two men jumped at the African and threw him onto a nearby table. Each wrestled with an arm and a leg as the African screamed in his foreign language and shouted for his heathen gods to protect him.

Once he was somewhat restrained and Imran Bey did not have to fear being kicked in the face, the bey cut off his loincloth with his knife and groaned in frustration upon seeing that the man's testicles had shrunken in fear.

"You shall have to hold him still, my friends. This will take some skill on my part."

"About the letter, effendi..."

"Not now, Atahan." the bey said as he grabbed the African's scrotum. As he did this the slave began to scream louder and got more violent with his writhing. Imran's cut would have to be swift and precise. He brought the knife in with one quick slashing motion and off came the slave's testicles. Blood soaked his linen tablecloth as the slave shrieked in pain.

"You were saying something about a message?" the bey said over the noise of the screaming African.

"It has a seal with an eagle on it, effendi."

"Why did you not say so earlier? Come, let us discuss the matter in my study. Leave the siyahi."

With that, Atahan let go of the arm and leg he was restraining so that Dastan was forced to do everything himself, including the act of dragging a profusely bleeding man out of the bey's house. The two Turks ascended a winding staircase to the bey's study while the African's screaming faded away as he was dragged outside.

"Hand me the letter," said the bey. As Atahan handed his master the rolled parchment, the bey ripped off the seal and unrolled the piece of parchment, scrutinizing every word.

"A message from the Polack colonel." the bey said as he rolled up the document once more. "The Christian claims that he has captured his prize and that the other half of the payment he promised for my Tatar mercenaries is ready."

"He was smart, that one." Atahan added, "Half now and half if they do their job and not run back to you."

The bey threw open the double doors to his study on the upper floor of his estate. The room continued his emerald scheme, with golden-trimmed green curtains covering everything from the walls to the ceilings. Maps of the various territories of the Ottoman Empire covered the walls, and a large map of the entire empire served as the floor decoration.

The Ottomans were a people that ruled over a vast swathe of humanity. They had conquered more land than the ancient Persians and Alexander the Great combined. Every man from Transylvania in the west to the birthplace of the Prophet himself in the east called the sultan lord; every spice, every exotic good, and every slave from the east flowed to and from markets touched by the sultan's hand. It was the largest contiguous empire in the world.

The bey traced his finger through a map of Poland as Atahan looked on.

"This is Jarlsberg Castle." he said, tapping on a tiny dot in the Swedish Baltic lands. "Before he left on his campaign the Polack told me that he was to capture it. If this is true then he has restarted the war with Sweden."

"The war ended?" asked Atahan.

"Yes, very recently. I understand it is difficult to keep up with events in nations that do not concern us, but these things are vital for people like me, as you will see. Atahan, what would it look like if we took our client prisoner?"

"It would look extremely bad, effendi. That would leave a mark on our reputation that..."

"It would look extremely bad to whom, exactly?"

"To the client's family and countrymen, effendi; they would never again trust us. We would not be able to have repeat business with them – ever."

"Has the Polish-Lithuanian Commonwealth ever had cause for commonality with the great Ottoman Empire?"

"No, effendi."

"This is the beauty of it. No Polish lord has ever dared buy product from a Muslim because we were never trusted in the first place. This single Polack became a rebel to the crown and now he expects me to simply stare at the fruit of his actions as it dangles in front of me.

"The king of Poland now has a rebel on the loose, Atahan. If I were a king I would not want to disrupt a peace treaty while the ink is still dry. He will be looking for names of collaborators, spies, and other traitors who would restart this war illegally. It is inconceivable that this man wishes to restart the war on his own. Colonel Jan Casimir is worth a lot of money to the king of Poland as a living prisoner. Besides I do not believe he could stomach the thought of one of his officers being held by an 'infidel' like me."

Atahan saw the simplicity in his master's plan. By allowing this Polish colonel to successfully retake a castle without the support of his government behind him, he was passively creating a valuable captive, whom he could capture with ease if he were disguised as an ally. The rewards would be immense.

"Surely he has sent word to his king, begging him to throw his army behind him in support of his illegal war. The idiot was raving on about the injustices of the Swedish peace as he was negotiating rates with me. He practically assured me that the Polish King would come to his aid. He is wrong. He commits this act of foolish treason alone. Whatever the case, we Turks have the advantage here – we can depart soon and present the prisoner before the appropriate client within the week. If we leave tomorrow with a sizeable force of mounted sipahi lancers and Tatars, we will arrive at the castle in perhaps three days."

Imran Bey left the map and walked over to his balcony. He reveled in the scene below – his sipahis, Ottoman knights known for their brutality and speed on horseback, were practicing their skills with the bow and sword, massacring row upon row of ripe melons.

"Unlike the Polish, I anticipated this event well in advance. We have been training for days. Tell the men the time has come to leave."

Chapter 23

Königsberg, Prussia

For four days Talbot Company had marched through hostile territory, avoiding major roads and large cities as they did when they first arrived in the country. Villages, however, were subject to the whims of the men's stomachs. Two more Polish villages razed to the ground on their way to Prussia.

Don Alfonso had refused to take part in either of the lootings, so the matter of pillaging was left to the cripples Warwick and Bjornsson, neither of whom had any problems about slaughtering a few peasants for the greater good. To ensure that the men's morale did not suffer as badly as it did when the company chose Catholic soldiers to burn down a Catholic church at Zalesie, Protestant soldiers were hand-picked to do the slaughter, as they thought that they did God's work through shedding the blood of the heretic Catholics. Some began to remember what the war was about in the first place, and there was a real danger of religious strife within the company.

However, when the first Talbot Company boot stepped into Prussian territory, MacRae had ordered the looting to come to a complete halt. Prussia was a Protestant nation and firmly in league with Sweden. Any hostile actions against Prussian citizens on its soil would be seen as an act of war against Sweden's valuable ally. They were fortunate to have acquired so much booty that they were no longer in need of a resupply, but passing through Königsberg was a geographical necessity, despite acquiring a surplus in supplies thanks to the looting.

"If I have not made myself clear," said MacRae as his men entered the large red brick gates of the city of Königsberg, "I want ye men to touch nothing. No tavern brawls, no fraternizing with the local lasses, no thievery, and no mischief. We are merely here to rest, and we will move on at daylight."

The citizens of Königsberg looked upon the mercenary horde with apprehension. A thousand men with their pikes and corselets covered with mud and blood were a sure sign of violent intent, and the city's militia was on edge. MacRae tried his best to smile and wave at passers-by, but how could a smile be charming, when one had but a single eye?

MacRae rode up to the marketplace and had one of the baggage wagons drawn up beside him. The officers then unloaded all of the unusable goods that the company had acquired and began to exchange them for solid coin with the Königsberg merchants. Iron bars, pottery, baskets, jewelry, and fragrant herbs went a long way towards getting coin for the men's food and other expenses.

They deserved some rest and relaxation, especially now that Jarlsberg was only three days away. The officers divided the coin equally amongst their soldiers but ensured that their sergeants kept watch for anyone who so much as passed wind in the wrong direction.

MacRae had allowed the men free time to roam the city until sunset. While Bjornsson and Warwick elected to stay and guard the baggage train on account of their injuries, Otto, treading a fine line, made a beeline for the tavern; Sophia, meanwhile, found that the fine colors and fabrics of Königsberg's tailors were enough to make her smile again; Gunther found himself at a cross street with a theater on one side and the town brothel on the other; and Don Alfonso had taken to sparring practice and drill lessons with Fletcher. Everyone else in the company was trying to find something to do to distract them from the war.

The Pregel River flowed through Königsberg, straight through a manmade island in the center of the city reminiscent of the islets of Venice that held the statehouse and the city's cathedral. Beautifully landscaped gardens with tall trees and flowering bushes would have contributed a calm, meditative atmosphere to the place if it hadn't been for the throngs of politicians, priests and college students that were gathered around in a large crowd, watching two foreigners duel each other in a courtyard under the shadow of the cathedral.

Don Alfonso held his sword at a low guard, his body leaning back at an angle. Fletcher, seeing an invitation to strike for his head, swung his hunting sword, but his blow was promptly parried while Don Alfonso's free hand simultaneously grabbed Fletcher's wrist. In the time it took to scratch an itch, the don had parried and countered Fletcher's overhand strike. The Englishman now stared down the length of Don Alfonso's sword.

"Stop attacking overhand, *señor leche*. Use moves that the enemy does not expect. Again."

Of course, this was no true duel. The Spanish captain somewhat enjoyed Fletcher's company, and was equally enthusiastic to practice his English. Fletcher, on the other hand, believed that he could find out more about the mysterious Italian girl through her mentor.

"So, milord, about Lieutenant Bianchi..."

Don Alfonso batted Fletcher's blade away with his sword and thrust home, just barely tapping Fletcher on his neck.

"*¿Otra vez? ¡Por que?* Why must you persist with the girl?" He sheathed his sword, and the crowd almost immediately began to disperse. Sparring time was over, and Fletcher's interrogation had begun.

Fletcher put away his own hunting sword and grinned, "I do not know, milord. She is... amazing. Her eyes are like the stars, her hair flows like water, her skin..." Fletcher stopped. Don Alfonso's eyes narrowed. "Eh... her skin is very nice."

"*Ante todo, señor idiota*, her name is not Lodovico Bianchi. That is a man's name, and her disguise has fooled absolutely no one. Her real name is Sophia Fortezza."

"Sophia..." Fletcher whispered. Her name was like sugar on his tongue. He almost began singing her name before the don put a stop to it by putting his hand on the Englishman's shoulder.

"It is obvious that you are in love. Do you deny this?"

"No..." Fletcher replied, his mind somewhere else.

"I am not one to stand in the way of your emotions, *señor leche*, but do you not find it difficult that you speak no Italian at all? No French?"

"Je parle la tongue de amour!"

"*Primeramente*, it is *la langue de l'amour. Secundo,* you are embarking on a path that will lead to ruin. You will doubtless be devastated if she dies, and I will have lost two comrades instead of just the one."

226

Fletcher suddenly turned serious, "I am prepared to risk my life for her, milord."

"...again." Don Alfonso finished, "By her account, you hid her in the bushes, and I saw you flogged for her sake. I do not doubt your conviction. I am simply saying what I feel needs to be said. However, I will not hinder your endeavor. What do you wish to know about our esteemed lieutenant?"

Fletcher's mind became giddy with thoughts. This was as close to speaking Sophia's own language as he could get. The first words to escape his words were,

"What is her favorite color?"

Don Alfonso reeled back in disbelief. "*Hijo*, no. You are wasting this opportunity. Ask something with a bit more substance."

Fletcher thought for a moment, putting his hand to his chin, "Sir, if I may be so bold to inquire – what stirs her soul? What drives her passion?"

Don Alfonso chuckled, "The dice, believe it or not. She is quite lucky with them. You know the only reason why she is here is because she fell into a massive gambling debt?"

Fletcher was slightly taken aback. He did not expect the beautiful, graceful Sophia to be a hard gambler. But as he thought about it some more, it did make sense. She was an adventurous risk-taker, jumping into things she knew nothing about in anticipation of profit. Perhaps he could gamble on his love for her.

Sophia Fortezza walked proudly through the streets of Königsberg wearing her new outfit – a blue and white silk dress decorated with ribbons, and tiny brass flowers. As a lady of Milan, she had impeccable fashion taste. She was laced up to the neck like a proper lady, but she still wore her broad-brimmed beret, which actually matched the dress even though it was considered a rather masculine item. Her old clothes she carried in a box.

It was good to be in proper women's clothing again. Although she had to admit that her costume was easier to put on, her steel corselet did not turn heads the same way a satin corset did.

With her shopping trip completed, she made her way back to the town square where the company had been ordered together. The men who saw her scarcely recognized her as she gracefully glided through the streets, the scent of roses from her new perfume lingering in her wake.

The soldiers stared at her slack-jawed. They could hardly believe that this was the same girl they had marched with. Her own swordsmen argued amongst themselves that this could not possibly be their commander. Sophia giggled as she passed them, content to hear them curse and shout at one another over her. Few hooted and whistled – everyone remembered what happened to the last man that tried that.

As she walked up to the baggage train to stow away her old clothes in her trunk, she caught Warwick's attention, who was sitting there with one of his men on guard duty. If it was not for her beret, he would not even have been able to recognize her.

"Buongiorno, Capitano Guarrico." she said as she gave a graceful, feminine curtsy. It made no difference how she acted now, since everyone knew that she was a woman anyway.

Warrick said nothing, his expression one of astonishment and confusion. The same awkward girl that trudged through mud and grass with them now stood before him, looking like an elegant swan. His soldier looked on with hungry eyes.

"Who... is Guarrico?" he managed to say in French.

"Why, you are." Sophia replied with a smile.

Warwick realized that the two had never truly spoken before, and that was just how Sophia pronounced his name.

"Sir," interrupted his soldier in English, "My man parts are bewildered. Was this not Lieutenant Bianchi?"

"Master Thatcher," Warwick said, continuing to stare at Sophia as she sat beside him, "shut your gob and go away."

"But, sir..."

"Go. Away."

As the soldier slowly shuffled away, mumbling something about man parts and "he-shes", Sophia smiled at Warwick and leaned closer to speak to him.

"Captain Guarrico, would you be able to teach me your language?"

Warrick furrowed his brow, "Whatever for? All the other officers speak French, and you know the language yourself..." Warwick found an explanation in his own query and smiled, "Ah... the peasant boy."

Sophia blushed and nodded her head.

"Permit me if I misstep myself, my dear, but... would you not prefer someone more... mature, perhaps? Maybe you would be better suited to wed someone with substantially more wealth?"

Sophia drew a dagger from her corset, but did not drop her smile, "If you touch me, even MacRae himself will not be able to save you."

Warwick swallowed, "I see. Your intentions have been made quite clear. What would you like to learn first?"

"How do you propose your love to someone in English?"

"Well, you could simply say, 'I love you', but those words are meant to be used..."

"I lava yo..." Sophia said, trying her best to sound romantic.

"We have much to work on, my dear."

Gunther Jaeger's clothes lay in a neat pile on a nightstand in the *Höllischer Hase,* or Hellish Hare guesthouse, one of Königsberg's lesser known but affordable houses of ill repute. Parts of the gaudy dress of a prostitute, with its prominent yellow stripe indicating the nature of her profession, lay scattered all over the floor.

The dress's former wearer, a skinny Königsberg strumpet with too much makeup and dyed hair, lay on a bed on all fours grunting loudly while Gunther took her from behind.

Gunther held a golden hunter-case pocket watch in one hand and the girl's rump in the other, as he pounded her back and forth, each smack of skin-on-skin corresponding with every second on his watch. As soon as the minute hand struck the forty-fifth minute, he allowed himself to ejaculate and made the slightest grunting sound. Satisfied, he withdrew himself from the girl and lay beside her on the bed. They both panted in exhaustion.

"We have about..." he glanced at his watch, "Fourteen minutes to prattle meaninglessly. You may ask me anything you wish."

The girl laughed in between gasps, "You are quite the different fellow, mister..."

"Customer."

"Of course love, we must keep things discrete after all. Would you care if I asked where you received those welts on your back, or would that be going too far?"

"Six I received for dropping a bucket of water, twelve for calling my commanding officer a 'lout', and fifteen for drinking while I was on watch. Next question."

"You are certainly very forthcoming with that information."

"We will never see each other again. I can discuss anything with you without fear of malicious rumors."

"I... see." The girl said, furrowing her brow. "That is actually quite true. Um, you did not seem to enjoy your time with me. You barely even smiled at all."

"Sexual release is a human need that clears the mind and prevents crimes of passion."

"My, that sounds rather... detached. Have you ever been in love?"

"No. Next question." He said, looking at her dead in the eye.

Taken aback, the girl turned to him, propped on her elbows, "Are you certain? No one has ever taken your fancy or made your heart skip a beat?"

"No." Gunther replied, his voice a monotone.

"Interesting. If you are without love, then what brings you joy?"

"Money."

"And what do you spend that money on?"

"Necessities – food, clothing, shelter, sex."

The prostitute shook her head, "That is a sad existence."

"Perhaps you are asking the wrong questions."

"Oh? I see the game you are playing."

"What game?"

"Your joy and your purpose of living are not the same thing. The question I should be asking is, 'what makes you feel alive', is it not?"

Gunther paused for a long moment. "When you clash in the heat of battle, with the dust clouds kicked up by men and horses obscuring your vision, and you hear the shouts of friend and foe all around you, the dying and the yet-to-die, when you feel your blade thrust into the clothes, flesh, and bone of a man who wishes to take your life – this is when a man knows he is alive."

"Ah, you are of the forlorn hope."

Gunther was now the one taken aback in surprise. "How did you..."

"Love, these legs have spread for many men. You are not the first. If I recall, you forlorn hope types receive double pay for dangerous work. You are notoriously resistant to death, you live hard, and you are quite the dying breed of men."

"Yes, originally my company had an entire platoon of men like myself, who loved nothing and feared nothing, as they say. I was once their leader. The men were always the first ones into the fray and we could never find enough volunteers to replace them. I am the last."

The girl chuckled, "How much longer do we have?"

"One minute."

"Would you care for a kiss, love?"

"Yes, that would be nice."

The prostitute smiled as her lips pressed against his.

At another tavern nearby, a drunken band of musicians played their hurdy-gurdy, drum, and lute to the tune of an ancient drinking song as Otto, still dressed in his armor, danced atop a table leading the raucous crowd in an out-of-tune chorus that Bacchus himself would be proud of:

In taberna quando sumus,

non curamus quid sit humus,

sed ad ludum properamus,

cui semper insudamus.

quid agatur in taberna

ubi nummus est pincerna,

hoc est opus ut quaeratur;

si quid loquar, audiatur.

Latin, normally the language of the Catholic Church, was now being used to sing about the joys of sinful drunkenness. The lyrics, mostly butchered by the drunken crowd, spoke about not caring about the troubles of the earth, the stresses of gambling and how money was one's servant in a tavern.

"Drink! Drink for all time!" Otto said in a slurred voice as he tried his best to keep from falling onto the floor that was apparently rolling like the sea. Despite his efforts, he slipped on his own foot and fell onto the wet, stinking floor. The crowd howled with laughter. "Whose dog pissed here?" he yelled. The crowd laughed harder.

Otto, laughing at himself, crawled to a bench and sat back down.

"Where is mead? I need more!" he spat.

A smiling patron poured him a tankard and passed it over to him. Everyone had been all smiles since he offered to buy a round for everyone in the tavern.

"Thank you, kind sir." he said, raising his tankard, "And now I propose a toast... to..."

Otto remembered the last time he proposed a toast in a tavern. Much merriment was had over that, but he did not seem to remember why.

"… His holiness the pope!"

A dead silence fell over the tavern for a long while, until someone screamed,

"Fuck the pope!"

Immediately followed by another patron screaming,

"How dare you speak of our holy father like that?"

Civilians drew their swords and glass bottles began breaking on the tavern walls as Otto calmly gulped his mead.

The city of Königsberg was a divided one. While the majority of the population was Protestant, there was a small Catholic minority in the eastern part of the city and a Jewish population to the north. The citizens tended to avoid topics concerning religion when drinking with strangers precisely to avoid a situation like the one Otto had created. It was funny how an argument about God was able to divide a city, even whole nations. Otto contemplated the politics of the war as a glass eye rolled across the table while its previous owner was getting his teeth violently removed.

Two wrestling drunkards landed on top of Otto's table and nearly spilled his mead. He took great offense to this and removed his gauntlet.

"Sirs, I challenge duel!" he said, slurring. The men continued to wrestle, ignoring his challenge.

"You dare acknowledge a noble? How dare you!" he belched as he threw the gauntlet down on the back of one of the two wrestling men. Their fight continued while Otto's gauntlet bounced off of them, rolling onto the floor and into the crowded mass of fighting tavern patrons. He groaned in frustration as he got on all fours, crawling through the spilled mead, blood and urine to get it. Several men tripped over him as he crawled under them. After wading through a sea of boots and unconscious people, he finally got a hold of his gauntlet – and that was when the tavern door burst open.

"Captain Koenigsherr!" a voice bellowed from the entrance. He knew that Scottish accent anywhere.

William MacRae had come to collect his men. Since this particular tavern had people and objects being thrown out of its windows, he rightly assumed that his drunken cavalry officer had something to do with it. MacRae stood in the doorway with a great scowl on his face while furniture and bottles flew around him. Eight of his men stood behind him.

"Search the place."

MacRae's definition of "search" involved punching, kicking, throwing, wrestling and biting. The soldiers rushed into the melee and began knocking people aside, breaking even more furniture and causing the even tavern owner to run out of his own establishment.

Otto was found trying to crawl out of the tavern through the back door. Two soldiers grabbed him by the pauldrons of his armor and fought their way back to the front door to drop the wretched German in front of MacRae.

"Ah, Master Koenigsherr." MacRae said, looking down at his officer like a disappointed father, "Welcome back. This be coming out of yer pay."

Gunther said nothing in response but instead showed a toothy, drunken grin. As he was hauled outside, MacRae took a last look at the state of the tavern, shook his head, and left; closing the door behind him just as a chair leg hit it.

Talbot Company, freshly restocked and well-rested, would continue their journey eastwards into Swedish territory. Spirits were high, bellies were full, and coin purses had been lightened. The men took every opportunity to distract themselves for they knew that in five days, many of them would not be alive to return to their fields and families.

Chapter 24

After days of marching through hostile Lithuania without encountering serious resistance, Talbot Company was now within the borders of friendly Livonia, a vassal state under the rule of the Swedish king. Jarlsberg Castle beckoned to the company.

Otto Koenigsherr and his cavalrymen were on an advance reconnaissance patrol, marching several yards ahead of the main body of the company. The memories of the village still distracted him as he walked through the cool pine forest, looking for signs of enemy troop movement. He hated the silence. In his state of sobriety, sometimes the screams of dying children would jump out of his head and project into the world around him.

The cavalrymen approached a clearing that led into an open field with low rolling hills dotted with white and yellow flowers. Beyond the hills, a structure broke the straight line of the horizon: Jarlsberg.

At long last, Talbot Company had reached its destination. After this battle, every man would either return home or return to his maker. The sense of finality made Otto hold his breath in a moment of tension.

There was something else he saw on the horizon. Banners waved in the cold Swedish breeze, displaying a gold cross on a blue field. The Swedish regular army had already arrived. Hundreds of men and horses had mustered outside the castle, waiting for Talbot Company to arrive so that, hand-in-hand, they would be able to drive the Polish into the dirt.

However, the sight of the Swedish colors made Otto wince. The last time he had seen them was at Breitenfeld, where he fought under the command of their king. He had deserted them during that battle, and the colors brought back painful memories. He was doubtlessly thankful for their presence as allies but prayed that no one would recognize him and call him out for his cowardice.

"Sergeant," he called out, his eyes still fixed on the Swedish flags, "Ride to Colonel MacRae and tell him that we have reached our destination at last. I shall ride to the Swedish commander and announce our arrival."

A few yards away from the Swedish main camp, Captain Henri Andersson and a small entourage of riders patrolled the forests surrounding Jarlsberg, ostensibly looking for deserters.

However, this was all part of Henri's plan. The night before, he had encouraged several of his men, all Finnish cavalrymen like him, to "desert the camp" so that they could meet in secret to plot against their Swedish oppressors. They were reported as missing the next morning and Henri had been ordered to bring them back to justice.

The bird call of a little grebe rang through the woods. This was the signal that the band of saboteurs had agreed on. Since grebes lived near water, there was no danger of being confused with the genuine animal, unless one were a keen listener of birds.

Henri and his men hastened towards the sound and found themselves in a small clearing, met by a dozen men gathered around the ashen remains of a campfire.

"Greetings, you fuckers." Henri said as he and his men dismounted. "Today is a fine day for subterfuge. You know why I have gathered all of you here."

"You promised us an honorable way to get out from under the hand of the Swede."

"I never said the word honorable." Henri said, waving his finger, "However you are correct. Tonight we plan our escape. You may be wondering – without the army, where do we go? What do we do?"

Heads nodded all around him.

"Fellows, are you not aware that all of Europe is wading up to its flesh pole in war? The opportunities for work in any of the free companies are vast, and if you desire to fight no longer, many villages have labor shortages thanks to the men being called up to fight. Our location and timing could not be more perfect. All we have to do is flee west. Poland itself will act as a vast buffer zone between us and the Swedish devils. Who wants to go to fight in the Netherlands? I know I do."

The men murmured in agreement.

"So, the plan is simple. The Swedes need food and ammunition, yes?" Henri gestured to one of the soldiers that had ridden in with him – an older man with a bushy blonde beard, "This is Sergeant Koskinen. The Swedes made the mistake of

240

entrusting their supplies to a Finn. He will make certain that our Swedish lords know the full extent of our displeasure."

"It is our goal to keep at the siege for as long as possible," said the sergeant, "To achieve this end, we must destroy our own artillery. I have placed impurities in all the charges of our cannon so that when they are fired even once, the guns will explode and be rendered useless. Stay away from our artillery. As far as the matter of food – do not drink the mead."

An angry clamor began to rise among the men.

"Unless you want to shit yourselves, speak to Satan himself, and possibly die a slow and painful death, stay away from the mead. I have mixed the essence of devil's trumpet into the barrels, which is masked quite nicely by the flavor of honey. Greve Stenbock intends to open the casks right before we assault the castle. When the Swedes drink the mead, they will believe that the grass is speaking to them and that they are falling into the sky. The cheap beer that they have us drink, however, is safe for consumption."

"Thank you, sergeant," said Henri, "Your heroic efforts will be sure to make this day will be memorable and entertaining. Men, once the Swedes are distracted by all this chaos and madness, we are to flee the field and head due south to the Lithuanian border. We will meet at the wooden church in the town of Joniskis, and from there we will begin our new lives. Does anyone have any questions?"

The soldiers said nothing, but all voiced their silent approval in their unique Finnish way.

"Good. Now, bind your wrists and let us tie you to the horses. You must look distraught and defeated for the Swedes to believe that we have caught you."

Otto Koenigsherr's mind raced with thoughts of uncertainty as he rode at full gallop alone towards the Swedish camp. What if they recognized him? Would he be arrested on the spot? Executed perhaps? What if the king himself was there?

"Think positive." he said to himself. The absolute best outcome was for no one to even acknowledge his presence. This was extremely doubtful. His black armor stood out even amongst Talbot Company's cavalry.

As he rode up to the perimeter of the camp, a Swedish soldier yelled at him to come to a halt. He obliged and pulled on the reins of his mount, causing it to kick up dirt and huff loudly, flaring its nostrils and shaking its head.

After a brief exchange with the soldier, Otto was escorted to the Swedish command tent. He could not help but notice that he turned heads as he passed, in the way that a crowd in a marketplace looks at a known miscreant. His armor betrayed his nationality, and the men's icy stares were making it clear that they did not trust Saxons.

The command tent was larger than the others, decorated in the Swedish national colors of blue and yellow as opposed to the tan or white of the common tents that surrounded it. A banner bearing the coat of arms of the Stenbock family – a rearing black he-goat on a yellow field – waved about on top of the tent.

Otto threw back the flaps of the tent and entered to find Greve Olaf Stenbock and his officers hunched over a map with wooden pieces decorated with Swedish, Polish, and Talbot Company symbols. They were discussing the critical role of cavalry, as their backs were turned to him. Engrossed in their meticulous preparations, they did not notice him enter. Greve Stenbock addressed his officers,

"My lords, it is safe to assume that Talbot Company will always have the numerical superiority. This is especially true now that we have potentially lost a dozen of our Finnish Hakkapeliitta to desertion. Hopefully, Captain Andersson can find them in time. Now..." the greve took one of the wooden pieces decorated with the Talbot Company dog's head and placed it on the right of a long line of mixed Swedish and Talbot Company pieces, "Assuming that their cavalry has enough strength to break through the enemy's defense, we will put them on our right flank to crush the enemy's left. Remember, my lords, that I desire a strong right above all things. Our left flank will be allowed to falter."

"A sound plan, my lord," said Otto in French, breaking his silence.

"Who are you?" said the greve in the same language.

"I am Captain Otto Koenigsherr, my lord." he said with a low bow, "I represent Talbot Company's carabineer cavalry troop."

"I am Greve Olaf Stenbock." the greve replied, looking Otto up and down, "It is good to meet you. Forgive me for saying this, but I believe I recognize your armor."

Otto said nothing, but watched as the greve's expression suddenly changed from neutral to irritated.

243

"You're a damned Saxon, are you not? Do not deny it, man."

"I am, my lord."

"I fought alongside the Saxon cavalry at Breitenfeld."

Otto gritted his teeth.

"You were all cowards and you almost cost us the battle. If it were not for the personal bravery and tactical brilliance of our king, that rout would have cost us the battle!"

Otto still refused to say anything.

Greve Stenbock grumbled, "What is Talbot Company's cavalry force composed of, pray tell?"

Otto replied in a near whisper, "Some Polish and Russians, but mostly Saxons, my lord."

The greve clenched his teeth and turned back to his officers.

"In light of recent information given to us by the commander of our mercenary cavalry, we must rely on our own Hakkapeliitta for flanking maneuvers. Talbot Company's cavalry, although more numerous than our own, must be kept in reserve. I will not risk another rout here."

Otto sighed in resignation.

"Is there anything else you wish to say to us, Captain Otto Koenigsherr of Saxony?"

"Yes, my lord." Otto replied, suddenly standing tall with pride, "Talbot Company has a little over a thousand men under arms, at least double the size of your forces. We will not disappoint you."

Otto's words were punctuated by the gradually loudening rhythmic beating of Talbot Company drums signaling the company's approach.

"And we are commanded by the finest officers in Europe."

While Otto sweat under his armor as he tried to project an air of confidence, outside MacRae grinned in actual pride as he rode in front of his great mercenary horde pouring out of the tree line. Gunther, Don Alfonso, Warwick, Bjornsson, and even Sophia rode behind him, all sharing the same grim expression born from weeks of violence and suffering. All of them knew that all their training and hardship would culminate in this – an assault on a pile of bricks and earthworks, defended by a lunatic who believed himself a hero.

Chapter 25

The allied camp was bustling with activity. Supply wagons and soldiers rolling barrels of black powder milled about, safeguarding valuable war materiel behind barricades. Greve Olaf Stenbock stood together with Captain Sven Bjornsson on a small hill that overlooked the whole camp and peered through a spyglass at the enemy fortification that was once his home.

"May I say, my lord," said Bjornsson, "that it is a great pleasure to be able to fight under your service once more. It feels good to be speaking the mother tongue again."

"It is indeed good to have you back, captain. What have you seen of the mercenaries while you lived and fought alongside them these past few weeks?"

Bjornsson looked towards Jarlsberg and breathed deeply, "I can say for certain my lord, that they are highly spirited and willing to be done with this as soon as God permits. They are reasonably trained and well-spirited, lord."

"And most importantly with their strength in arms, I am confident that we outnumber the enemy." the greve added.

"Forgive my impertinence, my lord, but what is stopping us from storming the castle now?"

The great oaken gate that had been breached during the siege had now been replaced with a hastily constructed wooden palisade gate made from fallen trees. It was nowhere near as sturdy as the original gate had been, and their new bronze cannons would make short work of it.

As far as enemy defenses, the leather cannons at the castle were still in place, augmented by the two longer ranged Polish six pounders that had originally caused the castle to fall. Breaching the walls or gate would not be a problem, but it was still something that the greve wanted to avoid.

"Crista is still inside."

Bjornsson had not forgotten about the day when he was dragged outside the walls to be toyed with by his Tatar captors. He had simply assumed Crista had met the same fate or worse.

"How did you come about this news, my lord?"

"Ratsherr Fegelein sent me a message via pigeon. Curiously the same message also hinted at collusion with the Turks." the greve said with raised eyebrows, "Although I do not see traces of a single Turkish Mohammedan here, I believe that we should not discount anything the ratsherr says."

Bjornsson nodded in agreement and added, "What of the walls, lord?"

"Yes, that will be a problem. I have already considered that cannon fire might topple the keep, and we do not know whether they are keeping my daughter in there, or in the barracks, or in any other building within the walls. I believe this is a matter that should be discussed with the mercenary commander and his officers. Perhaps they can divine a solution to this problem."

Bjornsson saluted his lord and walked off to find MacRae, leaving Greve Stenbock standing on the hill alone in contemplation. The thought crossed his mind that he was not sure if he could trust an army of paid ruffians to preserve the life of his pride and joy. However, he was not in any position to refuse their help. He had already given a letter of credit stating that he was willing to part with four thousand florins to pay the company and there was no taking that back now. The Swedish and Finnish regulars assembled outside of Jarlsberg numbered in the few hundreds and could not possibly hope to overrun a fortified position, while Talbot Company and its thousand men guaranteed that it would play a crucial role in the battle ahead. The matter was not up for debate – Crista's life depended on the strength of arms of strangers of questionable reliability motivated solely by money.

"Ye want us to do nothing then, sir?" MacRae said in French as he stood before Greve Stenbock inside the Swede's command tent. Standing together with MacRae were all of the Talbot Company officers, together with a few sergeants who were taking down notes. On Greve Stenbock's side of the tent sat the Swedish officers and Bjornsson.

The two groups had been debating for some time about how to assault the castle without having to breach the walls.

"No, that is not correct, monsieur MacRae."

"Colonel MacRae." the Scot corrected immediately.

Greve Stenbock shot him an annoyed glare, but MacRae stood as he was, refusing to acknowledge the greve's expression.

"... Colonel MacRae," the greve relented, "as stated previously, the castle must not be fired upon for the sake of my daughter's own safety."

"Can we not gamble the soul of one person over the necessity of a breach that will ensure victory?"

"I cannot believe you are arguing with your client, sir!"

"And I sir, cannot believe that yer men want mine to walk ladders up to a castle brimming with cannon and expect to make it out alive!"

"There was also the proposition of a battering ram..."

"Yes, a battering ram which would take till Christ's second coming to reach the walls of the castle, all the while being fired upon by cannon."

Warwick raised his hand and hobbled forward, still on his crutches, "I have a suggestion, my lords. What if we used sabotage?"

Greve Stenbock shook his head, "Sir if you believe that I shall give you any permission to tunnel under my home and destroy its structural integrity..."

"No sir, not like that at all. We merely need a very small team of my fox-walkers."

MacRae laughed, "Oh just like what ye did in Poland? That was time well spent indeed."

Warwick rolled his eyes, "No that was completely different. What I am planning is a ruse so simple that even a child could pull it off. Gentlemen, what is our primary concern?"

"We are required to breach the walls without using artillery." Greve Stenbock said, frustrated. He had gone over this a hundred times.

"Yes sir, but to what end?"

"Get to the point, man."

"Of course, sir. Our primary objective is to enter the castle and force its surrender. We can do this by sending a single highly skilled fox-walker over the walls at night to open the gates, after which a handful of others will trickle in to burn down everything that can be set alight."

Greve Stenbock sighed, "Sir you are forgetting that my daughter is still inside the castle."

"If that be the case then she should simply be rescued before..."

"And that property still belongs to me. Your idea is sound, but I believe that we do not need to burn down my entire estate. One man over the walls – and you are sure that he will be able to open the gate?"

"Absolutely. It is only a matter of walking along the ramparts until he reaches the gate, in theory. It is a wooden palisade, gentlemen. Only one man is needed to open it. The army will be standing at the ready, waiting for his signal."

"Which would be?"

"Ah, it shall be a red lantern that we can all see in the darkness. We shall find a lantern with red glass and have him hoist it up once the gates are open."

"And if it fails?" the greve said with suspicion.

"Then we will only have lost one man."

The English captain was right. The loss of only a single man would put barely a mark on Talbot Company's numbers, and sneaking a single person across an open field was much easier than trying to hide a dozen men, even in the dark.

"Your idea is agreeable, captain. Which one of your men do you have in mind for this perilous task?"

"A certain James Fletcher, my lord."

The crickets chirped in the meadow while the nocturnal denizens of the forest began to emerge from their hiding places. A lynx emerged from its den to begin its hunt, just as a certain hunter prepared to leave the safety of his camp and venture into the bowels of enemy territory.

James Fletcher, armed with his longbow, rondel dagger, and a grappling hook, crept up to the castle walls with the stealth and deftness of a small cat. His mission was simple – open the gates. The entire allied army had slept in shifts during the afternoon and was now standing by in the tree line waiting for the signal to attack the castle.

Fletcher chose his angle of attack – the western portion of the wall was far away from the barracks, according to Captain Bjornsson, but close enough to the gate so that he would not have to walk very far. The looming keep was the closest building to that part of the wall, and its immense size would hide him well. As Fletcher threw the grappling hook over the wall and began to climb, he could not help but think that something was amiss. The guards on duty on the wall had lanterns as he did, and he was supposed to simply light his lantern to signal the attack? He was certain he misunderstood something.

With the walls scaled, he looked around for any guards that might be patrolling the walls. Pausing for a while in complete stillness, he waited, watched, and listened. There were no sounds, no movement. He was about to proceed forward when suddenly he saw something from the window of the keep. An entire window frame, bars and all, came crashing from the fourth floor. This was immediately followed by a long rope that was apparently made of bed sheets and clothes that were tied together. A figure, dressed in what appeared to be a bright pink gown, began climbing down from the open window.

Fletcher could not believe what he was seeing. Part of him wanted to continue on with his mission, but the other part wanted to see what would happen to this girl.

Her descent was slow and awkward. She was swinging precariously, attempting to find footholds where there were none. She was likely about to fall.

Fletcher's conscience gnawed at him. He wanted to help, but could not risk the mission. If the girl fell he would have to live with it for the rest of his life. If he jumped off the ramparts now, the only way up again would be through the stairs that were likely well guarded. The drop from the ramparts was a little more than the height of a man, but the drop from where the girl was hanging was surely fatal.

Fletcher's choice was made for him when one of the girl's hands lost its grip. She now dangled from her blanket rope by the strength of her grip and five fingers alone. Fletcher cursed his luck and jumped off the ramparts, sprinting to where he believed she'd land.

At that moment, her strength failed her and she fell several feet, landing on Fletcher. The impact of a woman that weighed a hundred pounds was enough to cause him to collapse on the ground as he caught her, but at least she fell without screaming.

The first thing Fletcher noticed, aside from the pain in his back, was her distinct smell, like fresh peaches.

"Ach, min rygg gör ont!" the girl whispered as she climbed off of Fletcher.

"Almighty Lord, the continent is like Babel." Fletcher said as he lay on the dirt in pain.

"Engelska språket? You are English?"

Fletcher, stunned for a moment by the fact that this strange window-climbing girl was speaking to him in his own language, managed to stutter a reply,

"Well... yes. Yes, I am."

"What is you do here?"

Therein lay the problem. She did not speak it well.

"I uh... I was trying to open the gates."

"Varför?"

"What?" Fletcher said. He thought she sounded like a small puppy.

"Oh, sorry; why for?"

"Well... I believe we are trying to take back this castle."

"When jobber you for?"

Fletcher shook his head, "What?"

"I speak plainly, when jobber you for?"

Fletcher had had enough and stood upright, being careful not to make the slightest noise as he did so.

"Stay close behind me – if your intention was to escape, then stay with me."

"I understand. I shall follower you."

Fletcher shook his head as he took her hand. He could not see her face clearly in the darkness, but she had very soft and tender hands.

Fletcher crept close to the wall, trying his best to be silent, but the girl's long gown kept rustling against the short grass. Fletcher cursed at himself and turned to face the girl.

"Madame, please, stop and stay here."

"Yes, I stay." she said, "Hurry till back."

Fletcher sighed in frustration as he crept forward, hugging the walls towards the gate. He prayed that the guards would not find him. The gate was only fifty paces ahead of him, and he could see a single guard with his lamp standing on top of a staircase that led up to the ramparts, effectively blocking Fletcher's way.

Fletcher had no choice – he had to knock out or kill the guard to open the ramparts. Therein lay the problem – Fletcher had yet to kill a man at close quarters, but he knew it had to be done.

Fletcher's dagger unsheathed with a whisper as he crept up to the unsuspecting soldier. He could hear the man gibbering in Polish, probably complaining about how his life could be spent better elsewhere. His heartbeat raced, and his palms became sweaty. He was not sure how he was supposed to go about this. Perhaps it would be like sticking a knife into a deer's throat? He would attempt to stab him through his neck. Maybe he could cover his mouth with his left hand and deliver the murder stroke with his rondel. A man with no windpipe would not be able to summon the other guards. It would have to be swift and catlike.

He tried to brush the thoughts out of his mind that this man had a family, perhaps a child that he would go home to. He held his breath, not wanting the slightest sound to escape his body as his left hand extended ever so slowly over the guard's shoulder, while his right hand prepared to deliver the kill strike.

"Psst... English." whispered the girl from behind.

The Polish soldier turned around, and Fletcher, in a panic, thrust his dagger into the man's left eye, causing him to scream in pain and terror; shouts in Polish echoed from the barracks.

"You have now buggered us both, my lady." he said with an exasperated gasp.

"Sorry!" she said, still whispering.

To Fletcher's surprise, the Polish soldier was still alive. He yelled something at the Englishman in his guttural language and reached for his weapon – a long poleaxe – and swung it at him, who instinctively stepped back, causing him to tumble off the ramparts. He landed on the cold, hard, earth; which did little to cushion his fall. The Polish soldier, with the dagger still in his eye, descended the rampart's stairs to finish him off, screaming as he went.

The soldier now stood over Fletcher, about to deliver his killing blow, when suddenly he was tackled to the earth by the girl. Shocked, Fletcher stood up to see the girl stabbing away at the man using the dagger she had pulled out of his eye.

"By the grace of God, you are a violent one."

"Come! No time!" the girl said as she ran towards the gate.

Still in pain from the fall, Fletcher managed to get on his feet and ambled to the giant palisade doors. The heavy bar that locked the doors tight had to be removed before the troops could be let in. Clutching the bottom of the bar, he pushed up with all his remaining strength. It barely budged. The girl tried to help him by lifting from the other side, but even their combined strength was not enough to lift the great wooden beam.

The shouts in Polish were getting closer. The patter of feet could be heard in the distance – people were running their way.

Fletcher groaned in agony and frustration. He was likely going to die here. He thought that at least he was not going to die a virgin.

The girl had no such plans – she grabbed him by the hand and led him up the ramparts.

"Come, we jump!"

"What?!"

Before Fletcher could complain any further, the girl pushed him over the walls, and he fell screaming, falling a short distance before thankfully being caught by the downward slope of the castle's earthen defenses. The girl followed shortly afterward. Polish sergeants barked search orders behind the wall just as she jumped over.

Fletcher could hardly believe it – although he had failed his mission, he was alive, and it was thanks to this strange girl.

"Where is this house?"

Assuming she was asking about where he was supposed to go, he pointed to the tree line. Without a moment's hesitation, the woman ran off into the woods, beckoning him to follow.

Since the soldier's lamp had died with him, there was only moonlight to illuminate their path. Fletcher was glad that the Polish had chosen to search within the camp rather than look over the walls. Mustering the rest of his strength, he ran after her into the woods.

After they had run a distance to where they were comfortably out of sight of the castle's guards, they stopped to rest. Both were panting heavily, with their hands resting on their haunches.

"What is your name, milady?" Fletcher asked.

"Crista Stenbock." she said with a smile.

Chapter 26

Greve Olaf Stenbock, dressed in his armor and riding his war horse, waited with the full force of his Swedish regular army hidden in the tree line. Talbot Company hid with him, keeping his flanks and front covered with their pikemen and musketeers. The whinnying of the cavalrymen had to be kept quiet, so the combined allied cavalry force was placed far behind the main body.

The greve was growing impatient. It seemed that he had seen the English footpad sneak into the castle hours ago. Perhaps he was still trying to find a way inside, or perhaps he had fouled up somehow. The more the greve thought about it, the more worried he became. He was certain he heard shouting some time ago. Perhaps the poor boy was dead, for no red lantern lit the gates.

Just then, he saw something in the darkness: he could make out two figures, both walking slowly towards him. One was a male, walking with an awkward gait as if he were injured, and the other was definitely female – he could tell by the outline of her large, voluminous skirt. There should not have been any women out here except...

"Crista!" he yelled out, as he dismounted his horse and ran to meet her.

"Pappa!" she squealed as she ran to embrace him.

It seemed like it had been years. The two were finally reunited and shared a tearful hug. Greve Olaf Stenbock's little girl was safe, and with her life secured, his inhibitions were released.

"I'm sorry I was late coming home, my love." the greve said in their native Swedish.

"Oh, no, pappa. The guests were very rowdy, you would not have approved." Crista replied with a giggle.

"And whom do I have to thank for the safety of my daughter?" he said, switching to French.

Fletcher, unsure of what he said, stepped forward. "I believe you said, 'who', milord?"

Greve Stenbock grabbed him by the shoulders and gave him a great bear hug. His chest tightened against the greve's steel armor, making it hard for him to breathe.

"... Milord..." Fletcher managed to say between gasps, "...I thank you?"

When the greve finally allowed him to breathe, he clapped him on the back and said in French, "My boy, you may have failed your original mission, but nonetheless you did a great thing for us. By freeing my daughter from captivity, you have earned my eternal gratitude and..."

"Pappa," Crista said, tapping her father on the shoulder.

"Yes, my love?"

"While this man did manage to help me over the walls..." she stopped short. Crista was hungry for her father's acknowledgment and attention. She was always neglected at home, and her father was almost always away. She wanted to tell him something that he could be proud of. She wanted to tell him that she escaped the castle by herself, but that would be discounting Fletcher's efforts.

"Never mind, pappa."

"Silly girl," the greve said, giving her a tender kiss on her forehead. "Now where was I – yes. You, sir, have allowed us a great tactical opportunity. Now that my daughter is free, we may now begin using our artillery against that blasted palisade gate."

"I understood the word 'artillery' from that, milord."

The greve laughed heartily and slapped him on the back again, knocking the wind out of him.

"Boy, you may retire to the camp. Tomorrow, we assault the castle. But tonight, we open the good mead! Let us celebrate, for my daughter has come home to us!"

"Retire for mead, if I understood that correctly... yes milord, gladly!"

Fletcher took a slight bow and walked carefully back to Talbot Company's camp. The pain in his back had not subsided, and the greve's strangely affectionate hug may have made it worse. Still, he had little idea of what he did right, but he had correctly guessed that he had rescued the greve's daughter. He would have a little of the cheap mead from Talbot Company's stores tonight, mostly to dull the pain, for the next morning he feared that he might have to be sent out again.

The Swedes were more than grateful for Crista's heroic rescue. It would mean one less charge over the walls. As promised, the casks of good mead were unsealed and the men drank freely, with Finnish eyes watching them in mischievous anticipation all the while.

The sound of a dozen pops of mead corks was followed by the trickling of wine into tankards, canteens, and cups. The sweet honeyed golden liquid was taken together with fresh venison that the Swedish musketeers had killed that afternoon, and men gathered to tell stories around their fireplaces.

Captain Henri Andersson sat by a fire together with a few Swedish cavalry officers, calmly nursing his mug of beer. He politely refused their mead and preferred to listen to their conversation rather than take part in it.

A veteran cavalry captain named Nilsson took a gulp of mead and said, "I just want you to know, boys, that whatever happens tomorrow, you can rest assured that God will be with us. These Catholic dogs no longer represent His message, and it is our duty to cleanse the fatherland of their filth."

His statement was followed by cheers of "here, here" followed by the clinking of mugs and the downing of more mead.

Another officer by name of Hagman took a large swig of the golden brew and added, "If by tomorrow I have not killed more than a dozen men, then you have my permission to diddle my sister."

The men laughed and kept laughing for the longest time, for a joke that was not even that funny.

Henri sat silently, observing their eyes and gestures. Nilsson began staring at his hands, while Hagman began swatting at insects that were not there.

"Captain Nilsson..." whispered Hagman, "You should see the size of these little flying Catholics."

"I have no idea what you mean, sir – have spiders been living in our fingernails all this time?"

Henri, satisfied with a job well done, stood up and walked away from the fireplace. He watched as men around him yelled that the sky was about to swallow them whole, while others began flopping around on the dirt as if they were swimming. He had no idea how long the devil's trumpet poison would last, but it was certainly entertaining to watch.

Unbeknownst to Bjornsson, Gunther Jaeger was also in the Swedish camp. He had come by to borrow a sharpening stone for his sword but instead arrived to see an army of madmen. People walked around trees in circles, danced without music, and laughed at the grass. It was true insanity.

What Gunther managed to notice was that they all held drinking vessels and the whole camp stank of mead. Thinking quickly, he rushed back to the Talbot Company camp to warn the others.

The mercenary officers, meanwhile, had just sat down with the greve and his daughter in MacRae's command tent for a celebratory supper. A long table that was normally used for maps and lists was now laden with biscuits, fruit, various sausages, pickled herring, and soft bread. In the corner of the room, a large untapped cask of mead sat ready, beckoning to be drank from.

The officers actually arrived some time ago, but the food remained untouched. The two camp leaders – who shared opposing religious beliefs – could not decide how to say grace, and a simple disagreement had evolved into a bitter argument of passive aggression in French.

MacRae sat in his chair, hands folded in prayer, as he looked Greve Stenbock dead in the eye, "If his lordship would be so kind as to embrace the ancient and implanted traditions of Holy Mother Church that everyone here knows, then perhaps this food would not be growing cold."

"And if the good colonel actually remembers that he is in a country where we do not pay lip service to God but instead pray with our hearts, then maybe we can finally start eating." Greve Stenbock said between clenched teeth.

The other officers dared not speak a word, their eyes darting about at each other like embarrassed children at a family supper. Sophia slowly extended her hand, attempting to quietly reach for a moist piece of raisin pastry, but it was quickly swatted away by Don Alfonso, who gave her a scolding look.

"His lordship does not understand that more than half the people here present follow the Catholic faith. It would be highly fuckin' improper if grace were said in the local tongue which we do not understand." MacRae growled.

"And the colonel must be reminded that he is in Sweden under the banner of a Swedish noble and that his pay comes from Swedish coffers." the greve hissed.

Just then, the tent flaps were thrown open and Gunther entered, shouting in English, "Do not drink the mead!"

The whole room stared at him in awkward silence.

"I apologize for interrupting your supper, *Herr MacRae.* There has been a... development... in the Swedish camp."

The greve and Bjornsson stared anxiously at him as Crista translated what he was saying to Swedish.

"The men... they are... *es war Wahnsinn, mein Herr.* They are going mad."

Greve Stenbock stood up from his seat, "What is this about my boys going mad I hear?" he said in French.

"Apologies, *Herr Markgraf,* but I believe that your mead may be... rotten."

"That's impossible." the greve said, his eyebrows furrowing.

"I suggest you come and see for yourself."

MacRae shot Greve Stenbock a cheeky smile and said, "My stubbornness in my faith has saved us from this misfortune and ye know it."

The greve refused to acknowledge him and hurried out of his tent. MacRae rose to follow him, chuckling in satisfaction.

"Ye men may dine here while we see what all the kerfuffle is about. We have nary a need for every man to be there," said the Scot as he left with Gunther following behind him.

As the tent flap closed behind him, the remaining officers seated at the table: Bjornsson, Otto, Don Alfonso, Sophia, Warwick, and Crista, all sat and stared at each other for a while, until Don Alfonso made a deep, defiant scowl and made the sign of the cross, giving death stares to the Protestants who sat at the opposite end of the table. He then began to say grace in the Catholic manner,

"Benedic nos Domine et haec Tua dona quae de Tua largitate sumus sumpturi. Per Christum Dominum nostrum. Amen."

264

After crossing himself again, without looking away from the Swedes, he reached over the table and grabbed a loaf of bread. He nodded once and broke it.

Bjornsson, clearly offended, clasped his hands and muttered his own prayer, returning the don's stare.

Warwick slowly reached for a spoon, hoping not to be noticed, while Otto threw his hands up in apathy and began eating. The girls exchanged an awkward look of confusion.

As the three men ate in irritated silence, Crista thought it would be pleasant for them to have a go at civilized discussion,

"So..." said Crista in near-perfect French, "that's a very nice dress, miss...?"

"Fortezza, *mia signora*. Sophia Fortezza." For once, Sophia could say her real name without concealing anything. It felt somewhat liberating.

"Ah, you are Italian. *E cosí bello conoscerti!* That explains your impeccable fashion sense! I have seen many dresses of the sort adorning the women of high society in Riga."

Sophia smiled and switched to Italian herself, "You speak my language well. Where did you learn it?"

Crista's smile dropped, "I... had a good tutor. I prefer not to discuss her."

"I see..." Sophia said with genuine morose in her voice. The room was silent once more. The non-Italian speakers continued eating, oblivious to the tone of the conversation.

Don Alfonso now entered the conversation in Spanish, "So, what was it like, escaping from the tower? How did our man *leche* do it?"

265

Sophia clasped her hands under her chin and leaned in closer. "Yes, how did *freccia* do it?

"You two pronounce *Messere Fletcher's* name quite oddly." Crista said, chuckling, "But if you must know, he did nothing but catch me. I leaped out of the window myself." she finished the sentence with a proud smile.

Don Alfonso and Sophia exchanged puzzled glances.

Crista acknowledged their disbelief, "I know I may not look the part, but I am actually quite the athlete. I used to spend many hours horseback riding, and I ran foot races quite a lot when I was a child."

Sophia furrowed her brow in disbelief, "So... you chose that specific time on that specific date to jump out of your window?"

"Oh, heavens no. The window was barred for weeks. I reasoned I would never be strong enough to break the bars, but I noticed that the bars were built into a wooden frame. I was able to sneak a kitchen knife into my room one night and cut up the frame, little by little every day, until such a time that it weakened and I was able to kick away the window frame to freedom! Is that not truly amazing?"

Sophia narrowed her eyes.

Don Alfonso interjected, "You say you were a prisoner in the castle keep. How did you manage to sneak a knife into your chambers?"

"Oh, the guards posted at the castle were ordered not to harm me. After a while, they appeared as very large, living toy soldiers to me. A very strange sense of chivalry this Polish colonel has, willing to rape and murder servants and peasants but unwilling to do the same to noblewomen. If he had tried, I would have gutted him with my knife."

"How many people have you killed, exactly?" Sophia said, her eyes still narrow, slightly annoyed at Crista's exaggerated bravado.

"Until this evening, none." she stopped at the thought. "As I recall I saved *Messere Fletcher's* life. He was assaulted by a Polish guard and I had the opportunity to fend the brute off."

"*Signora,* do you take me for a fool?" Sophia said, visibly irritated.

"Why the hostility, darling? I am merely telling the truth. But in all fairness, *Messere Fletcher* did save me from what could have been a most grievous and painful injury. As I was climbing down from the tower dangling by a rope that I made of sheets and my less expensive dresses from Riga, the brave *messere* thought to catch me, but instead, I landed on him in a most comedic fashion." Crista let out a high pitched giggle.

Don Alfonso put a hand on Sophia's shoulder, urging her to calm down, "There is some gravity to *señorita Fortezza's* doubts, my lady. You do not seem like one who is prone to acts of violence."

"*Signore,* I do not believe I caught your name?"

"Don Alfonso Villanueva y Santiago, my lady."

"Ah, you are a Spaniard. *Señor Villanueva,*" she said with a smile, "when one is trapped as I was in my own home with little hope of escape, forced to watch as one's friends are butchered and raped, and given all the reasons in heaven and on earth to hate a man, then one develops a certain righteous anger."

Crista, still smiling, took the smallest bite of a grape and continued, "You know, I believe that I inherited my bravery from my father and my finesse from my mother – may her soul rest in peace. Illness took her while I was but in my cradle. From whereabouts did your parents come from, *signora Fortezza?*"

"Oh, my father was a textile merchant, *signora.* No one special."

"Ah, I see he taught you some of the finer things about clothing and fashion. Did you make that dress yourself?"

"No, I purchased it with my own money."

"Ah, excellent. Forgive me, I assumed that you commoner types would not have enough money to afford such finery. I have always felt so bad for you."

Sophia, scowling, wordlessly tapped her index finger gently on her temple, in that unique sign language that her people were famous for. She was calling Crista a fool.

Crista was stumped for the first time. She knew the Italian language but she was never taught any of its subtle hand gestures. She assumed that Sophia was being rude but kept smiling politely. She would play this verbal war game. Noticing Sophia's necklace, she remarked,

"That is an interesting looking necklace. Where did you purchase it?"

Sophia glared at the Swedish noblewoman, "I did not purchase it – I played for it in Schwedt." The mere mention of the town brought back painful memories.

"Ah, Schwedt is a lovely town. I have been there but once. Of course, it pales in comparison to Riga."

"What is so special about Riga?" Sophia cursed herself. She should have challenged her to dice to wipe the smile off her face, but instead allowed her to prattle on about this town she had never heard of.

"It is a fine place, love. Second largest city in the empire, you know. All the finest wines, silks, dyes, books and all those wonderful things can be found there. And I certainly believe that the jewelers of Riga would have been more kind to you than the German swindler who gave you that gaudy glass necklace. I myself have this necklace of pearls," she said showing her neck, "Its elegance lays in its simplicity. The glass one you have is in poor taste, darling. May I suggest buying something in gold instead?"

Sophia was seething, but trying her best to keep her composure. She was about to spit out a retort when she was interrupted by a whirl of the tent flap. Greve Stenbock, MacRae, and Gunther had returned with worried looks on their faces.

"Ladies and gentlemen," said the greve in French, "my regiment may be out of commission for some time. It appears as if the lot of them are overcome with a bout of laughing sickness. Our surgeons believe that recovery may take anywhere from overnight to three days. In the meantime, we must not assault the castle. We have agreed though, that it would be prudent to at least shell the walls to mitigate the enemy's defenses."

"How dreadful, pappa!" said Crista, wearing an expression of shock that somehow still managed to irritate Sophia, "Where are we to live while our own home is besieged? Perhaps we should stay with Aunt Rigmora in Riga?"

"Nonsense," her father scoffed, "we will simply have to wait out the sickness for a few days and deny them food and supplies."

Crista paused for a moment, her mouth agape, "Pappa, wait – do you mean to say that we shall be sharing quarters with... these..."

"Yes, we shall have to sleep and eat with the soldiers. Is this a problem, my dear?"

Sophia grinned. Perhaps miss pomp and arrogance would be put down a notch after all, she thought.

Chapter 27

Morning broke. Thomas Warwick was the last one to rouse himself from slumber. The Englishman was not severely late, but he blamed the foreign food for upsetting his humors and keeping him from rising.

"Bloody Swedes and their bloody herring – they should have some good, simple English cockscomb." He complained as he left his bed.

After he had a swig of ale for breakfast and changed into his red and white uniform, he grabbed his crutches, threw open the flaps of his tent and grimaced with frustration at what he saw.

Swedish soldiers walked, ran, and danced about the camp, chasing invisible insects, talking to inanimate objects, and screaming silently at the sky or the ground. The poison had clearly not worn off yet, but today was the day that the shelling was supposed to commence. The guns were lying unlimbered, pointing towards the enemy and ready to fire, but their crews were missing.

As he hobbled around the camp shouting in vain for the gunners, Warwick realized that it was like trying to summon a fish to heel like a dog. No one understood him, and no one was capable of understanding.

However all was not lost – Talbot Company had cannons of its own, however without gunners. The cowards who had once manned these guns had deserted the company during the battle of the bridge on the Oder River. Warwick would have to train a new crew to replace them, and he had one name that he had in mind above all others.

James Fletcher was interrupted from his curious task of collecting various flowers to "present to a certain officer" and selected for gunnery detail along with several other men from Warwick's irregular unit. They all spoke English, so giving instructions would not be as difficult as it would be if Warwick had to train a mixture of Swedes and Germans. Besides, manning the guns was a dangerous thing indeed. If Fletcher were to perish, perhaps he could attempt to console Sophia. Perhaps more would come of it.

Warwick instructed the men to position Talbot Company's guns alongside those of the Swedes to form a single combined battery. That way, there would be four cannons on an elevated place that would be able to fire as one. The issue at hand though, was that after the men had lugged the cannon up to the Swedish position and positioned themselves near the guns with six soldiers per cannon, they had yet to receive instructions on how to fire them. Warwick sought to remedy that issue. He hobbled along the line, giving his instructions as he went back and forth.

"Gentlemen, our first order of business should be to extinguish any sparks left in the gun from the previous firing. As these guns have never been fired before, there is no need to do that, but when the need arises – and it will – take yonder woolen sponge and dip it in water. We shall do this now to form a force of habit."

After a few seconds of hesitation, the one man per gun began grabbing their sponges and did as they were told, listening with great intent and focus.

"Drive the wet sponge into the breech of the gun and thrust and withdraw as if you were diddling a damsel."

Some of the younger men giggled but went to work just the same. Fletcher, who stood by the end of the gun, smiled with the slightest hint of embarrassment.

"Now that your woman is all wet and ready for you, insert your whore-stick into her. Grab one of the cartridges filled with black powder, and ram it in."

The giggles turned into low laughter and the men proceeded.

"Think of the powder as your liquid rapture. Too little will cause no pleasure at all, and too much will cause childbirth – and I know none of you boys want that! Measure powder to adjust how far your shot will fly."

The entire battery was now laughing.

"Now for the shot itself – serious business this is, boys. This is the thing that pounds your enemy harder than Captain Jaeger pounds his expensive whores!"

The gunners had begun to howl, and even Fletcher began slapping his knees. Some lunatic Swedish soldiers nearby, who understood nothing, laughed in unison as large iron balls were inserted into the tubes.

Strangely though, the Swedish rounds did not roll down and were very tough to insert. They had to be guided down with ramrods.

"Now, we poke through our little vents with our little pricks," Warwick said as he approached a Swedish cannon, "insert our priming wires and light our matches."

Fletcher along with the other cannoneers took spears with wicks on them and lit them as other men stabbed through the touch holes on top of the cannon and inserted fuses.

"And now boys, we touch our matches to our holes... and give fire."

The men did as they were instructed one by one, and the first two guns belonging to Talbot Company sent cannonballs careening towards the walls of Jarlsberg.

However, just as the lit match from the third cannon – of Swedish make – made contact with the touch hole, the gun exploded with a great roar.

The wooden gun carriage splintered into millions of pieces, sending shrapnel everywhere while the bronze tube of the gun warped and broke, forcing red-hot shards of metal to fly into everything around it.

The explosion threw Fletcher to the earth as bits of wood and metal zipped over and hit his cannon. Smoking bits of cannon littered the earth around him.

All the archer could hear was a loud tinny sound in his ears. His vision blurred, but he could make out figures of men crawling on the ground in front of him – many were bleeding. The Swedish soldiers around them were still laughing and did nothing to help. Slowly, the sun began to lose its light, and everything faded to darkness.

"Messere Freccia! Svegliati!"

Fletcher's eyes slowly opened to reveal Sophia standing over him. From the cloth ceiling, he could tell that he was inside the surgeon's tent. His head hurt and her voice had an echo to it, but otherwise, he believed that he was in good health.

Sophia stepped away as another face came into view. Calvert the archer and part-time surgeon now loomed over Fletcher, grinning from ear to ear like a child about to receive a sweet treat.

"I told you! I told you he did not die! By God's Blood at least we saved one of them."

Fletcher paused and wondered what he meant by that. Opening his mouth to speak, he managed to utter a single word,

"Warrick..."

Calvert's grin turned into a somber frown at the mention of the captain's name. He shook his head at Fletcher and remained silent. He wanted to say more, but darkness clouded his eyes once again, sending him into a deep sleep.

"Master Fletcher will be all right, my dear." Calvert said to Sophia in French, who stood over Fletcher with a look of anxiety on her face. "All he needs is his rest and he will be fit for duty in no time."

Calvert then covered Fletcher up with a blanket, hiding the bandaged cuts and wounds from the shrapnel he received. They were all minor, and most of them were from wooden splinters and very small bits of metal that were propelled by the force of the blast. Since Fletcher was standing on the right side of his gun when the explosion occurred, the gun itself took most of the damage from the explosion. Fortunately, it was still serviceable. The same could not be said for the other three guns, and neither could it be said for Thomas Warwick.

Outside the surgeon's tent, Talbot Company archers piled up the bodies of the fallen gunners and stripped them of their clothes and belongings. The dead were then covered with lime powder to help with the stench and prevent decay so that the bodies could be buried properly later.

Warwick, however, was different. The men did not remove his clothes for there was not much to salvage. He and the cannoneers of the third and fourth gun had body parts strewn all throughout the field. His once handsome face clung to his skull, but the blast had caused it to break, and now his head, separated from the rest of his body, looked like a bloody broken egg wearing a fleshy mask. Bits of his crutches were in the bodies of the other men, while his torso lay some ten paces from where he stood, split in two with his jacket torn to bits.

The explosion had been a grave misfortune, and there was to be a terrible reckoning. MacRae and Gunther had arrived on the scene of the explosion moments after they had heard it, and were now looking for signs of foul play. Cannon explosions did occur often, but most of the time it was due to the inexperience of a gun crew. Warwick had commanded artillery before, and this should not have been the case.

MacRae was trying in vain to get information from Swedish witnesses, who were still hallucinating out of their gourds that they could not tell illusion from reality. He would have had Greve

Stenbock himself interrogate his own men, but he had no patience, and the greve, by all accounts, was out hunting.

"What happened here, ye boy-buggering sack of herring shit?!" he said as he pinned a grinning Swede down on a rock. The colonel was very tempted to choke him to death and was trying his hardest to restrain himself. The Swede said nothing but made spit bubbles with his saliva, laughing as they popped. MacRae could not help himself any longer and began beating the soldier to a bloody pulp, screaming curses each time his fist landed.

Gunther, meanwhile, had gone to the Swedish munitions tent. He had gone through it and now held a powder cartridge in his hand. Many of the ammunition barrels were far away from the site of the explosion, and he wanted to be as thorough in his investigation as possible. The Swedish troops did not stop him from going through their supplies, as giddy as they were with laughter, so opening barrels that did not belong to him was an easy matter. These cartridges were much heavier than the others.

Opening one with his knife, Gunther found bits of metal such as musket balls, nails, and even caltrops embedded together with the powder. Someone had clearly been making these cartridges into bombs.

"*Voinko auttaa sinua?*" said a voice from the shadows.

Gunther turned to see the silhouette of a man in what appeared to be a Swedish uniform who was strangely not dancing, drooling, or delirious. Gunther did not know how to speak Swedish, but knew that whatever strange tongue the man was speaking was not it.

277

"Eh... *Bonjour."* Gunther said, gauging the situation carefully. He watched as the foreigner moved out of the shadows and into his field of view. He was an older man with a bushy blonde beard. In his hand, he held a strange knife-like weapon, shaped like a rectangle with a sharp tip. He eyed the cartridge in Gunther's hand.

"Monsieur," he said, switching to heavily accented French, "It seems that you have discovered something that you were not meant to discover. For this, you must die."

Without saying another word, the foreigner lunged at Gunther, raising his knife overhand.

Without drawing his weapon, Gunther blocked the blow by grabbing his opponent's wrist and twisting it, making him wince in pain and scream in surprise, dropping the knife. This was followed by a quick, snappy punch to the gut, causing him to reel back. The two now fought hand to hand.

Gunther's foreign opponent tackled him to the ground, landing blow after blow against his face. The German mercenary captain then pulled out his own blade, a short *katzbalger*, and thrust it into the side of the foreigner's rib.

In shock and pain, the foreigner yelled and gripped the side of his rib as blood came pouring out. Gunther, seeing an opportunity, then thrust his knife into his opponent's neck, killing him.

Blood from the man's neck wound splattered all over Gunther's face as he collapsed on top of him. Gunther pushed him off and got on his feet and watched as the foreigner thrashed about on the floor. He would no longer be a problem.

As a matter of habit, Gunther began looking through the dead man's things. He found a leather notebook tucked away in his belt containing accounts of food, clothing, ammunition, and war materiel. He reasoned that this must have been the Swedish quartermaster. If that were the case, he had just killed the man responsible for all the allied army's supplies. All this was important information that needed to be reported to MacRae.

The blood on his clothes and face did not need rinsing. It was proof to everyone that there was a murder involved. His jaw felt painful to the touch, and he could not be sure if all the blood on his face was that of his opponent.

Still in pain, Gunther shook his head and made his way out of the tent. The Swedish soldiers still ambled about aimlessly, but some had already collapsed due to exhaustion. Hopefully, when they woke up they would be sober. MacRae was still making his rounds outside, "interrogating" potential witnesses with his fist, shouting insults at them in a language they could not understand.

"Herr Oberst!" Gunther yelled out to him.

"What the fuck is it, Master Jaeger? Can ye not see that I am busy here?" MacRae yelled back as he held a bloody soldier by his collar.

"I believe, *mein Herr,* that I have found the cause of our mysterious exploding cannon incident."

MacRae turned to see Gunther's bloody face and clothes.

"I trust ye have dealt with the matter appropriately, Master Jaeger?"

Gunther nodded, *"Ja,* it was the Swedish quartermaster. He intentionally turned the powder cartridges into bombs."

279

"Why would a Swede want to sabotage his own fuckin' army?" MacRae said, dropping the wounded soldier he was beating.

"He was no Swede, *mein Herr*. He spoke... differently."

"A spy, perhaps? We must inform the greve upon his arrival."

Chapter 28

Sophia stood by in the surgeon's tent, watching Fletcher breathe peacefully in his sleep. While she knew that Calvert had done his best, she also worried that he might have been irreversibly injured.

"Freccia," she said in Italian, "I wish we could get to know each other more. You seem like a sweet, caring boy, but the fact that your language sounds like animal noises makes it hard for me."

The tent flaps flew open.

"Ah, come to check on the *messere* again, doctor?" Sophia said, still staring at Fletcher.

"Why, yes of course. But I am certainly no doctor." Crista said in Italian as she took her place on the other side of Fletcher's bed. "I must say, he looks quite handsome in the light. Shame about those scars."

Sophia scowled and whispered sharply in Italian, "Why the devil are you here? He needs his rest!"

"And why are you here, dear? Perhaps you fancy the boy? He does have a certain rustic charm..."

"Stay away from him." Sophia hissed. She suddenly realized she felt a tinge of jealousy. But she refused to believe that she could ever be threatened by this jezebel of a woman.

"Ah, so you admit it. You peasant types would be good for each other I'm sure." she said with a smile, "We of the nobility must not risk our reputations on such scandalous relationships; however, the temptation is still there."

Crista took her hand and placed it gently on Fletcher's shoulder. He made a small grunt.

"Precious boy." Crista whispered, "I have not had the chance to see a man of my age in so long."

Sophia was furious. She instinctively reached for her sword – which was not there. She had left her baldric with her other clothes. She would have to win this battle with words.

"You nobles always think you can get what you want, and when you cannot have it, you piss yourselves in a tantrum like small children!"

Crista's gaze met Sophia's. She was not smiling anymore, "We also do not swear as you country girls do; besides your way of life is dreadfully boring. May I remind you that if it were not for my father's contract you would be back in your village or wherever you are from, churning butter or whatever it is you do."

Sophia grit her teeth, "I am from Milan, you bitch. I was raised in a house, not a barn!"

"Hush, dear, do not wake the patient; and again with the swearing? So uncouth. You would make a terrible wife."

"And you, *signora,* would make a terrible doormat! Without your servants to do anything for you, you are useless!"

"May I remind you, *signora Fortezza,* that it was I who descended from my tower and rescued myself!"

"By falling on his back!" Sophia said in a shrill whisper, pointing to Fletcher. "Your adventure was nothing! I killed two men and watched them die!"

"Well, I killed one man with *Messere Fletcher's* dagger – while I was wearing my dress mind you, and I got not a drop of blood on it."

"Are dresses and jewelry and shoes all you care about, you harlot? I take stock in more in life!"

"Again with this unwarranted hostility." Crista said, rubbing her temples, "A peasant like you should know your place when talking to your betters. And I lied about the dress you're wearing. For a textile merchant's daughter, you do not seem to know how to dress yourself."

Sophia's face was turning red. Now she had insulted her family and her fashion sense, "I would slap you right now if it was not for him!"

Crista stared down at her, "Oh he will not wake, I am sure. Try it and see what happens."

Sophia gritted her teeth and balled her hands up into fists, preparing for an outright brawl. Before she could land the first blow, however, Don Alfonso entered the tent.

"Ah, *señoritas...* am I interrupting something?"

"YES." both chorused.

"Forgive me for prying, but..."

Crista turned and faced him, *"Señor Villanueva,* this is a private conversation. I suggest you leave."

Sophia, not even looking at him, said, "I appreciate your concern, *signore,* but I can handle this myself."

"But..."

"LEAVE." they chorused again. The don left without another word.

The two girls refused to acknowledge the fact that they just agreed on something.

Sophia pointed her finger at Crista, "Next time there will be no interruptions. If it was not for my ladylike demeanor, I would challenge you to a fucking duel."

"My dear, you have the ladylike demeanor of a common alley cat, but if you did deign to challenge me, I would have accepted."

Perturbed by her insolence, Crista left the tent, leaving Sophia alone once again with Fletcher, to whom she whispered, "If you touch her, I will cut your flesh pole off." After which she kissed his forehead.

"This is outrageous." Greve Stenbock said to MacRae as Bjornsson untied a bunch of rabbit carcasses off of a saddle bag behind him. The two had just come back from a hunt to find that only one cannon was left standing, and the explosion that had destroyed the other three had also damaged the gun carriage, making movement out of the question.

"Yes, the situation is fucked, but," said MacRae, "I have yet to stop the shelling."

Thankfully, Talbot Company gunners were firing single projectiles at the palisade gate of the castle, adjusting their elevation with each miss. MacRae's men would continue the siege as long as they had that single cannon working.

"I am thankful, colonel, that we managed to save one of the guns, but do not mistake my gratitude for complacency. What was the cause of the explosion?"

"Sabotage, sir. One of your men, some non-Swede, the quartermaster from what Captain Jaeger tells me, sabotaged your charges. He would have a lot to answer for if he weren't dead."

"You killed him? Idiot! He could have provided us with names, numbers, a motivation for this madness! Surely he cannot be working alone."

"Yes... well, sir, he attacked the good captain, who was left with no course of action but to defend himself. I am quite sure you understand the necessity for action when a fuckin' knife is coming down on you, do you not, sir?"

"Well, it makes no difference. I doubt any more ill could come of this siege. Have your men continue to concentrate fire on the gates. The sooner we get them down, the sooner we will be able to storm the castle. Lord preserve us, we may as well begin preparations for the assault now – a prolonged siege is no longer an option."

The allied camp was a mess. Dancing, giggling, and fainted Swedish soldiers were still scattered about, and the kitchen at the Swedish camp had been dry since the day before. The only sane people around seemed to be the Talbot Company mercenaries, the officers, the devious Finns and a single sutler lady.

Now, the sutler was an older Livonian woman who sold coffee grounds, sugar, and turnip bread to the soldiers. She had been pushing her little cart through the camp ever since the

Swedes had arrived. Now that nobody could buy her goods, she would retire home – to Jarlsberg.

Before the shelling had begun, no one had taken notice of the little old lady pushing a cart in and out of the city. She usually arrived in the small hours of the morning and left at sundown. When she returned, the palisade gates would open slightly for her.

Now that the Swedes were lobbing stone cannonballs at the fort, most normal people would be content to stay away from the large, noisy, whistling balls of death; but not Viktorija. Her routine was her routine, and nothing and no one would change that for her.

She descended from the hill, singing an old folk song as her rickety coffee cart traversed through the dirt trail that led away from the Swedish camp. The occasional whistle of cannonballs interrupted her tune, but she ignored them and kept singing anyway, as if she was in no danger at all.

The area between Jarlsberg and the Swedish hill was divided by a large field full of flowers – white oxeye daisies. Viktorija would often collect them and make them into ornate flower garlands that she would present to the girls at the castle. She wondered why those were no longer making them smile.

Another whistling cannonball overhead interrupted her thoughts.

She dismissed it and continued rolling through the field towards the fortress. Only a few more yards to go; even so, her old legs were still strong and they could walk for many miles if she kept at her own pace.

Suddenly, she saw the palisade gate shatter as it got hit by a cannonball. That would not be good for thieves, and the greve would be quite angry. She supposed that it was not her problem. She could hear screaming coming from within the castle. Of course, the soldiers would be upset. They would have to clean all of this up.

As she approached the gate, she greeted the sergeant of the watch, who simply yelled at her. It was strange that he used to speak Swedish and now spoke something else entirely. He even wore a different uniform. It mattered little to Viktorija.

Once she was safely inside the walls of Jarlsberg, she continued to push her little cart up to the palatial keep, where she would try to sell her goods to the young man that the greve had entrusted to keep his castle safe. A Colonel Casimir, she remembered. She did not appreciate all the people running in the streets or the yelling. That was dangerous.

She did not have to walk any further. The young man was on his beautiful white horse with that golden armor that made him look like an angel. He rode down the streets after the others who were running to the gate and crying out, but he stopped for Viktorija, because of course he would.

"Ah, *babcia*," the young man said in Latvian. He had a peculiar accent. "You know that I would be happy to buy your delicious coffee, but I am slightly occupied at the moment."

"Ah, a shame." Viktorija replied, "The dancing Swedes did not want to buy anything either."

"Dancing Swedes?" Casimir asked, intrigued. He stopped his horse and listened to what she had to say with genuine curiosity.

"Oh, you should have seen them, milord. They thought they were fishes on the land, swimming in the soil, laughing at the sky, all manner of foolishness."

Casimir rubbed his chin. "And what of their commander?"

"He seemed very upset. His men had a bad case of the giggles, wouldn't listen to him."

"I see. Thank you, *babcia.* I think some of that coffee would be good for my humors right about now."

Chapter 29

The Talbot Company gunner burst into MacRae's command tent, out of breath from having run so fast,

"Sir! We have breached the gates!"

Greve Stenbock slammed his fist on his table. "Good work, lad!"

MacRae let out a yell, voicing his frustration, "By the devil's thorny cock, if I had known we were going to assault the fuckin' place today I would have assembled the troops on the field of battle to be ready to enter the fuckin' breach! But ye! Ye sir, sit here and fuck it up!" Turning to the gunner, he said, "Get back out there, inform our officers, ride the fucking wind!"

The order of siege was wrong. Greve Stenbock's impatience and had cost the allies valuable time that the Polish defenders could use to repair any breaches in the wall or assign additional troops to defend it.

In a correctly planned assault, an army would be assembled outside a walled fortification, organized into proper regiments with every commander knowing precisely what they would do. It was not the case now.

Minutes passed before the gunner returned, completely winded, with all the Talbot Company officers. Otto Koenigsherr, Gunther Jaeger, Don Alfonso, and Sophia Fortezza entered the command tent wearing their full battle raiment and gathered around a large table littered with papers and maps. MacRae and the greve were still in the midst of their heated discussion.

"I will not have myself questioned by a mere mercenary! You will know your place, sir!" said the greve.

"And ye will acknowledge, sir, that ye are fuckin' your own assault in the arse! Many men will die for your negligence!"

The officers stood around the table in awkward silence.

"We should not argue in front of the children." MacRae said to the greve as he turned to his officers. Switching to English from his French, he said, "Men, our esteemed client has fucked us over. The castle gates are breached but we must fuckin' scramble like mice to assault the walls. Now, all of ye, hold your wheest and listen here.

"Master Jaeger. You and your men will be at the forefront of the assault, first through the gates. You will be commanding the pikes and muskets as the first regiment."

"Jawohl, mein Herr."

"Master Spaniard, you will take up the second wave of the assault with your halberdiers, if the pikes falter. Together, you and Lieutenant Bianchi will compose the second regiment."

"Tenente Sophia Fortezza, signore." Sophia said with a proud smile.

"Ah, so that be yer real name." MacRae said, switching to French, "Ye will stay behind as a reserve force. On the march, position yer men behind the first regiment."

"Capisco, signore."

"And as for ye, Master Koenigsherr..."

"The Saxon," interrupted Greve Stenbock in French, "will stay behind in the reserves. I will gather whatever remains of my cavalry. They will storm the breach when the infantry breaks the dam of Polish defenders. I do not trust in the constitution of his men after Breitenfeld."

MacRae stared at the greve for a long while. "As ye say, sir."

Otto reacted with a small sigh as the greve continued.

"The Swedish regular infantry will sweep away any stragglers after my Finnish cavalry charge through. When the battle is over, the Swedish colors will be raised over the top of the castle keep by Captain Bjornsson or myself. This is a matter of national pride. You understand, of course, colonel."

MacRae, shaking his head in annoyance, turned back to his officers and said, "Assemble yer men. This battle shall be befucked. We will lose many today, but I want to see nary a one of ye officers in the lists of the dead."

The meeting ended with the officers running out of the command tent in a panic. Men ran laps around the camp, barking orders in different languages to form ranks as some officers scrambled for their horses. Pikemen stopped playing dice, halberdiers left their guard posts, swordsmen woke up from their naps, and cavalrymen mounted up.

MacRae himself stood at the highest point of the camp on horseback, calling the deceased Warwick's irregulars to action in English, "My Scottish brethren, I grieve for the loss of your commander, Captain Thomas Warwick. A good man the fucker was, and a finer soldier. I now bid ye grant me the honor that he had and lead ye into battle! Ye are strangers to order, discipline, and the march, but that is why I keep ye! Wild savages ye are like the painted Celts of old! Yer battle cries make the enemy lay a shite in his breeches as a wretched stinking babe! Ye bring your fire to this, our final battle, and afterward, we can booze and fuck till our debaucheries kill us!"

The irregulars that heard this whooped and hollered, cheering MacRae's name. A Scottish fellow began to play a war tune on his bagpipe, and he was joined in by a drummer, who beat on his drums with the fervor of a man ready for the fields of war. An older Scottish mercenary, with a long beard and wrinkles covering his corpse-like face and hands, began to sing a tune familiar to the entire company:

Down in the devil's garden

There lies a wretched tree

That's watered by the blood

Spilled by the Talbot Company

The tree is always fruitful

The devil laughs with glee

His demons do not work

As hard as Talbot Company

Our colonel marches onward

From Spain to Germany

Our only home is on

The road with Talbot Company

It was with this tune that the irregulars carried as they marched out of camp to join the formations of pikes, muskets, and swords that were already assembling at the base of the hill.

As the music played on, the regulars started to sing along, while Gunther and Otto saluted with their weapons to the tune of Talbot Company's anthem. Sergeants barked their orders at the men as they counted heads and made sure that their men were spaced out properly.

As the irregulars took their place behind Gunther's first regiment, the thundering of Finnish cavalry arrived from the left of Talbot Company's formation, with Captain Henri Andersson leading it. The armored Finnish Hakkapeliitta formed a neat wedge and stood silently in formation.

Following the Finnish cavalry, a hundred Swedish pikemen and musketeers, surprisingly devoid of drool or laughter, also formed up, led by Captain Sven Bjornsson. They were the only sane soldiers at the camp that could be found, and were understrength, but they would have to suffice. Its standard-bearers carried the Swedish national colors and the black he-goat banner of the Stenbock family.

Greve Stenbock descended from the hill last and galloped in front of the men, drawing his sword as he called out the names of his regiments,

"Åbo och Björneborgs läns kavalleriregemente!"

The Finnish cavalry trumpeter blew a single prolonged note in response.

"Jarlsbergs läns regemente!"

The Swedish infantry gave a loud cheer, with their drummer and trumpeter playing proudly along.

Not to be outdone, MacRae called out for his own regiments in a pre-battle display of boastfulness. The captains had long ago come up with their personal slogans.

"Company of Pike and Shot, First Regiment of Foot, Vanguard!"

"Für die Feuer des Krieges!" Gunther's regiment responded as they stomped their feet.

"Company of Halberds, Second Regiment of Foot, of Christ our Savior!"

Don Alfonso cried out, *"¡Adelante!"*

His men responded with, "¡Para Dios y la Gloria!"

"Company of Swords, Second Regiment of Foot, Cruel Fate!"

"Ferreo cuore!" said Sophia alone.

Her men responded with, "Mai ritrattare mai arrendersi!"

"Troop of Horse, First Regiment of Horse, Black Riders!"

The trumpeter blew a trumpet followed by Otto's men crying, *"Für Geld und Bier!"*

MacRae looked proudly over the rows of men and horses, with their glistening armor, bristling polearms, and stern expressions. He was not so sure about the Swedes, some of whom still wobbled in their formation and all of whom had pupils the size of grapes, but he trusted that he could send his men into the mouth of hell itself and they would do it. They had gone through so much already, and this would be the final push before they would all go home. As agreed, Talbot Company would lead the charge.

MacRae gazed at the walls of Jarlsberg ahead. The oxeye daisies swayed slightly in the breeze, undisturbed for now. In moments they would be trampled by thousands of boots and blood would stain their white petals. Talbot Company's leader took a deep breath and exhaled slowly. Then in a loud, thundering voice, he went,

"Talbot Company! Forward – MARCH!"

Chapter 30

Talbot Company Center

Vanguard, 1ˢᵗ Regiment of Foot

"Company!" Yelled Gunther from horseback, "Forward, MARCH!"

The company drummers began rolling their drums to the tempo of a quick march as the musketeers and pikemen advanced. The faces of the men betrayed their fear, but some looked towards Jarlsberg with anticipation, and some others even grinned with the excitement that only battle could bring.

The musketeers marched with their weapons posted on their shoulders, while the pikemen behind them formed a porcupine of pikes, all raised up in the air for now; later they would come down upon the enemy's densely packed infantry and light cavalry. Their footsteps thundered as they inched closer and closer, Gunther looked through his spyglass and saw something at Jarlsberg – the gate was being opened.

Polish troops began leaking out of the castle like pus from a wound. The Polish commander rode out in front of them in his gold armor. Colonel Jan Casimir had chosen to sally forth with his Polish, Lithuanian, and Tatar allies behind him. The company's orders still stood. They would meet the enemy on the field of battle. It was better that way, the castle did not need to suffer any longer. It would all end here.

Casimir's Brigade Center
Levy Infantry, Lithuanian Contingent

Colonel Jan Casimir, upon hearing about how the Swedish defenders were unfit to fight, made the decision to form ranks and charge the enemy camp. With him were his Polish and Lithuanian infantry, armed with pikes and muskets, which formed his reserves and center, and Tatar cavalry, which formed his right flank, who had left the fortress from another exit to hide from the enemy. The hussars formed his heavy cavalry and would be kept within the walls, to be released in an emergency. Casimir was a little more than surprised to see the enemy army marching to meet him, and had formed no plans for engaging in battle in an open field.

The infantrymen, Lithuanian conscripts in their various mishmash of uniforms, looked at the enemy with puzzlement and fear. There was not supposed to be an opposing force this large. They looked upon their commander in his golden armor for courage – Colonel Casimir was truly the epitome of the chivalrous knight, leading from the front and courageous in the face of the enemy. He would not give an order that he himself would not follow.

"Regiment, HALT!"

The men's feet stomped the earth as their march came to a complete stop. The eyes of the Lithuanians stared unblinkingly into their enemy, but some could not help but tremble.

Casimir spurred his horse and galloped behind his infantry, as to not get caught in their line of fire. The foremost officer in the ranks, commanding an understrength company of pike and shot, was a Lithuanian captain by the name of Salius. His experience included many siege battles where he could sit back and watch the action from a distance, but had never before had to fight a pitched battle such as this one. He now stood quaking in his boots.

"Captain, prepare the men to fire!" Casimir barked.

Salius stood there with his lips quivering, trying to remember the words for the command that fear had stolen from his memory.

"Captain! I said prepare the men to fire!"

"C-Company!" Salius stuttered, "Order ARMS!"

Talbot Company Center
Vanguard, 1ˢᵗ Regiment of Foot

Gunther saw the enemy army before him – a few hundred musketeers and pikemen. His men only slightly outnumbered them. He could see the enemy soldiers ramming their scouring sticks in a panic, desperately trying to get off a shot before his men could do the same. Looking towards the faces of his men, he saw grim determination and the acceptance of death.

"Company, HALT!"

The clacking sound of wooden pikes and steel armor never got old to Gunther. They were the prelude to the violence that could never be found elsewhere in the natural world – only men were capable of such destruction.

"Order ARMS!"

At this command, the men struck the ground with the butts of their pikes and muskets.

"Musketeers, load!"

At this command, the musketeers began the arduous and time-consuming practice of loading their muskets. Their musket pans would have to be primed, their charges would have to be handled, their scouring sticks would have to be rammed down into the musket barrels, and their burning matches would have to be blown and set in the proper position. This laborious process took about as much time as it took to wash one's hands.

A series of loud pops was followed by the thud of several dozen Talbot Company bodies hitting the earth. Blood seeped through the soil as the men gurgled their last words. Those few that wore steel breastplates now had bits of both lead and steel in their bodies. The enemy had finished firing first, and the company had received its first casualties of the battle. The men, however, ignored the bodies of their dead comrades and loaded even faster so they would not soon join them.

"Musketeers, present ARMS!"

At this command, the musketeers raised their weapons to their shoulders and aimed down their sights to see that the enemy was now the one who was struggling to reload. Each musketeer chose his target.

"Give FIRE!"

Dozens of bangs rang out from the Talbot Company lines. The smoke obscured everyone's vision for a while, and when it cleared, dozens of enemy troops lay dead upon the field. The smell of gunpowder was intoxicating. A small sense of victory came over the men, but they knew the battle was far from over.

Gunther would not order his men to reload a second time. The battle had to be decided with a rout. Fear would have to be thrust into the heart of the enemy like the tip of a spear.

"Musketeers, withdraw by ranks!"

At this command, the musketeers gladly scrambled to the sides of the formation. The pikemen were now facing the enemy. Many swallowed in fear and all were breathing heavily. It was said that many pikemen would prefer to be anything else, as their particular troop type was little more than a bullet sponge, but Gunther knew this to be completely false. He came from the old school of warfare, where cold steel reigned supreme.

"Pikemen!"

An audible *"merde"* could be heard from one of the men.

"...advance your pikes!"

The pikemen lifted their pikes from the ground and brought them to their sides, preparing to march.

With another sporadic burst of loud pops, a second volley of enemy musket fire ripped through the ranks of pikemen. The impact of the rounds made loud clunks as they punched through the pikemen's armor. Some of the men thought it was madness, sending a formation of spear-wielding infantry against modern firearms, but Gunther believed in the power of the Greek phalanx and its long spears that conquered the known world. He was about to show it today.

"Company! Forward MARCH!"

Friedrich of Vienna no. III, who had once been a beggar in the streets of the Austrian capital, now stood amongst the crowd of pikemen. Once owning nothing but the rags on his back, he was now attired in his own corselet, helmet, and white sash of the Talbot Company. He marched along in well-practiced cadence to the beat of his company's drum, and he had gotten very familiar with the back of the head of the man in front of him. He was kept blissfully unaware that they were to go into a melee with the enemy infantry.

"Hey boys," he yelled out to no one in particular as they marched, "Who do we battle?"

"You mean you do not know?" answered the man on his left.

"I know as much as everyone else, I think."

"Idiot! We fight the Catholics today!"

"Do we? Thank you, good sir. May I know your name?"

"My name is Christoffer." the soldier said, refusing to look at Friedrich.

"Pleasure to meet you, sir. My name is Friedrich."

"It will matter little soon. One or both of us will be dead."

"I do not understand. The shooting has stopped. Are we not simply chasing the enemy?"

Gunther's command interrupted their conversation,

"Pikemen, charge your pikes!"

With this, the pikemen brought their weapons forward, so that their spear tips formed a bristling wall pointed towards the enemy.

The pikemen in the front row sweat in torrents as they watched the enemy musketeers withdraw, exposing the Lithuanian pikemen, who now mirrored them. Now pikes were going to clash on pikes. The men in the foremost ranks gritted their teeth and prepared for the initial clash of men and metal.

"What is happening?" Friedrich said, suddenly panicking, "Are we to actually fight?"

"Yes, you idiot!" Christoffer said, irritated by the sweat forming under his helmet and the fear of what was to come.

The formation came to a violent halt as wooden shafts, steel tips, armor, and flesh came crashing into each other from both sides. Those with enough elbow room in the melee made attempts to thrust at the enemy, while others pushed against the people in front of them to advance. Eyes, noses, and ears were lacerated by sharp spear tips. Talbot Company pikes were thrust easily into the unarmored bosoms of their Lithuanian counterparts. Thankfully, the enemy pikes could do little against the protected torsos and heads of the company's men. The battle was quickly going one way.

"Are we winning?" asked Friedrich, as he wiggled his pike at the enemy like a fire poker.

"I think so, my man, I think so!" replied Christoffer while he did the same. He did not see as many Talbot Company dead, and he could tell that the wide-eyed, screaming Lithuanian infantry were on the verge of routing.

Casimir's Brigade Reserves
Regular Infantry, Polish Contingent

Colonel Casimir rode at full gallop towards his reserve force of pikemen, waving his mace about his head and yelling a great war cry.

"Advance, you dogs! The heretics are upon us, and your brothers stand over there in the field overwhelmed!"

The captain of the reserve company, a large, heavyset Polish man named Korneliusz, raised his spontoon to heaven and cried,

"Raise the standard of the Blessed Virgin! Company! Forward, MARCH!"

The standard bearer, a youth of no more than fourteen years of age, carried aloft a large banner bearing a hand-made likeness of the Black Madonna of Czestochowa, and the troops crossed themselves before marching forward. With grim faces all around, they were resigned to fight or die.

Their comrades in arms lay a few yards away from them, locked in a deadly pushing contest with the enemy's own pikemen. The Polish soldiers could hear the screaming, but many could only see the blue coats and four-cornered hats of the men in front of them. The soldiers in front bore witness to the slaughter of their Lithuanian allies being skewered alive by enemy pikes as they were pushed from behind by the other men in the ranks.

Korneliusz could not bear to see his comrades suffer any longer.

"Double time, MARCH!"

With this, the Polish infantry quickened their steps, first to a slow jog, then to a run. They were charging the enemy formation, while the Black Madonna fluttered in the wind, leading the way.

The clash was spectacular. The Talbot Company pikemen were caught by surprise when a mass of quivering pikes rushed in from their right flank, killing several in the initial shock of the charge. Those of them that were already engaged on the right were trapped between their enemies to the front and their enemies to the side in a tangled forest of wood and metal.

Korneliusz himself joined the fray, drawing his sword to strike at the foreigners, finding gaps in their steel armor. He struck at mercenaries who could not fight back as they held their pikes keeping his own men at bay.

From out of the corner of his eye, Korneliusz saw someone charging the entanglement of pikes wielding a giant German zweihander – it looked like the enemy commander. The deep, chilling sound of his battle cry drew closer and closer until the five foot beast of a zweihander was on top of him. Withdrawing his sword to parry the blow, he found that he lacked the strength to do so, and the great German sword found itself embedded in his shoulder, bright red blood splattering the armor of his enemies and the clothes and faces of the men behind him.

Talbot Company Right
Of Christ our Savior, 2nd Regiment of Foot

Don Alfonso had chosen to fight dismounted and had given the order for his company of halberdiers to move forward to assist Gunther's pikemen, who were being flanked. He now spoke to them as they marched,

"The Lord will march out like a champion; like a warrior, he will stir up his zeal; with a shout, he will raise the battle cry and will triumph over his enemies. We go now into battle against these wicked heretics, and we show them that God has not favored them, for we are destined to win here this day! And as Gideon routed the army of the Midianites, we shall route them here! A sword for the Lord!"

"A sword for the Lord!" his men chorused.

"Halberdiers, charge your halberds!"

With a great shout, the halberdiers pointed their weapons towards the enemy as they slowly marched forwards.

Don Alfonso's heart beat rapidly in his chest. This was just another battle, he thought to himself. He had been through all of this before. The men would clash with the enemy pikemen, break their push, and scatter them to the plains. Some of them would die, but God would protect them.

Would God have approved of his actions at Zalesie though? He still felt the burning guilt that came from burning dozens of innocents, just as Herod slaughtered the babies of Israel. But not this time – this time he would be redeemed by the blood of heretics. Surely this was enough compensation.

As the company approached, the enemy began to come into clear view. The dark blue coats of the enemy contrasted with the shining plate armor of Talbot Company's pikemen, but Don Alfonso noticed something else.

"Santa Maria Virgen…" he gasped.

The forlorn image of the Black Madonna had her sorrowful eyes fixed on him. His legs suddenly refused to move forward.

"Company halt."

The sergeant immediately to his left could not believe his ears.

"Sir, did you say halt?"

"Si. Halto."

"Company HALT!" the sergeant yelled. The men came to a complete stop, their halberds still pointed towards the enemy.

There was an awkward, uncomfortable silence amongst the men as the battle raged on ahead of them. The don stared at the image of the Virgin, unblinking. It seemed to tell him that he would be committing a great unforgivable sin if he shed more Catholic blood on the field. The Blessed Mother wanted no sacrifice of blood like a heathen god. Her virtues were love and peace, and here he was, wanting to soil his blade with the blood of her children. No more.

"Company, order arms!" he said, commanding his men to withdraw their weapons and carry them at ease. He whispered an apology to the Virgin as he dropped his spontoon on the ground and fell to his knees. This was not cowardice – no, this was divine intervention.

Talbot Company Reserves
Cruel Fate, 2nd Regiment of Foot

Sophia did not need a spyglass to see that her mentor's company of halberdiers had halted just a short distance away from the mess that was the push of pikes. She stared at them standing there, motionless, while Gunther's boys fought tooth and nail against the enemy.

The enemy's push had to be broken.

"Compagnia!" she said at the top of her lungs.

The men gave each other looks. They had thought that their small company of a handful of swordsmen would get to avoid fighting completely. The halberdiers were more than enough to break an engagement of pikes.

"Attenti!"

One of Sophia's sergeants that stood nearby her approached her and said to her in her native Italian,

"Lieutenant, what are you doing? We have not been given the order to advance from the colonel!"

"I know." she said as she unsheathed her rapier. Raising it up in the air, she bellowed, "Forward MARCH!"

The company drummer winced, anticipating a swift and painful defeat, and reluctantly played the beat for the march as the company moved forward. Every sword but Sophia's was still in its sheath.

William MacRae watched from a hilltop, where he and his irregular reserves lay in wait, and silently applauded Sophia for her initiative.

"The lass shows promise. She would warrant a commendation if she can pull her scrawny hide from this battle unscathed."

Meanwhile, marching in the field of flowers below, Sophia breathed heavily. While she had certainly killed more men than Fletcher, she had never once faced an opponent in a fair fight. She also realized that she was not suitably equipped for battle. While she did have her old steel corselet and kidney belt on, she had little else in the way of armor. Even her men wore helmets and steel gauntlets. All of them carried their small steel bucklers.

The thought crossed her mind of simply taking equipment from one of her men since she was technically their leader, but she quickly banished the idea, not wanting to further alienate her swordsmen.

The pike battle raged on ahead of them. The clatter of wood and metal resounded throughout the field. Battle cries and screams of men in agony were drowned out by the clash of steel on steel. Now even the musketeers had drawn swords, battling desperately against their enemies while trying not to get stabbed by the swords and pikes of the enemy that seemed to poke out from every direction.

As Sophia marched along to the beat of her drummer, she remembered the way she danced with Fletcher. That was so long ago to her – she would have to remember to fight as she danced, with speed, grace, and ferocity.

"Company will prepare swords!" she yelled.

A barely audible murmur of curse words in various languages resounded from her formation as the men hesitantly drew their weapons. They would have to fight now – there was no way around it.

Sophia took three heavy breaths, and for the first time in a long time crossed herself in prayer. *O Lord, let me not make a fool of myself.*

"Double time, MARCH!"

Hearing this, the swordsmen slowly gathered up speed, then one after the other began to raise their swords and yell their wordless war cries as they charged the flank of the Polish regular infantry. A Polish soldier turned his head to see the charging swordsmen just in time to be met by a buckler to his face.

Amidst the cries of "forward!" and "lay on!" there were whimpers of fear and cries of pain, wailing and crying; all emotions that the human mind could muster save the joy of peace were thrown into the fray with pike and sword.

Sophia stabbed without any thought towards technique or direction at the crowded mass of Polish soldiers. Her blade drew blood as it pierced below the ribs of one of the unfortunate soldiers who was too busy holding off a pikeman in the tangled mass of men to fight back. This was no duel, this was not even a brawl. It was a pushing contest with bladed weapons.

Chapter 31

Imran Bey's Force

Southeast of Jarlsberg, the soft forest breeze carried the voices of foreigners through the trees. Horses snorted as they walked through the dense woods, carrying men covered from head to foot in chainmail armor, wielding lances, maces, and composite bows. Their shields, made of banded iron, bore the symbol of the star and crescent. The riders were Imran Bey's elite sipahi cavalry, and the bey himself rode at the front of the column. His adjutant, Atahan, rode close behind him together with his standard bearer who bore aloft the Ottoman tug, a staff adorned with the crescent of Islam and black horse hairs that symbolized that the troop was on a warpath.

It did not take long to hear the sounds of battle through the forest. The Ottoman commander, unaware that there was to be any fighting before he could claim his prize, brought his men to the edge of the woods that led into the open fields, ordering his men to remain hidden behind the trees. From this vantage point, the sipahis could witness how the battle fared in the distance.

"Foul circumstances have befallen us today, my lord." Atahan said as he looked on at the Europeans ripping each other to bits.

"Perhaps, or perhaps Allah *Subhanahu wa-ta'ala* has placed a fruit in our hands. See how the Christians have committed nearly their men to the fight? If the Polack is among them then our journey has been in vain. But perhaps we may yet gain some profit from this endeavor."

Imran Bey motioned with his curved sword to the top of a hill some distance away from Jarlsberg. MacRae and his irregulars together with the Swedes under Greve Stenbock stood in reserve.

"You see, there is a very small force up there on the hill. Behind them, doubtless, lies their camp. Within it lie spoils of war, treasure, captives... perhaps we can capture their commander and ransom him instead of the Polack. But we must bide our time, Atahan, for indeed Allah is with the patient."

The rumble of hooves in the distance forecast the shift in the tides of the battle. The Tatars had finally come out of their hiding place and were riding at full gallop towards the massive orgy of clashing steel and dying men that resulted from the push of pike.

"Ah, you see. There are the fighters that we sold to him."

Casimir's Brigade Right
Tatar Mercenary Cavalry

"Warriors, strike hard and quickly!" said the captain of the Tatar cavalry, "We must not get caught in the melee!"

The small but agile step horses of the Tatars swept in from the woods to the surprise of Talbot Company, who had thought that they were finally winning the battle. Gunther's pikemen, struggling in a bad war with the opposing Polish pikes, was preoccupied with their struggle and could not form up ranks to protect against cavalry with their pikes.

As the galloping horde came upon the already-engaged mercenary formations, the Tatars slashed at them with their sabers and knotted whips. The horsemen were careful not to get too close to the tightly packed melee as to not be dragged into the fight, but instead were content to attack those soldiers who stood at the edges of the fight.

Swedish Reserves
Åbo and Björneborg County Cavalry

"Captain Andersson," beckoned Greve Stenbock, "charge down the enemy cavalry."

The captain, barely containing a low chuckle, responded in the affirmative and summoned his entire Finnish cavalry force.

"Men of *Suomi*, hear me!" he said in his native Finnish, "Today we taste our freedom! We ride away from this field while the Swedes are defeated by their own pride and cowardice!"

A resounding cheer echoed after him, and with that, the Finnish cavalry charged down the hill and veered into the forest beyond, completely avoiding the battle.

Greve Stenbock looked upon the sight in disbelief.

Bjornsson furrowed his brow and exclaimed,

"My lord, I believe Captain Andersson has quit the field."

"Who by the name of Adam's sacred fuck gave that order?" said Colonel MacRae, peering out to the woods with his spyglass.

"Pray tell, what are ye to do now that yer precious light cavalry has deserted ye, sir?" MacRae said to the greve, giving an acknowledging smile to Otto, who rubbed his hands in glee.

"I... I..." the greve stuttered, suffering from a lapse in tactical judgment, "Send in our infantry."

Otto's face dropped.

Astonished himself, MacRae collapsed his spyglass with a forceful clap and stepped within a hair's length of his client's face, staring him down with the brim of his hat touching Stenbock's forehead.

"Sir, must I fuck ye in the eye for ye to see? Yer infantry be half mad! They shall likely piss themselves and retreat from the threats of a fuckin' daisy before engaging with the enemy! While here with Captain Koenigsherr ye have capable, brave Protestant riders, armed with musket and sword, and fitted with full plate! The choice is a fool's dilemma!"

Greve Stenbock returned MacRae's one-eyed glare with his own, staring up at the man that was a few inches taller than he. With a great inhalation as a warning, he bellowed out the command, launching flecks of spittle in MacRae's face,

"AVDELNING! Framåt MARSCH!" and bid his pikemen, with Bjornsson in command, to march towards the enemy.

MacRae grit his teeth and stepped away, exerting great effort in restraining himself from striking the greve; instead throwing his hat on the ground in contempt and frustration. He then yelled in English,

"May Lucifer himself bugger yer arse with his horns so that the wounds will form the shape of my banner for ye to remember this day as the day ye fucked yer campaign!"

Greve Stenbock said nothing in reply, content to watch the mercenary commander throw a tantrum.

Swedish Reserves
Company of Pikes, Jarlsberg County Infantry

Captain Bjornsson kept his military bearing – eyes straight ahead, steps in rhythm to the beat of the drum, and the blade of his sword resting on his shoulder in a stiff but elegant manner. However, the men concerned him.

All of the participating Jarlsberg Infantry Regiment's pikemen were the "survivors" of poisoned mead. While some marched towards the push of pikes, others wobbled, and others still shimmied to the fight. All of them had pupils as large as small coins.

Bjornsson, fearing for his life, began to pray out loud,

"Heavenly Father, I beg you to spare the lives of we who are your faithful sons, for we fight for your just cause and under your holy cross. May we come forth from this battle with our lives and with praise on our lips for you, Amen."

Many of the men responded with an "Amen" in kind, but some could only manage to let out "Ebbe" or "Blblff."

Bjornsson shook his head slowly and looked to the violent melee that lay ahead of him. He could see the bodies lying on the ground that had been run through with pikes and slashed with swords, as well as the Tatars that circled like vultures about the fray, shooting at random with their arrows and darting in and out to make slashes with their sabers.

"Avdelning, skyldra GEVÄR!" Bjornsson said as he braced for the worst.

At this command, the pikemen attempted to bring their weapons forward to present them to the enemy in a defensive wall of pikes, but the effects of the devil's trumpet were still inhibiting their motor skills, and the spear wall they formed was akin to an awkward-looking fence.

The Tatars took notice of this and began shooting arrows at the helpless pikemen as they ambled towards the fight.

Men whimpered and yelled in shock as arrows embedded themselves in their armor, while others were hit in their unprotected arms, faces, and buttocks. In their disarray, some of the uninjured men tripped over the fallen, causing their pikes to impale other members of their company.

Bjornsson hung his head in shame but continued to march onward. If these were the men he was given, then he would do the best he could. He would most likely die in the attempt, but he had to accept the fact that fate was cruel to him.

As first few Tatar cavalrymen charged upon his pikemen to break them, he drew his sword and praised king and country before the horses ran into him and his men.

Imran Bey's Force

The bey watched the battle with the patience of a vulture, waiting for more to die so he and his men could claim the spoils. He had recently seen a rather ungainly detachment of Christian troops descend the hill and join in the battle against the Polish.

They were not doing very well against the Tatar cavalry and were getting torn to bits slowly, as if the Tatars were toying with them.

As Imran Bey looked back to the hillside where the pikemen had descended from, he noticed that there was but a single armed force standing atop the hill.

The soldiers comprising this "mystery unit" were neither regular infantry nor logistical personnel. From his distance, he could tell that this group only had white sashes in terms of uniformity, and all of them dressed differently. They seemed to be nothing more than armed peasants.

"Atahan," Imran Bey whispered to his adjutant who, as always, hovered nearby, "what would our casualties be if we attempted to take yonder hill?"

"Very slight, milord; our armored horsemen and lancers will be more than sufficient for simple farm folk with pitchforks."

"It is done then." replied the Bey, "We shall attack the hill on my command and crush this Christian dog. We shall fight for the winning side here, and later, we shall see what other business opportunities Allah will give us."

Silently putting his spyglass away, he motioned to his men to ride very slowly out of the clearing. He then drew his sacred sword – a steel curved scimitar with a beautiful ivory handle and gold inlay, the weapon of a businessman, not a warrior – and raising it above his head, bid his men march forward towards the hill.

The armored horses stepped out of the tree line, grunting and neighing as they made their way into the clearing beyond them. Their walks became trots, and then trots became thundering gallops, as Imran Bey pointed his sword towards the

316

hill and ordered a charge, bellowing the universal battle cry of
the Prophet,

"Allahu akhbar!"

Talbot Company Command

Peering down into the plains below the hill, MacRae caught
sight of a large group of horsemen that had seemingly appeared
out of nowhere. They were heavily armored, but he was expecting
Polish hussars, not whatever these men were. MacRae's eye
widened as he realized that they were heading for the hill on
which he stood.

"Master Koenigsherr!" he yelled, "We are about to be charged
by enemy cavalry! Form up and intercept the bastards!"

Otto acknowledged the command with a wide grin and
summoned his horsemen, galloping down the hill to engage the
enemy.

"What are you doing?" asked Greve Stenbock in
consternation.

"I be saving yer army from the carrion crows!"

"The Saxons will simply melt away!"

"I trust Master Koenigsherr's ability to lead, Master
Stenbock. I know that he shall not fail us today, and when yer
pikemen lie dead and rotting on the field, know that my cavalry
would have saved ye from your disgrace!"

Talbot Company Reserves
Black Riders, 1st Regiment of Horse

"Make your peace with God, boys," Otto Koenigsherr said as he drew his two pistols from his saddlebag, "We may be meeting Him soon!"

The other riders, all armored from head to toe in steel plate, followed Otto's lead and readied their firearms. Spreading out in a loose formation as to not shoot at each other, they formed a wedge as they charged the Ottoman cavalry, with Otto at its spearhead.

The clacking of armor and the thundering of galloping horses was too loud for verbal commands, so Otto would indicate the command to fire by shooting his pistols first.

As the Muslims rode closer, he could make out their armored riders, covered with chainmail and lamellar, and the shields which they carried that would do them no good against modern firearms. As they came even closer, he could see their expressions – none of them bore a hint of fear, all of them looked confident of victory. He would change that.

Otto blew on his burning match cord to stoke its fire, and then aimed at the mass of enemy cavalry. With a pull of his finger, the match lit his priming pan and launched a steel projectile the size of a walnut into the upper lip of an unfortunate Turk. The man fell out of his saddle and was trampled by the horses behind him.

Otto's shot was followed by the sound of dozens of others in a glorious thundering hail of musket fire. Bullets zipped through

318

the ranks of the Turkish attackers as several of their number fell dead.

The enemy was within throwing range now. Otto fired his second pistol and immediately holstered both firearms, drawing his sword. He had always loved the rush of the clash of cavalry. It reminded him of the days of old when knights would joust at tournaments to win the hand of a fair lady, but that was a far cry from the reality of war.

Otto closed the visor of his helmet and held his breath as he braced for the charge. Through the slits of his visor, the world beyond seemed like it was barred by a cage, protecting them from him – or him from them. He imagined that this was what the crusaders must have felt like.

He locked his eyes on an approaching enemy horseman. A chainmail veil covered his face, and his armor glinted in the sun. He could see nothing but his eyes that stared back at him with hate. Otto watched as his enemy raised his sword.

The clash of horses was quick and violent. Men were thrown from their saddles in an instant, animals whinnied and screeched as their necks and heads were cut by the blades of the riders, while humans swung their swords about or were trampled underfoot by hundreds of powerful hooves.

Otto's sword clashed with the scimitar of his Turkish opponent, and both galloped on forward, losing one another in the mayhem of the battle. Otto wheeled around to give chase but was met by another enemy, who struck him with his shield. His armor protected him well, and he turned to face this new threat, only to hear the sound of metal-on-metal again as he felt someone strike him from behind.

Before he knew it, someone had struck his mount in the neck, causing the animal to buckle and fall as blood gushed out of its wound. Otto fell with it, his left leg crushed beneath the weight of a two thousand pound animal, preventing him from movement.

Looking up through the bars of his visor, he could see the Muslims and their mounts that looked down on him. One of them produced a spear and began to stab at him with it as he lay on the grass. He swung his sword about to parry it, but could not deflect all the blows.

Otto suddenly realized something – he could not save himself. He was surrounded, with his men otherwise engaged, and he could not run away or fight effectively. This was when he would have to make peace with God.

"Heavenly Father," he said, his voice muffled through his helmet, "I give myself wholly unto you. This day I shall be with you in..."

His prayer was cut short as a Turkish war horse stomped down on his head with enough force to dent the helmet and crush his skull.

Talbot Company Command

From his position on the hill, MacRae looked down at his cavalry troop through the lens of his spyglass and saw men being thrown from their horses and beaten to death. A Turkish lancer chased after a dismounted Talbot Company rider as he tried to run away, clutching his wounded arm; another unfortunate rider was speared through his open helmet as he fired into his assailant; a little distance away, a man knelt, cradling the head of his horse as it died.

"Well, we be harder fucked than a London whore's rotten quim." MacRae said as he collapsed his spyglass.

The greve, astounded by MacRae's apparent resignation, clenched his hands into fists and screamed at MacRae,

"Will you let your host fall like this, colonel? Attack them!"

"With what?!" MacRae barked in reply, "Before me be over a hundred skilled riders who slay my cavalry, and behind me be brave British boys, but too few in number, sir, and lacking the necessary arms. We shall not make our stand here where they will surely tear us apart like dogs."

MacRae turned to face his irregulars, and with a heavy heart yelled the command,

"Sound retreat from action!"

Shocked and angry looks came over the faces of MacRae's irregulars, who thought that they would be fighting and dying on the field today. Instead, they listened to the mournful tune of the horn blower as he announced the withdrawal from battle.

Chapter 32

Talbot Company Right

Of Christ our Savior, 2nd Regiment of Foot

The halberdiers still stood there, with their weapons rested on the ground, watching the battle in the distance. They knew they should have acted, but they were thankful that they did not have to die needlessly like the companies before them. Many who wanted to be cavalrymen before now saw the devastation in the ranks of the cavalry and praised God that they were but lowly halberdiers.

The sound of the horn caused all Don Alfonso's men to turn their heads to the hill. A general retreat had been sounded. The men were to leave the plains and return to camp – they had been defeated.

Don Alfonso relished the chance of going back to camp, fleeing to safety, avoiding the needless bloodshed. But he regretted the fact that the company could not count on him in its hour of need. He felt like a coward – worse than a coward, a traitor. The sin of his inaction would trouble him for the rest of his life. Perhaps this was his curse for burning down that church.

Suddenly, out of the corner of his eye, he spotted a great dust cloud, the kind that was kicked up by a stampede of horses. They were coming closer, and the don could not recognize the armor they were wearing, but could tell that they were neither Polish or allied soldiers. He did, however, recognize the shining symbols on their shields. The Stars and crescents yelled out to all that Allah guided their hands.

"Moros." the don spat. In his youth, he was indoctrinated that there was once a time that every heathen killed allowed for the remission of sin and made one that much closer to obtaining eternal life.

As God had once tested Abraham, now He tested Don Alfonso. There would be no faltering this time, no lack of courage. Here, fighting against the enemies of Christ – this would be his redemption.

"Halberdiers! The company will advance, right turn!"

Hearing the don's command, the halberdiers formed up and faced the oncoming enemy. Some looked on with fear, but most of them started with grim determination, glad that they would finally able to be of use to the company.

"Charge halberds for horse and draw swords!"

At this command, the halberdiers planted the butts of their weapons in the ground to brace for the oncoming charge, and with their right hand drew their swords to prepare to engage in melee.

The enemy cavalry fell upon them like lightning – swift, painful, and merciless. While some horses stopped short of the halberds for fear of being impaled, throwing their riders in the process, the Turkish bowmen found it convenient to circle around the formation and pepper them with arrows as they held the line.

"Form a circle! Give them no chance to flank us!"

They scrambled to their positions, forming a defensive ring around the don with their weapons pointed outwards. The Turkish horses continued to ride around them as sporadic arrow fire continued to whittle their numbers with the fast-flying Turkish arrows being able to pierce through the halberdiers' armor. The don was not sure how long he would be able to continue like this, but it would not matter in the end, for every man here would die a soldier of Christ.

Talbot Company Center
Cruel Fate, 2ⁿᵈ Regiment of Foot

Sophia heard the horn over the clashing of steel and the screams of men. She herself had just dispatched another enemy soldier, and her blade and armor were now red. Sweat and blood trickled from her scalp and into her left eye, while her clothes were tattered and bloody from the glancing blows of many foes. It was a miracle that she was still alive.

Upon hearing the call to retreat, she shouted for her sergeants and ordered the withdrawal in Italian. No one could hear her voice over the sound of sporadic musket fire and the clashing of steel. She grabbed the hand of the nearest allied soldier – a pikeman – and told him,

"They have sounded the retreat, you idiot! Fall back!"

The pikeman simply stared at her with fear-widened eyes, uncomprehending, and said,

"Den katalavaino." I do not understand.

Greek. Of the thousand men Talbot Company had under its command, she found one of only five Greeks that served as pikemen. She gritted her teeth in frustration and combed her way through the melee of pikes with her sword, sometimes grabbing onto pike shafts to push them out of her way, not sure where she was going. All the while she shouted in Italian,

"Go back! Go back! The colonel has called us to fall back!"

It was no use. Her tiny voice couldn't be heard over the cacophony of battle. She was amazed that no one else heard the horn besides her.

Seemingly from out of nowhere, an enemy blade thrust at her from behind. The strike glanced off of her steel armor, but she knew that the next blow would not be the same.

Turning, she faced her opponent – a Polish infantryman armed with a saber. This was the first time she faced someone in a fair fight. Behind her, the battle of pikes still raged, a tangled forest of wood and metal. In front of her stood her opponent, tired, but with the rage of battle still burning in his eyes.

Sophia swallowed and raised her sword to defend herself. With a great yell, the Polish soldier brought his sword overhead to strike. On instinct, she raised her own blade up high to block.

The strike was a feint.

The saber swept under Sophia's block and struck her low. Her thigh gushed bright red blood, and her jaws clinched from the pain, making her bite her own tongue.

The Polish soldier swung in for another blow. Panicking, she pointed her blade at him, only to have it struck from out of her hand. The expensive rapier flew several feet in the air before landing on the dirt.

Sophia could hear her own heartbeat as the world seemed to slow around her. Her opponent, not hesitating, brought his saber overhead to deliver the killing blow.

Sophia closed her eyes and accepted her fate. She had lived a good life – she had made new friends, experienced new things. She had gotten the adventure that she had always longed for.

The sound of metal on metal interrupted her surrender.

She opened her eyes to find the Polish soldier going blade to blade with Gunther Jaeger and his zweihander. The force of the larger blade was too much to block with one hand, and the soldier's parry failed him, letting the blade slip past his guard and slice straight into his shoulder.

The Polish soldier dropped his weapon, and gripped Gunther's blade with his one hands, desperately trying to free himself from the weapon. Gunther only pressed down harder and started to saw away with his blade in a rapid back-and-forth motion as if he was carving meat. He wore an uncharacteristically wide grin on his face.

Gunther's victim dropped onto the ground, screaming for God or the angels to take him. The German mercenary took pity on the dying man and stabbed him through the mouth with his bloody sword before turning to Sophia.

"Lieutenant Bianchi – how do you fare?" he said in French.

Sophia was too stunned for a moment to respond. She had already resigned herself to death and could not believe that she had just been saved.

"Have you not heard the horn? We need to get the signal to the other men, come on!"

"I... I have tried, *signore,* but no one understands me!"

"Impossible! Wait... what words have you been using?"

"Eh... torna indietro." Go back, she said.

"Mein Gott im Himmel. No one understands that! Say retreat instead!"

"Retraite... ritiro?"

"Yes, that. Now come on, we must get the word out!"

The two officers ran together across the field, shouting the command to retreat. Soldiers began to leave the push of pike to break ranks and run back. Sophia took no pleasure in watching her soldiers run, but Gunther valued the lives of his men. He would save a few now instead of wasting them all in a battle that was clearly lost.

Imran Bey's Force

As his men circled around the hapless company of halberdiers, Imran Bey saw that some of the pikemen and swordsmen had broken formation and were apparently routing back to the top of the hill in what could only be described as a chaotic retreat.

"Mounted archers, continue to attack these men – everyone else, with me!" he barked.

The bey reasoned that they were wasting their time picking off this small force, and if they allowed their enemy to regroup there would be more resistance to encounter once they raided the Christian camp.

The riders moved fast, closing the distance with the retreating Talbot Company infantry fairly easily. They then came in sight of their Tatar brothers, who greeted them with their peculiar version of the Turkish language as they slashed down fleeing Christians together.

"*As-salaam alaikum,* my brothers," said a cheerful Tatar horseman as he approached Imran Bey on horseback, his bridles and his horse's legs stained with blood, "it is a pleasant surprise to see fellow believers on the field."

"*Wa-alaikum salaam,* brother." Imran Bey replied, "We intend to capture the enemy camp beyond the hill. Will you help us?"

The Tatar stroked his beard in thought and looked towards his commander, Jan Casimir, who was in the distance rallying his men.

"I am quite sure that his grace will not disapprove of us chasing the fleeing enemy and cutting them down like the villains they are."

"Inform your commander, then. We will race up the hill – try to cut down as many infidels as you are able."

Talbot Company Center
Company of Pikes, Jarlsberg County Infantry

The initial shock charge of the Tatar cavalry had left Captain Bjornsson's force of halfwits in disarray. Many lay dead on the field, and Bjornsson himself had only survived by sheer luck.

Now he wandered about the battlefield with his sword drawn, dragging the tip of the blade along the ground.

He had given up all hope. His eyes looked skyward, asking God why he had allowed such a needless defeat. No answer came – it seemed as if the very powers that be mocked his efforts. No enemies came to face him in combat; all were too busy dispatching more dangerous foes, none of them considered him a threat.

The sound of horses' hooves surrounded him. Several riders breezed past, slicing into the bodies of fleeing men and the brave souls that dared to resist them. Bjornsson's apathy to the situation was his camouflage. The enemy was looking for men that were running towards them or away from them, not a ghost that walked the field.

Bjornsson thought he could hear voices in the distance, as well, besides the screaming. Voices that sounded like they were calling his name...

"Captain Bjornsson!" they yelled one after the other, "The retreat has been sounded! Fall back!"

Retreating was a coward's device. He would never do so, even now in his disheveled and beaten state. There was no tail to put in between his legs.

A hand grabbed him by the shoulder. He instinctively whirled around to attack, but he stopped once he saw who it was.

"The Italian girl and the German *förlorat hopp*." he muttered, mostly to himself. "Have you come to watch an old man suffer?"

"We need to retreat, you idiot!" Sophia yelled at him.

"No, no, I will stay here and be at peace. Go and do your coward's errand."

Gunther and Sophia looked at each other, then at Bjornsson. The next thing he knew, a fist obscured his vision as a sharp pain shot through his nose. The world around him suddenly went black as he fell to the ground.

"Why did you do that?" Sophia asked Gunther, who was shaking his hand from the pain of the punch.

"He will be better off unconscious. The enemy will take no notice of a man on the ground. Keep falling back, we must regroup at the camp."

Talbot Company Command
MacRae's Irregulars

The fading whine of the horn lingered in the air, and yet Talbot Company's Britannic irregulars stood their ground, unwilling to fall back to camp, standing in blatant defiance of MacRae's orders.

The Scottish colonel looked upon his countrymen with pride.

"So that is how it be, eh. Look over in yon plain below, how our numbers be swept up by the enemy's swords and cavalry. I know ye lot have fires in yer bellies and steel in yer hearts, and I will not hinder ye this day – so I bid ye, me bully boys, crash upon the enemy and rip open their throats with your blades, lay your great shites down their windpipes and slander their mothers all the while!"

The irregulars unsheathed their weapons with the rasping of dozens of scabbards and cheered with glee as their spirits were suddenly lifted again.

"Nary will a son of Eire, or a warrior of Alba or Cymru, or even a scrawny villain of an Englishman fall today without having his blade taste enemy steel. I care not how the deed is done. Disembowel them, pluck out their eyes, fuck them with your blade! But your war kin shall judge ye upon the number of noses that you have brought with you!"

The cheering grew louder; the shouts of the men were almost enough to wake up the war gods of old from their ancient slumber.

"Now go on ye wretched sons of whores! Up and at them!"

With this, the irregulars, with their eyes wide with bloodlust and their tongues hanging out like mad dogs, charged at the incoming enemy cavalry, not caring that they were at a disadvantage in numbers or arms.

The pikemen scrambling up the hillside were greeted with a rush of screaming Celts and Britons who jeered them for their cowardice as they charged downwards to the oncoming foe.

The Turkish cavalry nipped at the heels of the fleeing mercenaries and Swedes, eager to claim prisoners or booty later, but the warrior cries of the irregulars gave them a brief pause for thought. Who were these men, they thought, that so eagerly charged into the waiting maws of death?

The clash was spectacular. Scotsmen leaped at riders in their horses to tackle them down to the earth to fight like men. Turkish lancers speared red-headed Irishmen who still smiled, glad to die a warrior's death.

English and Welsh bowmen loosed their arrows to kill the advancing horses, just as their forefathers did in the muddy fields of Agincourt – but there were simply too many.

A wave of horses and men quickly overwhelmed the irregulars, brave as they fought. MacRae's men were trampled underneath the oncoming cavalry charge while he himself cursed his luck and galloped back to camp with the greve before the enemy could overtake them.

Chapter 33

James Fletcher's tent was cool and comfortable. The spring breeze wafted through the canvas flaps and over his cot as he lay there in peaceful sleep. He even dreamed that he heard an angel calling his name as she stroked his hair.

"Fletcher... Fletcher..."

Then came a hard whack against his cheek.

"Fletcher!"

The English peasant awoke to the sight of Crista throttling him awake. This was the first time that he saw her in broad daylight – she was beautiful. She had large, sapphire eyes, golden curls tied with a blue bow, a gentle nose and a mouth curled in a snarl that made her seem adorable in the way that an angry lapdog was adorable.

"Waken! Waken!" she said as she shook him by his shoulders.

"Calm down, milady!" Fletcher said, still groggy from his long sleep, "What is all this fuss?"

"Fiends come! They come to us!"

"Fiends?"

Fletcher paused for a while. He judged that there were no birds or forest animals that would normally be making all sorts of mating calls in the spring. Then he heard it, first a low rumble, then a crescendo of violent noise. War cries and thundering hooves were fast approaching.

"What is happening?" He said in confusion.

"I say the fiends come!"

Frustrated, Fletcher threw off his blanket and leaped out of bed. A jolt of pain shot up his back and side. His wounds were not completely healed, but now was not the time to complain.

A chilly breeze and Crista's awkward stare made him realize that he was covered only in bandages. His old clothes lay in tatters on a chair, but they would have to do. He put on his frayed breeches shirt in a hurry while Crista dashed to get his sword and bow, passing them to him with a sense of urgency.

He could hear the distinct sound of horse hooves right outside the tent. Not even bothering to buckle his baldric, he unsheathed his hunting sword and cautiously approached the entrance to the tent.

The silhouettes of two riders were visible through the billowing white tent cloth. Both of them were armed – Fletcher feared that he could not take two opponents at once, but he had no choice now.

The riders dismounted and walked with purpose towards the flap of the tent. As soon as he saw the hand of the intruder slip through the small opening in the canvas, Fletcher raised his blade and brought it down, but his injuries would not allow him to go as fast as he would have wanted to. He barely scraped

MacRae's hand as the Scottish colonel cursed and yelled in pain. Greve Stenbock took a step back in surprise.

"Ye be a jumpy one, boy. It is good to have ye protecting the Lady Stenbock," he said as he clutched his bleeding hand, "but we need ye elsewhere. Be not mistaken, I am glad that ye are awake, however, I was of a mind to fetch the lady alone." MacRae said as he looked at Crista, who was in the corner of the tent, holding a bone saw for protection. Turning back to Fletcher, he continued, "The enemy be at our doorstep so it seems. The company will form a defense behind the wagons. Bring yer bow."

Fletcher nodded in affirmation and reached out for his bow, but Crista whimpered for him to stay,

"Please sir, defend me?"

"You can come with us to the wagons where it will be safe."

"I prefer hide."

Greve Stenbock rushed over to his daughter. "I will see to her." he said. "Go now, form up – and may God be with you."

MacRae pointed an accusing finger at the greve, his eye wide with contempt,

"You shall be aware sir, that if I die, I blame this defeat solely on ye."

With those words, MacRae exited the tent with Fletcher not far behind him.

The sunlight was a shock to Fletcher's eyes, having been cooped up in a tent for the last day. The sudden weight of his sword made him realize how weak he was – he had not eaten in all that time, but there was certainly no time for bread and cheese now.

The wagons were as they had been arranged before – in a circle around the camp, allowing only one entryway. The sentinels who had remained behind to guard the camp and even some of the Swedish soldiers who had recently recovered from their devil's trumpet poisoning were passing around muskets and shot to fend off the rapidly approaching enemy.

Fletcher took position behind one of the carts and nocked an arrow in his bow, as MacRae took a musket and a bandolier to join his men in what could very well be their last stand as a company.

Talbot Company Right
Of Christ our Savior, 2ⁿᵈ Regiment of Foot

The Muslim arrows had whittled Don Alfonso's men to merely two dozen. They stood there, unwavering, some with tears rolling down their cheeks – angry, helpless, and frustrated that they could do nothing to fight back as long as the riders kept at a distance.

All of a sudden, the rain of arrows stopped. A Turkish horse archer yelled something in his strange tongue, and all of the men slowed down to a trot, then a walk, and then completely stopped, forming a circle around the beleaguered halberdiers.

Then, unexpectedly, the Turks simultaneously dismounted their horses and drew their sabers. As the don looked into their veiled faces, he could not decipher whether they were out of ammunition, toying with him, or appealing to their strange sense of honor. At least now, he thought, the playing field had been slightly evened.

336

The enemy approached slowly and cautiously, looking for signs of weakness or tiredness in the men that up till now had not shed a drop of Turkish blood.

With no warning, the entire Turkish force charged and dashed upon Don Alfonso's halberdiers like violent waves against rocks. Using their shields to block, they avoided the blades of the halberds, but could not come close enough to strike their own blows with their swords. It was now a stalemate that could only be broken by a lapse in fighting skill or a slip of a blade.

The don did not have to wait long. One of his men made the fatal mistake of trying to swing his halberd high like a headsman's axe. The Turk dashed under the blow and delivered a shield strike to the halberdier's face.

There was now a kink in the circle.

Turkish soldiers rushed to exploit the gap, all the while contending with the protruding spearheads of Don Alfonso's men. The don himself stepped in to defend the gap, meeting a Turk's scimitar with his own schiavona.

The curved eastern blades slashed against European plate armor while western broadswords cut and thrust against Turkish lamellar, neither having much of an effect. The battle was now one of willpower as much as it was of strength – if the men could stand on their two feet, then the slightest chance of victory was possible, even in these seemingly overwhelming odds.

Talbot Company's Routing Units
Vanguard & Cruel Fate, 1st & 2nd Regiment of Foot

Sophia and Gunther ran as fast as they could towards the hill. The pain of Sophia's wounds was only made worse by the exertion of running in armor, while Gunther urged her onward even as enemy cavalry rode around them, killing retreating soldiers at random.

"I cannot!" Sophia gasped as she ran, "This is a fool's errand! We run from horses on foot?"

"Better to run to safety than guarantee a painful death, idiot child! Now run faster!" Gunther barked as he urged Sophia onward.

The two reached the base of the hill. The tips of muskets extended out from the carts at the top – if they could reach them, they would be safe. Both sprinted up the hill, fighting the burning in their legs. The wagons on the top of the hill grew tantalizingly closer – Sophia felt as if she could almost reach out and touch them.

From behind them, the sound of a galloping horse grew louder. They could almost feel the animal's breath on the backs of their necks. A Turkish rider with a raised scimitar approached screaming his shrill battle cry.

Gunther turned around and presented his blade to the enemy tip first – the horse could not stop fast enough, and it was stabbed in the chest, causing its rider to be thrown onto Gunther. The two tumbled on the ground and the German released his heavy sword as the fight degenerated into a bout of fisticuffs and biting.

Sophia stopped and turned to see her friend wrestling with the Turk on the ground. She instinctively reached for her sword and remembered that it had fallen somewhere in the field.

338

A rock would do.

She scrambled to find a good-sized boulder and leaped upon the two grappling men, striking the Turk repeatedly with the rock she had in her hand. It made a satisfying metallic echo as it hit him, but Gunther protested,

"Take off his helmet you idiot!"

Doing so, Sophia then applied the rock to the Turk's head. His life blood came rushing out like a fountain. Sophia had killed again. Her conscience was increasingly burdened by what she had become.

"Ah, the stone; a smart choice – Cain's weapon." Gunther said as he stood up. "But come, we are not there yet – hurry!"

That remark made Sophia more than a little uncomfortable.

Gunther did not intend to stop to apologize or debate morality. Without another word, he ran on, urging Sophia to follow. With a sigh of exhaustion, she followed.

Her vision grew dimmer. She no longer looked ahead but at the passing dirt beneath her feet. She urged herself not to stop, but her legs would not heed her. They buckled and gave way, making her collapse onto the cold ground.

Sophia gritted her teeth. She could not die here, not of exhaustion, and not in such a pathetic state. She would get up, she would seek safety, and she would continue to fight for all she was worth.

As she propped herself up on two hands and looked upward, she was greeted by a friendly face. James Fletcher stood over her, smiling as he offered his hand to her. She had made it to the defenses.

Returning Fletcher's smile, she took his hand. The stickiness of the blood between her fingers turned what could have been a pleasant moment into a macabre reunion.

"Are you hurt?" Fletcher asked in English.

She put her bloody hand to his cheek, stroking it gently and leaving a trace of dark scarlet on his face. She did not understand what he said, but it was good to be with him again.

Gunther grabbed two muskets and bandoliers from a Talbot Company soldier that was passing them out. He thrust one of each into Sophia's hands, stopping her just before she could release her emotions on Fletcher.

"Do you know how to use this?" said the German in a gruff tone.

"N-no."

"Well, you will have to learn, and quickly. Look there." Gunther said, pointing towards the bottom of the hill. The Turkish riders had taken their fill of retreating soldiers and were now forming up to charge the hill.

The Talbot Company mercenaries aimed their weapons down at the enemy and prepared to fire. MacRae checked his musket then barked at his men,

"Right, ye lot, hold yer fire till ye can smell the piss on the enemy! Bite yer charges and load yer weapons!"

Gunther ripped off one of the cartridges from his bandolier and ripped it open with his teeth, keeping an eye on Sophia to make sure she was doing the same. The nervous girl put the paper cartridge to her teeth with shaking hands.

"Lady Fortezza..." said Fletcher, nocking an arrow into his bow.

"Che cosa, Messere Freccia?"

Gunther hit Sophia lightly on her shoulder, reminding her to load her powder into her weapon. She breathed heavily as she did so, her eyes darting from Gunther to her weapon to Fletcher.

"I... wanted to say something..." Fletcher said.

Gunther dropped his musket ball and wadding into his weapon, urging Sophia to do the same. She furrowed her brow and attempted to drop the little ball into the muzzle, her attention clearly divided.

Fletcher swallowed, "If we are to perish here today..."

Gunther interrupted, "Your scouring stick, lieutenant – take it out."

Sophia, exasperated, fumbled with the large metal rod and rammed the musket ball into down the muzzle of her musket.

Down below, the enemy cavalry was beginning their rapid ascent up the hill. The men could feel the ground shake beneath their feet.

Gunther removed his scouring stick and replaced it back in its holder, while telling Sophia,

"Replace your scouring stick and make sure your match is lit."

Fletcher and Sophia locked eyes. Her heart slowed down, and she felt nothing but calmness and longing.

"Sophia..." Fletcher said softly, skipping all his usual formalities, *"Je t'aime."*

Tears welled up in Sophia's eyes.

"Fire!" shouted MacRae.

The sound of dozens of loud bangs gave Sophia a violent fright, and she pulled the trigger of her weapon, sending her scouring stick flying out of her musket, impaling a horse through the knee as it charged up the hill.

Sophia let the tears flow as she dropped her weapon to grab Fletcher, just as he released his arrow.

As the arrow was in flight, she planted her lips on his and gave him a deep kiss that was equal parts sorrow and love.

Before Fletcher could wrap his arms around her, Gunther ripped them from their embrace and shook Sophia by the shoulders,

"We have no time for this! We are about to be overrun! Grab a weapon and fight, in God's name!"

Chapter 34

Casimir's Brigade Reserves
Winged Hussars

Casimir surveyed the field and breathed a sigh of relief. The Protestant enemy and their mercenary horde had been routed, and not a moment too soon. He feared that his pikemen would have broken if they had continued the fight but a minute more.

He was pleasantly surprised to see the heathen army break through the woods and rid his flank of the enemy. He felt that he would owe the Turkish bey a great deal after their victory, but any price was worth it.

At the moment though, Casimir knew he had to capitalize on his foe's defeat. Polish soldiers would triumph for a Polish cause, and the white eagle would fly proudly over the battlefield. The hussars would have this final triumph.

The colonel rode back to the castle alone, his men cheering him on as he raised his mace in victory. The castle gates opened for him, and there stood the pride of Poland's cavalry with their armor glinting in the sun and their weapons unsheathed, ready for battle.

"My brothers," Casimir said, barely containing his excitement, "the enemy has been routed. It is time for us to take the field and take the battle to them!"

The hussars did not need another word. On Casimir's lead, they charged out of the castle shouting their battle cry with pride:

"God, Honor, and Homeland!"

Then as if on cue, the infantry heard the rumble of more horse hooves in the distance. Bursting through the forests from the southwest, even more hussars appeared – their wide, white wings rode under a different standard. A giant banner emblazoned with emblems of Saint Michael and the white eagle of Poland made it known to all present that they were in the presence of the king of Poland.

Seeing the royal colors, Casimir nearly exploded with pride – the king himself had arrived to give his blessing for his campaign. The war against Sweden was back on, and his mission was accomplished.

Talbot Company Remnants

Of Christ our Savior, 2ⁿᵈ Regiment of Foot

The halberdiers' formation was broken. Dozens of men were now scattered around the field fighting in groups of two or three.

Don Alfonso pushed back against a Turkish sipahi who had gotten too close. An underhand cut with his schiavona made contact with the Turk's chainmail-covered thigh, doing little beyond giving him a bruise.

The Muslim's curved sword, in turn, merely nicked Don Alfonso's plate armor when it struck. The don could not stand for this stalemate any longer.

With a great yell, the don threw his opponent to the ground. Before the Turk could react, the angry Spaniard began repeatedly slamming him in the eye with his sword pommel.

The screaming Turk slapped the don in the face, causing him to lose concentration for a split second, just enough time for the Turk to flip him over so that he was now on the bottom.

The don's opponent raised his sword to deliver the killing blow, but the skull-crushing thwack of a halberd to the back of his head ended him before he could strike.

Don Alfonso scrambled back to his feet and found yet another opponent, clashing swords with him as well. Salty sweat dripped down his brow and into his eyes as his aching muscles screamed at him to give up.

The battle seemed hopeless. Men from both sides littered the ground around him, but there were more Christian dead than Muslim.

The ground shook. An ominous thundering accompanied the hundreds of Polish hussars charging straight for the already engaged halberdiers. This was where the don would die.

He gritted his teeth and shouted in his opponent's face in Spanish,

"I surrender to no one but God!"

As he said this, a gust of wind from a horse and rider swept by him, and to his surprise, his opponent now lay on the ground dead – killed by a mace strike to the head.

As the don looked around him, astonishment and confusion overtook him. Polish hussars galloped around lopping off Turkish heads and smashing in sipahi helmets with their maces, but no European blood wet their blades. It was almost as if God had granted them a battlefield miracle.

Casimir's Brigade Reserves Winged Hussars

Casimir looked upon his Tatar and Muslim allies slack-jawed as the king's hussars proceeded to tear into them with remorseless efficiency while his own hussars simply rode around in circles, too confused to engage with anyone.

King Sigismund himself rode up to Casimir, who immediately dismounted and bowed in the presence of his king. In truth, Casimir's gold armor and wings made him look like the greater of the two, since the king favored the simplicity of black half-plate armor and a plain felt hat, but what he lacked in extravagance, he made up for in regal bearing. The king's mere presence commanded respect. All before him saw the God-chosen ruler of the bulwark of Europe, not the sickly sixty five year old man that he really was.

"Colonel Jan Casimir." King Sigismund said as he looked down from his horse, "We always valued you for your loyalty and your patriotism, but this... this is treason."

"Majesty, I was..."

"You will not interrupt us again!" the king boomed.

Casimir knew this did not bode well for him. The king was speaking to him as an enemy to the crown, far from the warm praise he had expected.

"You would take the peace we had fought so hard for, at the cost of thousands of Catholic lives, and dash it as glass against a rock, simply because you believe that it would further Poland's honor? My boy, there is no honor in breaking a peace treaty! If we want the Swedish crown we will do it on our terms, not yours! You have no right to play our pawns for us."

"Majesty, may I speak?"

"You may."

"Poland was wronged. That crown rightly belongs on your head, and not on the head of some heretic like Gustavus Adolphus. By surprising them, we would have had the advantage, and we could have swept through Livonia like a great storm."

"A single host is no great storm. It is a fleeting gale that will wither away. If you thought your storm could borrow strength from the mountains of the Ottoman Empire," the king said as he pointed to the Turks being slaughtered in the distance, "then you are a traitor to your faith as well as to your king. We do not need the like of the Mohammedans polluting our land with their rapine destruction. If you were allowed to continue with this plan, every church touched by their hand would be a smoldering ruin, or worse, a mosque."

"Majesty, I did this all for you!"

"What you have done for us will not bring back the lives of the men who fell at Gniew, Kokenhusen, and Gorzno. It will only give the Swedes the excuse they need to bring a nation unprepared for war to its knees. Do not pretend to dictate policy. We are Poland – you are merely a dog. Once you were a good hunting companion but now you have grown mad and must be put down."

King Sigismund cast him a glare and motioned for his guards.

"Seize him. Put him in chains until this battle is won."

Casimir, defeated, did not attempt to struggle as the king's bodyguards hoisted him to his feet. As they stripped him of his armor, he thought to himself about how he had become so deluded, and how far he had fallen for the sake of his country.

Imran Bey's Force

"Atahan!" Imran Bey called out to his adjutant, "We have the infidels on the run! They occupy a hill on the far side of the field! We can win this now!"

Atahan, who was usually at the bey's side, was nowhere to be seen. The bey looked around for him but he had been separated during the initial melee with the enemy cavalry.

If Imran Bey had paid more attention, he would not have missed the sight of his faithful assistant scurrying off in the distance after he had caught sight of the king of Poland.

The bey dismissed Atahan's absence and raced his horse up the hill together with his cavalry. A single volley of musket fire erupted from the top of the hill and five of his men fell dead.

It did not matter. They could not possibly reload and fire again before they reached the top of the hill. The bey grinned as the enemy's wagon barricade grew closer. He could almost feel his steel against the necks of the infidels.

A scream from behind him interrupted his thoughts. The bey turned his head to see Polish hussars riding up behind him and hacking away at his men. How had the Polish suddenly turned on him? And more importantly what would he do now that he was sandwiched between two hostile forces?

He did not have to think about the question for very long. A flying scouring stick, of all things, tore through his horse's knee, throwing the bey to the dirt as his men raced ahead of him. The Turkish lord tumbled down the hillside as his men continued onward without him.

Thinking quickly, Imran Bey tried to roll sideways to escape the multitude of hooves that were kicking up dirt in his face. His efforts made him tumble down the path further, but he mercifully landed in a bush on the side of the hill trail.

Covered in dust, blood, and sweat, the bey picked himself up and saw his cavalry stop in front of the wagons of the enemy. The shouting of the enemy, the height of the wagons, and the sporadic musket fire made the horses too scared to jump over the wagon barricade, and their riders paid for their indecisiveness as musket balls ripped through their chainmail armor.

The men began to realize the futility of the assault and turned their horses around, only to be hacked to bits by advancing royal hussars. The Turks could not even retreat in peace.

The Christian mercenaries occupying the hill were momentarily stunned by the turn of events, but cheered in loud voices as the Poles cut down the dumbfounded Turks until only Imran Bey remained, hidden in his bush.

When the last cry for Allah was silenced, and only Christ's name could be heard up on the hill in the all the languages of the people that worshipped Him, Imran Bey cursed at the Europeans and slinked away through thickets below like a snake, swearing revenge on these mercenary dogs and the Poles that had thwarted him.

Chapter 35

At long last, the battle was over. Some Talbot Company and Swedish survivors cried tears of joy, while others simply fell to the earth from exhaustion. Others embraced each other in victory while some gave thanks to God.

Sophia and Fletcher, both reeking of blood and sweat, were locked in a long embrace. Sophia could not help but cry onto Fletcher's shoulder while he stroked her long auburn hair and whispered sweetness into her ear that she could barely understand.

Don Alfonso and his halberdiers praised the Lord with every psalm and prayer that they could remember. The don himself fell to his knees and closed his eyes as he lifted up his hands in praise. He said with great conviction that nothing but divine intervention could have won the battle for them on that day.

Sven Bjornsson woke up in a daze to the sound of cheering. He looked around him to find a battlefield littered with carcasses, but heard shouts of joy coming from atop the hill. He managed a weak smile and thought to himself that he was right not to retreat.

William MacRae roared with laughter at his survival, but for only a moment. When he surveyed the field and the number of dead around it, he walked over his men's bodies in solemn silence.

Gunther Jaeger ran down the hill to retrieve his zweihander, and immediately made his way to the spot where Otto's Black

Riders had been deployed. After finding his good friend's corpse and his skull crushed like an egg, he knelt beside him and allowed himself a good cry, even as Polish troops began removing corpses nearby him.

Greve Olaf Stenbock and Crista crept out of their hiding places – inside two large oaken barrels – upon hearing the victorious cries of Talbot Company. They embraced and kissed as they both laughed the sweet laugh that only comes from survival.

When the dust had settled completely, the king of Poland gathered MacRae, Greve Stenbock, Crista and all their officers to meet with him in a clearing just outside Jarlsberg to discuss reparations and to give his formal apology as king of the Polish.

Greve Stenbock stepped forward and genuflected before the king,

"Greve Olaf of the house of Stenbock – it grieves us to see your estate in such a ruin. Let it be known that our crown accepts the full responsibility of the damages to your home and the lands surrounding it, and rest assured that reparations will be paid in full post haste to ensure the goodwill and peace between ourselves and your ruling sovereign Gustavus Adolphus."

Greve Stenbock uttered "Thank you majesty" as he kept his eyes averted.

The king turned next to MacRae, who bowed only his head. William MacRae would kneel before no man but King Charles of England.

"Colonel William of the Clan MacRae, your men fought and died bravely here in defense of Sweden's honor and sovereignty, and for this I commend you. However, in good conscience, I cannot pay reparations to a mercenary host, especially one that inflicted so many casualties upon my people."

MacRae mouthed a "fuck" but let the king continue,

"However, I grant you safe passage upon your return to the west, and the sum of five hundred gold florins for traveling expenses."

The colonel rolled his eye, making sure it could not be seen, but muttered: "Thank ye majesty."

Turning back to Greve Stenbock, the king spoke,

"We return now to Warsaw, to bring the villain Jan Casimir to justice. We trust that you will inform your sovereign of the honorable rescue that we undertook on your behalf, to honor the treaty between us signed at Altmark. He will be given a fair trial under the law and in the eyes of God. If there is anything more I may do for you, now is the time to ask."

For a moment, there was silence, but as the king turned to leave, Greve Stenbock spoke up,

"Majesty, if it pleases you, I wish to challenge your prisoner Jan Casimir to a duel."

Intrigued, the Polish king inquired,

"And what satisfaction would you have to gain from it? The man has been defeated, and is now a prisoner in chains. He has

353

suffered the ultimate humiliation that can be afflicted on a person of his stature."

"I wish to lay my own hands on the wretch that took my home from me and slaughtered my people."

Thinking on the Greve's proposition for a moment, the king said,

"God is in all things, Greve Stenbock. He was there when you were in battle and He is here now as we ponder on Jan Casimir's fate. Whatever verdict is decided in this duel, we will view as divine judgment. It will save us the trial, and you will either receive redemption or death. Are you certain that you want to do this?"

"Yes, majesty. It would be a great travesty to see the man go without having achieved satisfaction from him."

"Very well then; we shall allow it." Turning to his men, he ordered the prisoner to be brought forward.

A confused Casimir was released from his chains and brought before the greve. Olaf Stenbock was not a short man, but the Polish colonel towered over him by at least a couple of heads.

Undaunted, the greve removed his steel gauntlet, looked up at the large, scowling Polish man and slapped him across the cheek with it. Casimir did not flinch.

"You have committed sins against my kin, my people, and my family." the greve said in Swedish, refusing to switch languages for the usurper. "For these, you must die."

"I accept." Casimir replied in his native Polish.

MacRae put a hand on Greve Stenbock's shoulder.

"Ye be mad to fight him. The Pole looks as if his pecker alone be enough to bludgeon ye to oblivion – and ye appear to have but the strength of a wrinkled walrus!"

"A walrus still has tusks, colonel." Stenbock said, still looking up at Casimir, who wore the same scowl on his face as he did when he charged the walls of Jarlsberg.

Crista ran up to her father with pleading eyes.

"Pappa, you must not do this. We have won, and you are safe! I fear that I may lose you!"

Turning to his daughter, the greve stroked her cheek gently, "My dear, God has already delivered us this victory. Surely He will grant me this bit of just retribution against my enemy. Have faith, my love." he said as he kissed her on the forehead.

"You should be saying farewell to your father, *kochanie*." Casimir said in a low voice, his eyes still focused on the greve.

Grimacing back at him, Crista hissed back, "Whatever happens I will see you dead, you monster; even if I have to kill you myself."

Casimir would have laughed if he did not detect the seriousness in Crista's tone and the hate in her eyes. This was the first time she had broken her ladylike demeanor, and he could respect her for that.

After both men had separated and allowed to prepare for the duel, they met again in front of Bjornsson, who served as an arbiter. Casimir stood arrayed in his golden hussar armor sans its cumbersome wings, while Greve Stenbock stood across from him wearing his rather simple steel plate armor and burgonet helmet. Neither was armed.

"The terms of the duel are as follows:" said the Swede, "Before the duel commences," he said, deliberately speaking slowly, "all efforts must be made to reconcile the two parties."

Greve Stenbock spat, "Your mother conceived you from being fucked in the arse, Catholic swine!"

Crista covered her mouth in shock, while Casimir offered no response.

Sighing, Bjornsson continued, "After all attempts have been made to reconcile, the challenged has no option but... to accept... the challenge."

"I accept the challenge." Casimir growled.

The Swedish captain rolled his eyes and turned to Greve Stenbock, whispering "My lord, this is insane – this man will crush you like an insect."

The greve offered no response, but simply gave Bjornsson a look that he was serious about avenging his honor.

Withdrawing from Greve Stenbock, Bjornsson shook his head and continued,

"This duel will end when the challenger is satisfied."

Speaking through clenched teeth, the greve hissed, "This duel will end when you are dead, Polack!"

Casimir maintained his calm composure and looked to Bjornsson, who continued,

"As per the code of honor, the challenged may choose the weapon."

Casimir crossed his arms and said, "I choose the mace."

Greve Stenbock nodded. Although he had little experience fighting with bludgeoning weapons, he reasoned that fighting with a mace was much less complicated than fighting with a sword.

"When the weapon is chosen," continued the captain, "the combatants shall arm themselves and begin the duel on my command."

A Polish hussar presented Casimir's mace to him. It had not tasted blood all day, and its flanges were still sharp. The Polish colonel longed to bash in the head of the arrogant old fool across from him whom he believed did not deserve his title of nobility.

The greve, meanwhile, was presented with a captured Ottoman mace, since the Swedish army did not have a habit of arming its troops with the weapon. The rounded head still had bits of crusted blood on it, but other than that it was a sufficient weapon.

The two combatants now faced each other once more – the greve's hateful glare met by Casimir's calm but calculating stare. The crowd that gathered around them was remarkably quiet considering its size, and rightly so. No matter who fell dead, someone was about to lose a great and powerful leader of men.

"Duelists, are you ready?"

Before an answer could be given, Greve Stenbock charged. Bjornsson leaped out of his way before his mace made contact with Casimir's own. The weapon was not meant for blocking.

Greve Stenbock's mace crushed through Casimir's parry and landed a strike on the colonel's chest, almost winding him and making a slight dent in his armor.

Not giving him time to recover, the greve launched another strike, but to his surprise, Casimir's mace flew into his wrist, breaking it and making him drop his weapon. The colonel's next blow flew into the greve's face and fragmented his skull into several pieces. Flecks of blood and loose teeth flew out of the greve's head as he fell to the ground, dead.

Crista, momentarily stunned, let out a loud scream of anguish as she saw her father's lifeless body slumped on the cold ground.

Casimir, his expression blank, sheathed his mace and said,

"I am sorry this happened, *kochanie*. Your father gave me no..."

A loud bang, followed by a metallic plink interrupted him. As Casimir looked down, he could see bright red blood gushing out of a hole in his armor. His legs suddenly felt like clay and he collapsed, beginning to gurgle blood at the mouth.

A very angry William MacRae entered the dueling circle, holding a smoking pistol. His eye and face was red with rage and his entire body seemed to quiver as he spoke,

"Both of ye are eedjits! Ye! Protestant moneybags!" he said, pointing to the greve's lifeless corpse, "Ye throw yer life away like ye fling shite at the moon! May Satan mangle yer stubby cock in hell, sir!"

Trudging over to the dying Casimir, he kicked him in the head and screamed, "Ye! Killed! My! Money! A pox upon ye, seven generations of yer family, all yer friends and yer dog! May they all be raped and eaten by wild beasts! When ye arrive in hell, I hope a devil shoves his thorny pecker into yer bullet wound!"

Crista came running from the sidelines to the side of her dead father. Tears streaked down her face as she wailed for her loss. She would have stroked her father's face but there was nothing to stroke. A flattened mass of skin, bone, and giblets was barely contained by the greve's open burgonet helmet.

"Pappa! Can you hear me?" Crista said into the greve's shattered face between sobs, "I just want to say I am proud of you – and I love you!" Her crying became louder as she rested her forehead against her father's chest. "What will I do without you? Who will I have coffee with in the afternoons? Who will walk me down the aisle when I get married?"

Crista's heart sank as her tears mixed with her father's blood. "You were everything to me after mama died. And now... I am lost." she bit her lip as tears continued to streak down her cheeks.

The king of Poland, sword drawn, walked up to Casimir, who could only gaze up at his king. Kneeling, King Sigismund placed his hand on Casimir's forehead,

"In the name of the Father, and the Son, and the Holy Spirit, may your soul find eternal peace in the embrace of God, who is our everlasting salvation, Amen."

Casimir closed his eyes as the king dispatched him with his sword. There was no final cry of anguish.

"I believe our task here is finished. God's judgment has been brought upon this villain. My men and I shall return to Warsaw."

The king was about to leave, when he glanced at Crista continuing to sob by her father's body. He approached her and put a gentle hand on her shoulder. "Lady Stenbock, I offer my condolences for your loss – but Jarlsberg still stands, and Sweden still needs a strong greve to defend its lands."

Crista looked up to him, realizing what he was saying. "Does that mean..."

King Sigismund nodded, "Yes. By the ancient laws of nobility, you are now Grevinna Crista Stenbock."

While Crista gave a weak smile, MacRae's grin curled from ear to ear. He rushed over to her side and knelt by her, and, still grinning, said loudly, "I cry for ye lass, I truly do, but I congratulate ye on yer succession as well."

Crista looked at MacRae, her brow furrowed.

"Thank you?"

"Now look at these men," he said gesturing to his tired, dirty, and bloodied soldiers, "do ye not think they deserve some sort of respite?"

"Yes?"

Pulling out Greve Stenbock's old crumpled letter of credit out of his pocket, he thrust it into her hand and said,

"Then sign this paper – as grevinna ye can authorize us to draw on yer father's accounts. We may all be paid and go home!"

King Sigismund shook his head and walked away, muttering, "mercenaries..." as his men dragged away Casimir's body.

Looking at MacRae dead in his eye, Crista did not appreciate his wide smile, especially as her father had just passed away.

"I will sign this, colonel..." she said in French.

MacRae, barely able to contain himself, yelled out,

360

"A pen! Bring me a fuckin' pen!"

"...but on one condition."

MacRae's smile dropped.

"And what condition would that be, ma'am?"

"That I join your company."

MacRae froze. He already had enough trouble with Sophia, and now another female wanted to enlist? It did not seem like he had much choice though. The company needed the money, badly. Gunther could probably turn her into something resembling a soldier, but...

"...as a properly commissioned captain."

MacRae grimaced, baring his teeth. He did not want to be known as Colonel William MacRae, leader of women – but again, he had little choice if he wanted the company to continue surviving.

Sophia came rushing up to them with a pen in her hand. She noted MacRae's expression and asked,

"Sir, is something the matter? You look like you are in pain."

MacRae said nothing but simply shook his head in dismay.

Crista smiled back at her in a gentle, friendly manner, "Without my father, I will need a family. You may not think this, but you are the most precious friends I have right now. You delivered me from my captivity, you saved my home from destruction, and I feel that I am indebted to you. I do not need to be here at Jarlsberg all the time, and Ratsherr Fegelein can look after it while I am away. He is a capable man after all."

"What are you saying?" Sophia asked, suddenly wary.

361

Rising to her feet, Crista kissed Sophia on the lips, to her shock, and said, "I am joining Talbot Company, sister."

Sophia's eyes widened as she let out a loud scream.

Epilogue

The funerals for Otto and Warwick were held in the small Protestant chapel of Jarlsberg after it had been cleaned up and hurriedly reconsecrated by a Lutheran minister. The new Grevinna Stenbock had allowed their remains to be buried in the churchyard as a sign of her gratitude to Talbot Company.

After the services, the company officers settled down for a simple dinner inside the castle, while the surviving enlisted soldiers drank themselves to oblivion outside. MacRae sat near the head of the table, while Gunther, tired and grieving, sat beside him. Sophia and Fletcher sat opposite of them, while Don Alfonso sat beside Fletcher, carving bread.

Crista, however, was conspicuously absent.

"I always knew that something stupid would kill him," said Gunther, his head in his hands, "but being stomped to death by a horse was not something I would have imagined."

"Captain Koenigsherr was a good man," said MacRae, patting Gunther on the back, "and he redeemed himself for his actions at Breitenfeld. But cheer up, ye lot. We are here, alive, and we have been paid! What more could an honest soldier of fortune wish for?"

Across from them, Sophia too, was not feeling her best,

363

"I can hardly believe it." she said to herself in Italian, "The bitch is my sword sister!"

"You were once in her shoes, were you not?" said Don Alfonso as he spread some lingonberry jam on his slice of bread, "Running away from your problems by seeking fame, fortune, and adventure?"

"Yes, but I am not a pretentious arse like Lady Crista!"

"*Culo.*" Fletcher chuckled, "That means arse. You must be talking about Lady Crista."

The archer was learning quickly.

"Yes," Sophia smiled at him, still speaking Italian, "yes we are."

"She is not so bad, I think. Perhaps a little showy and arrogant, but she is not a bad person."

Sophia's smile dropped. All she grasped from his words were that Crista was "not so bad."

Don Alfonso chuckled, "*Hija,* leave him to his opinions. We do not know her as you do, but perhaps even your opinion may change one day.

Suddenly, a large pair of double doors burst open, and Captain Bjornsson entered with an exasperated expression on his face.

"Presenting," he sighed, "Grevinna Crista of the house Stenbock, first of her name, protector of Jarlsberg and vassal to his majesty King Gustavus Adolphus of the Kingdom of Sweden."

Crista entered from behind him with her head held high, wearing the uniform of a Swedish cavalier, complete with its

364

yellow ochre doublet and laced collar and sleeves. On her head she wore a broad-brimmed hat just like MacRae's, while at her side hung her father's sword.

Her guests at the table looked on her with a mix of shock and confusion. MacRae dropped his silverware and muttered,

"By all the saints, 'tis the fuckin' butterfly pixie attired for war."

"Good evening, all you fine folk," she said with a polite smile, "I can only begin to imagine what fun we shall all have together!"

Meanwhile, miles outside of Jarlsberg, a man walked alone on a dirt road as his curved sword dragging behind him. He face was contorted into an expression of anger and hatred even as he walked with slow, limping steps.

Imran Bey walked with his hands balled into fists, cursing Talbot Company, the Polish, and the Swedes as he walked away from the castle. Revenge would be his, but patience was the greatest of virtues that Allah had bestowed upon man.

In time, he swore that he would assemble a great Muslim horde would sweep through Europe, and no one – not the Polish, not the Swedes and their mercenaries, not even the pope himself and his armies would be able to stop them. He would call upon the largest empire in the known world to seek vengeance for this defeat.

The End

Acknowledgments

This work, a fictional account set against the backdrop of actual historical events, would have been infinitely harder without the support of the many fellow writers and friends that have helped me believe in myself and the novel.

I would like to give special acknowledgment to Magali Hilfiker, Phil Madafferi, Adrien Lasbleiz, Nathan Mays, Andy Rattan, Eleazar Aurens, Brianna Mae, Stella Sauer, Lemius, and J.A. Morales for providing help with beta reading and constructive criticism and Sigourney So for her hard work designing the initial cover, even though it was ultimately not used.

I would also like to thank the men of Alpha Battery, 1st Battalion, 7th Field Artillery Regiment, United States Army for giving me the inspiration to begin this story while staring out into the vast nothingness of the desert at Fort Irwin.

About the Author

Michael was born in San Francisco but is never going back there again. He spent much of his life in the tropical islands of the Philippines, but returned to the United States to join the Army in 2016 as a cannon crewmember. He currently lives in Dallas, Texas.

FACEBOOK:
HTTPS://WWW.FACEBOOK.COM/MICHAELREGALBOOKS/

TWITTER: @MICHAEL_REGAL

EMAIL: MICHAELREGALBOOKS@GMAIL.COM

Made in the USA
Coppell, TX
25 January 2021

48786219R00203